Praise for JASPER FFORDE

"Every book of Fforde's seems to be a cause for celebration and a source of pleasure for many people, and for good reason."
—*The New York Times Book Review*

"Fforde's inventiveness remains a bookworm's delight."
—**Entertainment Weekly**

"This insanely clever novel from the author of the best-selling 'Thursday Next' series sounds like a cult classic for people who crave a rich brew of dystopic fantasy and deadpan goofiness . . . Every page of this high-concept novel (the first of a projected trilogy) glistens with ingenious details." —*The Washington Post*

"Mr. Fforde has his priorities right: First, be funny and entertaining. Second, make 'em think . . . *Shades of Grey* II and III are promised at the end of this book, and I'll admit it, until they're out, I'll feel a bit blue."
—**Karen Sandstrom, *Pittsburgh Post-Gazette***

"Fforde is an author of immense imagination. Not satisfied with just a few layers of Dickensian jokes and revisions of the physical universe, he creates an archeological treasure trove for readers . . . The coming-of-age story and manic-pixie-dream-girl romance don't need to be much more than icing on the cake to make *Shades of Grey* a fancifully satisfying concoction." —*The A.V. Club*

"*Shades of Grey* is absolutely [Fforde's] by-now-expected, over-the-top brand of storytelling . . . The world is wildly but closely imagined, so the result is as internally coherent as it is unlikely. Distinctive wordplay abounds. All the fooling around is built on a good mystery, and Fforde telegraphs no punches."—*Denver Post*

RED SIDE STORY

ALSO BY JASPER FFORDE

The Thursday Next Series
The Eyre Affair
Lost in a Good Book
The Well of Lost Plots
Something Rotten
First Among Sequels
One of Our Thursdays Is Missing
The Woman Who Died a Lot

The Nursery Crime Series
The Big Over Easy
The Fourth Bear

Standalones
Early Riser
The Constant Rabbit

Shades of Grey Series
Shades of Grey

The Dragonslayer Series
(for young adult readers)
The Last Dragonslayer
The Song of the Quarkbeast
The Eye of Zoltar
The Great Troll War

RED SIDE STORY

JASPER FFORDE

SOHO

Published by
Soho Press, Inc.
227 W 17th Street
New York, NY 10011

Names: Fforde, Jasper, author.
Title: Red side story / Jasper Fforde.
Description: New York, NY : Soho, 2024.
Series: Shades of grey
Identifiers: LCCN 2023056130

ISBN 978-1-64129-628-1
eISBN 978-1-64129-629-8

Subjects: LCGFT: Dystopian fiction. | Novels.
Classification: LCC PR6106.F67 R44 2024 | DDC 823'.92—
dc23/eng/20231208
LC record available at https://lccn.loc.gov/2023056130

Interior design by Janine Agro

Printed in the United States of America

10 9 8 7 6 5 4 3 2 1

For Carolyn with my admiration and thanks

Before I met Jane Grey, I was seeing only a fraction of my world. After, I saw more than ever. It terrified me then, it terrifies me still.

—*Eddie Russett, East Carmine, Red Sector West*

RED SiDE STORY

WELCOME TO EAST CARMINE

1.01.01.01.08(ii): The name of the Collective shall be Chromatacia; it shall be divided into four Sectors known as Red, Green, Yellow and Blue; each Sector shall be subdivided further into areas known as North, South, East and West. An administrative centre will be located in each Sector, and each area. For specific definitions see sub-note 1.01.01.02.08(iii)

—From Munsell's *Book of Harmony*

My name is Eddie Russett, but only for another two hours and nine minutes. After my negotiated marriage to Violet I will take on the prestigiously dynastic surname of deMauve, but within twenty-seven hours I find out that I was not Eddie Russett at all, but a subject termed HE-315-PJ7A-M. Three days after momentarily becoming Russett again I reluctantly take on the name of Mr. Hollyberry before quickly reverting to deMauve, but less than forty-eight hours after *that* I decide to dispense with a colour-based name entirely.

There is jeopardy, too: Jane and I almost catch the Mildew, a group of Yellows try to kill us and the ever-present Green Room beckons us towards its soporifically deadly charms. We also meet a Tin Man, a Riffraff and have an encounter with an Angel sent by our very own Creator, who then tries to kill us—three times.

But it's not all bad. At least Jane and I get to figure out the riddle of existence. Not *the* riddle, I should add, just ours, and we also learn there is a literal truth to the adage that you can't go home. And that's a problem. We're free and healthy and ready to live full and complete lives together, away from the Colourtocracy for good. That should be a cause for celebration, but it isn't: we wanted to improve our world, not abandon it. You'll be joining us there shortly, looking around our new home, sharing in our wonder, but for now:

THE 13:42 TRAIN pulled into the station with a punctuality that was within time parameters, but outside geographical ones. That is to say the train was on time, but the station was in the wrong place. There were strict Rules against non-punctuality, but nothing against the erroneous siting of a station. Such loopholery allowed us to maintain adherence to the strict Rules governing our society but still maintain a workable practicality.

The locomotive hissed in the warm air as the train rocked to a standstill, the gyros a soft melodious whirr as they kept the machine upright on its single rail. There were trains every other day—one in the morning, one in the afternoon—and their arrival was always an event: the quiet stasis of the village interrupted by arrivals, departures, post, news, freight and supplies.

The freight dispatcher moved to the far end of the platform to supervise the Greys as they swapped raw materials for finished rolls of linoleum, while the postman took the sack of mail and quickly departed. True to form, the stationmaster argued in a half-hearted manner with the train-driver about punctuality. I exchanged glances with the Arrivals Monitor, a dazzlingly unpleasant Yellow named Bunty McMustard. She was a few years older than me, had a small nose much akin to a button of understated ordinariness and insisted on wearing the Standard Casual

Girls #16, which was less of a dress and more of a bell tent. No one else wore one, not even ironically.

"None of your nonsense as we greet the visitors, Russett," she growled. "The council told me to report any infractions with *extreme* prejudice."

"You mean you get to exaggerate any potential misdemeanour?"

"In one—so watch it."

She meant it, too. Yellows took to their enforcement duties as a squarial takes to split pins and washers. Anything I could be demerited for, she'd get a cut. A Yellow who had amassed a large amount of merits had most likely done so not by worthy civil duty, but by snitching.

"You do your thing," I said, "and I'll do mine. Is your bow straight?"

Bunty quickly looked at her reflection in the train window. Her regulation-sized hair adornment was, of course, regulation straight. Yellows often used protractors on the hair bows of girls they considered sub-optimally attired, and if it was beyond three degrees plus or minus, it was five demerits. Tie knots for boys were the same, but type of knot, neatness and overly artistic interpretation added to the potential demerits. Woe betide anyone with an untucked shirt, poorly executed creases or socks not fully pulled up.

"My bow is *perfect*," she said, shooting me an annoyed glance, "as always. And you are wrong—as always. The sooner you are removed from this village, the better it will be for the rest of us."

"Did you ever think of starting up your very own charm school, Bunty?"

"There is no such thing as a charm school, Mr. Russett, so your comment is as banal as it is pointless. And don't call me 'Bunts.' That is reserved only for my closest and dearest friends."

"So no one ever uses it, right?"

Now that we had needled one another to our satisfaction, we stepped forward to greet the passengers.

The first to alight were a troupe of travelling players, all of whom wore Orange spot-badges on the lapels or blouses of their regulation Travel Casual #6s. They were lively and irreverent as players generally were, and I welcomed them to East Carmine while Bunty copied down their names and details on to the arrivals manifest. Quite why, no one knew: the manifests were diligently logged, filed, then recycled into blank arrivals manifest forms eight years later. The Rules demanded it. The Rules demanded a lot.

"We welcome your welcome and give thanks for your thanks," said the leader of the troupe, making a dramatic flourish to me, Bunty, then in the direction of the Grey Porters. "We are the Tangerine Players, and the Tangerine Players are us: famed all over Chromatacia for our bravado and spectrally compliant performances. A laugh, a tear, a smile—and after observing our lively frolics your resolve at the strength, brilliance and indivisible oneness of the Chromatic harmony will be for ever cemented. Apart We Are Together, but only together can we properly embrace that apartness."

"Well spoken," said Bunty, who was always eager to praise those who exhibited an unwavering support of the Colourtocracy.

"Thank you," said the Troupe Leader, eyeing Bunty's Yellow spot-badge and the 5,000-merit badge underneath. It told her Bunty was foremost a Yellow, and secondly, quite good at it. As the enforcers of the Rules, Yellows were universally loathed within the Collective. Some said it was a coincidence, but accidental face-down drownings in swamps were three times more likely if you were a Yellow.

The Troupe Leader stared at me for a moment then said:

"Haven't we met before?"

I knew instantly who she was, as I rarely, if ever, forget an interesting nose: small and snub, like a child's. It was as though her nose had ceased development at age nine, and her adult body had simply grown up around it.

"Jade-under-Lime," I said, "three years ago."

I had helped set up the stage and had been allocated the job of prop master: stagehands were always picked from the village to assist, along with any bit parts, usually from the Amateur Dramatic Society. My good friend Fenton had a walk-on part with two lines and told everyone who would listen he was going to be an actor, but without any yellow in his vision he was not going to be an Orange, so acting was never going to be open to him.

"I recall Jade as a very appreciative audience if a little inclined towards the cough," she said, "but sited in pleasant enough countryside."

She looked around at East Carmine's lugubrious surroundings as she said it. The landscape was hot and dusty, the grass dead in the summer heat, the railway station tired and worn and without hue as we had next to no synthetic colour in the village. High colourisation, usually delivered by colour feed-pipes, was for the wealthy and connected, generally those within the periphery of Emerald City, the nation's capital.

"It's been a hot summer out here in the Fringes," I said by way of apology. "Without regular night rain I daresay we'd have none at all."

I should have been happier living here in Red Sector West with people of my own hue, but there was a downside: the Rules ensured that anyone remotely troublesome was shuffled to the periphery of the Collective where they would be less influential. It made the Fringes more loaded with those of difficult disposition, which made life more challenging—but probably a good deal more interesting.

"Anything further out?" asked the Troupe Leader, indicating the hills to the west.

"We're right on the edge of the known world," I said, following her gaze. "There's nothing beyond here except wild rhododendron, megafauna, ball lightning, Riffraff and peril."

"The Red Side of the nation," she mused. "What did you do to be transferred out here? I'd say life was easier and more colourful in Jade-under-Lime."

"I was accompanying my father," I replied defensively, "who is now the village Swatchman."

In truth, I had been sent out here to conduct a chair census—the sort of pointless task usually reserved for those who have shown a level of innovation, curiosity or independence of thought that wasn't quite enough to send them to a re-education facility commonly known as "Reboot." My innovation was nothing seditious: simply a more efficient method of queuing. The Prefects didn't like the idea much, but I can happily report that my "take a number and you'll be called in turn" system has been adopted here in East Carmine and is something of which I think I can be justly proud.

"I see," said the Troupe Leader, who was only making small talk while Bunty over-diligently filled out the arrivals forms. "Any idea when the last troupe of travelling players passed through?"

"Twelve years ago."

The Tangerine Players all nodded and appeared relieved. There were only eight three-act plays, twelve one-act plays and forty-six educational vignettes permitted to be performed, and constant repetition to audiences only ever diluted the interest and applause.

Once Bunty was done with the manifest, I directed them to the Model T Ford which was waiting outside the station building. Our Janitor, Carlos Fandango, was already in the driver's seat, ready and waiting.

"We have a grass-banked auditorium," I told them. "Mr. Turquoise, the Blue Prefect, will meet you in the main square to show you around."

The players walked off down the platform towards the waiting car, talking and chatting in an enthusiastic manner that, had they been anyone else, would be demeritable on volume *and* frivolousness.

The next few passengers were more run-of-the-mill: a naturalist from Green Sector here to study bouncing goat, two Greys who would be sharpening the millstones, then the Sector co-ordinator for the Jollity Fair games, who was here to give a final talk before the Fair commenced.

"I hope your Penny-Farthing riders have got their act together," he said anxiously. "Red Sector needs to win this year more than ever."

"They have been practising most diligently," said Bunty. "I saw to it myself."

"Good show. Apart We Are Together."

The overused salutation had become little more than a murmur, its meaning lost to repetition and now merely word-grease to lubricate the wheels of social engagement. It was so oft repeated that no one even stopped to *think* about questioning it. When you did, people died.

NATIONAL COLOUR

Technological Leapback IV was due in three years, and everyone feared the worst. It was speculated that single-rail trains would be removed along with Model T Fords, electric light, heliostats, bicycles and telegraphy. Any of them would spell severe annoyance on their own, but taken together it would be a disaster: Chromatacia would become a darker world with transportation, sports and communications much reduced, the villages and towns and Sector capitals that made up the nation ever more dependent upon themselves.

—Ted Grey: *Twenty Years Among the Chromatacians*

"I despise the slack of hue, shy of toil and weak of manner," said Bunty while we waited for the next passenger to emerge. She was referring to the players, I think, as their non-productive role was often regarded as valueless to society.

"You are very equitable with your disgust," I said. "You seem to hate all colours, of whatever shade, in equal measure."

She observed me carefully for a moment to decide, I think, whether I had strayed into a demeritable level of discussion. Bunty McMustard was not just another Yellow: after Courtland Gamboge died she was bumped up to be the village's Yellow Deputy Prefect, her position within the village Yellows decided during her Ishihara eye test two years before. The Ishihara was the life-defining moment within the Collective: once you knew which colour you could see and how much, you knew precisely where you sat in the rigid hierarchy of the Colourtocracy. You knew what to do, where you would go and what was expected of you. In return, you accepted without question your position within society as laid out in Munsell's *Book of Harmony*. Your life, career and social standing decided right there and then, and all worrisome uncertainties eradicated for ever. I'd had my own test last month, and scored exceptionally high in my red vision—something I was still coming to terms with.

"The slack-hued, as you call them, are of as much use to the Collective as any other," I replied, paraphrasing the Rulebook as Yellows love to do that to others, and rarely enjoy in return. "Between Yellow and Red lie the Oranges, for entertainment and artistry, and between Yellow and Blue lie the Greens, for plant husbandry and applied outdoorsology—all necessary to the smooth running of the Collective. But tell me, Bunty, does your definition of slack-hued also describe the folk who lie equally between Blue and Red?"

She glared at me, for those folk would be defined as Lilac, Fandango, Lavender, Plum, Mauve, Magenta and eventually Purple—the highest echelon in society.

"The sooner this village is rid of you, the better, Russett. Once you are safely consigned to the Green Room for killing Courtland you will find none happier than I, with the possible exception of his mother."

"I didn't kill Courtland, Bunty."

"So *you* say."

It should be noted that Bunty McMustard had been betrothed to Courtland Gamboge, and Courtland's mother was the current Yellow Prefect. Not wise to annoy either of them, really, but aggravating Bunty had a peculiar pleasure to it, despite the risks.

"You say the sweetest things, Bunts."

She opened her mouth to say something but shut it again as the next passenger approached us. He wore a showy nickel-plated splashy paint-tin badge on his right lapel that denoted he was from National Colour, and by the looks of it, a low-level operative, someone learning the ropes before moving on and up.

"Welcome to East Carmine, sir," I said to the operative. "Our home is your home. Apart We Are Together."

"We certainly are," said the operative, whose name we learned was Jason Applejack. "I travelled from Emerald City this morning and will return on the next train. When is it?"

"The day after tomorrow."

"Then I am your guest for two nights."

"And we are to prove ourselves excellent hosts," I said. "May I ask a question?"

"Is it about colour feed-pipes and full colourisation?"

I nodded. National Colour weren't asked much else. A piped CMYK colour feed meant the potential of a full-gamut Colour Garden, visible to all, the hues to the flowers and grass and trees fed by pipes and capillaries beneath our feet.

"I'm sorry to say that new feed-pipe extensions are currently on hold until scrap colour drives have improved," he said. "We'd all like to have full-gamut Colour Gardens, but without the raw materials supplied by good people like you, full colourisation will never be complete. So: How is your colour mining going?"

"Not as well as we'd hoped," said Bunty in a quiet voice.

"Then you better pull your finger out. I thought the Red Side Fringes were brimming with scrap colour?"

"It's mostly mined out around here," I said, "but we're trying to open new colour fields further away."

To assist in the colour-based economy, scrap colour left by the Previous was mined, sorted and shipped to National Colour and reprocessed into raw Univisual colour for us all to view. Without it, we had only the natural shades that our sight gift bestowed upon us. To me as a Red, the poppies, to the Greens, trees, to the Blues, the sky. Visual colour to Chromatacian citizens was *everything*. It ran the entire social order, legal system, economy and health service. But most of all, colour was aspirational. National Colour didn't simply distribute colour, they were the suppliers of a dream-goal: to bring to our discoloured world the bounteous joy of full colourisation.

"Until such time as the Grid reaches us," said Bunty, "would National Colour open a colour shop out here instead?"

You didn't have to rely on colour feed-pipes to enrich your chromatic surroundings. Colour was also available in tins, paper rolls, tubes, food colouring, fabric dye and stained glass. Even if you weren't on the Grid, you could still enjoy synthetic colour, but always at a price. Oranges were two merits a half-dozen, but an *orange* orange cost that much for one.

"I'll be honest: it's unlikely," replied Applejack. "Retail colour outlets are generally reserved for the larger towns. So," he added, "can you recommend any lodgings?"

"The Fallen Man offers good food at a reasonable price with rooms that are clean and tidy, close to the central streetlamp and generally free of vermin," said Bunty.

"The Fallen Man?" he echoed.

"A local . . . *legend*," I replied, having chosen my words carefully. "He fell from the sky, strapped to a metal chair."

"Recently?"

"Thirteen years ago—if he did. Which he might not have."

Bunty sighed.

"The fallen man is *Apocrypha*," she said, "so we shall only speak of it as the name of an establishment."

If something in our surroundings—object, person, rule or

phenomenon—didn't fit within the strict terms of definition of the *Book of Harmony*, then it was conveniently dealt with by being ignored. There was an Apocryphal Man in the village named Baxter who it was forbidden to see, so who was steadfastly ignored. This meant he could do what he wanted with impunity— and this usually manifested itself in theft of clothes and food and wandering around naked. Baxter was seen and yet not seen all at the same time.

"A swan came down near Lincoln-on-the-Water," said Apple-jack, who clearly didn't think Apocrypha Rules applied to him. "Turned out it wasn't living at all, but made of metal and wires."

"Metal and wires?" I echoed. "Like Leapbacked technology?"

"More like the insides of a ripping turtle, if you've ever seen one."

"I've seen a picture of someone looking at a picture of one," I said.

"Liar," said Bunty, "there's no such thing."

"It's tortoise-like and the size of a dustbin lid," said Applejack, who sounded as though he'd taken a dislike to Bunty.

"It has six legs and spends its time finding and ripping out copper, brass, zinc and bronze from anywhere it finds it," he added, "which it piles into neat heaps, presumably for collection by a means long forgotten. Useful for anyone with jewellery as a hobby."

"Is that a fact?" said Bunty.

"I think it is," said Applejack.

She *did* know all this, but denied the existence of all Apoc-rypha because it was policy, and Yellows always promoted policy. She knew as well as I did there were twelve beasts in the nation generally regarded to be of manufactured rather than biological origin, and the ripping turtle was one of only three that were still known to function. It had been long suspected that swans might also be of non-biological origin, except the Rules stated they were real, and the Rules were infallible because it said so. In the Rules.

"Was it covered in feathers?" I asked as I hoped to clinch the swan issue one way or the other.

"They were painted on, yet quite realistically."

"Ah. What happened to it?"

"It was deemed *not* a swan but a 'swanesque' Apocrypha. They couldn't ignore it as it was too big, so burned it. Gave off a nasty odour and then exploded, taking a foot off an overly inquisitive Grey. Nasty business. They dumped it in the river beyond the Outer Markers. The Fallen Man, you said?"

He tipped his hat to us both, then took the waiting cycle-taxi into town.

MR. CELANDINE

3.09.11.67.09 (iv): The Ishihara test shall be taken in the year of a resident's twentieth birthday, and all must attend. The Colourman's test shall be final, the level of sight gift immovable and without recourse to appeal, change or review. Failure to accept your gift or attempts to sway the Colourman's views and opinions shall render the guilty resident and any associates forfeit of one hundred merits and/or Reboot, at the Prefect's discretion.

—From Munsell's *Book of Harmony*

"You ask far too many questions," said Bunty, "and really, what's the point, enquiring about swans and Apocrypha? Swans are simply swans and this time next week you and the ghastly Jane will be tallow and bonemeal with the unwanted remainder shredded and fed to the clutching bramble—and in that form a great deal more use than you are at present."

One's civil obligation to the Collective did not end with death. Your life and mind and compliance belonged to the Collective—as, ultimately, did your body, once you had no further use for it.

"When I want an intelligent or unbiased opinion I will seek the wisdom of a slug. Besides," I said, "the disciplinary hearing is to be conducted strictly in accordance with the Rules. We were on a fact-finding trip to High Saffron—we all knew the risks involved, and that includes Courtland. Jane, Violet, Tommo and

I are innocent of the charges and the rendering shed will have to carry on rendering without us. And just for the record, Jane is far from ghastly."

"Your endless denials speak heavily of guilt," said Bunty. "A model and upright citizen would defer to the better judgement of the Prefects and accept whatever punishment they thought appropriate."

"Is that what you would do?"

"In a heartbeat."

"You have a heart?" I said. "News to all of us. And denial doesn't mean guilt, it means we had nothing whatsoever to do with his death."

Courtland, Tommo, Jane, Violet and myself had been the team tasked to evaluate whether the abandoned coastal town of High Saffron could be opened to the mining of scrap colour. Violet and Tommo turned back early so just Courtland, Jane and I made it to High Saffron. Only Jane and I returned. Courtland had been the village's Yellow Prefect-in-waiting, so his loss was a big deal. And since he was also betrothed to Bunty in a roundabout default maybe perhaps if-no-one-better-comes-along sort of way, it made her dislike of me very personal.

"Everyone knows you and the dangerously volatile Jane Brunswick are guilty," said Bunty. "My beloved Courtland died as a direct result of your malice."

"If he was so beloved, why did he never pop the question and instead devote his downtime to Melanie Grey?"

Bunty went the colour of a beetroot and narrowed her eyes dangerously. The woefully small village marriage market made one's spousal choice a question of who was available and of how much colour they could see. If you came out of a marriage thinking: "that could have been a lot worse," it was generally agreed a happy life might await you both.

"He was practising with that Grey girl so he would be at the top of his game when ready to fill me with his adorable Yellow babies," said Bunty, shivering at the thought of it and conjuring up an image I could definitely do without. "Courtland was *exceptionally* generous in that manner."

"It's the only possible explanation," I replied.

"Are you and Jane still sticking to your 'Courtland got eaten by a tree while rescuing you' nonsense?" she asked.

"It's the truth," I replied.

"It's demonstrable nonsense," she said, "and you know why? Courtland would *never* have rescued you. Such selfless acts were entirely out of character. A Yellow resident with as high a sight gift as Courtland has a duty to protect themself from harm so their true value to the community can be properly exploited."

It was a very good point. The story wasn't a great one, but the truth would have been unthinkable. We didn't kill him—the Collective did.

"Courtland was taken by a yateveo while rescuing me," I said, sticking to the plan. I'd been taken by a carnivorous tree twice myself and I can reliably report that it is not a pleasant experience, even with the big plus that you'd drown long before you were digested, so long as you had the extreme good luck to be deposited head down in the digestion bulb. Jane rescued me, but it didn't mean I owed her big time or anything: she was the one who put me there.

"So *you* say, Russett," said Bunty. "My troubling level of stress-induced constipation is all your doing. I shall be honoured to be a part of the group that consigns you forcibly to the Green Room."

Barring an unexpected, violent or other unlikely end, most of us would choose to depart via the Green Room once our burden to society outweighed our usefulness. We'd voluntarily enter, gaze upon the restful shade of green known as *Sweetdream* painted on the walls and ceiling and then, in a manner similar to the buoyant pleasures of Lime or Lincoln we would feel a sense of restful contentment, giggly joy, indescribable pleasure and then ecstasy, where the pleasured cries of engreened souls would drift across the playing fields for all to hear. Little wonder people took the Green Way Out. If you had to go before Your Time, it was a good way to do it.

"Sally Gamboge will supply that proof," said Bunty, "or a near enough approximation as to make no difference. Now pay attention: our last passenger has held themself back so as not to have to queue. They will alight presently."

"Must be a Prefect."

"Of course—so don't run your mouth."

Jane had told me she would gladly poison Bunty McMustard, and while I shared the sentiment in a wishful-thinking kind of way, I never agreed or encouraged Jane on matters like this. I loved Jane, but there was little doubt in my mind that she was capable of such a thing. And if she hadn't already killed someone, it was only a question of *when*.

The "Prefects only" compartment door opened and I moved closer to help the passenger climb out. He waved my hand away, alighted from the train and then looked around disdainfully.

"Welcome to East Carmine," I said politely. "Apart We Are Together."

He inclined his head in acknowledgement and returned the mantra of the Collective in a murmur. He was about twice my age, that is to say, about forty, and he had a soft jowly face whose nose seemed as though made of inadequately risen dough. He carried with him an air of arrogant never-questioned authority and seemed utterly unimpressed by the desolate rural environment that surrounded East Carmine. Unlike villages in the more affluent sectors with their well-appointed hedges, Colour

Gardens and raked gravel paths, East Carmine was scrubby, dusty and unkempt.

"It's the Greys," explained Bunty, following his look, "we don't have enough of them, and those we do don't work nearly hard enough. One died last week and with that single selfish act, six houses were left without a cleaner, the Prefects lost a bootboy and we are one less on the linoleum factory late shift."

"An intolerable state of affairs," said the Yellow. "Greys are as indolent and untruthful as they are lazy and obstinate—sometimes I think they die on purpose, simply to vex us."

He wore a large Yellow Spot of Univisual hue on his light robes, which were themselves probably natural yellow although I couldn't know that.

"The Outer Fringes do not agree with me," he announced as he held a perfumed kerchief to his nose. "A place without morals, society or hue. I trust the stockwalls are well maintained? I have no desire to make acquaintance with megafauna while on my visit."

"I supervised this morning's Boundary Patrol myself," I said. "Bouncing goat get in, but they harm no one and bounce out soon enough. Both rhinosaurus and ground sloth have not been near the village for years, although a herd of elephant did pass by the week before last."

"And the squarial?" he asked.

"The squarial come and go as they please," I said, not sure why he thought them a threat. Indeed, the tree-based mammal had the useful propensity to hoard nuts, screws, washers, split pins and bolts, which were useful for mending things, always supposing you could find the hoard. My best friend Fenton's great-grandmother came across a centuries-amassed heap in an empty oak tree outside Jade-under-Lime, and used it to start a hardware store still profitable today.

"My name is Hawtrey Celandine," he said to Bunty so she could write it in the manifest, "here for three days, Yellow Prefect of Dog-Leg-Lake. Would you be Bunty McMustard?"

"I am, sir."

"Then you have my sympathies regarding the loss of Courtland. I understand you and he were betrothed?"

"In every single way but physically, legally, and affectionately," she announced as if that were somehow a fine boast, "and since the Lemon brothers here are low-grade material in every meaning of the word, it means I am once more available for marriage. If you have any high Yellows in Dog-Leg-Lake eager of a union with an upright Yellow with good prospects, I come with a dowry of two thousand merits and my tuba playing is much spoken about."

"Born here or sent here?" he asked. It was a loaded question, and doubtless to put her in her place, as he probably knew the answer. Reports about potential spouse material were routinely compiled and shared.

"I was born in Buckfastwii, Yellow Sector North," she replied in a bold voice, trying not to make her presence in East Carmine the humiliation it was. "Sent out here six years ago to study the nest-building habits of . . . cuckoos."

The pointlessness of her mission and the fact that she'd never been recalled suggested they'd disliked her almost as much as we did. She'd slotted in here well as the Gamboges were about as awful as she, and Yellows generally looked after Yellows.

"Good to know," said Celandine as we walked towards the station exit. He took a moment to look me up and down. "You seem young. I trust I have not been met by someone weak of hue?"

According to the Book of Munsell, any visiting Prefect had to be met by a "Significant Shade," and I had been one of those since my 86.7 percent red vision was revealed during my Ishihara. There was no breaking-in period—I was thrust instantly into a world of responsibilities that befitted my new-found status.

"No, sir," I said, as our spot-badges only ever designated one's hue, never one's spectral proficiency, "I am one of the highest red sighters in the village; Head Prefect deMauve tasked me to greet you."

"Then despite your youth you will have to do."

While unexpected, my promotion from "likely high red sight gift" to "exceptional red sight gift" was really from one level of spectral privilege to another. By contrast, Jane had been a Grey before her Ishihara, and a very light Green after. She transferred from the Greyzone to an unused apartment in the Green part of town, where she would be expected to mingle and marry and work in a job dictated by her new hue. Worse, she and I with our complementary Red and Green colours were expressly forbidden to fraternise with anything more than "distant cordiality." It was one of the crueller Rules. You might be good friends or lovers or even engaged, but come the Ishihara test, if you were on the opposite side of the colour wheel, you'd be compelled to be on nodding terms for the rest of your lives.

"There was a Riffraff alert just before we departed Dog-Leg-Lake," said Prefect Celandine when Bunty asked if his journey had been agreeable, "but we saw no one. I am proud to say that we have embraced the policy of extermination on the advice of Head Office. It's the kindest way to deal with the Riffraff, especially as they have a well-known tendency to steal babies, probably because they eat their own. Some suggest that they have babies only to eat, a view I am inclined to believe. Do you have much problem with vermin down here?"

I had to admit that we didn't. Riffraff was the more usual term for *Homo feralensis*, a sort of wild human, who despite their recategorisation as "vermin," seemed peaceable enough in the few encounters I had shared with them.

"In all honesty I doubt the baby-eating stories," I said, somewhat daringly, "given that it must take considerably more energy to grow a baby than could possibly be liberated by eating one."

"So you're expert in midwifery now, are you?" sneered Bunty.

"Theoretical nutrition."

"They are *savages*," snorted Celandine disapprovingly. "Base, vulgar and ignorant. I heard they engage in procreative behaviour simply for *fun*."

"Shocking," said Bunty. "Congress without benefit to the community is congress wasted."

"I could not agree more," said Celandine. "Mrs. Celandine and I had congress only when the demand of a child required it, and even then we took steps to ensure there was no enjoyment to either party."

I didn't want to know how they might have achieved this, and Celandine continued:

"What about swan attack?"

We all instinctively looked up. There was nothing to be seen in the clear grey sky. East Carmine's swans appeared regularly at around ten every morning and five in the afternoon. They adopted that curious figure-of-eight pattern above the village for about twenty minutes before moving on.

"East Carmine has not seen so much as a broken arm in living memory," I said, which was true. The "Days since Swan Attack" sign had long ago reached 999, the highest it could be, and had stayed there, never reset.

"You are indeed fortunate," he said. "A swan swooped down and took a toddler in Greensdale-on-the-Vale only a week ago. We must remain perpetually vigilant."

"Why would a swan take a toddler?" I asked, but he didn't

answer my question as it was not a question that could or should be answered. Like many of the existential fears foisted upon us—lightning, the night, Riffraff, swans, Pooka—none of them was particularly fearful when placed under even the most cursory level of scrutiny. Little wonder curiosity was so frowned upon. A frightened population, Jane told me, was a compliant one.

"I will be attending the disciplinary hearing," he added to move the conversation on, "as by the Rules enshrined in the good book and to ensure impartiality, an investigation into the loss of a Deputy Prefect cannot be led by the resident Yellow Prefect if she is related."

I understood now why Celandine was here. If left to her own devices, Sally Gamboge would already have found Jane and Tommo and me guilty of her son's death. At least with Celandine here, there would be a veneer of impartiality. Violet, we knew, would be unlikely to face any charges.

"And we are very grateful for your assistance," said Bunty as she shot a glance at me. "Your transport awaits."

THE VILLAGE

Torrance Redwing invented the term *Loopholery* and made the skill his own. He began by finding a way around the Rules to allow him to keep fish, then made trifle available to all, wangled a way to wear a beret on Thursdays, and have hair that went over the collar. Although regarded as something of a hero, you won't find his exploits recorded. He lives on only in the covert and unregulated oral tradition.

—Ted Grey: *Twenty Years Among the Chromatacians*

We stepped out of the station building and Prefect Celandine stopped abruptly at the sight of the Ford. It wasn't the ancient car that annoyed him as nearly all cars were Model Ts since the ban on automobiles during Leapback III ninety-six years before. If the Model T had not been museum exempted and subsequently declared "surplus to collection" in an inspired piece of loopholery, we wouldn't even have those. I read in *Spectrum* magazine there were several stripped-down Hispano-Suizas in Blue Sector used for ploughing, and somewhere in Red Sector South an Austin Allegro was used to transport dung, a role in which it was surprisingly able.

No, it was the Tangerine Players who were sitting on the flatbed that irked Celandine. Oranges were generally creatives: artists and poets and actors and whatnot and seen as dissolute: footless, feckless, and often, meritless—both financially and personally. By the look on Celandine's face, he thought them little better than Greys, or worse, Riffraff.

"I shall not travel with them," he announced sniffily. "They shall walk."

He waited while I explained to the players that I would send the car back for them, and after glaring daggers at the Yellow Prefect, they went to stand in the shade of the station canopy.

"Welcome to East Carmine," said Carlos Fandango, our resident Janitor, speaking from the driver's seat. "I have a brother at Dog-Leg-Lake who clerks in the council chambers."

"How fascinating," replied Celandine. "Drive slowly or I will have you demerited. And I have no desire for banal conversation."

Carlos nodded in reply, knowing better than to backchat a Prefect. Fandango was *technically* Purple, but so mild as to be inconsequential. Higher Purples often referred dismissively to their lower-hued brethren as simply: "Bluey-Reds."

The car ran on discarded cooking oil, so as soon as the engine burst into life there was a smell like the communal kitchens on chip night. After I had removed the brick from under the T's rear wheel and joined Bunty sitting on the flatbed, we set off along the Perpetulite roadway towards the village.

"That is our linoleum factory," I said, pointing to the large red-brick building from where the sound of muffled clanking could be heard. "We supply the entire Collective with linoleum."

"A worthy boast," said Celandine, "and a success I understand much attributed to Mrs. Gamboge. Is it true she has the workers on sixty-eight-hour weeks?"

"It is," said Bunty enthusiastically, as Gamboge's excesses were well known, "and seventeen years without a holiday."

"How does she manage that?"

"She persuaded the Council to adopt a Standard Variable that holiday entitlements must be taken at either retirement or death," said Bunty. "Retirement tastes so much sweeter when well earned, and who needs holiday after death?"

Prefect Celandine chuckled to himself.

"An admirable solution to an intractable issue, and one which I am sure to implement. Keeping workshy Greys in check is nothing short of a wearisome burden with which I can empathise—Dog-Leg-Lake's factory makes cutlery and we often miss production targets solely due to the Greys' characteristic indolence."

This was indeed interesting. Not his negative attitude to Greys, which was fairly standard among the higher hues, but the cutlery factory. I had a potential spoon problem workaround planned.

"Really?" I said, then added a little stupidly, "But you make no spoons?"

"Of course no spoons," he said in a sharp tone, scolding me for the banality of my comment. Due to an unaccountable error in Munsell's *Book of Harmony*, spoon manufacture was prohibited. At the last spoon census it was estimated there was only one spoon per eleven residents, not counting ladles and other implements of a serving capacity. Spoon sharing was now permitted as a Standard Variable, as was eating custard with a fork. If you thought that Rule was daft, consider gloves: we were permitted to make them, but never to wear them.

"If it were not for my team's constant harassment of our workforce," said Celandine, "the entire Collective would be eating with its hands."

We pulled to the side of the road to allow a three-man peloton of Penny-Farthings to pass in a whirl of spokes, the riders' faces a mixture of concentration, exertion and fear.

"For Jollity Fair?" asked Prefect Celandine.

"I think we may win the sprint and miles covered in an hour," said Carlos. "They practise a lot, and seemingly have no fear."

"How did Penny-Farthings escape the bicycle gearing ban of

Leapback III?" asked Bunty, a question doubtless couched more in search of an infraction, rather than curiosity.

"Unicycles were exempted from the geared bicycle ban," I replied, "so by extension that included the Penny-Farthing, as the smaller second wheel had been deemed a 'stabilisation aid' rather than a wheel in its own right."

"Humph," said Bunty.

"Although the large wheel of the Penny-Farthings give the bikes a usefully fast speed," added Carlos, "there are drawbacks: their high riding height and extreme rapidity make them potentially dangerous, and riders are routinely killed attempting new records."

The chief cause of fatalities was not only speed—it was also while competing in the profoundly insane "urban freestyle" event of back flips and spins in mid-air.

"I will be attending Jollity Fair," said Bunty proudly, presumably in an effort to impress Mr. Celandine, "in my attempt to win 'lowest note sustained' on my highly modified subcontrabass tuba. My entry will be below a human's frequency range, but should be able to induce an extreme mooing event in a cow."

"I wish you the best of luck," said Mr. Celandine without any interest at all. "If there is any way at all I can assist in this effort, please keep it to yourself."

"Thank you," said Bunty, mishearing him.

We drove on for a minute, past the lumber yard, cheese-making facility and donkey mill.

"You are here to make judgement upon young Mr. Gamboge's death?" asked Carlos Fandango. As village Janitor he was driver and maintainer of our small fleet of Model Ts, the central streetlight and much else besides. He saw 14 percent across the blue and red fields, which was only just the mauve side of nothing at all, but his coveted Janitor status did afford him odd perks, such as being able to speak to someone like Mr. Celandine without being spoken to first.

"I will listen to all the party's testimony with due diligence, look upon the evidence dispassionately and without bias, then weigh all the factors to arrive at a verdict that supports Mrs. Gamboge's initial finding: that her son's death was foul and unnatural and that the perpetrators be punished forthwith."

"You have already made up your mind?" asked Carlos as he glanced at me.

"I am not here to impugn upon the word of a much-respected Yellow," he said. "I am here merely as a formality. Do any of you know this Edward Russett fellow?"

"Quite well," I said. "It's me."

He stared at me.

"Your asinine questions over spoons and swan attack are now easily explained," he said. "You and Cinnabar and Jane Brunswick are not being *punished*, but are sacrificing yourselves so that everyone realises the importance by which the Rules are penned, and that the defiling of the harmony bruises the Collective's ability to enjoy a life unsullied by confusion and malice."

He made our death sentences sound almost noble.

"Do you do many of these hearings?" I asked.

"My time is spent doing little else. My forthright manner and Yellow-centric demeanour puts me much in demand."

I didn't doubt it, although it didn't have to be like this: the Rules weren't the problem, it was their unchangingly rigid interpretation that made them unworkable. It was how these Rules were interpreted in order that fairness could be attained that marked out a good Council from a poor one. On a day trip once to Viridian to buy some food dye, Dad and I went into the Council Chambers for some free entertainment and watched an interesting case: the Head Prefect, instead of charging a woman with murdering her husband with a pair of garden shears after he stole intimacy without consent, decided instead she be charged with "irresponsibly running with scissors." She was duly found guilty, fined fifty demerits and undertook an afternoon's additional scissor training. Her husband's remains went straight to the rendering shed without fanfare. No one denied it was anything but a good result.

"That is our crackletrap," said Bunty proudly, as she pointed towards the domed copper device atop the village's flak tower, "a civil project devised by our very own Sally Gamboge to keep lightning strikes away from the community."

Lurid tales of lightning strikes where residents had their brains boiled inside their heads were the third most popular article in *Spectrum* magazine along with swan attack and Riffraff baby stealing. In truth, the crackletrap had only two attributes that were incontestable: it had cost a vast amount of communal cash merits in its construction, and was of no use to anyone at all.

"Impressive," said Celandine, but he was more interested in the flak tower. Since city, town and village layouts all conformed strictly to the Architectural Uniformity Protocols, towers randomly placed or anything at variance with the approved layout gave a unique identity, something of which East Carmine could be rightly proud.

"Any idea of its function?" mused Celandine, as there were no flak towers in Dog-Leg-Lake.

"None at all," said Bunty, "but they are mentioned in the *Book of Harmony* so presumably Our Munsell has a plan for them."

The vast, mildly tapered structure was at least three times as tall as the town hall, and like the town hall and Council Chambers it had been grown out of building-grade Perpetulite. The tower might have been a storehouse, lookout, or even a store of Perpetulite itself, waiting to be called into use as something else, but never was. Like so much around us, the past was not only unknown, but *unknowable*.

We lapsed into silence as Fandango drove us through the East Gate and into the village, the centre of which was laid out as a large open square with the prominent hues' residences at the north end and with the cafés, shops, library and artisans' workshops making up the remainder of the periphery, all in their prescribed position, the exact same in each "C"-sized town. The main hall sat in the middle, outside the main doors of which was the twice-lifesize statue of Our Munsell. Beyond the central square were the lower hues' quarters, kitchens, workshops and granaries with hay barns, dairy and Carlos's workshop a little way distant, with the rendering sheds, tannery, Green Room and Greyzone downwind and most distant of all.

Carlos stopped outside the Gamboges' house, easily recognised by the bright Univisual yellow door. Sally Gamboge was waiting on the doorstep and greeted Mr. Celandine warmly.

"That's the one who killed my son," said Mrs. Gamboge, pointing a bony finger at me. "Note him well."

"I despise him already," returned Mr. Celandine. "You have my unwavering support in this matter."

"I thought this was to be a fair and free hearing?" I said as I placed Celandine's valise on the ground next to him.

"How *dare* you?" said Mrs. Gamboge. "Your suggestion of a predecided outcome is insulting, demeaning and unruleful. Your book, please."

I sighed and handed over my merit book and was fined twenty merits for "impugning upon the reputation of an elder," ten for "speaking out of turn," and five for "additional nonspecific impudent intent."

She handed me back my merit book and I thanked her for my punishment in order to avoid a further demerit due to "inadequate acknowledgement of personal failings," then departed quickly before they could drum up some more charges.

"I hope you and Jane have a good strategy in place," said Carlos once we were out of earshot. "Those two will try anything to get you into the Green Room."

Despite my involvement in the plot that saw Carlos's daughter and Dorian run away together, he seemed not to bear me much ill will. That would change dramatically if he knew what had ultimately happened to them. I would have to ensure he never did.

"We've got a plan," I said.

"You have?"

"Yes; it revolves chiefly around a large helping of delusive hope, and failing that, a good pair of running shoes."

TOMMO CINNABAR

The Cinnabar family had been big in the crimson pigment trade until illegal price-fixing which led to their downfall and made them fairly toxic in the marriage market. When all Cinnabars had no better option than to marry a Grey, the family would be no more. Once in the Greyzone, all fallen hues were rendered equal—until someone married up-hue and the whole thing started over again.
—Ted Grey: *Twenty Years Among the Chromatacians*

We parked the Ford outside the Janitor's workshop and climbed out. While Carlos conducted the post-drive maintenance checks and logged the mileage in the book, I had a look around. Any Janitor's garage—not just Fandango's—was a wondrous collection of exempted old tech in which it closely resembled Cobalt's Museum of the Something that Happened. The village had two Ford Model Ts, the first for general use, and the second for hunting ball lightning: the car was mounted with a crossbow in the rear loaded with a copper spike that trailed earthing wires when launched. Both vehicles were at least a millennium past their design life, and the vehicles had been so oft repaired that they bore only a passing resemblance to the original Ford—we knew, because there was a picture of one pinned to the wall.

Also in the large workshop were a forge, a lathe and a milling machine, all powered by an exempted Everspin, which ran a series of pulleys and belts from an overhead shaft. It was thought another Everspin generated the electricity for the central streetlamp, which burned carbon rods to produce an arc of pure white brightness, but no one knew for sure as the generator room was locked, and no one had the key.

But by far and away the most interesting thing in the garage was Fandango's pride and joy: the gyro-bike, East Carmine's entry for Jollity Fair's stored energy sprint race. The bike was beautifully hand-constructed by Carlos himself and was a low-slung two-wheeled vehicle with tyres a foot wide, a low single saddle and short stubby downward-facing handlebars inboard of a tight fairing.

Jane had been in the frame to pilot the bike, but with our future up in the air, an alternative was being sought. Amelia Cinnabar—Tommo's first cousin—was the assistant Janitor under Fandango and, having ridden the bike on numerous tests, was the next fastest in trials around East Carmine's velodrome.

"Are we in with a chance?" I asked.

"Technically we've got a good bike," said Carlos, laying a hand on the sleek, polished steel-and-black machine, "but Jamie 'Mad Dog' Juniper representing Green Sector is the rider to beat, and that will be difficult."

"Difficult or impossible?"

"Somewhere between the two. But we do have an edge: most teams store the bike's energy in six spinning weights, but I've squeezed in another two. Takes a little longer to wind up to full speed and the compensating mechanisms for turning safely are more complex, but it should help."

"The bigger issue," said Amelia, who was also present, "is ensuring Jane is around to ride it. I'm fast, but not as fast as her."

"I asked deMauve to defer your hearings," added Fandango, "but he said Gamboge wouldn't have it."

"She's not a fan."

"So I heard. There's a meeting later on this afternoon to finalise plans for our team this year—you ever competed at Jollity?"

"My shade of mustard won 'best runner-up' last year," I replied, "but I didn't attend, just sent in the numbers over the telegraph: 33-71-67. But unless Jollity introduces the sport of 'improved queueing methods,' I'm not sure I'll ever compete."

Tommo walked up, greeted us both and joined in the conversation.

"If you want to compete at Jollity you could always start a 'most people in a mandated-size wardrobe' team," he said. "I'm sure there are enough people in this village stupid enough."

"I'm not so sure we'd be competitive," said Amelia. "The wardrobe-stuffing event long ago reached maximum stuffage, so the event is really about longevity."

"The Greens dominate the event," added Tommo, "and often spend the whole of Jollity Fair locked inside a medium-sized wardrobe. Fatalities are common and there are unfounded yet undeniably salacious rumours of cannibalism."

I would have liked to have dawdled longer in the workshop, but Tommo and I were actually there to pick up a couple of hoes. Although well above farming duty, dealing with the advance of pernicious aliens was deemed the work of higher Chromatics. We signed out the implements and walked off in the direction of the East Gate.

"Hey, Eddie, guess what?"

"You're going to live a blameless and honest life from now on, and renounce all your schemes and misdemeanours?"

"Not a chance. Guess again."

"You've volunteered to become the village's ornamental hermit?"

"What? No. I've been given the job of editor and photographer at the East Carmine *Mercury* following Dorian's departure."

He looked pleased with himself as it was a plum job—you could poke your nose pretty much anywhere. But on the downside, say the wrong thing and you could be poorer by several hundred merits or, in the worst-case scenario, sent off to Reboot. The canny newspaper editor reserved themselves to jam harvests, parroting the words of Munsell, repeating the Prefect's many speeches, then trumpeting the impressive yet wholly fictitious village manufacturing figures.

"I see," I said, as the previous editor's fate was not something I was that happy about, "and I'm assuming this means you're not facing charges with Jane and me over the High Saffron fiasco?"

"You guess correct. Mrs. Gamboge agreed to dismiss all charges in exchange for an in-depth feature in the *Mercury* about how the Yellows are far better than anyone had thought—making special mention of their probity, adherence to procedure and transparency. They want me to cover your and Jane's hearing, too: testimony, defence, guilty verdict, punishment—that sort of thing. I'll be watching from the public gallery."

"So Sally Gamboge let you off? That was excessively kind of her."

"Not really," he said cheerfully. "I've been—how shall I put it? Laying down some favours for a rainy day."

"Is there anything you wouldn't do to get ahead?" I asked, as Sally's semi-regular bedroom usage of Tommo was an open secret, and just one more reason why no one would trust him an inch.

"I've had all charges dropped and am now the editor of the *Mercury*," he said. "Figure that one out for yourself."

"I suppose Violet will wriggle out of the hearing too, what with her father the Head Prefect."

"Hadn't you heard? It's been established 'beyond all doubt' that Violet had absolutely no part in Courtland's death. She has been exonerated from all wrongdoing and been awarded 'aggrieved bystander in need of sympathy' status and signed off work for a week."

"That's not a surprise," I said.

"No," agreed Tommo, "and since Violet doesn't actually do any work, she was given the cash alternative."

"Figures."

We walked past the colour sorting room, grain store and flak tower and soon arrived at the village boundary, a high dyke-and-ditch structure that encircled the village and was topped by a defensive hedge of clutching brambles, a carnivorous plant that would constrict its victim until death by starvation or fatigue, then live off the decomposing nutrients as they leached into the soil. The clutching brambles kept out most animals aside from bouncing goat who could leap clean over, although the ground sloth and elephant had been known to simply push their way through.

"My first Useful Work assignment was slopping unwanted render on to the roots of the clutchers," said Tommo. "Even then the Prefects didn't much like me."

"My first Useful Work was shredding the village's glove allocation to be used as stuffing for toys and quilts," I replied.

Despite the ban on wearing gloves, their manufacture was at a mandated level. Stockpiling them would have been impractical, so they were recycled almost as soon as they arrived in the village.

"Did you ever try one on?" Tommo asked. "Y'know, for kicks and giggles?"

"Maybe."

"Daring of you. I heard Bunty McMustard was caught wearing a pair of work gloves last month," he added, "while trimming the clutchers. I think her hearing will be the support act to yours. She'll get off, what with being a Yellow and Celandine here to help preside. Should be quite a show—there are six infractions being heard before you. I'll be doing refreshments at half-time and renting cushions by the hour. Disciplinary hearings are always popular and a good way to make a few extra merits."

We exited the village by way of the underground tunnel that went through the steep earthen bank and was secured at the far end by a heavy wooden door, then took off our spot-badges and placed them in a locker, as Riffraff were reputed to kidnap and ransom those of high hue. But like many fears, there was little if any evidence to support the suggestion. As we moved outside the village I felt an imperceptible relaxation, as though a weight suddenly lifted. It wasn't uncommon to feel an urge to simply walk away and never look back, come what may. There was even a term for it—*wanderlost*—but the foolishness of such an enterprise was soon quashed by thoughts of the many genuine perils that awaited the hapless traveller outside the comfort and security of the village. People *did* go missing—quite a few if the adverts in *Spectrum* were anything to go by—but it was impossible to say whether that was wanderlost or something more sinister such as beasts, the night, exposure, starvation or even the mythical "Pale Rider" whom death always followed.

We loosened our ties and then pulled our shirts from our elasticated waistbands in celebration of quiet defiance and moved away from the village, but were careful not to stray past the ring of stones that delineated the Outer Markers, as that would require permission from the Prefects, which we didn't have.

"There's a contender," said Tommo, pointing at one of the alien invaders we had been tasked to destroy.

The rhododendron had been encroaching upon the land for a very long time, and as Head of Invasive Alien Eradication, it was my job to ensure that they—and other invasive species—did not gain a toehold anywhere within the village. We quickly dug it out. It wasn't big, barely a seedling, and to the untrained eye, little more than a weed.

"Actually," continued Tommo as we carried on, scanning the

ground for any more seedlings, "I didn't take the *Mercury* job to write inflated nonsense for the Prefects. I'm more interested in taking photographs. Dorian taught me how to use the camera and darkroom before he left, and I think I've got the hang of it—look."

He showed me a picture of Daisy Crimson in front of the library.

"I get enough chemicals to coat four glass plates and make thirty paper prints a month, and that got me to thinking—do you think you could persuade Jane to pose without her clothes on?"

"Whatever for?"

"Market research has revealed to me that a naked picture of Jane would be mighty popular; twenty-six villagers have already pledged five merits each for a look, and eighteen merits to hire the picture for the evening, the profits of which I would gladly share with Jane—and you for facilitating the deal, naturally."

"You can go down to the river any day of the week and see as many unclothed bodies as you want," I said, "Jane included. Why would people pay to see a picture of something they can get for free?"

"It's *different*," he said, "and about desire. Everyone reads the Very Racy Story in *Spectrum* magazine, either on their own or with a special one—this is a similar deal, although it would work a lot better if Jane could offer up a 'winsome come-hither' sort of look."

"Winsome come-hither?"

"Yes," he said, "or 'impudent coquettishness.'"

"You're kidding?" I asked.

"Not kidding at all. I reckon this could be a lucrative business and I'm surprised no one's thought of it before."

"I think," I said, "Jane's answer would be a punch in the eye followed by swift kick in the plums."

"I thought so, too," said Tommo, "which is why I'm asking you to be the middle man at considerable financial loss to myself."

"Ask her yourself," I said, "and good luck getting anyone to take part."

"Clifton Grey and Sophie Lapis-Lazuli jumped at the chance and I've already sold three prints of each. Clifton *really* took to the challenge as he's got about the most impressive physique in the village. He swapped the 'winsome come-hither' look for 'rugged and willing.' I can see why Violet chose him as her Grey-on-the-side. Do you want to have a look?"

"No thanks, and I'm not sure the Prefects will look kindly upon your little scheme."

"You'd be surprised. Prefect Yewberry *himself* has already enquired if I might have the models pose together in the same picture—and standing daringly close to one another."

"What's that noise?"

We ducked behind an old phone box which was half-sunk into the soil. The years of corrosion had reduced the metalwork to a delicate spiderweb of rusty iron; if you sneezed, it would likely collapse into rust. We exchanged a nervous glance until we heard the familiar swish of a zebra's tail.

We moved quietly forward through the underbrush until we came within sight of a small group of coded zebra, their barcode incorporated into their stripes. There were a half-dozen of them and they had not seen us, so I quickly whispered out their barcodes while Tommo logged them in his book.

"Medium, broad, thick, heavy, thin, thin, medium, thin, heavy, broad, medium, thin, heavy, broad . . ."

Once we were done on all the zebras we transferred the code into a number and then did a checksum calculation to ensure we had read the bar correctly, and after ten minutes of adding and multiplication all the numbers came up as correct. We were just in time, for a noise startled the zebras and they were soon gone in a cloud of dust. We sat down and consulted our animal-spotting books to see if we'd seen them already.

"I've logged five of these Taxa numbers before," said Tommo thoughtfully, "but the remainder is a foal—two years old if your barcode-reading is up to scratch."

Animal Taxa numbers were mentioned in the Rules so could be legally traded, swapped, studied and collated with impunity. The heavy-hitter animal-spotters collected megafauna numbers—giant sloth, elephant, woolly rhino and the like—but it was a hobby that could be done in the safety of one's own home, too, simply by logging the barcodes on rats, cockroaches, homing slugs and possums.

"We can sell or swap the newbie's number, but the others I think are well known—there's a shop in Vermillion that trades in numbers and most zebras have been logged."

The brief excitement over, we shoved our books back in our pockets and carried on our way.

"Ever wondered why everything has a barcode?" I asked.

Tommo looked at me and raised an eyebrow.

"Why would you *want* to know? Things don't have to have a reason or explanation—isn't life vexing enough without mysteries and unknowns to divert us from happiness? When I found out how rainbows worked it didn't improve my life, so neither will the knowledge regarding zoological barcodes."

"Wait, you know how rainbows work?"

It was well known that the same single band of colour in the sky was observed by others of a different sight gift; it was supposed a rainbow had six colours, but the loftier Purples claimed seven.

Tommo shrugged.

"Sort of. Lucy explained it to me. Something to do with light and raindrops. I'm a little hazy on the details. But the point is, knowing stuff doesn't change your life—and if it does, then that's proof it was better off not knowing. I'd rather to be a happy fool than a dead expert."

"Being a happy fool is working out for you?"

"So far it's been highly lucrative."

I examined the enlarged nail of my own index finger, and the unique set of lines that grew out of the nail-bed. Human barcodes were so far unreadable, but considered to also be Taxa—hence the name "index finger." The lines were very fine, and double the quantity of a standard code. A *lot* more information. I'd tried deciphering it once and came up with a thirty-six-digit number that defied decoding.

Tommo showed me his—at some point in his life he had damaged the nail and the lines had fractured and now grew out as dotted lines.

"No Taxa code on me"—he grinned—"so I'm not collectable. But seriously—knowing where the Fallen Man came from will not help you or me one iota."

He had made the comment because we had arrived at the spot a man had unexpectedly thumped into the earth more than a decade before.

THE FALLEN MAN

Chromatacia was built upon the ashes of a world that belonged to another species of human known as *Homo ambitiosus*, or more simply, the Previous. They were tall, had full colour vision and were handicapped by anger, avariciousness and greed. Little is known about the Something that Happened, but it was thought to have been a conflict of some sort, as the detritus of what one supposes were fighting machines still abound.

—Ted Grey: *Twenty Years Among the Chromatacians*

The remains of the Fallen Man were surrounded by a low wall about forty foot in diameter, the area within kept short and neat by a small colony of charmingly plump and very industrious guinea pigs, the usual go-to solution for maintenance-free grass cutting on a budget. We sat on the low wall for a rest as the afternoon had heated up like an oven; even the flies seemed languid and of low cheer. Although serious work, there was little fun to be had in pulling up rhododendron seedlings, and so long as we logged a dozen destroyed in the invasive aliens book, everyone would be happy. I was actually thankful that the notweed and him-and-layman balsam were less prevalent around these parts; back in Jade-under-Lime there had been an entire team of low Greens doing little else.

We sat for a moment in silence.

"How could this *not* impact your life in some way?" I asked as I pointed towards the Fallen Man, and all the unanswered questions his presence brought. No one knew where he had come from, nor the mechanism by which he had. The only two things known for sure were that he appeared overnight thirteen years before, and his name: Martin Baker, which had been painted on his metal seat. Baker wasn't a colour, so he was either a baker— unlikely—or National Colour, which was also not likely, given that he didn't have a splashy paint-tin logo anywhere on his uniform. There was nothing that related to people falling from the sky in metal chairs in the *Book of Harmony*, so the Council officially deemed him Apocrypha: something to be ignored. In truth there shouldn't have been a wall around him at all as there was technically nothing for there to be a wall around, but sometimes it was handy to know what we shouldn't talk about. The Fallen Man existed, but only to define the context in which he didn't.

"Knowledge that fails to further the good of society is knowledge better forgotten," said Tommo, parroting the words of Our Munsell as he withdrew to safer pastures. "Seeking answers to unknowable questions beguile the good citizen from the glories of social obligation. The Previous got it wrong, Eddie, and they died out in the Something that Happened as a result of division and unhappiness. This way, the Munsell way, apartness is celebrated. Everyone knows their position and can celebrate the stability and harmony that it brings. Do you want to end up like the Riffraff: Base, feral and lacking in all social graces?"

"Endless repetition doesn't make wrong things right," I said, "and I'm not convinced knowing stuff *necessarily* leads to social fracture."

The Fallen Man and his crumpled chair were now half buried in the soil, partially covered with lichen and with a small ash sapling growing out of one corner. His helmet and boots were sun-bleached but largely undamaged, the few exposed parts of the skeleton now crumbled to white powder by the elements. The chair, a riveted box-like structure and once painted a reported olive green was decorated by bottles and pipes and had been partly squashed with the fall; ripples could be seen from the impact, which must have been substantial. But although it looked as if it had fallen from a great height, no one knew or had attempted to find out where he and the chair had come from. Even Lucy Ochre, who was rarely short of speculative ideas, had no plausible explanation for his purpose or origin.

"I think the real issue around the Fallen Man is not where he came from, but why no one has any particular desire to know," I said.

"I'd keep that to yourself," said Tommo, "and when you do find out, do me a favour? Don't share. I really don't want to know, and if you know what's good for you, neither do you."

As if to punctuate his contempt for things he did not wish to understand, Tommo picked up a stone and threw it as powerfully as he could towards the Fallen Man. His aim was surprisingly good, and the stone struck the chair with a resounding *crack*. There was then a fizzing noise, some smoke and with a dull roar the back of the seat ignited with twin plumes of reddish fire six foot long, and a split second later the chair was torn from the soil and propelled by an unseen force along the ground as the guinea pigs scattered in alarm. The seat hit the low boundary wall, where it was directed vertically upwards at great speed, trailing a shower of soil, stones, bones, boots and the rotted cloth of the Fallen Man's uniform. A couple of seconds later and, at perhaps three or four times the height of the flak tower, the fire from the base abruptly ceased and from the back of the chair a bundle of fabric was ejected, which caught the air and then blossomed into a large mushroom-shaped canopy, which floated in the breeze with the remains of the Fallen Man dangling beneath. The chair, now seemingly discarded, came wheeling down from the sky and fell to earth quite near us with a thump.

We watched silently as the spectacle floated down to make landfall in a gingko close by, the remains of the Fallen Man suspended by the multiple strings, the canopy, now deflated, draped over the tree. The white smoke that the chair had expelled during its fiery journey drifted past and smelled acrid, like overheated metal from a blacksmith's forge.

We said nothing for several seconds.

"What just happened?" I asked.

"Nothing happened," said Tommo. "We didn't see anything. Let's get out of here before someone arrives."

"We can't be punished for looking closer at something that never happened," I said, and walked over to where the Fallen Man was suspended. I eased the skull from the helmet. It was missing a jaw and was badly weather-corroded, but I'd seen one like it before.

"Look," I said, holding it next to my head to show how different the skull was, "it's one of the Previous. I thought they went extinct during the Something that Happened."

"It's possible pockets of Previous survived," he said, taking the skull and running his hands over its peculiarly rounded shape, small eye sockets and lack of a bulge at the rear. "*Spectrum* magazine reported a Previous living with the Riffraff in Blue Sector North. Lucy thought it was a Riffraff–Previous hybrid. She said it was utterly repellant and scientifically fascinating all at the same time."

The Chromogencia had long argued that if the Riffraff could breed with the Previous, and the Riffraff could breed with us, then it was likely we could breed with the Previous—which made them more closely related to us than we thought. Without warning, an illogical thought popped into my head. It wasn't an abstract notion, either; it was a fully formed idea with several steps.

"I need to gather up his remains," I said, and set off to search among the grassland for the Fallen Man's remains, with Tommo reluctantly following my lead. After half an hour we had found perhaps two thirds of a skeleton, along with his helmet, two sun-bleached boots and a glove containing what had once been a hand. Tommo being Tommo, he searched the glove and found a small wedding ring. More interestingly, I found a steel tag stitched into the laces of a boot that had always faced away from casual observers, and it had a name on it: Hanson, Jacqueline, and a number, 897452-BB9, then the word UTOPIAINC capitalised, and that was all. I turned to Tommo.

"The Fallen Man wasn't a man at all," I said, showing him the tag, "and not named Martin Baker, either. It was a woman named Jacqueline Hanson."

"No one's interested and no one cares," said Tommo, reading the tag, "and what colour is 'Hanson'? I've never heard of it. What's that?"

Attached to the Fallen Woman's harness was a small bag. It contained several plastic pouches that had hardened with age but looked as though they once contained food, a packet marked "First Aid," a water bottle—still sealed—and a small cylindrical object marked "ELT" with a serial number, barcode and a very small lightglobe no bigger than a petit poi—which as we watched made an audible tone and then started to flash every couple of seconds.

"What's that?" asked Tommo.

"I don't know. Listen, did you ever tie four pieces of string to the corners of a handkerchief, attach a stone beneath it and drop it from a high place to watch it float down?"

"Yes," said Tommo slowly, realising where I was going with

this. "You think what we just saw was a bigger version of that? One that could support a person?"

We both looked upwards, but there was nothing to be seen aside from a few doughnut-shaped clouds that had stretched and twisted in the upper winds.

"She was meant to descend safely beneath the mushroom of material," I said slowly, "and separate from the chair. But there was an error. She never left the chair and the canopy never opened. She landed at speed. Her death was . . . an accident."

It was quite a leap of thought.

"How could she be in the air?"

"There were *once* flying machines," I said, thinking about the swan of metal the National Colour operative had spoken of, "and maybe there still are."

Tommo frowned.

"Really? Like from *where*?"

"Maybe Jacqueline Hanson came from . . . somewhere else."

"Somewhere else?" he said. "Like, what, Blue Sector?"

"No," I said, suddenly feeling myself flush with the realisation I might have just come up with an abstract concept all on my very own. "*Somewhere Else* meaning 'somewhere not here on Chromatacia at all.'"

Tommo gave a patronising scoff.

"The Book of Munsell *specifically* stated that we are all there is—the chosen ones, the survivors, who moved society from a bad place to a good place."

"What if . . . the Book of Munsell is wrong?"

"The Book of Munsell *can't* be wrong," he said. "That's the whole point of it."

"Forbidding the manufacture of spoons is an error," I said, "and the banning of the number that lies between seventy-two and seventy-four has no rational explanation—all arithmetic calculations that are above that number must have the absence calculated into the answer to stay within numerical accuracy targets."

"I know all that," said Tommo, "and yes, we're not allowed to count sheep, use acronyms or wear gloves. But look: What if all that is perfectly rational—just at a level beyond the understanding of Mr. fancy-pants-know-all Eddie Russett? Your trouble, pal, is you've been listening to Jane, and she's put all sorts of fantastical ideas into your head. This is pointless, dangerous talk, Eddie, and even broadminded little me has limits."

He stared at me with a look that spoke more of fear than indignation.

"Never mind, Tommo. Help me bury the bones."

"Why?"

"I don't know. It just seems . . . right."

Tommo shrugged and decided to humour me, so together, using our rhododendron hoes, we dug a small hole in the place where the chair had been—it gave us a head start—and we placed everything in the hole, aside from the wedding ring and the tag with her name on it.

"I think this is a daft idea," said Tommo once we had patted down the soil.

"Think what you want," I said, then scratched "Jacqueline Hanson" on a flat stone, then, as an afterthought, added "Fell to earth 00483" and placed it on top. I stood up and regarded the stone for a while, wondering who she was, the true mechanism by which she arrived here, and if somewhere, someone had missed her. Perhaps, *still* missed her. I looked at her identification tag for a moment and showed it to Tommo.

"Does Utopiainc signify anything to you?"

"No. Are you done? I don't much like it here."

I stared at the flat stone with Hanson's name on it for a few more seconds.

"Okay," I said, "now I'm done."

We continued on our walk, still attacking the aliens but both preoccupied by what we had seen, and Tommo, sharp-eyed as usual, spotted a swan high overhead, which he only made comment upon as the afternoon swan wasn't due for another hour. By the time we had checked the hoes back in and I'd filled in the aliens book, we'd missed teatime, so I headed across to see Jane but was waylaid by a small bundle of Yellow nastiness in pigtails that went by the name of Penelope Gamboge.

"Hullo, Penelope," I said, "snitched on anyone today?"

"Only ever those who deserve it, Russett," she growled, the enmity obvious—she was Courtland's niece and Sally Gamboge's granddaughter. "You're to go to the Colourium to see your father."

"For what purpose?"

"Head Prefect deMauve wants to talk to you both."

"Why?"

"Does he need a reason? Do as you're told."

THE COLOURIUM

"Toshing" was the name given to any activity that searched through the waste of the Previous. As a child I would often pan for buttons, keyboard letters and human teeth in the local river, hoping to earn a few extra merits. Although most former towns and villages were covered with several feet of accreted soil, remnants of previous habitation were easy to spot: intriguing grassy mounds, streetlamps poking out of the earth, the odd building still standing, that sort of thing.

—Ted Grey: *Twenty Years Among the Chromatacians*

The waiting room to Dad's Colourium contained several assorted villagers and Tania, Violet deMauve's sister-in-law. I'd seen her about, but she'd never made eye contact and we'd not been introduced. There were also a dozen or so of the village's higher-hued children all sitting patiently, ready to attain their musical proficiency. My good friend Fenton had acquired trombone skills in the same manner, by viewing the appropriate learning shade of "Trombone 675" when he was eight, and played until his parents decided not to pay for a refresher. The skill then quickly fell away. I myself played the cello, but had learned the cheaper, old-school way, through repetition and practice, one string at a time.

I learned from Dad's admin staff-of-one, Lucy Ochre, that he was out, stitching on the arm of a worker who had been caught up in machinery over at the linoleum factory.

"They are torn off so frequently I wonder if it's worth stitching them back on at all," said Lucy with a grin.

"Dad once sewed a left hand on to a right stump," I said, as the accident in question had been devastating for the victim, and he felt he had to do *something*, "and it held. In fact, the recipient was left with two wrist joints which allowed them novel and possibly unique levels of dexterity."

"Was that useful?"

"For accessing those hard-to-reach drain blockages it paid massive dividends. Dad wrote a paper for the Guild of Swatchmen entitled: 'The Use of Bilateral Swaps to Extend Civic Use for Those Damaged in Industrial Accidents.'"

"Impressive," she said. "When my dad was the Swatchman he just sewed them back together again—with string if nothing else was to hand."

Lucy was a slim girl with dark hair, a small button nose and one of the sharpest intellects I knew. Her overriding interest at present was the mechanism by which lightglobes shone, Everspins rotated and hotpots boiled water—all without any apparent method of energy input. She thought this energy was transmitted invisibly through the air by something she called "harmonic resonance."

"How's the ear?" I asked, as she too had had a body part stitched back on recently—only not lost to linoleum machinery, but a particularly violent bout of hockeyball. Ears, as everyone knew, came off quite easily.

"It's okay," she said, touching her still-bandaged ear gently, "and oddly, led directly to my inclusion on the Red Sector hockeyball team competing at this year's Jollity Fair. The selection board regard losing an ear as a positive—it shows I was making an effort."

"I heard Daisy Crimson and Violet deMauve also made the

team," I said, "and I think Doug, Oscar and Earl are competing in the Penny-Farthing events. We saw them out practising this morning."

"They've got a good chance of winning something, too. Never mind about Jollity Fair," she said, giving me a playful punch on the arm. "Are you and Violet *actually* going to get married?"

"I was asked to come over here and meet deMauve, so I guess the answer is 'sadly, yes'—but only to legitimise the child of mine she's carrying. But it's all up in the air at present. The Overseeing Yellow Prefect just arrived and I think he and Sally Gamboge are two poisonous peas in the same pod—she wants to send Jane and me to the Green Room."

"What about Tommo?"

"He pulled some strings."

"And Violet?"

"Granted victim status."

"Ah," said Lucy, "can they convict you without a shred of evidence? You've got over eighty percent red, so your word carries weight."

"I agree," I said, as the Rules were very clear: the higher in the Spectral Hierarchy you were, the greater was assumed your truthfulness. With my 86.7 percent red sight gift I could see more red than even the incumbent Red Prefect. I should have had his job as soon as my sight gift was revealed, but I was accused of murder, so by Rule 2.4.3.21.6 my service had been deferred.

"These are Prefects we're dealing with," I said. "*Anything* could happen."

"That's true. Has anyone asked Yewberry to retire so you can be Prefect? That would solve a lot of problems for all of us."

That wasn't going to happen. I was simply a high-ranking Red without authority—and if Sally Gamboge had her way, one that was about to head into the Green Room.

"When was the last time a Prefect retired and voluntarily gave up all their privileges?" I replied. "Yewberry likes his house and his extra pudding and his unlimited shoelace allocation."

"You have a point, but seriously, Eddie, they won't send an eighty-six percent Red to the Green Room. Or at least, not until Violet has been safely delivered of your child—and potentially several more for a spare and future breeding stock—perhaps as a swapsie for a powerful Blue from somewhere."

I was thinking of pointing out that I had 87 percent if you rounded up, but said instead:

"That happens?"

"Not officially, but yes. But look, with your red you'd be invaluable in the sorting room."

"If we had anything to sort," I said. "There's a National Colour operative in town enquiring about scrap colour targets."

"Is there? He'll be delivering this month's swatches, too, I guess."

The door opened and two Greys walked in.

"Begging your pardon, Miss Ochre," said the first, holding out a piece of paper, "me and Bobby have a chit here for a skills upgrade."

"Hello, Sid, Hello, Bobby," she replied as she took their chit and read it, "Prefect deMauve after some home improvements?"

"Fancy newel posts for his stairs," said Bobby, "and linenfold panelling for the deMauve dining room."

"They're all in order," said Lucy, indicating the forms. "Do you want to wait or—"

"We'll wait, miss," said Bobby. Skills upgrades had knock-on effects. If these two were upgraded to master wood carvers, then the six to eight weeks until it wore off meant that everyone else could have a few extra finials, carved toys and decorated headboards. Maybe even a new oboe.

They went and sat down next to the children and I turned back to Lucy.

"I was over at the Fallen Man just now, and something happened."

"Oh?"

I outlined what had occurred and she blinked at me several times but couldn't offer much by way of explanation—except to agree that the Fallen Woman probably fell from a flying machine. I asked what she thought of my 'Someone Else living Somewhere Else' theory.

"It's possible, I suppose," she said, "but if there *was* a Someone Else, you would have thought they'd make themselves known by now. By the way," she added brightly, "do you think your dad and my mum are going to get married? They seem quite fond of one another and they've been up to so much *youknow* that Mrs. Cinnabar next door was thumping on the wall to either make them stop—or alternately yell out a running commentary so everyone could enjoy their congress in a vicarious fashion."

"Does that ever actually happen?" I asked, pulling a face.

"Not unknown."

"I'd like them to get married," I said, as Velma seemed good stepmother material, and Dad hadn't had any relationships to speak of since my mother died.

"So would I," she said, "and it would also make us step-siblings, which would be fun. I've never had a brother."

"When Head Prefect deMauve has me marry his daughter it would make Violet your sister-in-law."

"Oh yes," she said, face falling, "I daresay that wouldn't be fun at all. But if Mummy is happy, I'll accept the unpleasantness. Speaking of which, any ideas how I can stop Tommo from proposing to me? It's been going on weekly since we were nine, and although he's not bad looking, has a useful greased-piglet way of getting out of trouble and somehow always has some cash, being married to Tommo does have one massive drawback."

"The 'being married to Tommo' part?"

"In one."

"I could tell him you died."

"I've tried that. He's *very* persistent. What . . ."

The door to the street opened and my father walked in, closely followed by Doris G56, his Grey head nurse. He looked at the large group of people waiting for him.

"Sorry for the delay, folks—be with you as soon as possible. Lucy, would you send out to the Fallen Man for a jug of their finest puddle water and some biscuits? I think I saw the National Colour man walking this way, so better send him through when he arrives. Hello, Eddie, what are you here for?"

"DeMauve wants to talk to us both."

"That'll be about Violet. Come into the office."

I followed him into his consulting room, and once inside, he carefully shut the door and washed his hands. His shirt, I noted, was badly bloodstained.

"Bad one?" I asked.

"Torn off at the shoulder," he replied with a sigh. "I can stitch limbs back on and flash them a nerve-and-muscle rejoining hue, but it's never the same. It makes them clumsy even with frequent skill refreshers and before you know it, it's been ripped off again. Gerald G67 has lost three hands, two legs and so many fingers I've lost count—Sally Gamboge swears he's doing it on purpose to get off work."

"Shouldn't he be retired or put on to lesser duties?"

"That's got my vote," he said, "but the linoleum manufacturing targets have to be met and since the Rules state that even Greys can't start working until the age of eight, I don't see how they are going to keep the factory open at all by this time next year—unless someone devises a way for Greys to work in their sleep."

There was a knock at the door and after Dad called, "Enter," the National Colour operative walked in. He ignored me, introduced himself simply as "Agent Applejack" and handed Dad a battered leather satchel.

"Your new swatches," he said, "fine-tuned for you to better treat the citizenry."

"Thank you, Mr. Applejack," said Dad, opening the satchel and scanning the list of new hues, each designed to cure a particular ailment upon viewing, or, as my Dad thought, *induce the body to effect a cure*—a subtle distinction upon which Lucy agreed.

"We have a hue now to cure ingrowing toenails?" asked my father, still reading the list.

"Not once they are established," said Applejack, who presumably didn't want to be a courier all his life and eventually hoped to be part of the mixing team. "It works best on those with a *propensity* for ingrowing toenails, so you might have to do a survey. I think you will find the shade to relieve haemorrhoids much improved, and they've reformulated the anti-deafness hue to attain a higher-frequency response."

"Bats," said my father.

"I'm sorry?"

"Bats—it's always nice to hear them."

"Oh," said Applejack, "yes—I agree."

"No new skill hues?" asked Dad, as between healing and skills, the latter was more remarkable: skills you had previously never possessed, immediately available. There were many, and not all about trades and dexterity—you could have a new village up and running within a week by showing the admin skill hues to a random and previously ignorant set of individuals.

"They take longer to formulate," said the courier, "as you might appreciate."

"I was hoping perhaps a few of the 'off-book' skills might be licensed—to responsible thinkers within the Chromogencia, obviously, rather than given out willy-nilly."

There were over two hundred hues "retired and redundant," most of which gave one skills related to old technology such as electricity, engineering, and numbers. I'd had my suspicions for a while that these might be the source of Lucy's superior understandings. That she might have had a random flash, a chromatic coincidence, somewhere in nature. It happens. To Reds, a walk in an autumnal forest had been known to induce the entire works of a Previous poet named Longfellow.

"If Head Office deems it necessary or desirable you will be told forthwith," said Applejack, maintaining the aloofness that was National Colour's trademark.

"We live in hope," said Dad. "Here you go."

He handed Applejack a file that would have contained a meticulously kept list of which colour had been administered, to whom, how long, noted effect, that sort of thing. The records were compiled monthly and sent to National Colour to further research into the use of healing and skill-acquiring hues. It was, as far as anyone knew, the only regular transfer of records to Head Office, and healing and skill hues the only technology permitted to advance, with the possible exception of the gyro-bike.

The exchange thus completed, they shook hands, thanked each other, said, "Apart We Are Together," and Applejack took his leave.

"My Swatchman knowledge was from a skill hue," said Dad, "a shade of yellow, I think it was. I have to view it every month to keep it going. It's a complex business: The shade of blue that cured hiccups in a Grey can bring on shingles in a Green. Were you ever shown a skill?"

"Embroidery."

He snapped his fingers.

"I remember."

To finish the village quilt in time for the winter solstice celebrations back in Jade-under-Lime I had been co-opted as part of the embroidery team. For two months I could not have been more expert with stitches French, Stem and Chain, and took the opportunity to make myself a couple of shirts before the skill faded. Today, I'm quite good with buttons, but that's about it. I was going to tell Dad about the Fallen Woman but the door abruptly opened and deMauve walked in.

He didn't knock. Prefects never do.

HEAD PREFECT DEMAUVE

Due to a somewhat strict interpretation of the Rules regarding the postal service, everyone had to have a postcode to ensure your post *could* be delivered, because post *had* to be delivered. Dad and I were of a middle-ranking RG6 postcode, and the deMauves were the hugely prestigious W1D. Most Greys were run-of-the-mill SN3s, IP4s or even DD1s. Having a child without a postcode retention certificate risked your offspring being in contravention of post delivery Rules, and worse, being a non-person, ineligible even to have an Ishihara test.

—Ted Grey: *Twenty Years Among the Chromatacians*

"Ah," he said, "perfect. The two of you in one place. Good afternoon, Swatchman Russett."

"Head Prefect."

He looked at me with poorly concealed contempt.

"Edward."

"Head Prefect."

My marriage to deMauve's daughter was still up in the air, having been postponed from when it was meant to happen, the day following my Ishihara. I didn't want to marry her, of course, but with marriage to Jane out of the question, it did make sense. As a deMauve, I'd have access to all kinds of things I could never have as simply a Russett, and Jane and I needed to open doors to figure out how best we were going to change the Collective.

"Would you care for some puddle water, Head Prefect?" asked my father. "I've just sent out for some."

"I won't, thank you," said deMauve.

East Carmine's tea had run out the month before so we had reverted, as always, to drinking muddy water in an impressive range of tastes and colours. Some drank muddy water even when there was tea around, and others swore they couldn't tell the difference.

"I shall get straight to the point," said deMauve. "There has not been a single death by Mildew these past seven years, and I wonder why this is so?"

The Mildew, the Rot, OmniNecrosis—whatever you called it—was always fatal. It began with numb elbows and brittle ears and progressed rapidly to a growth of fungal spores in the lungs, and death within one to six hours.

"I've been here less than a month," said Dad, "so my knowledge is limited. Perhaps the citizens have built up a natural resistance."

"Possibly, possible," said deMauve in a distracted manner, then continued: "no one welcomes the Mildew of course, but one cannot deny that there is a certain . . . *convenience* to it. Especially to make space for new residents."

The Mildew took people, villages, and once even an entire Sector. But the Mildew wasn't entirely random: it was especially devastating to the socially and physically imperfect.

"Convenience?" said Dad in an innocent-sounding voice. "In what way?"

"Underpopulation is a pressing issue," said deMauve in a quiet, measured tone, "and we need youth to replace the aged. The Mildew is apt to spread throughout those of low moral worth or lazy demeanour by a 'subconscious auto-infection response' brought upon by their failing obligation to the Collective, which begs the question as to *why* the Mildew has given East Carmine a wide berth, and left us carrying the unwanted burden of citizens whose usefulness has waned? We barely have enough workers to keep the factory open as it is, let alone meet manufacturing targets."

DeMauve spoke in couched language, and I knew why. The Mildew had a dark secret in that it wasn't a disease at all—it was the body's reaction to a colour—and most chillingly, it was administered clandestinely by the Collective once certain key parameters had been met, usually as a way of disposing of the old and broken, societally useless or those inclined towards criminality, idleness or independent thought.

"So what would you have me do?" asked Dad.

"I'm not asking you to *do* anything," said deMauve, who wasn't going to spell it out. "I'm just asking why you think this situation has arisen?"

Not showing anyone the Mildew put Dad in difficult territory: a Swatchman who was not doing as the Prefects and the *Book of Harmony* decreed was one Swatchman not doing what was expected of him. Dad may have to face a dilemma: show the Rot, or be shown the Rot. The previous Swatchman had refused to do the same, and was disposed of.

"May I speak freely?" I asked.

DeMauve stared at me.

"Do you have to?"

"Not all Eddie's ideas are complete nonsense," put in Dad.

DeMauve flicked his eyes to Dad, then nodded reluctantly.

"Perhaps," I began, "this problem is twofold: we need to meet unrealistic manufacturing targets at the linoleum factory, while at the same time free up postcode allocations to enable new children to be born."

DeMauve narrowed his eyes.

"I concede that you may, by complete chance, have stumbled upon the heart of the issue."

"The first problem is easy," I said. "All production targets are fixed at one hundred and five percent of production in order to encourage output. But since we can *never* meet those targets, I suggest we go back to normal factory hours and submit to the Controller of Production whatever we make."

"Don't be ridiculous," said deMauve. "That would reduce productivity and the Controller would send us a 'special action required' memo rather than a 'missed target memo.' And I *hate* getting those memos."

"It would be only for the first week," I said. "You can tell them it was a linseed oil tank rupture or something. After that, you'd be back to missed target memos again—which you are currently getting anyway—and everyone gets to work a quarter as hard."

An empty moment seemed to swell in the room, fuelled by ignorance and fear. I could almost hear the cogs going around in his head. Dad and I exchanged glances. Smarter villages than us knew *exactly* how to work the Rules. It explained why East Carmine always had so little cash. If you wanted to prosper, you *had* to game the system—loopholery wasn't just an amusing distraction from the mundanities of life, it was a life-saving endeavour.

"That *might* offer a solution," said deMauve at length. "And the second issue?"

"There can only be a finite number of people within the Collective," I began, "as there is only a finite number of postcodes. We all have one, and no woman can be shown the ovulating shade without a postcode retention certificate, usually from a deceased relative."

"What's your point, Russett?"

I had to tread carefully. A centuries-long policy of the culling of undesirables under the umbrella term of "Reboot" or the "Night Train to Emerald City" had dramatically reduced the postcodes in circulation: you didn't take much to Reboot or the Night Train, but you definitely took your postcode, and it was lost with you. Oddly—perversely, even—postcode depletion was the leading causal factor in the Collective's current underpopulation, which led directly to the overemployment crisis. It was definitely not what Our Munsell had intended.

"I was thinking that if village residents surrendered their reserved postcodes," I said slowly so he could grasp the concept, "those same codes could be offered as incentives to lesser hues and Greys in other villages to move out here. How about this for a marketing slogan: "East Carmine: you *may* lose an arm, but you *will* gain a child.""

DeMauve considered my words carefully.

"I concede that postcodes are antisocially guarded but the Rules do not disallow it," he said, probably because he was hoarding several dozen himself.

"We need to find more spoons," said Dad, and strangely, he was right. The rarity of postcodes was linked to the rarity of spoons. To stave off theft, all spoons were engraved with the postcode of the owner—and were now seen as retention certificates in themselves. Find an orphaned spoon with a postcode, and you had a child allocation.

Spoons equalled children. It was simple logic, really.

"That's a good point," said deMauve, turning back to me. "You had some success in finding spoons on the Rusty Hill trip to secure the Caravaggio last month. Maybe you could undertake something similar?"

"Not all spoons have postcodes," I said, not happy at where this was heading.

"That isn't a problem," he said, warming to the idea. "Even

if the spoons don't have a postcode, they can still be traded. A dented teaspoon could be worth up to three hundred merits in Vermillion—and we need all the cash we can get. The loan on Gamboge's crackletrap is due, and we don't have the money."

"I think Rusty Hill is all spooned out," I said.

"I agree," he said. "I was thinking of sending you up to Crimsonolia instead."

"Crimsonolia?"

"Yes. You can look for scrap colour at the same time, which will get that National Colour johnny off my back. You'll take Cinnabar along with that horribly impertinent Jane Brunswick, who can drive. It will be a risky undertaking, as I understand Riffraff and megafauna abound in that area, so we should send only those we can afford to lose."

Most high-jeopardy expeditions functioned in this manner. No one of any value was permitted to participate, so deMauve's meaning was clear: he could afford to lose us.

"Jane and I have a disciplinary hearing the day after tomorrow," I said, "and need to work on our defence."

"I'm not so sure that will be time well spent," said deMauve. "If you do not return, then the council will have saved valuable hours of its time, the potential ambiguity of the hearing's outcome will be removed and, best of all, you will be safe in the knowledge that you died attempting to ease the village's underpopulation issue."

"Why would we want to go on a spoon hunt for the village with the spectre of the Green Room hanging over us?"

He sighed as though I were an idiot.

"Because everyone is expected to undertake the obligations of their citizenship in as useful a manner as possible and to the furtherance and betterment of the Collective as a whole at all times and without question, at any time and irrespective of consequence."

It was verbatim from the *Book of Harmony*.

"In that case I'll go—but only for two hundred merits per spoon," I said. "It's a risky endeavour and we have much to lose."

According to the Rules, any expedition beyond the Outer Markers was voluntary.

"Out of the question," he snapped back, "and it is not seemly to horse-trade with a Prefect."

"One hundred and fifty."

He glared at me angrily.

"Your greed literally plucks the food from the mouths of our children and infants," he said. "I will go only to one hundred per spoon and no further."

"Deal," I said, "so long as we are paid in transferable cash merits only."

He stared at me and narrowed his eyes. Book merits were easy to win and lose and had little real value: bearer merits could be traded anywhere, for *anything*.

"I agree to your terms, albeit extremely reluctantly," he said, "and your manner confirms my worst suspicions: that you are a vulgar individual concerned only with yourself and whose permanent absence from this village would be a blessing to us all. Which brings me on to your marriage to my daughter."

I BECOME A DEMAUVE

Marriage prospects were mostly dependent on your sight gift. Simply put, the more colour vision you and your partner had, the higher was your child's. Personal advancement wasn't possible within your own lifetime, but through careful and diligent Chromogenics over several generations, your descendants could rise to the top. The inverse, of course, was also true: unwise investment in your partner might see you revert to Grey in as little as two generations.

—From Munsell's *Book of Harmony*

Marrying Violet was not a surprise to me. Trading in your children's colour vision futures was entirely normal and deMauve had grand plans for his family. He produced a completed marriage certificate from his pocket and laid it on the table—I noticed that Violet had already signed it.

"You will bear the surname deMauve as an honorific only, and your father will be paid one thousand merits as a dowry. If I find that you have lain with my daughter for any other purpose than that of a purely procreational reason, the displeasure of myself and Mrs. deMauve shall be terrible, and our vengeance frightful."

"I assure you there is little chance of that," I said.

"I agree," he said, handing me a pen. "We brought up our daughter to be a young lady of impeccable good taste and restraint. Sign here."

"That's a lower price than we agreed," said my father, looking at the certificate. "You said ten thousand."

"I think it's very generous given the circumstances," said deMauve. "We knew nothing of Edward's unsociably murderous nature when we first agreed to the deal."

"I'll sign it after my hearing," I said.

DeMauve turned to my father.

"Swatchman Russett, instruct your son to sign it."

"My son is of age and free to marry whom he wishes."

DeMauve glared at him, then at me, then at Dad again.

"One of you better sign or there will be trouble."

Violet was already pregnant by me, but not because I liked her or even for fun—she had coerced me in case I didn't return from the trip to High Saffron. It was easy to see why: the deMauves were currently the bluey side of Purple so given the amount of red I could see, our child's vision would be sufficiently balanced in the red and blue sight gifts to ensure the dynastic future of the deMauves. The marriage was purely to legitimise that child. I was breeding stock, nothing more, and this was simply to validate the pedigree.

"I *will* marry your daughter," I said finally, "but with a proviso."

"I'm listening."

"My father is to gain two thousand merits and have a job guaranteed here for ten years minimum."

"The first I agree, the second I cannot. *Anything* might happen."

"Then your daughter gives birth to a bastard. They will have to carry a generic Purple name like Plum or Grape, and *that* family, not yours, will carry the Purple you so badly need to protect your dynastic ambitions."

He glared at me, the veins throbbing on his forehead.

"Very well," he said at last, "I accept your terms."

He grumbled as he wrote a letter of understanding to my father that outlined his employment terms, then pushed the marriage certificate across the table to me. I signed my name on the piece of paper and was now married to Violet and a deMauve, eleventh in the Chromatic Hierarchy of the village.

"Here's your copy of the marriage certificate," said deMauve, tearing off the docket at the bottom of the form, "and I offer you congratulations only because protocol demands it. Don't imagine for one single moment you are going to live long enough to accompany my daughter to Purple Regis, or enjoy any of the other trappings of our lineage."

He then changed my name in my merit book and counter-signed it, pretty much in the same manner as you might transfer the title of a pig. Marriage for love was a rarity in Chromatacia.

"I will inform Violet of her marriage and just for appearance's sake, you may show limited affection towards one another in public. The sooner your tenure as my son-in-law is brought to a close, the better."

DeMauve departed without another word, and we were left alone in Dad's consulting room. We both took a deep breath.

"Thanks for the ten-year extension," said Dad, "but you better find some spoons with postcodes on them or the Prefects will find another way to dispose of any unproductive resident."

"I'll do my best."

He thought in silence for a moment, then said:

"I've had twelve orders to induce the Mildew on residents since I've been here."

It was unguarded talk. A month ago I'd not thought the Mildew was anything but an illness. Much had changed, and I liked it that Dad knew he could trust me with this. It wasn't something you shared, for very obvious reasons. I paused for a moment then asked:

"How does the order come through?"

"Tennis elbow. I'm meant to pull them in for a check-up, flash them a shade of delayed-action Mildew and they'd be in the rendering shed in under forty-eight hours."

"What if someone *genuinely* has tennis elbow?"

"I'm not sure there is such a thing. But if there was, then an order like that would not come from the Council, but from the PE Supervisor."

He selected a swatch from the packet Applejack had given him and placed it in the gas lamp. As soon as it caught fire he dropped it on the desk where it burned furiously. I didn't need to ask what hue that was, and what it would do to anyone who viewed it.

"There'll be no Mildew on my watch," he said.

"Won't they do to you what they did to Robin Ochre?" I asked, as the previous Swatchman had been murdered in the Green Room.

"It was unusual, killing Ochre in that way," he agreed. "Usually they just call for the Supervisory Substitute. They'll do any job that a Swatchman refuses to do."

"I've not heard of a Supervisory Substitute Swatchman," I said.

"And you should hope you never do."

Up until recently Dad had struck me as a mildly dull but solid and dependable member of the Collective. He wasn't anything like that at all, and I wondered how many others like him were risking everything with their low-key resistance.

"What did Mum do to be diagnosed with tennis elbow?" I

asked in a quiet voice, as she had succumbed to the Mildew when I was eight. Dad hadn't been a Swatchman then, and knew nothing of the job.

"I think she went to Jollity Fair once too often. The first time was just an excuse for the Rainbow Room."

This was the place where women could go to surreptitiously increase the chroma of their offspring. With Mum's 23.4 percent red and Dad's 50.2 percent, it didn't take a genius to figure that my 86.7 percent came from somewhere other than Dad—and someone with almost pure red vision. A Prefect, most likely, needing some extra cash, or just a Red fundamentalist eager to increase core sight gift.

"But she attended the Jollity Fair celebrations anyway," continued my father, "and she saw something or met someone or learned something and went back every year, masquerading as a member of Jade-under-Lime's Slam Brass Band."

"She wasn't given the Mildew for lying over her abilities with the French horn."

"No," said Dad, "she wasn't."

He stopped what he was doing and folded his arms.

"Jollity Fair lies somewhat just outside the Rules—the *Book of Harmony* permits the two-day event to allow for a certain randomised mixing of peoples, events and information exchange. Your mother likened it to a pressure-relief valve or an expansion joint on a bridge—something that doesn't bend will ultimately break, and that when the Collective is viewed as a whole, a few days of relative freedom was necessary, despite the risks. After all, having the freedom to discuss change doesn't dictate that you will follow those words with actions—but the disruptive chatter may in itself be enough to keep the malcontents from doing anything disruptive."

We both fell silent for a moment.

"So what was Mum doing at Jollity Fair?"

"I don't know, but she used to come back with skills she hadn't had before."

"Such as?"

"Geometry, and her head clock kept time when asleep, although it gave her nightmares if she'd eaten cheese. More importantly, she said that if you ever grew up to be curious, then you needed to go there—and seek out the Herald. It's located somewhere near the sideshows, where preserved specimens of human anthropological interest can be seen alongside various animals with two heads."

I'd seen a Herald once before, during a brief time when Jane had rejigged my eyes to be immune to the Mildew. It was why she and I had been spared at High Saffron, and Courtland had been taken. Other people saw Heralds from time to time, but dismissed them as Pookas.

"How do you find this Herald?" I asked.

"You don't. It finds you."

"Did it find Mum?"

"She came back full of stories. There was a being, she said, an *entity* that controlled our lives: all-seeing, all-powerful, omniscient and omnipresent. An entity that knows what we do, where we are and, ultimately, controls our destiny."

"Higher than Our Munsell?"

"She said this entity *created* Our Munsell, National Colour, the world we live in, the animals that share our space and even ourselves. The Heralds exist so the Grand Creator can communicate thoughts and ideas."

"I've seen one," I said. "They're inside your head."

"Your mother said the same. But the Creator sends physical

messengers, too: Angels, riding on silent-winged horses that descend at night from on high, to take residents for study, or smite those who have displeased him."

"Sounds like the Pale Rider."

"It does, doesn't it? Legends have to start somewhere, although I'm not sure Flying Monkeys were ever a thing."

"I agree. Did she have a name for this entity?"

"She called him *Utopiainc*."

I thought of Jacqueline Hanson, and dug her identification tag from my pocket.

"The Fallen Man wasn't a man," I explained. "It was a woman."

I handed him the tag.

"Utopiainc," he read. "She carries the name of the Creator. What are you saying?"

"I don't know," I said. "Maybe Hanson was an Angel who fell to earth accidentally and who met their own death rather than meting it out to others."

He passed the tag back.

"It all sounds a little far-fetched," he said. "All-powerful beings, Heralds and Angels who bring death from the skies. And it gets weirder: your mother also said that if you wear gloves, it renders you invisible to the swans."

I breathed a sigh of relief. My mother now sounded like something of a fantasist, which placed all her other claims in the far safer "not likely at all" category.

"I know what you're thinking," said Dad, "that your mother might have been a little soft upstairs. She made claims, yes, and sometimes some very odd ones—but it was always with a steely sense of reality."

"I think I should go there and find this Herald," I murmured, wondering how I could wangle a pass and join the lucky fourteen who would go to Jollity Fair—and that was assuming I'd survive the next couple of days.

Dad pressed a button on the intercom.

"Lucy, send in Sid and Bobby for their carpentry skill hues, would you?"

He looked up at me.

"Eddie?"

"Yes?"

"Be careful. If you lift the carpet, all you ever find is dirt."

ASPIRATIONAL LIVING

A village of East Carmine's size was required to have one "luxury" retail outlet. If we hadn't have had an Aspirational Living shop it would have been a hatter's, taxidermist, coffee shop or fancy dress outlet. Given that we were only permitted three types of hat, coffee was strictly rationed to select personnel, only squarials were permitted to be stuffed and it was forbidden to "pretend to be something you weren't," Aspirational Living seemed like the best choice.

—Ted Grey: *Twenty Years Among the Chromatacians*

I took my leave from the Colourium and walked six doors down to East Carmine's Aspirational Living shop, sandwiched between the repairers and the Fallen Man tearooms. The bell tinkled as I entered and I was relieved but not surprised to find I was the only one there.

"Good afternoon, Mr. Russett," said the sales assistant. She was my own age, had eyes that sparkled with steely determination and was possessed of the most charming retroussé nose, something which no one ever mentioned unless they wanted a punch in the eye. She was the person who had opened my eyes to the iniquities of our society, was the reason I was facing the Green Room and had tried to kill me twice. Despite all that, I was hopelessly in love with her.

"Hullo, Jane," I said, "how is retail suiting you?"

"What happened to 'pumpkin'?" she asked.

"I thought you said pet names were nauseatingly pointless?"

She shrugged.

"I've never had a boyfriend, not even a starter one. I'm trying to readjust. I may call you 'googly bear' if I can bring myself to say it without vomiting."

Clearly, the fine details of our relationship were a work in progress.

I started again:

"Hullo, pumpkin," I said, "how is retail suiting you?"

She raised an eyebrow.

"*Never* call me pumpkin."

"I thought—"

"—I changed my mind. I was right. It *is* nauseatingly pointless."

Less than a month ago Jane had been Grey and on manual labour. At her Ishihara she'd been deemed a light Green, so now worked in retail.

"But in answer to your question," she said, "running a shop that sells valueless objects is both meaningless and draining of my spirit. I am indeed fortunate that few people can afford the junk that I'm pedalling."

"It might have been worse," I said. "At least you have something to do. Over in the library they sit and twiddle their thumbs all day."

Natural wastage, age, mould, fire, worms and damp had denuded the shelves of all books. There was no mechanism in place to print more due to an error in the Rules, nor was it permissible to allocate the staff to other duties. Librarians now outnumbered books five to one.

"At least a library has noble intent," she said. "Selling an elephant carved badly from soapstone, a footstool cunningly made to look like a Highland cow or a cheaply framed photograph of pebbles serves no useful purpose I can see. So," she added in a brighter tone, "in what way can I assist you?"

I looked left and right to make sure no one was watching and we both leaned forward and kissed. It was not hesitant or hurried, despite the fact that it was forbidden. With the Green Room or self-banishment hanging over us, we could afford to be bold.

"Talk retail to me," I said. "I love it when you talk retail."

"We have a special on scented candles this week," she replied in a husky whisper, our lips still close. "Only ten merits each. Something for the special one in your life, or simply to relax in a bath of mandated duration and mandated temperature with your unmandated partner."

"D'you sell many?" I asked.

"Six in the past eight years," she said. "Our best seller is inspirational placards."

She nodded towards some plaques on the wall that repeated well-worn messages of the Collective, the most obvious being "Apart We Are Together."

"Since they are repeated so much since birth, a plaque is barely needed to remind one. Would you like to buy a piece of wood carved into two links shaped like hearts?"

"Is there a point to that?"

"I think it's a way of making people *think* you are romantic if there's little chance of them guessing whether you are or not. To be honest I think death would be a welcome relief after a week of this," she said. "I spent the afternoon painting the phrase 'Believe in yourself' on river pebbles. You?"

"I valiantly killed six rhododendron seedlings. But more interestingly, the Fallen Man was actually a Fallen Woman—named Jacqueline Hanson."

She raised an eyebrow.

"Tell me more."

I told her everything that happened and she nodded sagely.

"Do you know what 'ELT' might mean?" I asked when I told her about the box with the flashing light. "I think it's an acronym."

She had no suggestions, and I then added what deMauve had said about ridding the village of the societally useless.

"Your father needs to watch himself," she said. "There's only a limited shelf-life for a Swatchman who won't flip a citizen the Mildew when the Council tells them to."

"I think he knows that."

I told her what Dad said about the Supervisory Substitute Swatchman and the tennis elbow coded message.

"Do you think the whole of Rusty Hill had tennis elbow?"

It was a good point. The entire village—only ten miles to the south—had been lost to the Mildew four years previously. The official story was "Indolence related Mildew which should be a lesson to us all" but what actually happened was anyone's guess. The thing was, Prefects and the Swatchman would have to have Mildewed *themselves*, which was unlikely. I told her what Dad had said about my mother, the potential relevance of Jollity Fair—and the notion of a Greater Being who had been the creator of Munsell, us and all the creatures, and who watched over us, all-seeing and in control of our destiny—and then the nonsense about the gloves, for balance.

"That's a bit of a stretch," she said. "Sounds like a carry-over from the Previous who were well known for their fancifully supernatural ideas."

I then told Jane about the Herald and the Angel.

"The only Herald I've seen repeated themselves word for word as though reading the same sentence from a book," she said, "and the only person I met who said they'd seen an Angel was off their face on Lincoln."

"Dad said they descend at night on silent winged horses and then either kidnap people for study or smite those who have displeased him."

"That does sound like the legend of the Pale Rider."

"It does. Might explain Rusty Hill, too—and the vanishings."

People regularly went missing. Adults were written off as nightloss, lightning or swan attack, missing children on the Riffraff. Parents told their children it was Flying Monkeys to ensure good behaviour, but no one believed such a thing. Perhaps it was just another word for Angels and Pale Riders.

"Where does this Creator live?"

"I don't know," I replied, and suggested the best course of action was to go to Jollity Fair and speak to the Herald that my mother had spoken of, and hope that it would find us, so long as we went with honourable intent. We might learn more—and, as a bonus, see an animal with two heads, always a plus, although I was as yet undecided on seeing specimens in jars, even if they were of human anthropological interest.

Jane nodded thoughtfully.

"That sounds like a plan. I'll definitely be on the Jollity Fair squad if I survive the hearing. They'll want me to win the gyrobike sprint race for them."

"Can you?"

"It's not likely. Jamie 'Mad Dog' Juniper has won almost everything she's ever entered. She's pretty fearless and has a reputation for winning at any cost."

The door rang as another customer walked into the shop.

"I have several novelty teapots you might like," said Jane to me, switching tone in an instant. "The one of a kitchen range is particularly fine, look here, there is a ceramic cat moulded in."

"Yes," I said, feigning interest, "very . . ."

". . . aspirational?" suggested Jane.

"You're not kidding anyone," said Bunty McMustard. She must have seen us talking from the street as she walked past on her way to tuba practice; her subcontrabass tuba was outside on a wheeled cart. It was so big, in fact, that someone once died when it fell on them, and used so much copper in its construction that all the cold-water pipes in the Greyzone had to be requisitioned.

"Oh, hello, Bunts," I said. "What a fantastic pleasure to see you again."

"Spare me the faux politeness, Russett. Fraternisation is *strictly* prohibited between complementary colours of Red and Green. And it's *Bunty*."

"I'm *technically* now Purple, Bunts," I said.

"Only just. It's still disgusting, and the Council has a broad remit when it comes to dealing with the sordid couplings of those with opposite sight-gifts, irrespective of hue-by-marriage."

"Perhaps," I said, "but serving a customer is not fraternising."

"But this is," added Jane, taking hold of my tie and pulling me very gently towards her and kissing me again, but with more lingering tenderness than the stolen kiss of a few minutes ago.

"Utterly revolting," said Bunty indignantly, "and just the sort of behaviour I would expect from a jumped-up Grey without a shred of morality—but as a high hue, Edward, you should know better. I am reporting this as an illegal osculation with a grade IV lust infraction as I suspect one or both tongues may have been used."

"Do that," said Jane, "but be warned: take your Yellow nonsense one step too far and you may find yourself surrounded when you least expect it—next week, next month, next year, perhaps—and then have a blanket placed over your head and beaten so hard with sticks you will see permanently with double vision."

Bunty blinked twice.

"Are you threatening me?"

"Not at all," said Jane. "I'm just pointing out that actions have consequences."

"You would not dare touch a Yellow Prefect-in-waiting."

It was a fact unwise to ignore. With Courtland now dead, Bunty would eventually succeed Sally Gamboge as the next Yellow Prefect.

Jane just stared at Bunty in a dark manner, and Bunty bit her lip. Jane *would* dare touch a Yellow Prefect-in-waiting, and I think everyone in the village knew it.

"It's been fun," said Jane, "but we really mustn't keep you."

"I shall leave when I choose to leave," said Bunty, but Jane didn't stop staring, and after a few moments, Bunty mumbled something about "needing more tuba practice" and departed.

"She'll come to a sticky end," said Jane in a way that sounded more threatening than idiomatic. Jane had sort of tried to kill me on a couple of occasions, and while she didn't *actually* kill Courtland, I think she was capable of it. And this made her *more* alluring, *more* exciting and *more* dangerous, all at the same time.

"So," said Jane, "what's this about you becoming a deMauve?"

"Oh yes," I said, thinking I should have mentioned this first, "me and Violet are married."

"Congratulations, that's wonderful news."

"I'm not sure it is. Violet is the most poisonous person in the village, not counting Bunty or Sally Gamboge. Even the other deMauves don't like her. I think I'd prefer to be bitten on the face by a skink."

"I mean from access to the Head Prefect point of view. If we want to find out about the inner workings of the Collective, then you need to end up as Red Prefect."

"The Head Prefect could block my advancement on the ground of moral turpitude—I'm not exactly blossoming with positive merits."

"Not *yet*," said Jane breezily. "I think a couple of decades of unswerving adherence to the Rules should do it."

"A couple of decades?" I echoed, as this was the first time Jane had mentioned any sense of a time scale to our project.

"Or three," she said, thinking carefully. "Violet will be the next Purple Prefect, and you as the Head Prefect's husband is a good place to be, even though persuading Violet to like or respect you is going to be quite a challenge."

"Any suggestions?"

"Being as uncaring and high-handed as she is would definitely turn her head. And I don't mean *pretending* to be mean and nasty when she's watching, then rescuing puppies from storm drains when she's not—Violet would see through that little caper in an instant. You can't just *do* obnoxious, you've got to *be* it and *live* it and *embrace* it."

There was a hollow pause as the next thirty years of my life suddenly took on the air of something closely resembling my very worst nightmare—being the person I didn't want to be while married to the person I least liked. The Green Room suddenly didn't really look so bad after all.

"Just how committed are you, Red?" asked Jane, sensing my reticence. "Did you think we were going to accomplish this in a month? I have to make sacrifices too. Thirty years of retail with only annual stock takes and the very occasional purchase of a crystal or shabby-chic chair to dent the tedium. Think I want that?"

"No. And after thirty years?" I said. "Then what?"

Jane shrugged.

"I don't know. It's an evolving plan."

"Perhaps," I said after we'd been standing in silent contemplation for a while, "all we can hope to do is loosen a single brick in a very large wall."

"I think you're right," she said. "Overthrowing the Colourtocracy could be a team event spread down over the centuries. Our names and our contributions may not even be recorded."

"So we could actually be doing something that may make no difference, might have already been done and no one will ever know what we did if one day someone succeeds?"

"Something like that," she said with a rare smile. "Still on board?"

"Totally," I said.

"Good. Carlos wants me to give the gyro-bike another test run. Want to come and watch?"

"Sure."

"Okay then. Before we go, do you want a set of flying ducks to go on your wall? Old stock so they're discounted."

"How old?" I asked.

She consulted her stock manifest.

"Three hundred and eight years."

MEL & THE GYRO-BIKE

Despite the extra work and lack of opportunities, being Grey had perks: residing in the Greyzone afforded one privacy and relative freedom and a place where Rules exhibited a certain flexibility as the Prefects were often hesitant to intrude. Being Grey also freed one from village politics, expectation and responsibilities. The higher up the Chromatic Scale you were, the more rigidly the Rules applied, the greater the freedoms restrained.

—Ted Grey: *Twenty Years Among the Chromatacians*

We set off in the direction of Fandango's garage but only got as far as the twice-lifesize statue of Our Munsell when we were joined by Melanie Grey.

She was a willowy girl a few years older than myself, and given her cheery manner, sharp intellect and striking looks, it had long been hoped by young men of limited hue that she would show some colour at her Ishihara and take up with them. She hadn't and didn't and not by accident. Melanie's family had been "Long Greys" for at least eight generations, and diligently kept it that way.

"Hullo, Jane," said Melanie in a sing-song sort of voice. "Hullo, Eddie—or is it Mr. deMauve?"

"News travels fast. Good to see you, Mel."

"Enjoy the honeymoon while it lasts," she said, "and here's a spot of advice: do anything she asks of you, and agree with everything she says."

"How is that a recipe for marital harmony?"

"Clifton was until recently her Grey-on-the-side," said Jane, meaning her brother. "He answered back once and she hit him with a shovel while he was getting dressed. We never found his tooth. I think he swallowed it."

"She keeps a shovel in her bedroom?"

"I guess so. That is quite worrying, isn't it?"

Mel giggled, waited until we were away from prying ears, then asked Jane:

"You sent word there was someone you wanted me to shake down?"

"A National Colour officer. Taking the train out the day after tomorrow."

"Not a problem. What do you want from him?"

"Anything you can get. Work number, a copy of his merit book, that sort of thing."

"Okey-dokey," she said. "If I'm not what he fancies, I can always ask Jerome to step in. Either way, we should come up with something."

"What are you doing?" I asked.

Melanie gave me a disarming smile while shaking back her long hair. She was almost ridiculously lovely.

"This is very wrong," I said.

"Why?" she asked.

"That no one should have to, well, I mean that is to say—"

"Look," said Mel, "this is my decision, my choice. I have no issues with what I do, and I'm not a victim who needs to be saved or cared for, or someone you can feel sorry about. I do what I do because it needs to be done and I need a new project because I'm still annoyed over Courtland's death and want to feel useful again."

"I'm sorry for your loss," I said.

"I valued him less than the steam from my gran's piss," said Melanie in an even tone. "I'm only annoyed because I put out for five years for no tangible benefit. With him as Prefect one day and me on his pillow, the Grey community could really have benefited."

"Melanie has a unique skillset," explained Jane, "and helps the cause considerably."

They both looked at me impassively, waiting for me to make some sort of value judgement or comment, but Mel was right: she was a grown woman, and this was her decision.

"A contact in Emerald City would be useful," I said. "Think you can strike up a longer acquaintance?"

Melanie stared at me and raised an eyebrow.

"You want me to engineer a relocation?"

"Can you?"

She thought for a moment, then looked at Jane who nodded.

"Game on," she said with a grin. "I like a challenge and a visit to Emerald City would be an amusing distraction. Where is he?"

"The Fallen Man," I replied, and Melanie bade us a cheery goodbye and was gone.

"Before I forget," I said to Jane, "you're coming on a spoon scavenge to Crimsonolia tomorrow."

"Pointless. Dog-Leg-Lake would have picked it clean years ago."

"I know."

I outlined what deMauve had said and Jane said it sounded like an assignment chosen specifically for its jeopardy, so long as you believed the Riffraff were inherently dangerous, which they weren't. But it would be a day out for us, and a jaunt away from the village could be something to enjoy.

"If we shake off Tommo we can make some colour in the open air. That would be good."

"It would be more than good."

There was a very sound reason why most physical trysts were conducted outdoors, usually beyond the Outer Markers, and during the day. At the height of the event and for a very brief moment, the whole world was suddenly in full and very beautiful colour—everything from the leaves to the water to the sky to the flowers, before fading away again almost instantly. A half-second of pure chromatic and physical pleasure.

"Ah," said Fandango when he saw us approach the garage, "just in time."

The gyro-bike was parked outside Carlos's workshop, and was quietly humming to itself while Amelia read gauges and made notes on a clipboard. Tommo was also there, along with others who were keen to watch Jane ride the bike—even Red Prefect Yewberry had turned up, but he wore a cloak over his suit and badges, a way of denoting that he was not there on official business and could be safely ignored.

"How's she running?" asked Jane.

"Pretty good," replied Amelia. As Janitor's assistant she could defer marriage indefinitely and although that suited her perfectly, I don't think it was the reason she chose the job. She just liked tinkering and mending stuff. She and Jane fell to talking about the bike in a technical language that I didn't really understand. They mentioned "gyros going in and out of phase" at one point, then the difficulties of avoiding "precession deceleration" when the bike went around a turn. I sidled up to Tommo.

"You, Jane and me are on a scavenger hunt to Crimsonolia tomorrow. To find more spoons, mostly."

"I know. DeMauve spoke to me about it just now."

"Are you coming?"

"Nope. There's Riffraff and Mildew and Pookas and other assorted jeopardy in Crimsonolia and besides, the last time I went on a trip with you someone got eaten by a tree."

"He'll pay one hundred merits per spoon with a usable post-code on it—and a ten-merit bonus for ladles and so forth."

"That's twice what he promised me," he said, "but still no."

"It's in cash," I said, "not book merits."

"Cash?"

"Yes."

I saw a look of scheming cross his features but I wasn't going to ask what it was. The less I knew of his wheezes, the better. If he wasn't vaguely likeable and one of the few people I knew well in the village, I daresay I'd have nothing to do with him at all.

"I'll be there," he said.

Carlos joined Amelia and Jane in their technical conversation, and after a few more minutes of impenetrable jargon they decided to go ahead with the test. Jane donned a pair of goggles and then swung a leg over the bike while Amelia checked the speed of the gyros and Carlos listened intently to the bike's whirring internal weights with a stethoscope. Jane had told me they only ever practised at 80 percent flywheel spin-speed and reserved full power for the race, given the risk of gyro failure.

There was an oval banked track next to the playing fields that was used mainly for Penny-Farthing endurance and speed training and was about three quarters of a mile in length overall and made of Perpetulite, so the road surface was an ideal mix of smoothness and grippy texture. The Penny-Farthings barely made it a quarter way up the steep banking but gyro-bikes being faster and more powerful could rise almost to the top where the bank was vertical, but had to be careful not to fly off the top and crash beyond. To help prevent this, a white safety stripe was painted a foot down from the top. Risk of accident was what made the gyro-bike event the huge danger that it was—along with the close proximity to the other riders, and a bike that carried its energy stored in heavy discs rotating at ludicrously high speeds. Six years ago, the Yellowtown gyro-bike suffered a devastating flywheel failure on the third bend, killing the rider and four spectators. The damage it did to the Perpetulite delayed the race for an hour while it repaired itself.

Tommo leaned over to me as we walked with the small group to the track.

"Did the National Colour man deliver some swatches?"

Peddling photographs of villagers in racy poses wasn't Tommo's only side hustle. He and Courtland had been running the village's illicit trade in Lincoln, to be used when the mild euphoric of Lime failed to bring the exuberant delights the user craved.

"You're not getting your grubby paws on them," I said. "That gig died with Courtland."

"I thought you might say that," he said. "Did Lucy talk about me when you saw her?"

"Sort of."

"Good things?"

"Sort of."

We reached the track and Jane lined the bike up on the start, and after more jottings on the clipboard by Amelia and a final check, she was off with a mild squealing of tyres. She accelerated rapidly down the straight and then, just as she hit the first bend, she leaned the bike sharply and rose rapidly up the banking to sit perfectly on the white line.

"That makes me nervous every time," said Amelia, who was standing close by. "If two bikers head for the same optimal position on the banking, things can get a little hairy."

"What makes 'Mad Dog' Juniper so good?" I asked. "Reflexes? Timing?"

"All of the above—and an ambivalent attitude towards her own death or serious injury. She makes a point of saying a tearful farewell to her team members and parents before she lines up on

the grid. As far as she's concerned, every race she enters is potentially her last."

"I heard she had 'Do Not Resuscitate' embroidered on her
jacket."

"I heard that too. Jane's good, but she's not going to die for a
ribboned coat or the selfish hope of a moment's fame."

Jane stuck to the white line on the banking until the bend
started to smooth off and then, in another fluid movement, she
was down on the straight once more, keeping herself tucked tightly
in behind the fairing. To be a successful gyro-biker you needed to
be not just fearless and fast, but have an intuitive understanding
of the conservation of energy, and the knack of reducing drag to
a minimum.

Jane negotiated the next bend with the same elegance of movement, and during the entire three minutes she was out there, only
once did her tyres stray above the white line, much to the small
crowd's consternation. She coasted to a halt just past the finishing
line, kicked out the stand and climbed off the bike.

"Jane seems pretty quick to me," said Tommo, "but do you
think she can beat Mad Dog?"

"I don't know," I said, "but the whole subject is rendered moot
if we're found guilty the day after tomorrow."

"You could drop it all in Jane's lap," he said. "They'd not question your testimony if you told them that she pushed Courtland
under a yateveo, then threatened you with death if you didn't back
up her story."

The odd thing was, Jane and I *had* discussed this. Jane, prosaic
as always, was keen not to do the right thing by others, but the
right thing by us to complete our mission statement: the disman-
tling of the entire apparatus of Chromatacia. If snitching on her
made me look as though I would be a better Prefect in Gamboge
and deMauve's eyes, then it would be worth doing—but since we

had already sworn that Courtland rescued me from the carnivorous yateveo tree only to be taken by another, it would be difficult to reverse the story without alerting some suspicion.

"Is that what you'd do?" I asked. "Blame it on Jane?"

"In a heartbeat."

While Carlos recharged the flywheels, Jane swapped places with Amelia to let her have a practice. We chatted some more before Tommo and I left them to it and headed back into town. We passed Melanie and the National Colour man heading off towards the river for an afternoon dip, towels in hands. As we passed the granary, Doug Crimson approached me.

"Hullo, Eddie," he said. "I just wanted to say thank you."

He grasped my hand and pumped it vigorously.

"What for?"

"Why, marrying Violet, of course," he said with a broad grin. "Now you have, I won't have to—and all of a sudden my life has never looked so rosy. I owe you a big one."

"I may not live long enough to collect."

"Even so," he said. "Thanks."

Tommo said he had "business to attend to" regarding the following day's trip to Crimsonolia, so made himself scarce while I walked back towards the town square. There was a meeting regarding the East Carmine entries to the Jollity Fair sporting events about to start in the town hall. Since I needed to get there, this seemed as good as any a chance to figure out a way, so I stepped inside.

THE GRAND PRIZE

Irrational belief systems were well known to be a quirk of the Previous. There were large abandoned buildings whose purpose seemed purely ceremonial, and irrationality was something we were warned was one of the agents of the Previous's downfall: and us too if we allowed thoughts to enter our heads that were incompatible with Munsell's teachings of rational factualism. There was only one truth: the Rules, and the noble aim of Chromatic betterment that they promoted.

  —Ted Grey: *Twenty Years Among the Chromatacians*

Chairs had been set out in the town hall, and anyone remotely involved in the Jollity Fair events were present. Red Prefect Yewberry was the Jollity Fair co-ordinator for the village, and he was standing on the stage with the Sector co-ordinator I'd welcomed at the train station earlier. As our head clocks indicated *precisely* four thirty, he began.

"Thank you for coming," he said. "The fire exits are clearly marked, but Chromatic order will be maintained: ensure those of a higher hue are allowed to escape before making an exit yourself."

The speech was similar in tone to about every other Jollity Fair pep talk I'd ever attended. Firstly he reiterated about how all hues—not just Red—should give everything for their Sector, embracing Our Munsell's "Palette Doctrine" which dictated that colours *had* to mix to a certain extent to ensure that all hue-specific jobs were filled. I felt happier as a Red living in Red Sector where being of the dominant hue gave us advantages—as there were to Greens in the Green Sector. The *Book of Harmony* described this as "an equitable spreading of unfairness," which sounded reasonable until Jane pointed out there was no Sector for Greys.

Yewberry talked on for a while, the main point being that Red Sector had a chance of walking away with the Grand Prize this Jollity Fair as we were that far ahead in the points. There were several cheers at this, and applause. It wasn't just a silver cup the Sector won, it was a substantial boost of colour feed-pipe infrastructure.

"So," said Yewberry, "let's talk to the team leaders. Where are we, where do we need to be?"

The team leaders outlined progress so far, and made final nominations of team members who would then be vetted by the Prefects to ensure they would "properly represent the village" before allowing them permits.

Mrs. Lilac was the Clerk-to-the-Prefects and ran East Carmine's speed topiary team. She thought winning the speed event was a strong possibility, but had doubts about extra points for artistic interpretation. Her nomination of Sophie Lapis-Lazuli would not be problematical, as despite peculiar personal habits, she was an upright supporter of the Colourtocracy. Hockeyball was Violet's event and she gave a good account of the Red Sector squad, whose skill with the sticks was equalled by plausible deniability when it came to outrageous fouls, always a mainstay—and quite possibly the attraction—of hockeyball. I could see that Lucy Ochre might be a problem for a permit, but if Violet wanted her, she could swing it.

The inexplicably popular loganberry jam event was probably the most contentious, as loganberries were scarce, and sole representative Lisa Scarlett had been practising for years on the more abundant raspberry. The Penny-Farthing events were talked about at length, with team captain Doug Crimson fairly confident that he and Earl from the Greyzone could pair up competitively for the endurance event. There was a possible win in the speed trials as Oscar Greengrass was blisteringly fast, but Doug conceded defeat on the "urban freestyle" disciplines which involved various hair-raising and gravity-defying stunts that, given the size and weight of a Penny-Farthing, would probably mean one or two competitors' permanent injury or death.

After Tania deMauve had given a brief display of extreme juggling—with three spaniel puppies, who seemed to enjoy the experience—talk moved on to the gyro-bike. The victor of the sprint gained not only a shedload of community merits, but sixty points—a massive chunk of the score needed to win the Grand Prize outright. It would be a feather in the cap for East Carmine, and that would have positive consequences chromatically.

"The bike has never been better," said Carlos, who was still breathless after running to get here from the track. "Amelia and I have switched to the denser gold-centred flywheels, and an improved form of gimbals will allow us to corner fast without gyroscopic forces throwing us off the racing line, with a harmonic crossfeed that keeps opposing flywheels at precisely the same speed."

"That's impressive," said Yewberry without understanding a word. "What are our chances against Green Sector's woman? I heard she was dangerously insane."

"Jamie Juniper will be hard to beat," said Carlos. "I can't deny that, but with Jane riding the bike, winning *is* a possibility."

The inference wasn't lost on Yewberry.

"I can't let Jollity Fair requirements interfere with the processes of justice," said the Red Prefect. "Winning the Grand Prize is a massive deal for the Sector of course, but the *Book of Harmony* can never be bruised in pursuit of this goal. When—I mean if—Jane is convicted, then we'll take our chances with Amelia."

Bunty McMustard swiftly took the opportunity to sycophantically support Mr. Yewberry's views that the Word of Munsell could never be compromised, then outlined her training for the "lowest note sustained on a brass or wind instrument" solo event in which she hoped to play "Amazing Place" in a key so low she would be able to separate water from semolina.

The talk wound up with a call for all team members to step forward and be logged in the manifest for their names to be considered by the Council, and for all those either competing or in ancillary roles to do whatever they could for the good of the sector, and the village.

I hid behind a pillar as I didn't want to bump into Violet until I absolutely had to.

"Who are you hiding from?" asked Lucy.

"My wife."

"Wise move. I heard you were going up to Crimsonolia tomorrow. Would you run some harmonic power tests for me?"

We all knew about Lucy's pet project, the "vibrational energy" that pervaded the Collective and powered up Everspins and whatnot. She told me it was not a natural phenomenon, but how the Previous managed their power distribution.

"I think it's still around because there's no one to turn it off," she explained after I'd questioned her further, "and I'm trying to find the source as its power varies according to location."

I agreed and asked her what she wanted me to do. In reply,

she took a small metallic object about the size of a bantam's egg from her pocket and popped it under her foot. She released it and it rose slowly upwards before coming to a halt about chest height.

"Floaties seem to gain their upward force by harmonics," she said. "The quicker they rise, the greater the harmonic power. Do you have a good head clock?"

"Accurate to within a second in an hour."

"That's good. I don't have one at all."

"You don't?"

"No, never have. Courtland didn't have one either and Tommo's internal time loses a minute every half-hour—which he uses as an excuse for always being late."

An accurate clock in your head was something we took for granted. Given the number of broken timepieces we uncovered it was obvious the Previous couldn't do this. Bedside clocks were used to reset yourself every morning when you "lost the clock" when asleep, and my friend Fenton back in Jade-under-Lime could time things to an accuracy of one hundredth part of one second, which was impressive, if a little pointless.

"But you can gauge distance?" I asked.

"Oh sure," she said, "to within a tenth of an inch over sixty yards—and volume too. Just not time. A pen pal of mine in Green Sector West can do compass direction as well as distance and time, which means she can navigate to a spot with pinpoint accuracy even if blindfolded."

"Is that a fact?" I murmured, as internal measuring skills were indeed useful—especially for ensuring portions were equal during meal times, water rationing and carpentry. The town hall striking the hour wasn't strictly necessary, but useful if your internal had drifted off while daydreaming or dozing.

Lucy gave me a kiss on the cheek, squeezed my hand and told

me I was a good sport, then was gone, as it was, apparently, her bath night.

I wandered home myself to have a wash and brush-up, and to change into my Smart Casual #1s as it was not often the theatre came to town.

THE TANGERINE PLAYERS

A "Standard Variable" was a legal circumvention of an annoying Rule. *Spectrum* only covered Standard Variables if they benefitted the Word of Munsell in some way, but otherwise Variables were transmitted by word of mouth, but even this was limited as few moved around, and those that did were often worried about saying the wrong thing to the wrong person at the wrong time—so stayed silent.

—Ted Grey: *Twenty Years Among the Chromatacians*

Dinner had been early so the evening's entertainment could finish before it became too dark to see. The Prefects were front and centre on a raised grassy mound with everyone else taking their self-allotted seat without thinking and strictly in accordance with the Chromatic Hierarchy. Supporters of the Collective pointed to the subconsciously perfect social shuffling as proof of the Colourtocracy's legitimacy and perfection.

"Well, well," said Violet, who had arrived so suddenly on the scene that I jumped. She was the same age as me and we'd had our Ishihara on the same day, but other than that, entirely different. Ever ambitious, she had earmarked Doug Crimson as a potential husband but not signed anything binding in case someone Redder than Doug chanced along. She was a good-looking woman, even though possessed of a nose which was barely anything at all, and wore her hair in Female Style #3: bunches. She also had an affected "bouncy little girl" thing going, which might have been amusing or alluring to some but I just found annoying.

"Hello, Violet," I said.

"Hello, husband *dearest*," she said, sliding her hand up my lapel to touch my neck in a tender manner. As head of the Amateur Dramatic Society, I figured she was good at pretending. I didn't flinch; so was I.

"You heard, then?" I said.

"I insisted upon our nuptials, sweetheart. Daddy was a darling to arrange it, but I was *most* disappointed you used the opportunity to extort favours."

"It's a skill I learned from my wife."

She leaned forward as though to kiss me since we were in company, and it was likely all eyes were upon us. In fact, the speed at which village gossip travelled, I think everyone knew about our marriage within ten minutes of deMauve signing the chit.

"We're going to be so very happy together during our short marriage," she whispered tenderly in my ear, "and I shall be *devastated* when you are sent to the Green Room. In public I shall be inconsolable, but in private I shall use your tallow to grease my door hinges."

"Squeaky doors *are* annoying," I conceded, "but I'm not going to the Green Room."

"I shall be mortally offended if you do not," she replied, then softly kissed me again with just the smallest amount of tongue and added: "And you would not want little wifey mortified, now would you?"

"I'm pretty sure I could live with that," I whispered back.

"You're not really getting this, are you?" she replied in a low growl. "I'm trying to make this easy. You should be grateful that I have granted the fruit of your scabby loins a decent life."

And she pinched me hard on the arm.

"Hello, Violet," said Tommo, who had just walked up. "Pulled the wings off any live dragonflies recently?"

"Can it, Cinnabar. Come, my husband, you will watch the performance with me in the Purple section as befits your new station, and you shall sit at my feet during the performance as a mark of respect."

It made more sense to play along, so I took her proffered hand and we walked towards where the rest of her family were seated. The East Carmine deMauves comprised Violet, her father, mother, paternal grandmother, elder brother Hugo and his wife Tania, who had been at Dad's office earlier, and their two children. They all nodded towards me in a friendly manner, each keenly aware that we were being watched by the entire village. Old Mrs. deMauve even allowed herself to be hugged and took the opportunity to tell me that her unborn grandchild would never once utter my name, nor know what I looked like. Violet's brother shook me by the hand then told me in a quiet voice that he didn't need to know my name as there was really no point. Tania, however, was more honest, and told me in a whisper: "It's a nest of vipers—get out while you still can."

Her husband—who had heard the comment—glared daggers at her, and she smiled sweetly in return. Violet said: "Don't talk to the drudge, husband. She came to us through *Spouse Mart* as a bargain Magenta but turned out to be closer to Lilac. We couldn't return the goods," she added as she gave her brother a glare, "as they had already been spoiled."

Tania regarded me with a resigned look. I'd seen her around

and witnessed her juggling skills earlier, but we hadn't spoken. It was best to steer clear of Prefects' families.

"Jolly bunch, aren't they?" she said.

I sat at Violet's feet as she had commanded, with Hugo's wife sitting next to me, also at the feet of her spouse. She gave me half her liquorice, which was good of her.

"What are you doing?" I asked Violet, who had opened a copy of Munsell's *Approved Plays for the Betterment of the Collective* and was consulting a handwritten list.

"Father tasked me to ensure the performances are *exactly* as scripted. Ad libs attract a ten-point demerit, unless deemed a 'Chromatically compliant whimsical aside.'"

"How can you tell the difference?"

"I'm head of the East Carmine Amateur Dramatic Society, so an expert in all things theatric. I have learned more just now while chatting to the Troupe Leader. She told me a 'proscenium arch' is a painful inflammation of the foot caused by incorrect 'treading of the boards,' which is how we make creaking noises off stage."

"She told you that, did she?"

"Yes. And 'exit stage right' means you have left the stage in the correct fashion, unlike 'exit stage wrong' which means you haven't. Do you want me to carry on?"

"No, I concede you are a complete expert."

"Agreed. I'll also be on high alert for 'ambiguous emphasis' on certain words and 'looks to the audience intended to convey a different and off-Chromocentric meaning.'"

"And what if they do these things?" I asked.

"Fines, usually, but Reboot is possible. The Noted & Lively Orange Players performed a non-approved version of *The Scarlett Letter* to a village over in Blue Sector South, and they were whisked off to be re-educated on the next train. But that won't happen," she added. "All they need to do is see me following the plays. They'll not stray from the path."

The troupe started off by doing a comedy sketch that revolved around cleanliness, and how if you didn't wash sufficiently before meals and the toilet and working in the kitchens and the rendering shed, then disease and the Mildew would almost certainly follow. Next up was a short sketch about the safe handling of methane briquettes in the solidifiers, and then a play about how the continuing hunt for scrap colour was essential, and the players mimed the mining and cleaning and sorting that were essential to the colour-based economy in a comedic manner that made everyone laugh, which, I suddenly realised, was rarely a communal activity; it was something you did in ones or twos— and only out of earshot of Prefects. "Frivolity," Munsell wrote, "is the bedfellow of indolence."

After that, there was a warning farce against passing oneself off as a greater hue, with a pompous fellow getting into all kinds of difficulties by insisting his social station was higher than it actually was. Despite the obvious meaning and function of the play, it was actually very funny, with everyone laughing uproariously, especially Mrs. Lapis-Lazuli who choked on a biscuit and had to be taken away to recover.

There was then a colour-based quiz show that challenged individuals to name all the seventy-eight red hues in order of colour and intensity, which was won by Lucy Ochre, and after that there were some amusing monologues: a skit about a small child who dodges the yateveo only to be eaten by megafauna after straying beyond the Outer Markers; a cautionary verse about the twin dangers of swan attack and lightning; a short vignette extolling the simple elegance of monogamy, and another warning that although *youknow* could be purchased from the Riffraff for as little as half a cabbage, the certain outcome would be a large and painful wart that might damage marriage prospects. And then, with a drum roll and a Parental Advisory warning, the main event began.

The play was a full three-act production and although I'd heard about it and performed in the musical *Red Side Story* upon which it was based, I'd not seen it before. The players began with a prologue:

Two households, opposite in colour,
In fair Violetta, where we lay our scene,
From ancient and very wise taboo breaks to new stupidity,
    Where uncivil hues make civil hues unclean.

From forth the fatal loins of these two hues A pair of idiotic
    lovers ruin their life;
The better Book of Munsell's Rules
Does punish them both with the Prefect's strife.

Now that I was throughly aware of the Collective's pernicious hold on pretty much everything, I thought I wasn't going to enjoy the play—but I did. With a ti-tumpity-tum-te-tum sort of rhythm to the speech and a clear and fluid understanding of drama, *The Tragedy of the Chromatically Non-compliant and Clearly Idiotic Romeo and Juliet* was oddly hypnotic and powerful—clearly the intention, as it depicted in unambiguous terms what happened when complementary colours ignored the social stigma attached to opposition and indulged in behaviour considered quite outside the bounds of polite acceptability. Set in the town of Violetta in Red Sector East, the eldest son and daughter of the opposing Madderhue and Capulime families fall in love, much to the disgust of their parents and the village, who are so appalled by the selfish and unseemly conduct of their children that within a short space of time six people lie dead, including the two people at the heart of the whole sorry business. There was little room for interpretation of the play, and during the performance there was lots of tutting and muttered cries of "serves them right" at the death of the two protagonists, who voluntarily enter the Green Room together, agreeing that their deaths are the only way to properly atone and mend the social ruptures that their selfishness had wrought upon the community.

The play ended with a short verse lifted from Munsell's *Book of Harmony*, exhorting all citizens to observe positive Chromatic values, which are there for the good of the whole community, and whose denial leads only to recrimination and despair. The players gave a low bow while the entire village rose to its feet to show its appreciation, although I noted the Greys and lesser hues did so without much enthusiasm and doubtless only for good form's sake. Personally, I thought the play dangerous nonsense, obviously penned by an insanely rabid supporter of the Colourtocracy.

DeMauve walked down to the stage, waved his hands to halt the applause, then made a speech thanking the players for "their most excellent work," declared that "Apart we were indeed together" and exhorted all the villagers to "think twice before entering a relationship that would only bring shame upon the village." He called for an encore, and the players dutifully complied with a ten-minute sketch that revolved around a Grey who worked hard and, by his applied industry, attracted a wife who could see a pale blue, and ended on a high note with them both being greeted into polite Chromatic society, even though at the very lowest rung.

There was more applause after that—muted again from the Greys—and the evening's entertainment was over. While the players chatted to the Prefects, everyone began the slow meander back to the village, the conversation abuzz with heavy praise and wonderment as the sun dipped below the horizon and the pockets of shadow turned to the deepest black. Night would soon be upon us, and night was not a place anyone liked to be unaccompanied.

AT HOME WITH THE DEMAUVES

Of the five most powerful dynastic families that have ever been, the deMauves have been the longest lasting. Since history is archived and sealed after a hundred years, little is recorded before this, but oral histories from the deMauves themselves suggest they have been a dominant force for the past two hundred years, and have at least three branches in every Sector.

—Ted Grey: *Twenty Years Among the Chromatacians*

"Come along, husband," said Violet and then, insisting on walking two paces ahead, led me back towards the deMauve residence, the largest house on the main square.

"I shall be playing Juliet Capulime in our own staging of *Red Side Story*," she said, talking over her shoulder to me. "I will have breakfast with the players and give them the benefits of my thoughts on their production."

"You could die for real in the final act," I replied. "I think you'd get a standing ovation."

She stopped and glared hotly at me.

"I enjoy spirit and accept chaffing as much as the next girl, Eddie, but don't push your luck: that level of impudence will not sit well with my parents."

"With the threat of the Green Room hanging over me," I retorted, "it will not matter much either way."

"Perhaps not," she conceded, "but your father will doubtless marry Velma Ochre, and that will give us two people to punish in your stead."

As we entered the main square, Carlos struck the carbon arc of the solitary central streetlamp and with a fizz and a flicker the bright white light punched out from the glass lantern and spread across the square like a white sheet on a slate floor. In reply, the clockwork heliostats that had tracked the sun to reflect light into the indoor areas during the day now swivelled towards the streetlamp to do the same for the night. Within another forty minutes an inky blackness would creep though the village, beginning with the shadows that were transformed into ebony, then enveloping all that was not lit by the streetlamp. The night was not dark, it was *black*, and one had to be either a fool or reckless to venture out.

The front door to the deMauve residence was a Univisual purple, and once inside, Violet and I paused in the main atrium, a double-height chamber with paintings of previous deMauves looking down upon us, along with three Titians that should probably be available for public viewing. The interior was opulent, and I presumed in degrees of purple, although to me it looked like varying shades of dark red. The effect was a sense of abject sombreness, like the colour of blood in different stages of drying.

"Am I moving in with you?" I said as she hung her robes upon the hook.

"I have what I need from you," she said. "I am with child—*my* child, I hasten to point out. You will remain here until just before lights out and then you will go home. The conception was this evening, and not before the High Saffron fiasco. If you say otherwise my father and mother will sign an affidavit that they heard you shout out in pleasure as I delivered a near-perfect level of bedroom artistry. Are we clear on this?"

"You've got it all worked out, haven't you?"

"The deMauve dynasty comes first, Eddie, so I'm going to ask you again: Are we clear on this?"

I took a deep breath.

"Yes."

"Yes what?"

"Yes, we're clear on this."

"Good. You will go and assist the drudge until twenty minutes before lights out, when I shall return to see you out. The kitchens are through there."

She turned on her heel and vanished into the living rooms that were ablaze with the warm glow of a log fire. I paused for a moment and walked along the servants' corridor to the kitchens, where I found Tania. She was probably about thirty, had a largish nose with a prominence upon the bridge, luxuriant dark hair plaited tidily, and was dressed well. She smiled easily, but I also noticed that her hands were red and raw—it looked as though the deMauves liked to save money on servants.

"Hullo," she said, giving me a friendly smile. "Here to deliver some Red seed into the viper?"

"She took what she wanted earlier," I said. "I'm here this evening as the cover story."

She nodded.

"Rumour says you're going to be found guilty the day after tomorrow and sent to the Green Room."

"Word gets around. I liked your puppy juggling."

"Thank you. It only works with spaniels—other breeds don't like it at all."

"Is that your competition piece for Jollity Fair?"

"I actually don't stand a chance," she said. "I'm just after a few days away with the kids. You going to the Fair?"

"Not if Violet has anything to say about it. What's your story?"

"I used to be a Magenta," said Tania as she placed some washing up in the sink and poured some water over it from a hotpot, "over in Skye, Blue Sector South. Don't believe that 'low hue Lilac' nonsense. The lack of Purple is not in me, it's in Hugo. Mrs. deMauve hoped to birth a deeper Purple by going to the Rainbow Room but got scammed and was sired by a Grey. Cost her four thousand cash merits and all they got was a son who isn't even Chromogencia, let alone Prefect material. Sort of funny, really—and serves them right. What's perfect about it was that the deMauves didn't know they'd been scammed for twenty years, when Hugo had his Ishihara."

She gave out another peel of laughter.

"And Violet?"

"No, she's the product of them both, and she'll be the next Head Prefect. Seventy-one percent averaged across the channels, but *definitely* straying towards the Blue, which is why she needed you."

"This is a lot of information," I said, dazzled by her lack of discretion.

"I despise them all. Look, I've been in a bit of a self-imposed drought recently, do you want to have some *youknow*? I've given the deMauves the two children that obligation requires, so I don't let Hugo anywhere near me these days; he's involved with Patsy Cornish-Blue, in any case. The laundry room is clean and cosy and warm, and smells of beeswax and clean linen and soap—we can go there right now if you wish."

She smiled, then held my hand in the most affectionate manner.

"I have someone," I said.

"I heard about that," she said, gently letting go. "It's Jane, isn't it?"

I nodded.

"They tell me she's dangerous but I've never had a problem. She tore Jabez's eyebrow off for some reason, and there were rumours she killed a man."

"Really?" I said, not as surprised as I should have been. "Tell me more."

She indicated a seat at the kitchen table and put some more water in the hotpot, then placed it near ground level, so it would boil.

"There was this Blue named Jeremy Duckegg who had his own definition of consent that he thought he should impose on others. He vanished one day after games eighteen months ago and wasn't found until the following year. Or rather, his personal effects were found. The organic parts of him had been absorbed by the Perpetulite roadway, and the indigestible parts—buttons, fillings, belt buckle, coins and his spot-badge—were found at the edge of the road."

"So why do you think Jane had anything to do with this?"

"Went missing at the same time, came back sort of changed."

She thought for a moment.

"Do you love her?"

"I do."

"Does she love you?"

"I think so."

"I'd like someone to love and be loved by," she said wistfully, "but they rarely let me out of their sight, and even when they do, no one would dare lie with me, what with me being a deMauve and everything. Can we hug, like tightly? No strings attached, no obligation. I just want to feel some kind of intimacy."

"Sure."

So Tania and I hugged, there in the kitchen of the deMauve's house with the smell of cooking and warmth of the range. I felt her draw me in tight and she put her head on my neck so I could see her nape which was covered in light down and freckles. She smelled of expensive soap, probably bought from the Aspirational Living shop, perhaps from Jane. After about half a minute, we cautiously disengaged.

"I think that's made it worse, not better," she said, fanning herself with her hands. "Are you sure you don't want any *youknow*? I'm very good at it."

"I'm sure you are, but no thank you."

She took a deep breath and her mood changed.

"Eddie, can I level with you?"

"Sure."

"If I'm not pregnant by you this evening, Violet will beat me violently with a broom handle."

"Oh," I said, suddenly understanding, "so that's why you were in the Colourium this morning?"

"Yup," she said with a sigh, "your dad flashed me the ovulation shade so I'm very hot to trot right now."

It made complete sense in a Violet sort of way. Since I was being Greened the day after tomorrow, Violet was leaving nothing to chance: she needed a spare. If hers didn't carry to term or died in infancy, she could just take Tania's.

"And you thought you knew how hideous the deMauves were," said Tania. "Believe me, you have no idea."

"Would Violet have rewarded you if we had?" I asked.

"Unusually, yes. She said she'd let me join the Jollity Fair squad and compete in the Juggling event. Better still, I could take the kids."

"Then let's just *say* we did," I said.

"She'll have me tested in a week," said Tania, "and if I'm not with child she'll ban me from Jollity Fair and *then* beat me for not trying hard enough."

I had an idea.

"That linen cupboard you were talking about. Is it on the ground floor?"

"What are you thinking of?"

"Is it?"

"Yes."

"Leave the window unlatched and spend the night there. I know someone who knows someone who might be able to help out."

"Even if I am a deMauve?"

"I think so."

She stared at me intensely for a moment and then gave a mischievous grin.

"*Make sure they're Grey,*" she whispered, "without a speck of colour. Let's really hit this family where it hurts. And a looker," she added as an afterthought, "who might want repeat business."

She gave me another hug and returned to her chores. We chatted while I helped her with the washing up and she told me that Head Prefect deMauve was far less interested in the well-being of the village than he was about the advancement of the deMauve dynasty which now had thirty-two Head Prefects in place; their annual Convention was due just after Jollity Fair at a place called Purple Regis.

"Hugo and I had our honeymoon there," said Tania. "It's amazing—so long as you have the requisite sight gift down the red and blue channels. Purples know how to look after themselves, and the waiters and cooks and servants are all Lilacs, so no Greys or other hues at all. It's on the coast, booming waves, fresh fish for dinner most evenings. Some people actually swim in the sea, despite the presence of the Under Toad ready to pull you under and devour you, but I never quite dared myself."

"I've seen the sea three times," I said, "so I'm something of an expert. I've heard of the Sea Beasts."

"The fishermen rarely go far because of them. Giant tentacled creatures with eight legs that can crush a fisherperson's head with one bite of its mighty beak. If the Squidling doesn't get you, the

Kraken certainly will, or even the deadly whirlpools, or the tidal ripper that can strip a horse to bones in under a minute."

"Good job I'm not a horse."

"The future is deMauve-shaped," mused Tania, "and if I was the future I'd be worried. Life is already pretty shitty—under a deMauve-centric regime it might conceivably get worse."

I didn't say so, but I agreed.

VIOLET WAS WAITING in the lobby at a half-hour to lights out, and insisted she search me in case I had stolen any of their spoons.

"I haven't stolen any spoons, Violet."

"So *you* say," she said, going through my pockets. "Did you and the drudge have fun?"

"*Tania* and I had a lot of fun, Violet—don't renege on the juggling gig at Jollity Fair."

"You have both done well," she said with a rare smile, and once she'd ascertained I'd stolen no spoons she pulled my tie demeritably askew, mussed my hair and gave me a passionate kiss on the doorstep.

"Thank you, darling, that was wonderful," she said for the benefit of Mr. and Mrs. Crimson who were hurrying past, then added in a loud voice so there was no mistake, "we shall expect the patter of tiny feet this midwinter."

She then shut the door behind me and I walked home.

MRS. OCHRE WAS at our house when I got in, and at this late hour she would be "visiting for the evening and staying for breakfast." I liked Velma, mostly because I liked that she liked my dad, and I think they suited each other, too. Both quietly seditious. She was the village telegraph operator, having taken over when Mrs. Blood retired.

"Hello, son," said Dad, who was playing Scrabble with Mrs. Ochre.

"Dad."

"Hello, Edward," said Velma. "I understand you are now married to Violet deMauve. How hideously unpleasant for you, I trust you are not taking it too badly?"

"I would probably head for the Green Room," I said, "if I wasn't already heading for the Green Room."

"I do not think you will be convicted," she said. "Natural justice has a way of smiling upon those of honourable intent. I heard you were popping up to Crimsonolia tomorrow. If you see a spare cheese grater lying around, bring it back for me, will you?"

"Sure."

"Ah-ha," said Dad, "flame." He placed the tiles on the Scrabble board and added up the score. Since only words describing colours were permitted, there were precisely one thousand, five hundred and six words available. The blanks were not permitted to be used, so they were instead upcycled into cufflinks and worn by the reigning village Scrabble Champion.

"Good move," said Velma, and then changed all her own tiles. A complete Scrabble game could sometimes last months.

"Dad," I said, "can I ask a question?"

"That sounds like a serious tone of voice," he said. "I trust Velma implicitly, but if you're happy we can talk alone."

"No, that's okay. The entire village of Rusty Hill was lost to Mildew, but what mechanism would they have used to achieve this? A mass diagnosis of tennis elbow?"

"Your son asks dangerous and interesting questions," said Velma. "Oooh, I've got 'madder' on the Double Letter Score."

"We've discussed the Rusty Hill issue at length," said Dad, indicating Velma and himself. "The Rules exist to cover all eventualities so no one ever has to make difficult decisions. All that is needed is an unwavering belief that the Rules must be followed."

"I'm still not sure what Rusty Hill might have done to deserve it," I said. "I mean, killing *everyone?*"

Dad shrugged and changed all his tiles again.

"I used to go along to the Guild of Swatchmen regional dinners," said Velma. "Stuffy affairs, but there was always some good green to be passed around. Not standard Lime or Lincoln, but illegal off-swatch shades that made you feel as though you were floating."

"I never saw that," said Dad, "but then I lived in Green Sector, where the dominant hues are less affected by the buoyant pleasures of the soothing greens."

"Anyway," continued Velma, "tongues are loosened and strange tales start to seep out. One old girl got a little too greenfaced and spoke of 'strangers not of this place who came in the night,' following which everyone in the village was dead by the Rot in twenty-four hours."

"And this was Rusty Hill?"

"No," she said, "this was Brunswick-on-Sea, Green Sector East. Similar story, different place."

"But why an entire village?"

Mrs. Ochre stopped rearranging her Scrabble tiles.

"This woman said it was beyond the capacity of any team of Swatchmen she knew, and thought it was the work of an unknown other, with greater powers than we possess. She thought it was the Pale Rider. Not a legend, but real."

"Arriving in the night on a silent winged horse," said my father, "and death following with them."

We were all silent for a moment.

"She referred to the eradication of Rusty Hill as a 'C-Notice,'" added Velma, "but she didn't explain what that meant."

There wasn't time to speak anymore as the lights would be extinguished in six minutes, so just enough time to prepare ourselves and the house for bed. A sprinkling of ash across the threshold to ward off the Pooka, doors secured, a glass of milk, teeth brushed. I was in bed and staring at the ceiling with fifteen seconds to run, and almost exactly on time the light went out, and the sable cloak of darkness washed over the village. Not simply dark, but inky blackness, as close to having no eyes as I imagined it to be.

There was a couple of seconds pause before news, messages and views began to be tapped out in Morse on the radiators of the now-redundant central heating system.

It started off with someone exclaiming how attractive the actor who played Romeo was, then more general chitter-chatter about the evening's entertainment, several comments over mine and Violet's marriage, then a more protracted conversation regarding Jollity Fair and our chances at winning the Grand Prize. While generally free gossip, none of this happened without prefectural oversight as someone—doubtless Bunty—was always ready to jam any inappropriate or disrespectful chatter with a noisy series of random strikes on her radiator with a wooden spoon.

Going on beneath these multi-threaded conversations was the bedtime story, gently tapped out with a fork: you could hear the reverberations of the tangs. This was once more *Renfrew of the Mounties*, which I had heard once through already, so ignored. All these noises were essentially the village bedding down for the night. But the night, while usually just darkness, radiator-chat and the distant cry of the wood hyrax, was something more to me right now: for when the night came, so did Jane.

JANE BRUNSWICK AT NIGHT

The Apocryphal Man's existence was, as his name suggested, apocryphal. But unlike the Fallen Man who was
deemed as such because he defied explanation or cat-
egorisation, the Apocryphal Man was mentioned in the
Book of Harmony as "the man who shall observe, but not
be observed" making him both existing and not existing
at the same time. He was a historian, who theorised that
Chromatacia existed to give him something to study.
    —Ted Grey: *Twenty Years Among the Chromatacians*

I had moved my bedroom to the ground floor as soon as we'd
all got back from High Saffron. The reason was not that I slept
sounder or wanted a cooler breeze or even that the decor was
better. No, it was because the night was no longer my prison.
Unusually, Jane could see in the dark. Not *completely* in the dark,
of course, like in a cellar, but outside under moonlight or the faint
collective glimmer from distant suns which had been reduced to
pinpoints of light by distance. I could not see them, but Jane
described the moonless night as a place of incalculable beauty:
stars so numerous that in places they were only a milky blanket
that stretched in a swathe across the night sky.

    For me, the greatest advantage to Jane's night-sight was that
she could visit, and often without me even hearing her enter my
room. The first I might learn of her presence was the swish of

her dress as it came off over her head, the subtlest sound of a bare footfall upon the tiles or even the sound of her breathing. Tonight, I simply heard her whisper in the darkness.

"Are you awake?"

"I am awake."

I felt her lips on mine. Warm, immensely soft.

"That felt good," I said. "Join me?"

I felt the cover pull back and with a faint creak of the bedsprings she climbed in, and we held each other as close as possible, the intimacy of skin on skin a joy hard to describe. I no longer wore pyjamas, in anticipation of Jane's visits, and for the next twenty minutes we let the physicality of our shared passion speak for us, along with the dangerously exciting frisson of a Green and a Red bonding together in contravention of all the Rules and taboos and regulations.

Once we had got our breath back Jane whispered: "This is sort of like *The Tragedy of the Chromatically Non-compliant and Clearly Idiotic Romeo and Juliet.*"

"With a happier ending, I hope," I replied. "Oh, and before I forget: Do you know of a Grey who would like to have some babymaking *youknow* with Tania tonight?"

"Which Tania? There are three."

"DeMauve."

"Ooo-hoo. This sounds juicy. What gives?"

So I told her the whole story. She tutted at Violet's efforts at engineered Chromogenics, then giggled at Tania's plans for continuing the tradition of deMauve dynastic sabotage.

"I think I know someone who would happily help out," she said quietly. "Leave it to me. Anything else?"

I told her about how Rusty Hill's Mildewing wasn't the only one, how the Swatchman who got over-Limed talked about a "C-Notice" and how "strangers not of this place who came in the night" might have done it. I didn't mention the Pale Rider legend as I wanted her to take me seriously.

"You mean 'not of this place' as in off-Sector?" she said. "Like Blue Sector or the DAC-lands?"

"No," I said, eager to see how Jane would accept the concept, "the people who killed everyone in Rusty Hill may be *Someone Else* from *Somewhere Else.*"

"*Someone Else,*" she said, speaking the phrase out loud and savouring it slowly, like a fine custard, "from *Somewhere Else.* I think you might be on to something, Red. The Fallen Woman adds weight to your conjecture. If she were meant to have fallen to the ground safely, it would suggest flight technology is still possible. But if it is," she added, "why haven't we seen any?"

"They come by cover of night," I said, "in silent flying machines."

She nodded.

"Nightseers; above and beyond the Rules, last line of protection for the Munsell Doctrine. I didn't know if they were real, but I guess so. But machines that can fly?"

"We know they existed once," I said. "Maybe they still do, just in the Somewhere Else. I think that's what swans are, just without people in them. The National Colour officer had seen one that was made of metal and wires."

We were silent again for a moment.

"I'm not going to have a view on the existence of the Someone Else until I meet one," said Jane. "Besides, where would they be if not here?"

"The only place there is: the other side of the water."

We lay in the darkness for a moment until she rolled silently out of bed.

"Better get dressed."

"Why?"

"I want you to meet some people."

We dressed quickly and I followed her to the window in the inky darkness. Moving across the room in the pitch black was no problem and even climbing out of the window presented little difficulty. But once she started to lead me around the buildings, it all got a little more fearful.

"How did you acquire this skill?" I whispered.

"I was shown a hue to cure rheumatic fever when I was thirteen," she whispered back, "and this was the side effect. Rare, but not unheard of."

"My friend Fenton back in Jade-under-Lime was being routinely hued for whooping cough," I said, "and afterwards he could remember the entire libretto of *Greys and Dolls*. It put him in much demand as an all-parts understudy."

She led me across the town square—I could feel the warm pantiles beneath my bare feet—then the cooler compacted soil of the area between Carlos's workshop and the rendering shed. Then there was some grass, a gentle slope down and we slowed as we negotiated the more cluttered yard within the small street of terraced-style houses that made up the Greyzone.

"Where are we going?" I asked.

"You'll see."

She squeezed my hand, then rapped very softly three times on an unseen door. There was a pause, then two raps back. The door opened and we stepped inside, the cool tiles under my feet replaced by the warmth of wooden boards. I knew I was not alone in the room, for I could hear the slight movement of clothes and the huff of breathing, and lingering on the air was the faint smell of briar tobacco.

As soon as the door clicked shut someone removed a black drape from a dozen or so lightglobes that were piled in a wooden bowl in the centre of the room. I gasped, for lightglobes were banned technology. Any dug up in the fields or exposed by alluvial erosion were placed in weighted sacks and dumped in lakes; shallow bodies of water sometimes glowed at night.

I blinked and looked around the room. I was in the Greys' community hall, and although I didn't count heads I guessed perhaps forty or so were present—and mostly Grey aside from the Tangerine Players and Lucy Ochre, who was sitting very close to someone I recognised as Jonny Grey, one half of East Carmine's window-cleaning team. She gave me a shy wave as she realised that she'd been rumbled—the rejection of Tommo had a stronger, deeper reason. Also in the room were the sixteen people technically known as "unlicensed supernumeraries." These were the ones who would long ago have been shown the colour that led to Mildew or sent to Reboot, but had escaped and washed up in East Carmine— and were living here protected by the Greys, presumably with food liberated from the kitchens. Harbouring an undocumented supernumerary was instant Reboot—death, essentially—for knowing about it and not speaking out. Jane's mum and dad approached us.

"Hello, 'He-who-runs-with-scissors,'" said Stafford, using the name by which I was known in the Greyzone, "the Stropgoblin tells us that you may have hidden depths, given time."

"The Stropgoblin?"

"Thank you, Dad," said Jane, the first time I had seen her even the tiniest bit embarrassed. While Jane went off "to action that deMauvian plan we discussed," I chatted to Jane's parents.

"You've raised a fine daughter," I said.

"It depends on your point of view," replied Belinda. "Her headstrong ways may spell the end for all of us—and you. It's odd," she added as she looked at me intently, "you don't *seem* her type."

"What is her type?"

They both shrugged.

"We don't know. She's never shown the slightest bit of interest in anyone until you. Has she tried to kill you?"

"Yes, but I think if she'd wanted to she would have done so."

"We think so too. I think it means she likes you."

"*Not* killing me makes you think she likes me?"

"It's a big deal," said Belinda, "and she talks about you at home."

"Really? What does she say?"

"About how she's not going to kill you."

It didn't help. When people talk about the things they are *not* going to do, it generally means they are thinking of doing them. So instead we chatted about Jollity Fair and Jane's potential win on the gyro-bike, which they thought really boiled down to who cared least about losing their life in pursuit of a win—her or Mad Dog Juniper. Belinda said that Jane wouldn't go that far, but Stafford wasn't so sure.

"When the Grey Mist comes down," he said, "I'd not like to think what she's capable of."

We didn't get to talk anymore as Jane had returned. I said my goodbyes and she took my hand and led me towards an empty sofa.

"Who did you line up for Tania?"

"My brother Clifton. He's a sort of male version of Melanie. Highly adaptable and Grey to the core. Tania knows him as he used to be Violet's Grey-on-the-side, so it won't be awkward, he knows the layout of the house and if anyone sees him about they'll think he and Violet are still having a thing. I'll take him over later."

We sat down together, our public association no longer a matter of secrecy: the abundance of shared demeritable infractions in the room created a sense of instant community between us all. I felt relaxed, and with a strong sense of belonging. Not to my hue, but to something else, a shared sense of purpose in the almost deafeningly unsaid notion that everything we knew and understood about the Collective was fundamentally wrong.

"Eddie, this is Daphne," said Jane, introducing me to a woman sitting next to us. She was of late middle age, and seemed to have both legs beneath the knee actually *missing*. I'd not seen such a thing before, and may have stared for too long.

"The linoleum factory," she explained cheerily. "The safety features were removed to allow for speedier production. Swatchman Ochre sent me to the Greyzone, then signed me off as 'unable to work due to Mildew-related death' and the rendering staff fudged the numbers. No one goes down there much anyway; the Prefects accept the figures without question."

She giggled at the wickedness of it all.

"Do all villages have hidden supernumeraries?" I asked.

"From what I've learned," she said, "I'm nothing particularly unusual."

Two people approached our sofa and we budged up so they could sit down.

The one sitting closest to me was the Apocryphal Man.

"Hullo, Eddie," he said. "Welcome to the East Carmine's flipside."

With the Apocryphal Man was another man who from the neck down was much like the rest of us, but from the neck up was unlike anyone I had ever seen. In place of his nose were two holes, and he had no chin or, as far as I could see, jaw. He had one eye—his right—on the side of his head that was undamaged, and which he used to regard me carefully. I figured he was the other guest in our house, the one who lived upstairs with the Apocryphal Man.

"This is Harold Lime," said Baxter.

Harold extended a hand and we shook in a friendly manner. When he spoke it was in an odd throaty monotone. I couldn't figure out what he was saying to begin with, but soon got used to it.

"You can call me Harry," he said, "and thanks for the food and drink back at the house. It was very kind."

"You're—um—welcome."

I'd never seen such a healed facial wound before, but then I suppose I wouldn't. Traumatic injury—along with blindness, birth defect, mental aberration—in fact, almost everyone not considered "normal" as narrowly defined in the *Book of Harmony's* Appendix vii(B) caught a variant of the Mildew and was carried off. The more you thought about it, the more iniquitous it became. My younger brother died of Mildew when he was only six months old having failed to walk or talk sufficiently well. I felt myself shiver involuntarily.

"So what's your story?" asked Harry, who seemed to speak when he was breathing in, rather than out. "Sent here on a chair census, I heard?"

"Pretty much," I replied, and told him of my limited time here in East Carmine—the recovery of the Caravaggio and the trek to High Saffron to look for scrap colour.

"You found only death there, didn't you?"

"I did."

We'd found the place where anyone who had ever been consigned to Reboot ended up, or those sent on the euphemistic "Night Train to Emerald City." Both trips were a ruse, a way by which the Collective removed unwanted people.

"What about you?" I asked.

Harry pointed to his face.

"I lost half my face in the pressing shop of the kitchen enamelware factory, over in Greenfield. I can see sixty-eight percent of green, so the Room named after us has only a non-lethal sense of dreaminess about it, so I was told I had to go to Emerald City on the Night Train for 'specialist care.'"

"You'd heard the Night Train was a one-way trip?"

"My uncle was the Swatchman and he told me to get out while I still could and then told the Prefects I'd died in the night. I walked out at dawn and after sleeping roughly for several months, ended up with the Riffraff."

"What were they like?" asked Lucy, who like all of us was listening intently.

"A mixed bag," continued Harry, "but basically residents of the Collective who had run away mixed with people whose descendants were likely Previous. Small family units, led by the eldest woman. They do Collective parenting, speak in an odd slangy way, and some of them look almost identical to the Previous."

"Were they very different to us?" asked Lucy.

"Little in temperament and intellect between us, but I noticed that the more Previous you looked, the less the healing hues had any effect. To those poor souls, even an open wound can occasionally inflame—and even kill."

The entire group was silent, hanging on his every word. As far as Head Office were concerned, Riffraff were regarded as vermin and should be destroyed on sight.

"Can they see in full colour?" asked Jane.

"They see it selectively, like us. But it does not signify anything socially. A Red is a Blue is a Green is a Grey is a Yellow. In fact, free interbreeding among long-established Riffraff has apparently given some trichromatic vision, albeit to a small degree."

"Do they get the Mildew?" asked Lucy.

"No," said Baxter, the Apocryphal Man, "but when their numbers get too big, I've heard they die in whole encampments, always overnight."

Jane and I exchanged glances.

"I suspect it is a culling, but for what reason and by whom, I do not know."

"A *what?*" asked Jane.

"A culling," he said, "an old term meaning 'to destroy pests' like we do when there is a plague of mice or frogs."

Jane squeezed my hand. I think we now knew what a "C-Notice" meant. Rusty Hill, and others like it, had been *culled*.

"What happens if a Red and a Green have children?" asked Lucy. Such a question was never posed, let alone answered—there was no such thing as a Greeny-Red, after all.

"Nothing at all," said Harry in his odd throaty wheezy voice, "but the Riffraff did have some odd rituals, the most grisly that all infants have their index finger removed at birth."

He raised his index finger, the one with the barcode in the nail-bed.

"If I'd wanted to stay beyond six full moons, I would have to have had mine removed too. The procedure was known as 'Off-gridding' but the purpose was never revealed, if they even knew themselves."

"Were they untamed savages?" asked Daphne.

"When the need required it," he replied after a moment's reflection, "but in general they were warm and loving and loyal and kind. If a member transgressed the rules they could be uncompromisingly violent, but I saw no baby-eating or baby-theft. Perhaps *unsophisticated* would be a better description, but their excesses were no worse than ours—and on most occasions a good deal better. Best of all, there was no Chromatics, no Munsellian Doctrine, no Ishihara, no Prefects—they lived naturally as I think humans probably once did, and chose their leaders by merit."

"By merit?" echoed Lucy, unsure of how a concept might exist, let alone be workable.

"Yes; the most competent person was chosen to be leader."

"I like the sound of that," I breathed.

"How did you wind up here?" asked Jane.

"After I left the Riffraff I joined one of the Jollity Fair sideshows as 'Johnny no-face' and took fourth billing after the two-headed sheep, a chicken that could peck tunes on a xylophone and 'Rita, the amazing one-legged woman.'"

This was more interesting. I'd always wanted to see a two-headed something—it was never considered a proper Jollity Fair if there wasn't one, and while the human anthropological curiosities in jars were popular, something two-headed was always the star attraction.

"I shared the sideshow tent with 'Janus, the two-faced boy,'" continued Harry, "who aced the attendance figures as he was intriguing rather than shocking, but I had the edge as I was alive and not in a jar. When we all ate Rita after a disappointing showing in Green Sector East, I was bumped up to second billing."

"You ate a one-legged woman?" asked Daphne, shocked by the admission.

"Rita was *also* the name of the sheep," he said. "I guess that is a little confusing."

"Oh," I said, disappointed that I might not see a two-headed sheep if by any chance I did get to Jollity Fair.

"But I was bumped back down to fourth billing when a tinker-trader brought in a Tin Man that still functioned, albeit in a limited fashion. It could follow basic commands by walking around the show tent, and even balance building blocks on one another. It would have been deemed Apocrypha anywhere but Jollity Fair."

"I think they're powered by harmonics," said Lucy, "the same as lightglobes and hotpots. They'll keep on running for ever."

"It certainly needed no sustenance," said Harry, "and often went out at night, a glimmering figure in steel with a halting walk, until one evening it made a 'pop' sort of noise, exuded some smoke which smelled of burned-out Everspins, and that was that.

I remained there," he added, concluding his story, "until Mr. Baxter found me. We've been together ever since."

We weren't the only ones chatting away—most everyone else was talking in a delightfully unguarded fashion, with the primary topic seemingly the many iniquities of the Colourtocracy and prefectural overreach. Lucy told us more about her hobby of noticing complex patterns in numbers. She could, for instance, arithmetically predict the way in which the seeds in sunflower heads formed by using a simple number progression, but I found it all a little hard to follow.

As soon as all our internal clocks indicated to us that it was eleven, Stafford stood up. He was the senior Grey in the village and had risen after thirty years of diligent work to the position of Village Porter, which conferred upon him "lesser hue status," meaning his level of expected subservience was reduced, and he could attend village meetings, though only as an observer.

"Welcome to East Carmine's flipside," he said in a voice practised to project at the lowest possible volume. The Greyzone was a long way from the village, but it always paid to be cautious. He looked around the group, then to me, "And we have a new member. His name is Eddie."

"He is married this day to Violet," said someone near the back. "A deMauve can *never* be trusted."

This fact was agreed upon by several others.

"A pair of eyes in the Purple camp is an asset worth protecting," said Jane, "and he has also ensured his father's work can continue. Eddie is one of us, and has already proven himself."

"My daughter vouches for him," said Stafford, "as do I. Eddie will be welcomed as one of our own and anyone who thinks otherwise can speak now."

There was silence, so he continued.

"Good. Now, instead of the usual discussions as regards the

impossible linoleum production targets and other circumventions of the nonsense perpetuated by the Prefects, we have entertainment from the Tangerine Players, who have kindly agreed to perform a banned play for our entertainment."

THE PLAY'S THE THING

The Daclands, DAC-lands or Daclans were the area to the north of Blue Sector North, and which were a harsh and sterile mountainscape composed of hard calcite, home only to lichens and the occasional pocket of soil. The scrubbing engines work day and night, apparently pulling carbonate out of thin air. Their function is so far unknown.

—Munsell's *Book of Harmony*

The Tangerine Players rose, readied themselves and then once more launched into a performance. They spoke their lines quietly, but with a practised sense of muted intonation, annunciating the words carefully so the low tones did not fall into mumbling. I thought for a moment the play was the same one they'd performed earlier, until I realised the words they were speaking conveyed an altogether different meaning:

> *Two households, both alike in dignity,*
> *In fair Verona, where we lay our scene,*
> *From ancient grudge break to new mutiny,*
> *Where civil blood makes civil hands unclean.*

And then, more:

From forth the fatal loins of these two foes
A pair of star-cross'd lovers take their life;
Whose misadventur'd piteous overthrows
Doth with their death bury their parents' strife.

And that wasn't the only difference. Sure, the bodycount was the same, but the two lovers—still a little dappy, agreed—had fallen in genuine *love* rather than in lust, and in defiance of their parents and the accepted order cast everything in front of them as they attempted to be the one thing they wanted more than anything else: together. Their deaths were not of their own choosing, but manifestly the result of their family's unspoken yet utterly pointless feud. Jane squeezed my hand tightly, for the parallels were not lost on me, either. More strikingly, all references to the Colourtocracy were omitted, and I soon realised I was watching the play as it might have originally been performed: *before* the Epiphany, *before* the deFacting, *before* the Something that Happened.

The players acted with far more commitment this time around, and the play, by turns funny, tragic and violent, had most of us in tears. This was no cautionary tale; this was a tragic romance of lovers kept apart by social conventions and a wasteful dynastic agenda, with an end that suggested reconciliation of the families, not a dry speech about the stupidity of contravened flawed orthodoxy.

The play finished some two hours later, nearly twice as long as the earlier rendition, and the patter of index fingers on thighs—the flipside version of applause—went on for a full ten minutes as the players bowed and took in our adulation, mouthed "thank you very much" and "no, really, you're too kind" as we showed our appreciation. Afterwards, the Apocryphal Man stood up and thanked the troupe, saying that he had never heard the play's text spoken more trippingly on the tongue. Lucy Ochre asked how they kept the text hidden so well when possession of such a play would be instant Reboot, and the leader of the troupe smiled, and tapped her head, and told us that players had handed down the original text from group to group in an unbroken chain all the way from the first Leapback when the hue that taught all the plays was withdrawn from use and replaced with the new, non-hue texts, rewritten to convey a more Chromocentric agenda. The plays they performed to the public were cover for their private performances, where delivery, timing and entrances and exits could be rehearsed, practised and maintained so that when the plays could be performed openly again—even if not for a thousand years—the very next night would be the opening night. No rehearsals or try-outs, read-throughs or faltering speech or flubbed entrances: the plays would speak again, instantly and without a hiccup, as though they had never been gone at all.

It seemed the players spent their lives not performing, but *preserving*.

"When was the play first performed?" I asked.

"Difficult to gauge," said the Troupe Leader. "We have a good idea that *Romeo and Juliet* was definitely performed in the pre-Something yearly notation of 2163, and that it was at least five hundred years old then. Add that to the 00496 years since the Munsell Epiphany and it gives us over a thousand years—minimum."

This could only ever be an estimate as we didn't know how close 2163 was to the Something that Happened. We talked some more with the players but they didn't want to be drawn on the shortcomings of the Collective as it was not something that ever concerned them.

"The plays are the only thing," said the youngest, a girl no older than myself. "It is for others to take society in a different route.

We will do nothing that places our fond remembered plays in jeopardy. It is the cause, it is the cause."

The others all nodded and murmured "it is the cause."

"We'll wait however long it takes," said the lead player. "Generations if need be. We have only one directive, and it is clear to us, and all must play a part."

We thanked them for their performance as they made their exit with a lightglobe wrapped in a towel so only a chink of light escaped to lead them to their lodgings. They would be gone on the next train to the next venue, to perform a corrupt play in public before a real one in private. The remainder of the globes were doused as the door opened, then uncovered again as it closed.

Jane and I then fell to talking with Lucy and Stafford about when the Epiphany had actually taken place, which no one knew, as the last pre-Something date ever found—on a receipt for Wensleydale cheese—was dated 2296.

"They're all rare above 2280," said Stafford, "which might point to societal strife up until that point."

"Or that paper was no longer being used," added Lucy.

"We should ask Baxter," said Jane, nodding towards where the Apocryphal Man was sitting on the sofa, playing chess with Harry. "He was around not long after Munsell's Epiphany."

The Apocryphal Man had no first name, or at least, not that he could recall, and it wasn't known whether Baxter was his name, or some kind of label like "Saddler" or "Chef." One in an identical series of ten, he'd been known officially as Baxter #4 and was blessed with not only full colour vision but negligible senescence, meaning he aged only slowly, if at all. He was trained to observe and record until he would be asked to submit his findings, something which had never occurred and he now thought never would, as either his relevance had so reduced to make him redundant, or that given the long passage of time he might have been forgotten.

"Mr. Baxter," said Jane, who always favoured the direct approach, "how could we figure out the time gap between the Something that Happened and Munsell's Epiphany?"

The Apocryphal Man looked up and thought for a moment.

"Several comets would do it," he said. We looked blank so he continued: "Eight years ago, in the daytime sky, you recall an aerial phenomenon?"

I did recall. A bright object in the sky, with a tail—most spectacular at dusk. Like Baxter, it was Apocryphal. There was nothing in the Book of Munsell to explain it so we were instructed to ignore it.

"That comet has visited before," said Baxter. "In my four hundred and fifty-two years on this planet I have seen it five times, regular as clockwork every seventy-six years. The Previous will have observed them too. All I need do is to consult an almanac of when the Previous saw them, and compare the periodic return of three or four, find a match and we have a date for the founding of Chromatacia. I'll get back to you."

"It's as easy as that?" said Jane. "The 'Date of the Epiphany' conjecture has been the mainstay of Chromogencia meetings for, like, for ever."

He shrugged.

"No one's ever asked before. I'm here to study you, not to be questioned."

"Who asked you to study us?" I asked. "Head Office? National Colour?"

Baxter looked across at me.

"I don't know," he said. "We thought of them only as the 'Creators.' They breathed life into me, you, all of us, then set us on our way."

It was similar to my mother's claim.

"Why are they called Utopiainc?" I asked.

Baxter frowned.

"That's not a name I've heard for a long long time. It's all a little hazy, but I think the Creator made you as a better version of himself; one that could live without strife."

"Could this Creator be Someone Else from Somewhere Else?" asked Jane, and Baxter looked at her and smiled.

"The unseen other? Now that is a possibility—an unknown unknown."

"On a clear day from the white cliffs on Green Sector East a land mass can be seen," put in Stafford. "Some say it is a small island, others an undiscovered country."

There was then one of those silences that portend either a disappointing and safe return to small talk, or an advancement to conjectural thought beyond one's knowledge or understanding. Luckily it was the latter, and was instigated by Jane, who said what was on all our minds, but through long force of habit we were reluctant to vocalise.

"Maybe we should go back to basics," she said. "*What do we actually know for certain?*"

Harry answered—it was becoming easier to understand him—and he outlined what we all learned at school: that we lived on a watery planet that orbited the sun and that there were five other planets in the solar system. We had a moon which drove the tides by way of gravity, which held all the planets around the sun, and the moon to us, and us to the earth. Ours was the largest and only inhabited island on the globe, and travel by sea was far too dangerous to attempt due to the aforementioned Krakens and giant octopuses and, of course, the hideous Under Toad and the tidal ripper, which now I thought about it, would need to be either quite large or have a lot of mouths to strip the flesh off a horse in seconds.

Historically, there were even fewer facts. The Previous had all died out in the Something that Happened, a great disaster brought upon themselves by a reckless level of individuality, lawlessness and greed. Following an Epiphany by the Great and Wise Munsell, the survivors were gathered together and reorganised according to Munsell's *Book of Harmony*, and the Collective was founded. The *Book of Harmony* was purposely vague when it came to facts and told us the past was best deleted, as learning about what the Previous did wrong was simply an invitation for "thrill-seekers and disruptionists" to repeat it. "The longer the Munsell Way endures," the argument went, "the greater is the proof of its perfection."

We all thought about this for a moment, and something struck me.

"Everything we have been told might be false," I said, finally finding something intelligent to say and feeling quite proud of myself. "We can only trust knowledge from *before* Munsell's Epiphany as anything afterwards may be tainted by Chromatic bias."

Everyone nodded their agreement and Jane said we'd better start with the basics: Mr. Baxter could furnish the *when*, so we needed to know the *where*.

Jane took out her notebook and carefully unfolded a copy of the Parker Brothers' celebrated depiction of the world, which was more usually known as the "RISK map." Although regions were marked—Irkutsk, Kamchatka, Brazil, Congo, Canada, Siam, to name but a few—none of them seemed remotely related to anywhere that we knew, nor were they Chromatically named with the obvious exception of Greenland, and given that the nation's capital of Emerald City was in Green Sector, it was always assumed that's where we were.

"It *never* made sense that Greenland is coloured yellow on the originals," said Mr. Baxter after we had discussed the RISK map for some time, "and I have my doubts it's where we are, but we know the rough shape of our island from Beck's."

The only map of Chromatacia we possessed was the Munsell-sanctioned "Beck's Schematic Railway Map," which showed the relationship of each town to one another and the existing rail network, which suggested the island—our island—was shaped roughly as a reversed capital "L" with a bulge on the western flank. Jane made a sketch of the familiar shape and placed it on the floor next to the RISK map so we could all stare at it.

"It's certainly not shaped like 'Greenland,'" said Harry.

"How about this one?" said Lucy, pointing to the island that had the regions Venezuela, Brazil, Peru and Argentina marked upon it. "They told us at school we were the largest and most important island on the earth."

We stared at that for a while and then thought not as it was the wrong shape and upside down, and the same went for the island that contained the Africas and the Congo.

Mr. Baxter spoke up.

"Let's suppose the RISK map *is* a correct generalisation of the world's land masses, and the map we have extrapolated from Beck's *is* a good idea of the shape of our island. Ignore everything you've been taught and ask yourself this: Which part of the map looks like a mirrored capital 'L' with a bulge on its western side?"

Once he said that, no one had any doubt of the most likely candidate, a small island in the centre of the map, dwarfed by everything else that surrounded it. There was an island to the left, and a landmass to the right, as might have been observed from the chalk cliffs.

"Great Britain," said Jane, reading the name written across the island.

We stared silently at the map. We'd been told we were the biggest and most important island, but it now looked as though we were geographically . . . insignificant.

"That's a lot of Somewhere Else out there," I murmured, "and potentially populated by thousands of Someone Elses."

"Millions," said Harry, in another huge leap of thought that left us all a little stunned.

"What would they all do?" asked Lucy, but no one had an answer.

The night bell clanged once in the distance. It was 2 A.M., and we had done enough for one night. Lucy wished me good luck on the journey and not to forget her harmonic measurements, and once we had all agreed that anything spoken here went no further, the lightglobes were doused, Jane took my hand in hers and we left the warmth of the Grey meeting room and retraced our steps back towards my father's house, climbed quietly inside, got undressed and snuggled up to one another in the darkness. She'd sneak out in the pre-dawn, when I was asleep, her absence in the morning a reminder of not only how close we were, but how dangerous our relationship.

I fell asleep with the night's conversation rattling around inside my head. We now knew *where* we are, and might figure out *when*—but this added another question: *What* were we doing here?

WE TRAVEL NORTH

Ball lightning, unlike its poor forked cousin, was a law unto itself. It drifted along with the breeze, starting fires and generally causing mischief. It could find its way into people's houses and was oddly sticky, and would attach itself to anything organic. Once it had, you were pretty much incinerated alive, and not quickly. But of all the nasty ways to die in Chromatacia, ball lightning still only came in about sixth.

—Ted Grey: *Twenty Years Among the Chromatacians*

At dawn +1, Carlos brought the Model T around to the muster point, having already ensured it was fuelled, oiled and a fresh flower was placed in the small vase on the dash, as was customary. He gave us a can of water for the radiator, and said we may need to top it up on the way back. Jane would be driving; when Grey she had been licensed to use the Ford to gather firewood.

"Where's that wretched Cinnabar fellow?" asked deMauve in his peeved voice. He had come to see us off, as was his civil obligation. He would probably return to bed once we had departed, though not necessarily his own, if the rumours were correct.

"I woke him up," I said. "Twice."

"Little pest, that boy—always has been."

"Stole the midwife's wedding ring on the way out, I heard," said Jane.

"I'd not put it past him," said deMauve. "Are he and that Ochre girl going to get married? I've not seen any paperwork, and we do need more young, even if it is a Cinnabar."

"I'm sure it's on their minds," said Jane.

"Anyone who isn't matched and with child within a year of their Ishihara is failing their community," he said, looking at Jane pointedly.

He may not have approved of her, but he could value her potential fertility.

"I'm considering a few marriage proposals," said Jane.

"Don't leave it too late," he said. "You've got five years to produce a child. If you don't, we can always issue a mandatory pregnancy order."

Jane made no reply to this, and we all fell silent.

"That's odd," said deMauve, whose bored gaze had chanced skywards. "One doesn't usually see swans out this early."

We followed his look and there it was, flying languid figure-eight patterns, presumably to ride the thermals to gain height before moving off to look for prey.

"It's too early for thermals," murmured Jane.

"And now I'm fed up," said the Head Prefect. "It's really very important that Cinnabar goes on this trip—without him we may have to postpone."

"With our disciplinary hearing tomorrow," said Jane quite daringly, "we may not have any time to postpone this *to*."

"True. We'll find someone else. Thank you for gracing us with your presence, Mr. Cinnabar."

Tommo had appeared. He looked as though he had slept fully clothed to save time, and was carrying what appeared to be a heavy rucksack.

"I'm sorry, Head Prefect," he said, "it shall not happen again."

"It had better not, but I shall not demerit you as I want the mood during this trip to be positive. Remember you are on village business and to acquit yourself with restraint, dignity and if at all possible, without anyone being eaten by a tree."

He then wished us good spooning and strode off.

We climbed into the Model T with Jane in the driver's seat, me in the passenger's and Tommo in the flatbed sitting on a bundle of flour sacks. Carlos cranked the engine into life and after ensuring the motor was running smoothly we headed off out of the village to the north, along the Perpetulite roadway. Jane and I were probably thinking of the same thing: just how big the world was, the nature of Everywhere Else and who might be there, and what sort of robust defence we were going to lodge at our hearing tomorrow to ensure our liberty. Tommo was more chatty and not particularly interested in the mission. He seemed more concerned about how to convince Lucy Ochre to like him.

"I've got an idea," said Jane.

"Yes?"

"Stop being a massive tit."

We drove the first couple of miles with the comforting surroundings of the fields and railway line until we reached the gorge, where the railway branched to the right and only the road and river carried on through the narrow valley to the countryside beyond. I'd not been this far, even though it was only two miles from the village centre, and it was very different from the managed landscape we had just left. The Perpetulite roadway was clear and perfect as always, but the forest grew right up to the road's edge, beginning with ancient oak, then beech and yateveo. As the valley sides steepened, this changed to silver birch, hawthorn, mountain ash, and finally grassy uplands. The environs all sounded different, too, as the lush foliage muted the sound of the engine, and I felt myself suddenly on edge.

After thirty-six minutes of pretty much nothing happening at all, we turned a corner and coasted to a halt as a rhinosaurus was lying dead across the roadway. Jane shut down the Model T and we climbed out.

"Not been this close to one ever," said Jane.

"A male," I murmured as I read its massive barcode, about the size of a bath mat, "one hundred and twenty-one years old and, since there's no sign of combat, probably died of old age."

The creature was thirty-eight feet and seven inches nose to tail, was scaly and already half-absorbed into the Perpetulite. The roadway was one of the few technological wonders that had survived the Something that Happened in a more or less fully functional state. It was an organoplastoid, which not only self-cleaned, self-heated and glowed in the dark, but would also self-tidy—any boulders or detritus would be slowly inched to the side of the road using a soft rippling motion. It didn't do any of that for free, which was why it was slowly digesting the rhino-saurus. Writings from the pre-Epiphanic era spoke of "millions of lives being lost on the roads," so it was a fair assumption the Previous fed their roads daily with human sacrifice.

"Oooh," said Tommo, trotting up to the creature's head with a hacksaw he'd taken from the T's toolbox, "twenty merits apiece to artisan chess piece makers."

We drove on once I had taken several measurements for Lucy's harmonic experiments with the floaty, and in which time Tommo had sawn two of the teeth out—we said he could take the rest on the way back.

The thirteen-mile trip to Crimsonolia was otherwise uneventful and we soon reached the junction where the road split. To the right, Dog-Leg-Lake and the Blue Sector border town of Bluetown and to the left, Crimsonolia, with a faded "Mildew Outbreak" warning sign. We took the left branch but it did not go far. About twenty yards in, the Perpetulite had been severed and pinned with bronze spikes. Despite this, the road had spalled into grey tentacles which had grown outward in a vain attempt to reconnect itself with the lost section, and were now wrapped tightly around trees, rocks and a rusty land-crawler.

Jane stopped the car and we climbed out, stretched and looked about. The land here was well-grazed upland punctuated by outcrops of rhododendrons, giant redwood and the odd clump of yateveo. A small herd of okapi were grazing a half-mile away, and from somewhere to the north we could hear the distant sound of elephants trumpeting. Ruins of the town surrounded by a tight grove of ash and silver birch were visible about a mile distant, the blackened tops of the buildings poking out above the canopy. While Jane and I readied ourselves for our task, Tommo sat himself upon the ground, removed his boots and drew his rucksack closer.

"You have to at least *try* to make an effort," I said.

"Oh, I have," he said, opening the rucksack to reveal a veritable treasure trove of spoons. Jane and I exchanged glances. Normally, all found spoons were deemed village property and surrendered for nothing more than an extra custard or shoelace ration, but now I understood why Tommo had come on a potentially dangerous trip: all spoons that returned with us would become legitimate finds and could be converted to cash, as deMauve had promised.

"All yours?" I asked.

"Goodness me, no," he said. "Once I put the word round, there were thirty-nine spoons that villagers were reluctant to surrender but eager to cash in—my end of the deal should be two thousand, maybe more. It depends how many postcodes I can engrave before we get home."

"Nice hustle," said Jane, who couldn't see any downside to hoodwinking the Prefects.

"Was that a compliment?" said Tommo.

"I think it might have been," replied Jane.

"Then while you are in a good mood," he said, seizing the opportunity, "did Eddie mention a photographic proposal I had suggested?"

"I did not," I said, "and I would caution you to keep it to yourself."

"Oh," he said, "another time then. Look, are you still going into Crimsonolia? It burned down after the Mildew outbreak, so there won't be much to find. I can say you found six of these spoons, so long as your reward is paid directly to me."

Jane and I looked at one another. We'd spoken earlier about finding a way into Crimsonolia's Council chambers. The Perpetulite from which the Council chambers was made would be fireproof. Sensing any high temperature, all windows would have morphed shut and internal water migrated to the exterior of the walls to keep it cool. It was possible the volumes of *The Word of Munsell* might still survive in the Council chambers, and if so, reading the strictly Prefects-only books might offer up some clues.

"We'll go anyway," I said.

"I'll book you a slot at the renderer's. Have fun, children."

And so saying, he took out an engraver's tool and, after consulting a list of fictitious but plausible postcodes, started to engrave DD6 9QJ into the handle of a battered utensil that was really more dent than spoon.

CRIMSONOLIA

Choice of hairstyle shall be free to the owner, so long as over eighteen years of age. Male hair length is to be above the collar, female hair length below, but above the small of the back. Styles are logged in Appendix viii (with pictures, diagrams and instructions) but can generally be categorised thus: Males: short back and sides with parting right, left or centre. Females: plait, ponytail, bunches, bun, beehive, bouffant. Fringes may be used in combination with all styles. Natural wave is permitted, topknots forbidden.

—Rule 2.02.34.59 of the *Book of Harmony*

Jane led the way towards the town and we kept a careful eye out for any movement. We knew Riffraff had been seen up here, but the usual tell-tale signs were absent.

"On reflection," said Jane, "Tommo's spoon haul is probably *exactly* what deMauve planned. He'll enter them as found spoons on the register so it's all legal and above board."

"You think this trip is actually a spoon laundry?"

"Looks like it. Explains why deMauve wanted to postpone. What was that business proposal of Tommo's?"

I outlined to her what he had proposed and why.

"I'm not sure I have a 'winsome come-hither' look."

"He was hoping you'd improvise."

"That boy is a complete arse. He should ask Clifton and Sophie. They'd *definitely* be up for that sort of thing."

"I think he already has."

"Sophie's a lot of fun," she mused, "and being a Lapis-Lazuli means she gets away with a lot. Clifton's a good brother—more or less—but he does have quite a lot of trouble keeping his clothes on. I hope he and Tania get on."

"She's very lonely. So who proposed marriage to you?" I asked, recalling her comment to deMauve.

"All the eligible Green bachelors," she said, "which number four. I had them all through my letterbox the morning after my Ishihara."

"What did you say?"

She shot me a glance.

"Are you jealous?"

"No. Yes. A little bit."

She smiled and touched my arm.

"Eddie, I'm going to have to marry *someone*—I'm not ending up in the Pool to be lotterised like a surplus heifer. Besides, even when I do tie the knot it'll be on paper only—the kid will be yours."

"That'll cause some ructions on their Ishihara," I said, "able to see green *and* red. What would the Colourman say? We'd be rumbled in an instant."

She shrugged and gave out a giggle.

"We'll cross that bridge when we come to it. By the way," she said, pointing skyward, "have you noticed that swan has been following us all the way from East Carmine?"

I had not, but looked up and there it was—so high it could almost not be seen at all, but flying the same figure-of-eight pattern.

"That's unusual, isn't it?" she asked. "To be followed, I mean."

"Maybe it fancies Tommo as a snack. He has been getting a little weighty recently."

"If they are made of wire and steel as that courier suggested," said Jane, "no swan has ever eaten or taken anyone."

For the first time since I was nine, I felt uneasy about swans. The swan *was* following us, and I thought about what my mother had said about gloves making us invisible. It didn't make sense, but it would, in time.

We stopped at the dilapidated gatehouse, where the doors were now simply scorched wood-rot attached to rusted hinges. Usually we would stop a safe distance from any settlement and observe for half an hour or more, but here there was no need— brambles stretched across the street and trees were growing up out of buildings that had collapsed long ago and there was little to no sign of human visitation. Stories of Riffraff habitation were just that. Stories.

I made to move forward but Jane stopped me.

"Hang on," she said, "what about the Mildew?"

"What about it?"

"We have to assume Crimsonolia was culled, yet we don't know how a C-Notice works. The colour of Mildew could be painted on walls—or even by changing the colour of the Perpetulite on the town hall."

"I'd not considered that," I replied. "Is it possible to change Perpetulite's colour?"

"I've not been able to do it, but then road Perpetulite is different."

Jane, it should be noted, had limited control of Perpetulite through a bronze bob she wore around her neck.

"But since we *can* take precautions against the Mildew," added Jane, "it makes sense that we should."

She dug a compact from her bag, flicked it open and stared at the colour within, then turned it to me. I *felt* the Gordini blue swatch rather than *saw* it—a sort of syrupy sensation. My left side went numb, I felt pins and needles, then, as if like a jack-in-the-box, a young man appeared in front of me. I knew he wasn't real as he seemed vaguely transparent, but he was wearing a neat grey suit with the National Colour logo embroidered on his lapel. He also looked like the Previous, from the many pictures we had of them—taller, reduced skull size and with creepily small eyes, the pupils not the attractive small dot, but wide open, which made his eyes seem hollow, as though a bee might be able to fly in one eye and out the other.

"Good afternoon!" he said in a cheery voice, *exactly* the same way as he said it the last time I viewed the hue. "Thank you for accessing Gordini Protocol NC7-Z. Please be patient while reconfiguration is in progress."

"Have you got the Herald yet?" asked Jane. "He's coming up now."

"If you suffer any undue discomfort during reconfiguration," continued the young man in a jolly sing-song sort of voice, "you may wish to seek assistance from customer services, available on ♩♩♩♩. National Colour. Here for your convenience. And remember, feedback helps us help you."

He vanished and the smell of freshly baked bread returned, some jumbled memories and then Violet's singing voice. After that I could see in full colour. Not the short moment that accompanied the culmination of *youknow* but long enough for me to look around, and savour the moment. It was more dazzling and beautiful than I could possibly imagine, but then I started blinking uncontrollably and heard dogs barking, starting off with a small yappy terrier and getting larger, all the while my senses cross-firing from light to memory to touch. I could suddenly *see* the colour of music, and *sense* the softness of red. The dog's barking grew louder until suddenly, it all cut out and everything seemed to swim back to normality.

"You okay?" said Jane.

"I'm okay. I got that man again. He said *exactly* the same thing."

"A lost page from a missing book," she said with a shrug, snapping the compact shut.

"Where did you get it?"

"Zane, my old mentor, stole five hues from a National Colour operative over at Rusty Hill. They were in skill hue slipcases, but no hint as to what they were, so Zane, me and Felicity Pink did some blind viewings to see what would happen."

"That was a little reckless, wasn't it?"

"Yes," she said. "It was. Zane tried the first one and eventually found out he was immune to the Mildew—it's how he survived the cull over in Rusty Hill. The second hue made him a Perpetulite maintenance engineer and able to access its inner workings, a skill he shared with me. I tried the third unknown skill hue and that's the reason I can ride the gyro-bike potentially better than Mad Dog Juniper. I seem to be able to *sense* the machine—understand precisely when the wheels will break out on a turn and ride it through the smallest of gaps and with much faster reaction times. I didn't know that straight away, of course, but it soon became apparent, and was permanent after only eight viewings. Felicity tried the fourth swatch and . . . things didn't turn out quite so well."

She fell silent.

"What happened?"

"Felicity suddenly *knew* things," said Jane quietly. "*Astonishing* things. She said she could predict with pinpoint accuracy every position of a ball's arc once you had thrown it, so long as she knew its mass and the speed and angle with which it was thrown."

"How could she possibly figure that?"

"She said there were mathematical rules that predicted motion. Lucy's right when she says there was a lot more to mathematics than the four disciplines of addition, subtraction, multiplication and division. Felicity said she knew other things, too, that gravity wasn't a force, but merely the effect of morass upon taste-time."

"The effect of morass upon taste-time? What does that mean?" Jane shrugged.

"I *think* that's what she said. She then started to gabble, and said that gravity had clear and definable laws that governed its properties, and that knowing these laws one could calculate with extreme accuracy the way in which the moon and the earth travelled around each other, and the effect of the sun on both of them. She then went on to say that the tides don't go in and out at all; the earth simply revolves around inside a bulge of water caused by the gravitational attraction of the moon."

"Is that true?"

"Who knows? She also said that two objects of different weights but identical shapes would fall at the same rate."

"That's patently not true," I remarked.

"Have you tried it?"

"No."

"I have," said Jane, "with Lucy. It's *completely* true. Felicity went on to say that a feather would fall at the same rate as an anvil if there were no air."

"But there *is* air," I said, trying to sound knowledgeable.

"Felicity became more excited after that," continued Jane. "She said the mechanism that drives the sun is based on a complex principle of physics whereby mass is converted into energy, and then talked about energy induction by harnessing the Van Allen belts. She used an odd, semi-intelligible language and then started bleeding from the nose. She stopped talking, looked at me oddly and one of her eyes rolled backwards into her head and she collapsed and died. Never even regained consciousness."

"What did she die of?"

"She drowned," said Jane quite simply, "in knowledge. Her mind became congested with insights of such manifest brilliance that her brain was unable to function in any normal way—sort of like trying to compress a gallon of soup into a pint tin. But it showed us," she carried on, "that skills are not just physical, but can be *intellectual*, too."

"All that knowledge from within a shade of colour?"

She tapped her head with a slender index finger.

"Zane saw it another way: that these skills *are already in our heads*, in the same way as animals have instinctual behaviour. No one trains the cuckoo, but it knows precisely what to do. The hue simply draws out that knowledge to a place we can make use of it. Zane described it as 'back of house' and 'front of house.' The hue simply transferred one to the other."

I felt my temples.

"You mean we *all* have that knowledge?"

"It seems so," she said. "We can already do Morse code at birth, draw with great accuracy and are able to tango, lambada and foxtrot. No one taught us, and while evolution gave us opposable thumbs and made us bipedal for a very good reason, the same can't be said of the lambada—and I'm not sure the foxtrot would help us survive in a hostile environment either."

I frowned. Now that she mentioned it, our instinctual knowledge skills did seem a little arbitrary. Most of Walter de la Mare's poems were firmly cemented in our memories from birth. There was quite a lot of Tennyson, too, and a bit of Wilfred Owen. Mind you, the lack of context in any of it made much of it intractable, but it had a pleasant rhythm to it that helped when trying to sleep, or pumping water from the well.

"Everyone who learns the guitar from a skill hue plays it pretty much the same," she carried on, "but if you acquire the skill from practice and repetition the sound becomes uniquely your own. And those drawing skills of ours. It's *always* the same style. If you and I drew the same dog, our sketches would look pretty much identical."

"We're using someone else's skills," I said. "Ones they learned the hard way."

"That's quite a profound thought, Eddie. But this I know: we can already do potentially anything—all we have to do is access it."

"All of it?"

"No," she said in deep thought, "no one's ever managed to hold more than three skills. There must be a limit—you'd have to lose one before gaining another."

"Maybe that's what did for Felicity," I said. "Too many skills at once. Did you try viewing the fifth swatch?"

"No," she replied, "not after what happened."

We stood in silence, pondering on what this meant—it was a big discovery, but as far as I could see, there was no point to any of it. Why have skills in your head that you weren't able to access?

"The Herald we just saw," I said, breaking the pause, "he's *also* stored in our heads?"

"I reckon he's our very own skills manager, right there in our heads. You could ask him for a skill to do, say carpentry, the same way you might order a Chelsea bun from a waitress."

"Is this the form the Herald in Jollity Fair might take?"

"Perhaps," she said. "I don't know."

We left the gatehouse just that little bit smarter and more

aware, and carried on along the village's main thoroughfare. As we walked we noted that unlike Rusty Hill, which had been abandoned only four years before and was still in a reasonable state, Crimsonolia's buildings were now entirely roofless, and most of the walls had started to crumble and collapse. But it was a soft death, as much of the fabric of the town was now either swathed in ivy and brambles or carpeted with grass. Wooden window frames and doors had either burned or rotted away long ago, and as evidence of the ongoing deterioration, fresh blocks of masonry and bricks occasionally peppered the grassy underfoot.

We headed towards the main square as our plan was unchanged: to try and enter the Council chambers. We walked past the twice-lifesize statue of Our Munsell and to the Perpetulite town hall/Council chamber complex, which unlike the rest of the town was in a reasonable state—Perpetulite always absorbed any ivy, lichen or moss that tried to grow on it, so was clean and smooth and looked incongruously new.

We quietly trod the steps to enter by way of the open doorway as respectfully as we would have at home. The beam of light currently penetrating the chamber was not vertical as was usual since the heliostat was missing, but pierced the building at a jaunty angle that reflected off the floor and illuminated the painting on the ceiling of *The Seven Labours of Munsell*. Now that Jane had mentioned it, the drawing style was similar to ours. The robes in *The Expulsion of the Experts* and the old tech in *The Closing of the Networks* were pretty much as anyone might draw them.

Then, she appeared. A woman, wraithlike and ethereal. I'd seen her before over in the town hall at Rusty Hill, when I'd looked at the ceiling the townsfolk had decided to augment, over and above the muted tones of the Perpetulite. Her appearance may have been a combination of the hue we'd just viewed and some residual effect of the partly painted ceiling at Rusty Hill, I don't know, but in any event, she was transparent—I could see the building behind and *through* her.

"You getting this?" I asked.

"Yes," breathed Jane. "Close your eyes and see if she's still there."

I did, but the Herald sort of half remained. She wasn't in the room, she was in our heads. And if what Jane had just said was true, she had *always* been in our heads—just waiting for a time to be called into action. She walked up to us, smiled sweetly, then spoke.

"Welcome," she said, "to your initial orientation meeting upon arrival at *Insert Destination Here*. You will not return home, nor ever know where home was. We hope you will be prosperous, and live long and productive lives and—"

She abruptly vanished and was replaced by the young man again.

"I'm sorry," he said in the same sing-song sort of voice, "but we are experiencing technical difficulties. Please seek assistance from customer services, available on ♪♫♪♫. National Colour. Here for your convenience. And remember, feedback helps us help you."

And then he vanished too, leaving us alone in the town hall among the moss and the grass and the empty abandoned sadness.

"I got that error message again," I said, "from the same Herald as when we viewed the anti-Mildew."

"I didn't get that far," she replied, "just a woman with a crackly voice welcoming me to orientation at *Insert Destination Here*."

I told her what the Herald had said about journeys and not going home, nor knowing where it was, and to be prosperous. I asked her what she thought and after a moment or two she said: "We don't have enough information to understand what's going on, so we stick to Plan A: see if we can get into the Council chambers."

"You're sure about this?" I asked. Viewing the book without being a Prefect was so utterly forbidden that it made me feel cold and sweaty just thinking about it.

I don't think Jane felt the same way. She didn't really do Rules.

THE TOWN HALL

Perpetulite's chief source of nutrients was leaf litter, fallen trees and random dead animals. Roadway starvation could become an issue. During the "Great Road Hunger" of 00423 everyone was warned not to pause for thought while crossing lest their shoes begin to be absorbed. To counter the threat, waste organic material was deposited on the roadway until it was sufficiently satiated and safe to cross.

—Ted Grey: *Twenty Years Among the Chromatacians*

We didn't need to go far—the Council chambers were part of the town hall, the same in every town and village, again, part of the Uniformity Protocols. The house in which we'd lived back at Jade-under-Lime was identical to the one we lived in now, the interior furnishings the same, the cupboards, *everything*. When you spilt something at a friend's house, you didn't need to ask where the mop was. Years ago Dad had swapped the location of a tin of kidney beans with some pear slices, and was demerited by a random spot check. The Yellows do like their spot checks.

We walked across the floor of the town hall and found a faint outline where the door to the Council chambers would have been. The building had sealed itself, presumably as a firebreak when Crimsonolia went up in flames. Tunnelling through Perpetulite was impossible as it either repaired itself almost immediately or became spiky and petulant, so it looked as though we'd come all this way for nothing.

"Well, that's that then," I said, probably sounding a lot more relieved than I had intended. Unluckily for my inner coward, Jane had other ideas. She removed the small bronze bob from around her neck and placed it on the wall next to where the Council chamber door should have been.

"You can talk to buildings as well?" I asked.

The bronze bob Jane carried was from Zane, and was principally a key to unlock, study and even manipulate the Perpetulite roadways. In the time of the Previous, vehicles—both passenger and freight—weren't carried with internal motive power like the Model T, but by simply placing inert objects on the roadway and letting the Perpetulite move along by a rippling wave action beneath them—the same manner, in fact, as the Perpetulite cleared the roadway of obstacles.

"Construction Perpetulite is more refined and allows for delicate shapes and mouldings," said Jane, "but I've never tried this before."

We waited for a few moments and then, with a crackling noise, the smooth wall of the town hall transformed into a sunken panel about the size of a mattress, with writing and knobs and a keypad and a few numbers, all of raised Perpetulite and which reformed as we watched them. The Previous had been, it was agreed, astonishingly smart. I thought of harmonics, of floaties, of remote viewers, of lightglobes and hotpots and Everspins—and legends of flying machines faster than sound itself, and vehicles that flew so high the sky turned to night. In one of my smarter moments I likened our era to someone arriving late to a concert, just as the final chords were hanging in the air.

Jane stared at the various sliders and knobs and buttons, each with the odd language beneath. She pressed a button that seemed to suggest a schematic drawing, and almost immediately another panel opened up to the left of this one, depicting exactly that—the building in plan and elevation.

"Let's see how similar this is to roadway Perpetulite," she said, and pressed a finger on the pictured elevation. Almost immediately a list of choices came up—a door, a window, a serving hatch or a niche for a sculpture. She pressed on the door to select it, then was given more options: open in, open out, clear opening, swing doors. There followed several more options as to size, placement and edge profile, and Jane selected all the options in order to create an opening through to the Council chambers, but was then greeted by a keypad, similar to the ones we had seen on numerous parts of old tech.

"I think it wants a numerical code to make the changes," she said.

"Do you have one?"

"No. Mind you," she added, "what's the worst that could happen with a wrong guess? Make a note in case I'm correct."

So I dug out my notebook and she punched in numbers, with me jotting them down as she did. A lucky guess might have been possible if it had been a two-number code, unlikely if a three, but once we had entered seven digits without result, we realised the chances of guessing would be vanishingly small. After she'd pressed the tenth number, all the numbers vanished and a cross came up.

"Wrong one," she said.

"I'm not sure we can guess this number," I said. "It's pretty big."

"It's been done before," she said. "Milton Grey over in Green Sector North spent twenty-two years trying to unlock a six-digit code on a remote viewer. It would have taken him less time, but it locked him out for a day after every third wrong attempt."

"Did he get any useful knowledge from it?"

"History does not relate. I hear these snippets, but it's like trying to guess the picture of a jigsaw with only nine pieces."

She tried again, and I jotted the numbers down again. On the third attempt, something finally happened. The panels sank from the walls leaving only a warning message:

You have entered three incorrect Passcodes, please contact customer support.

And after a few moments the panel melted back into the wall as though it had never been there at all.

"Hmm," I murmured, "at least we know we *could* manipulate public buildings if we had the correct code."

"Well now," said a voice behind us, "I think we've got ourselves some strangers."

We turned and found ourselves facing five men at the door who wore bright Yellow spot-badges on their Outdoor Adventure #9s. Most badges were left at Home Village Outer Markers, so wearing them here and now was to telegraph their intent, which was plain to see: they were all armed. Three carried farm implements, one a long pole and the last a cricket bat.

But I didn't think they were here to do any farming or play games.

"Oh, hello, Toby," said Jane to the one on the far left of the group, nodding to him in the same way you might an acquaintance on the street, "how are you doing?"

"We've never met," he said unconvincingly.

"Sure we have," she said. "You must remember: we hooked up when Dad and I visited to help with Dog-Leg-Lake's plumbing. I was underage at the time, and you gave me twenty merits cash not to tell. As you can see, I did not keep my part of the bargain. D'you want the money back?"

"You must be mistaking me for—"

"Your friends I don't know," continued Jane, cutting him off, "but you all need to go home before things get . . . silly."

"Is your resolve compromised by your relationship with this Grey?" asked the one who seemed to be in charge, the one who spoke first, the one who held the cricket bat.

"No sir," said Toby, "she is nothing to me."

"Good," he said, as he turned back to us, "my name is Torquil Celandine, Yellow second-in-command and son to the Yellow Prefect at Dog-Leg-Lake. Where's Cinnabar?"

If they knew our names, they were not here by chance. And that being so, *we* were not here by chance and it was likely this wasn't just a spoon laundry expedition. These were Yellows out to avenge the death of their own.

"You want Tommo," said Jane, "you find him, and good luck. That boy is as slippery as an eel."

She was bluffing. Tommo would be easier to find than the sky.

"We mean him no harm," said Torquil, "so long as he plays ball. You two, on the other hand, will have no need of a hearing tomorrow."

"Murder us," I said, "and you defile the *Book of Harmony*."

"You're wrong," said Torquil. "The *Book of Harmony* supports what we are doing. It's simply a question of interpretation."

There was a pause.

"Okay," said Jane, "now we know that you are as deluded and stupid as you are violent and misinformed, let's get down to business: Five against one? Doesn't strike me as a fair fight."

I might have taken umbrage that I wasn't worth counting, but she was probably right. Aside from on the sports field, which isn't the same thing at all, I had never been in a fight in my life and wouldn't know what to do if I was. Or maybe she was downplaying my competence to put them off guard. No, probably the former.

"I'm happy with these odds, Brunswick," said Toby.

"I meant it doesn't sound like a fair fight for *you*," she said. "I'll hang around while you fetch another two, if you like."

The grin fell from his face.

"I heard you were spirited, Brunswick," he said, "but we outnumber you and are well motivated: revenge adds ferocity, and Courtland Gamboge was a fellow Yellow, friend and mentor."

They started to walk towards us in the spacious hall, but concentrated their attention on Jane. It made sense; take out the dangerous one first, then mop up the remainder. They'd done this before. I looked at Jane but she didn't take her eyes off them, and instead dropped her knapsack on the ground, presumably to free up some weight and make it easier to move. I thought she was just going to go for them, but she didn't need to. There was a noise outside the door and a sixth person entered the town hall.

YELLOW AND DEATH

Physical violence, although utterly forbidden, did occur, and usually by Yellows who were outraged over some transgression that had gone unpunished. They didn't see it as wrong; they saw it as levelling up. Such off-book acts were known euphemistically as "Chromatic Easement."
—Ted Grey: *Twenty Years Among the Chromatacians*

The new entrant was probably the tallest man I'd ever seen, and was dressed in a hooded cloak which seemed incongruous given the heat. His eyes were hidden behind dark glasses of the sort that had leather hoods on the side, and his mouth was pursed closed in a thin line that betrayed little emotion. His nose, I noted, was unlike any I had seen before: large and authoritarian.

He walked slowly towards us and stopped in a position that gave no outward affiliation with either party. From the Yellows' demeanour they were not expecting him, and since we reacted with as much puzzlement as they, it was probably clear to them he was nothing to do with us either. In light of this, the Yellows with the farm implements changed their stance to clumsily indicate the weapons were of agricultural capacity. The one with the pole leaned on it as though it were a stick, and Torquil, who held the cricket bat, absently tapped an invisible crease on the dusty floor.

"Well, now," said the stranger, "looks like I've gatecrashed a party. I am an inspector, and you shall do my bidding."

This was impressive: a National Colour Pipeline Inspector would be in charge of the feed-pipes that brought liquid visual sustenance by way of the Grid. But since Crimsonolia was both abandoned and a long way from anywhere, his presence here didn't make much sense. I felt my sense of curiosity move to one of foreboding.

"Now that I have your attention," he said, indicating Torquil in the silence that followed his introduction, "account for yourself."

"Torquil Celandine, your Colourfulness," he said, "Son of the Yellow Prefect, Dog-Leg-Lake. These are my associates. We were here on a scrap colour expedition and ran into these two."

"I see. And the risk of the Mildew, biting animals and the Riffraff?"

"The economics and importance of useful scavenge demands the citizenry accepts risks."

It was a good answer.

"Okay," said the Inspector, turning to us. "What about you two?"

"Eddie deMauve and Jane Brunswick," I said, "from East Carmine. We're looking for spoons."

There was then an awkward silence, and when the Inspector made no indication he was about to leave, Torquil said:

"We don't want to keep you from your duties, sir."

The Inspector looked at us all again in turn.

"Okay," he said, "we're not hearing the whole story so we're going to play the Truth Game. There are two rules. One: you all tell me the truth. Two: there are no more rules. So, you two," he said, looking at us, "why are you really here?"

I looked at Jane, then at the Yellows from Dog-Leg-Lake.

Snitching was something no one liked to do, mostly because it was the preserve of the Yellows. But snitching *against* Yellows was kind of okay.

"We were sent out here to lend credibility to a spoon laundry," I said, then looked pointedly at Torquil, "but I'm having my doubts as to whether there was a more sinister motive."

"I agree," said the Inspector. "The tools they carry speak volumes. Is that true?"

The question was directed towards the Yellows, to whom he now turned. Torquil looked at me and Jane, then raised his chin in defiance.

"DeMauve and Brunswick murdered a Yellow Prefect-in-waiting. Their Council believes they will *not* follow Reboot orders after their disciplinary hearing tomorrow. The Green girl is a notorious Rule-defiler who has a pernicious influence upon Edward deMauve, and she has beguiled and enticed him with unthinkably sordid bedroom favours, and a highly ranked Red gone to the dark side of the Chroma is of such a high potential hazard to the smooth running of the Colourtocracy that . . . necessary yet regrettable action needs to be taken."

"I see," said the Inspector, "and you don't think the Book of Munsell, in all its glorious perfection, can deal with a few bumps in the road on the way to full colourisation?"

"I do not make these decisions," said Torquil. "We have simply been tasked by those better acquainted with the facts."

There was a pause as all this sank in.

"So here's what's going to happen," said the Inspector. "The Yellows shall return to Dog-Leg-Lake and tell their Council that Brunswick and deMauve could not be found. That's it. Off you toddle."

The Yellow named Torquil thought for a moment then

glanced at one of the others—the one he could most rely on, probably.

"We had a National Colour operative in our village once," said Torquil in a confident tone. "Moving through, they were, like you. They died in the night—either too much green or too much grey, or maybe too much of both. We sent a telegram to National Colour, kept her effects safe and then had her rendered. Thing was, the telegram docket slipped behind the desk in the telegraph office. It was never sent."

"Does this story have a point?" asked the Inspector.

"D'you know how long it took National Colour to send someone out to look for their missing operative?"

"Tell me."

"Nine years. And if we hadn't explained what happened, they would have moved on and searched elsewhere. They didn't know where she was, and I'm willing to bet good pudding they don't know where you are either. On your own?"

The man in the cloak didn't say anything.

"I thought we were playing the Truth Game, sir?"

"I'm on my own," he said in a quiet, measured tone.

"Then here's *my* offer," said Torquil. "National Colour does not get to meddle with the internal affairs of villages on the Outer Fringes. You go on your way now, or no one will ever find out what happened to you. What do you say to that?"

The Inspector seemed completely unfazed by Torquil's threat.

"I say that's bold talk from someone who has woefully misread the situation."

Three of his compatriots said nothing, but Toby suddenly had misgivings.

"I didn't sign up for killing an Inspector, Torquil, I mean, are you *insane*?"

"Shut up, Toby, or be laid by their side. We had orders to avenge Courtland, and I am not returning home with my tail between my legs. We're Yellow. We follow orders."

The Inspector changed his stance to one of readiness. It was a subtle move, and in that slightest of movements, there was an abundance of threat.

"I'd also like to leave," said one of the other Yellows.

"That option is now closed," said the Inspector, not keeping his eyes off Torquil. "Your fate is bound to your leader—who has led poorly."

As he was talking, the Yellow carrying the spade made his move. He brought it up to strike but the Inspector reached into his cloak and withdrew a sickle that was attached to a long handle and folded in the centre by a locking hinge. With an impressively fluid movement, he flicked the handle into a single long length, and with both hands swung expertly with all his weight—and took the Yellow's head cleanly off at the shoulders. Despite having undertaken rendering shed duties I had never seen anything like this before, and I felt a lump of bile rise in my throat as the Yellow's body paused for a moment before collapsing into a heap while his head bowled across the floor like a hairy cabbage to end up at Toby's feet, where the freshly severed head blinked at him, seemed to mouth words, and looked confused.

"Shit," said Torquil, and they all dropped their implements.

The Inspector shook his head sadly.

"I *so* wish you hadn't seen me do that," he said, wiping the blade of the sickle on the dead Yellow's back.

"We won't tell a single living soul," said Torquil. "We will return to the village and do *precisely* as you asked—and anything else, too. I have a sister who folk say is very fair, and she has many, many, friends and all would be willing—"

"We are past the time for words and bribery," said the Inspector as he hinged the handle of the sickle and stowed it back inside his cloak. He then took a device from his pocket that looked like a lightglobe and tossed it into the air where it hovered for a moment before it started to make wide orbits of the chamber, until he snapped his fingers and the chamber was suddenly flooded with a bright, greeny-red light that put me in mind of the colour I had seen up at High Saffron, the colour that killed, the colour of Mildew. Almost instantly the four Yellows gave out small coughs and I felt Jane clasp my hand as the Inspector walked to the back wall of the town hall and touched it with a bronze fob of his own, then expertly started to enter a series of commands into the control panel.

"Of them I care nothing and their loss is irrelevant," he said over his shoulder, "but you two seem like decent people. The Rot they received was Yellow-specific; you will not be harmed by it."

Jane and I exchanged a nervous look as the Inspector continued to enter instructions upon the control panel. The Yellows fell to their knees as the shortness of breath took their strength. If this was Mildew, it was quick-acting. The Perpetulite control panel asked the Inspector for an access code and once he had punched it in, the panel started to count down from ten with a low warning noise.

"Your aggressors will be dead in under twenty minutes," said the Inspector, as he turned back to us. "I've put the building into reset mode. It will reduce in size, absorb any organic matter within, expel any indigestible contents into the foundations and rebuild itself like new. The Yellows will become part of the fabric of the building in a very real and meaningful way."

He sat down on the steps that led up to the stage, and indicated for us to join him. He removed his dark glasses so we could see his eyes, then pushed back his hood. He was fair-haired and perhaps just approaching middle age, but what struck us both were his small eyes, large pupils, and skull of limited proportions. There was no doubt what he was.

"I thought the Previous had all died out," said Jane.

The Inspector smiled.

"As you can see, we have not. I'm neither an Inspector nor National Colour. My name is Hanson."

It took a second or two for the information to seep in.

"I'm sorry for your loss," I said, and reached into my pocket, found the Fallen Woman's wedding ring and handed it to him. I saw his eyes moisten as he looked at it, then pushed his cloak aside to place the ring in his top pocket. The uniform underneath was recognisably similar to the Fallen Woman's tattered clothes, and Hanson's name was on a patch next to the word UTOPIANINC. I had a *lot* of questions.

"Jacquie went missing thirteen years ago," he said. "I didn't find out what happened until yesterday when the ELT started to ping. I visited the site last night. You buried her?"

"I did."

"I hadn't planned to say anything to you at all today, just leave a gift where you could find it next to your transport—but then those idiots turned up and you were outnumbered and I owed you. Okay," he added as he climbed to his feet, "time to get going. You didn't see me, I wasn't here. Do you understand how important that is?"

"Can I ask a question?" said Jane.

"I'm afraid not," said Hanson. "Contact with subjects is forbidden. Again: I wasn't here, you didn't see me. We agree?"

"Yes," I said, before Jane could ask another question, "we agree."

He nodded, and pulled a package from his coat.

"Here's the gift. I understand they are a tradable commodity."

I took the package. It was lumpy and heavy. Spoons, was my guess; teaspoon, steel, stamped rather than cast.

"Give me twenty minutes then leave the town hall yourself," he added. "The reset will kick in about then and you don't want to be trapped inside. Thanks again."

We thanked him for the package and he stood up, began to walk towards the exit, but stopped. There was a man and a woman, also in uniform, standing at the doorway, gazing in our direction.

"Shit," said Jane.

"Yes," said Hanson, "you took the word right out of my mouth."

THE ANGEL

Chromatacia was built upon the ashes of a world that belonged to another race of humans known as the Previous. They were tall, had full colour vision and were handicapped by anger, avariciousness and greed. Little is known about the Something that Happened, but it was thought to have been a conflict of some sort, as the detritus of what one supposes were fighting machines still abounds.

—Ted Grey: *Twenty Years Among the Chromatacians*

Hanson told us to "sit tight," an expression we'd not heard before, then went to speak to the newcomers. He was there less than five minutes and the conversation seemed one-sided and not in our favour. The orbiting lightglobe came over to us at the command of one of the newcomers, and flashed brightly. I felt pins and needles in my arm, and I hoped that the anti-M we'd viewed earlier protected us from *all* Mildews.

"I'm really sorry about this," said Hanson when he returned. "It's not what I wanted but the rules are very specific."

"It's fine," said Jane, "really."

"No, I just feel I'm really treating you shabbily. Came down here to thank you, give you a present, then have to give you the Mildew. In my favour it *will* weigh on my conscience and I'm going to get into a bit of trouble from my superiors."

"Anything we can do to help with that?" I asked, taking Jane's lead.

Hanson smiled and looked at us both in turn.

"You are *such* nice people," he said, "and seem to be taking this very well indeed."

"We would have been dead anyway," I said. "Killed by the Yellows."

"So you've given us another twenty minutes of life," added Jane, "and we don't get to be bludgeoned to death, so *we* should be thanking *you*."

"Well, look," he said, visibly moved, "seeing as you're being so darned decent over this, is there anything I can do for you before you're put to sleep?"

"We could do with some answers," said Jane, "since we're going to die."

The town hall gave a shudder, and several drips of water fell from the ceiling.

"That'll be the reset," said Hanson. "It's started early. We've not got much time. What do you want to know?"

"I know that we're prisoners," said Jane, "of an unjust society led by an immovable dogma that cares only for the continuance of the Rules."

"That's not really a question, but correct so far."

"We also know," continued Jane, "that when you get sent to Reboot or the Night Train to Emerald City, you end up at High Saffron where the Mildew takes you and you're absorbed into the Perpetulite. So here's the question: Why have that mechanism when you can just Mildew us in the comfort of the village and under cover of darkness?"

Hanson cocked his head to one side.

"High Saffron, as you know it, was originally the only go-to option for the disrupters," he said, "but generalised fears are far more effective these days: fear of swans, lightning, Riffraff and the night keeps everyone pretty much in check. In an ideal world we'd cancel Reboot but we can't alter the Rulebook, or the experiment would be invalidated. What else?"

"Experiment?"

Hanson took a deep breath.

"It's a long story and we don't have the time. Another question?"

"Are swans manufactured in origin and made of metal and wires?"

"They are. We call them drones."

"Like a bee?"

"No," he said, "nothing like a bee. It's how we know where you are. We picked you up yesterday because you were so close to Jacquie's ELT when it pinged—it's a sort of beacon—and it's how I tracked you both here today."

"What about Tom—"

"What about what?"

"Nothing," said Jane. "We're on an island named Great Britain. Is it still called that?"

"No," he said, "not for a very long time. We call the small group of islands the Albion Archipelago, or Reserves Twelve and Thirteen to be technical. I have a question for you: Subjects don't bury their dead—why did you bury Jacquie?"

I shrugged.

"I don't know. It just felt like the right thing to do."

"We call that a *vestigial recollection*," said Hanson, "a subconscious window into a small trove of customs and beliefs that you are not currently permitted to access."

The building settled in on itself, and the walls started to glisten with moisture.

"I'm really really sorry about this," he said as he glanced towards where the two others waited at the door, "but it will be fast, I assure you of that."

Jane gave out a cough, and again I followed her lead. The only way to survive the Pale Rider was to make him think we were dying. If we could survive the next ten minutes, we could figure out a way to survive the hour—and both looked doubtful.

"In return for burying your wife," I said, "you can tell me something."

"Like what?"

"Anything. Something I don't know and never could."

He stared at me for a moment.

"You don't have a name. You're HE-315-PJ7A-M and generation twenty-four from Time Zero. You popped up on our database twenty years ago and your entire life is eighteen hundred lines of text, almost all of it geographic movements. Have you procreated yet?"

"Yes, though the child—*cough*—is not yet born."

"Then you and all your twenty-three forebears have done all that is required of you."

"What about—*cough*—me?" asked Jane.

"JK-768-OY9K-F," he said, "your record is even shorter."

"By what mechanism—*cough*—does the 'drone' track us?" I asked.

Hanson said nothing and instead tapped the barcode on my index finger.

"The drones scan by line of sight only. All specimens on this Reserve work on legacy tech five centuries old. Your barcodes allow us identification data, nothing more, so positional data has to be drone-assessed at twice-daily intervals. Reserve Thirteen to the west of here uses epidermal QR. Twenty-seven data points that include twelve physiological parameters . . ."

His voice trailed off as he realised he was saying too much and had lost us, which was true, as it turned out, on both counts.

"Never mind," he said. "Barcodes are crude, but effective."

Out of the corner of my eye I saw Jane wrap a hand around the barcode that was growing out of her nailbed. The swan had followed us from East Carmine and the reason Hanson didn't know about Tommo was because the barcode on Tommo's finger was disrupted—he could not be seen. My mother's assertion that gloves rendered one invisible to swans suddenly made perfect sense.

"Are you—*retching cough*—an Angel?" asked Jane quite suddenly. "Sent by the Creator to smite us from—*cough*—on high?"

"I hoped not to be that today, but it didn't work out that way."

"Can we speak to our Creator?"

"I think we're sort of done here," said Hanson as the town hall shifted and flexed and started to move inwards as it reduced in size. "And once again, you have my thanks—and my apologies. Take it from me that few ever get as far as you have, nor know as much at so young an age."

He called to the globe which came to his hand as a dog to its owner, then walked past the bodies of the fallen Yellows and out of the entrance while we made more coughing and retching noises. We saw him pause by the wall outside and he must have opened a control panel to close off the entrance, as the doorway reduced to nothing as we watched, trapping us inside.

I looked at Jane in the semi-gloom, the only light now coming through the roof-lantern high above, the *Labours of Munsell* on the ceiling now looking dim and unappealing.

"What was all that Angel Creator-smite stuff?" I asked in a whisper.

"I wanted him to think us timid and overawed in his presence," she replied. "I needed him to underestimate us. How are your elbows?"

"Numb."

"Mine too."

"Was any of that coughing for real?"

"None of it."

"Same here. Let's hope the numbness is as bad as it gets and that the anti-M we viewed earlier keeps us alive."

I looked around as the building shuddered again, the moisture now dripping from the ceiling as the Perpetulite contracted. It had an odd musky, seaweedy, long-dead sheep sort of smell to it.

"Surviving the Mildew won't add up to a hill of much of anything at all if we can't escape."

"That's true," she said, "and I really hope you were paying attention back then."

"Yes, I was," I said, "but since we're a team, I only concerned myself with the last five digits. Did you—?"

"I did," she said with the most radiant of smiles, "and that's it. You and I are joined as one—trusted and indivisible unto death."

"Married?" I said.

"Marriage is for hopeless romantics," she said. "What we have is bigger than that."

"Love?"

"Nope. Love fades, and entanglements of emotion lead to irrationality of decision. We have a bond of mutual trust and understanding, forged in the furnace of shared jeopardy."

"Oh," I said. I must have sounded disappointed, for Jane asked: "Why, would it help our relationship if I told you I loved you?"

"Not so much now you've diluted it with preamble."

She looked thoughtful for a moment.

"I understand. Another time, perhaps. We should be finding a way out."

I tried to get up but felt tired and listless, with pins and needles down the left-hand side of my body. The numbness in my arms had spread to my hands and fingers, which felt large and pendulous and useless. Jane scrambled to her feet with a similar level of difficulty and we headed for the far wall, where she opened up the panel and expertly changed the town hall layout to include an escape door in the back wall, pretty much where we were standing. When it asked for an access code we used Hanson's: we had both been looking over his shoulder when he keyed it in. She had the first five digits, I had the last. The Perpetulite was more languid now that it was in reset mode, but a door of sorts opened lazily in the back wall, leading into a patch of hawthorn and bramble, and we could see an escape beyond. Jane was about to dive through and into the open air, but I stopped her.

"What?"

"We're meant to be dead," I said, showing her my fingernail with the tell-tale barcode. "We can't let a swan see these or Hanson will know we're still alive—and he'll be back to ensure the job is complete. What he told us was not meant to be recalled or repeated."

"Good thought, Red."

So we each tied a handkerchief around our respective fingers and made our way out of the building. We looked around carefully, then darted inside a disused building and secreted ourselves within a house whose roof was a network of ivy and brambles, and we sat panting, not out of exertion, but fear and the knowledge of a close call—and witnessing that beheading which is still with me today.

We were there for an hour before we felt the residual effects of the Mildew begin to fade, and by that time the town hall had shrunk to little more than the size of a hay wain. As soon as that happened we heard a humming noise and three vehicles dashed past our hiding place at great speed.

"Those looked like gyro-bikes without wheels," said Jane.

"And with the Angel Hanson riding one of them."

We decided to wait another hour, just in case he or they planned to return. The town hall kept regrowing, and as we sat and waited, a small orb of ball lightning drifted from west to east to vanish from sight over the trees.

We ventured out as soon as we had convinced ourselves it was safe, then stood in an abandoned street and looked nervously about. The sun still shone, the birds still sang, nothing seemed much out of place—aside from the town hall, which was busy regrowing back to its original size and shape, the soft Perpetulite like unhealed scar tissue. It would be fully grown in an hour or two, but it would be empty again. The Yellows would be fully absorbed and their tools, belt buckles, spot-badges and anything that might have identified them would be firmly embedded in the foundations. Sadly, so too would all the volumes of Rules in the Council chambers, which had also been part of the reset.

"Did all that just happen?" I asked.

"I think it did," said Jane. "What's the cover story?"

"We saw no one," I replied, "but let's have a nose around in case anyone asks more probing questions—and there might be something to be found, after all."

Jane always maintained that if you needed a sound alibi for two hours of your time, then spend a *different* two hours together and use that. We'd done it several times before.

TIN MAN

Tin Men were once numerous after the Epiphany and were in those early days found blundering around the landscape, apparently without purpose. Impossible to destroy, they were discarded down mineshafts or dumped in lakes. There was a story about a Tin Man that crawled out of a lake in Blue Sector North all corroded and covered in weeds, but that might have just been a story to scare children.

—Ted Grey: *Twenty Years Among the Chromatacians*

We walked in silence past roofless, fire-blackened buildings, now open to the elements and overtaken by bramble, hawthorn and silver birch, until we found a row of shops with the roofs still vaguely intact and which seemed to have survived the fire. The first was the village café, and we pushed the door half open against detritus and squeezed in. It was dry inside, and most of the furniture was broadly intact, along with the counter tops, coffee machine and tea urns. Stacked cups were still on shelves behind the counter, all with a thick layer of dust and birds' nests. A bramble had made its way in and had grown across the ceiling, but the tearooms were not a lot different in form and function to the Fallen Man back home, just long abandoned.

We had a nose around but found nothing except a kitchen knife, which were always highly prized, then moved next door to the general store. It was dry here too, and a carpet of accreted detritus covered the floor. On the wall was the faded legend "Apart We Are Together." The statement was now an ugly joke; apartness kept us prisoners—the Greys from freedom, the other hues from progress.

"I think we just met an Angel," I said absently as I rummaged through a pile of old papers and forms that seemed to have been saved from the recycler.

"A Pale Rider," she said. "Death followed with him. What have you got there?"

"Back issues of *Spectrum*."

I continued to rummage while Jane went through the shop looking for anything worth salvaging. The youngest copy of *Spectrum* I found was dated 00461, which gave us a rough date of Crimsonolia's abandonment—about thirty-five years before.

"Hanson said we were *subjects*," said Jane as she looked in a cupboard that contained only rusty tins, "living on a *Reserve* and *generation twenty-four*. What does any of that mean?"

"No idea," I replied. "The only context for 'subject' I know is in a sentence. Or a person being 'subjected' to prefectural scrutiny."

"True," she replied, "and a 'reserve' is something you keep back in case of an emergency."

"He intimated there was *another* Reserve, numbered Thirteen, and to the west of here. Any ideas?"

"No. But we know he's affiliated to Utopiainc as his uniform suggested, and given his power of life over death and seemingly without scruples or much guilt, then he and his companions look upon us the same way as Prefects look upon the Riffraff: base, low, and little better than vermin."

"It doesn't make for a very benevolent Creator, now, does it?"

"None of it makes any sense," said Jane, "but one thing I do know, is that Hanson wasn't meant to tell us any of that. We, as a people, are not meant to know any of what he told us—and on pain of death."

We were both quiet for a moment as we considered what this meant. Our world—*the* world as far as we knew—had at least been ordered and understandable, if wholly unfair and dangerously corrupt. Hanson had overturned that completely. There was another part to our life—and it was a huge part—of which most of us knew absolutely nothing.

"You know when you turn over a rock and woodlice scurry for cover, confused and distracted?"

"Yes," I said, "I think that's us right now. Something huge is going on behind a curtain we can't see, and until recently, we never even knew was there."

"I agree. And I've had a bad thought."

"Such as?"

"We can't change the system without knowing what's behind that curtain, as I have a rather nasty feeling that Hanson and the Creator want us all just the way we are. He said it was impressive we'd found out so much at so young an age. If people start to fuss and show an interest, then it's over."

"So," I said, trying to figure this all out, "Pale Riders are there to ensure that when the Chromatic harmony fails, there is a fallback solution to keep things as they are?"

"I think so," she replied. "The Creator *wants* to keep the Chromatic Hierarchy going at all costs, and all malcontents and disruptionists are removed."

"Why would they have an interest? And who are they anyway and where do they come from?"

"I don't know," she said, "but it looks as though your Someone Else from Somewhere Else theory was right after all, and as we know from the RISK map, there's a lot of Somewhere Else for them to be from."

We fell silent for a moment, excited yet annoyed that our goal was no longer the goal. It was as though we had to get the puck into an impossibly small net, only to find there was another net, smaller and further away than the first. We both fell silent, then carried on our search for an unopened jar of jam or other luxury comestible.

"Found anything?" asked Jane after a few minutes.

"Some OmniGreen food colouring, suitable for salads," I said, holding up a tube, "but it hardened long ago."

"It could be brought back to life with cooking oil," she said, and I popped it in my bag.

Finding nothing more, we moved next door, which was the old repairers shop, the place where almost anything, no matter how worn or damaged, could be somehow brought back into service. The aged brass plaque by the door told us the last Master Repairer was Dorothy Crimson, and once inside we could see the roof had partially collapsed. Items either repaired or waiting in vain to be collected were now in a jumbled mass and mostly domestic and agricultural implements with egg whisks, butter churns and patched-up shovels now rusted beyond use, along with the corroded remains of a twin tub washing machine, taps, ballcocks and other hydrologically related ephemera.

"I can hear voices," I said, as the faint sound of conversation reached our ears.

"In the basement," added Jane, and nodded towards a closed door that presumably led down into the workshop below.

We tiptoed across and pressed our ears to the door, but the conversation was muted, and seemed to be interspersed with music—a little like a play. We pushed open the door and were greeted by the musty odour of dust mixed with funghi and sewing-machine oil. We picked our way down the concrete steps and could easily see where the conversation had come from: a working remote viewer was on the desktop. The visual play seemed to be of several men talking to one another in a spacious living room with a large fireplace.

It wasn't all that was down there. There were lathes and milling machines and pillar drills, each lit by a functioning lightglobe, the glow faded and discoloured by the industrious action of moths. We could see that old tech had been cannibalised to ensure more mundane machines could be kept working, but one item in particular caught our eye: a dull-grey machine that was standing in a corner, covered in dust and cobwebs. He appeared as though he hadn't moved since the village was abandoned, but that didn't mean he was inert. Tin Men were notoriously difficult to destroy. Lucy Ochre claimed they ran on harmonic induction, which might explain why some still worked five hundred years past manufacture.

"There's one of these at Cobalt's Museum of the Something that Happened," said Jane in a quiet voice, "but theirs is a deactivated composite."

This one, we could see, was still at least partially working—his single functioning eye followed us as we walked down the steps to the workshop floor, our feet kicking up the dust of decades. We reached the bottom and approached warily. There was no record of one ever hurting anybody, but they grew unsteady with old age, and people had been killed when they fell on them. It paid to remain a few paces away. We looked at him for a moment while his eye moved between the two of us, and I got the feeling he was sizing us up.

"Do you think he can understand us?" I said, as unlike the shredding turtle, the Tin Man was thought to be possessed of cognitive ability.

"I don't know," said Jane. "It's said they could once speak."

His eyes swivelled to look at Jane, then at me.

"I can still speak," he said in a rusty sort of voice. "Neither of you is Dorothy. Where is Dorothy?"

He must have meant the repairer, whose name was on the door.

"I think she might have died," I said.

There was another pause.

"Define 'died.'"

"Permanently deactivated," said Jane, and the Tin Man's eye swivelled to look at her.

"I understand," he said at length. "I think I may have been *temporarily* deactivated. I am different to Dorothy. I am different to you."

Jane looked at me and I shrugged. We'd never come across anything like this before.

"I like to repair things," continued the Tin Man. "I can repair almost anything. And in leisure, I play chess. Dorothy and I were playing a game shortly before she became died. Would you like to resume the game, new Dorothy?"

We noticed that there was a chess game in progress on the table near where the Tin Man was standing. The pieces were covered in dust, fragments of plaster and a long-desiccated jackdaw. Jane picked the dried bird from the game and laid it carefully upon another surface.

"Do you play?" I asked.

"I play very well," said the Tin Man, "and with a seventy-eight percent likelihood better than you."

"I was talking to Jane," I said, probably a little abruptly, but the Tin Man made no comment.

"Fifth Junior runner-up at Sector Championships," said Jane.

"White is to play," said the Tin Man.

"I'll play with you," said Jane. "Do you have a name?"

"Define 'name,'" said the Tin Man.

"It's an arbitrary label used to identify individual people, entities or objects. 'Dorothy' is a name."

"Dorothy labelled me 'Hoss,'" he said simply, "after her favourite Cartwright. I believe I *once* may have had a different name or an operating number. I mended things for Dorothy, and now I will mend things for you."

He indicated the remote viewer, which was still playing.

"I am watching episode thirty."

"Episode thirty of what?"

"Of a series called *Bonanza*. The episode is titled 'Feet of Clay.' Dorothy liked *Bonanza*, even though it was forbidden. To keep me company she played an episode every night for me on a loop. This was the one playing when she died. It has played ever since."

We didn't really know what he was talking about, but we did know that remote viewers could play entertainment in the form of plays.

"Which one am I?" said the Tin Man.

"Which one are you what?"

"Person, entity or object?"

"What do you feel you are?"

"I do not know. Entity, perhaps, but being a person seems to offer social advantages, despite the lack of longevity. I believe I was manufactured, so perhaps I am an object."

"What were you built for?"

"I do not know."

"Who built you?"

"I do not know."

"How old are you?"

"Define 'old.'"

"The passage of time. Since Dorothy left is a passage of time, from when we entered the room is a passage of time. The time since the last play was made in the chess game is a passage of time."

The Tin Man looked down at the chess game, then around the room, presumably at the decay.

"Entropy has increased," he said simply.

"Define 'entropy,'" said Jane.

"Entropy represents the unavailability of a system's thermal energy for conversion into mechanical work," he said.

"I don't understand."

"In simpler terms, disorder," said the Tin Man. "In a closed system disorder will always increase. It is a law of thermodynamics. You are currently ordered, but you will eventually be disordered, as you were before you were ordered. Is that what you mean by the passage of time?"

Jane and I looked at one another.

"It's how Felicity Pink spoke," said Jane, "just after she viewed the mind-expanding shade."

"I do not know this Felicity Pink," said the Tin Man.

"I was speaking to Eddie."

"What is Eddie?" asked the Tin Man.

"I am Eddie," I said and he stared at me, then at Jane.

"I am Jane," said Jane.

"Jane," said the Tin Man. "Dorothy had a smaller version of herself labelled Jane. She started small and became large, then I saw her no more. Water with point nine eight four percent sodium chloride by mass came from Dorothy's face when that happened. The water was also found to contain a quantity of organic compounds. Would you like me to list them by volume?"

"Maybe another time."

He paused, then looked at the dusty game again.

"Your last unanswered question: I do not know the passage

of time from my inception," he said. "Old Dorothy was the first thing I recalled upon reactivation."

"How can you tell you were reactivated and not simply activated?" I asked.

The Tin Man pondered this for a long time.

"I have faint images that appear randomly when in sleep mode," it said. "Artefacts from another place and time that are not this time. I disordered things and brought dying events upon people who looked like you. Then, that ended. I was buried for a passage of time, then Dorothy found me and mended me and reactivated me, and then I mended items for Dorothy. We last played the chess game fifteen thousand, three hundred and thirty-three light/dark cycles ago."

"That's around forty years," said Jane after some mental arithmetic.

"Is that too long a time to resume this game?" asked the Tin Man.

"No."

So while I searched the room for anything of value, Jane gazed at the chess match in progress, trying to figure out how the game arrived at where it was now, and then figure out the strategy of white to take it forward from there. All the while the Tin Man stared at us both in turn, but it was impossible to know if he had the gift of consciousness, or whether he was just reacting to the situation by an applied set of rules. Chromogencia meetings had often spoken about such matters regarding non-biological life forms, but ultimately concluded that while something manufactured in origin could *convince* one that they were sentient, we could never know for sure—on the rather simple basis that each of us could be only fully certain of one person's consciousness—our own.

I found four spoons, all in need of repair, but still valuable.

There was a drawer full of lightglobes, too, and various other bits of old tech whose use I could not even guess.

After a few minutes of thought Jane moved the rook to king one. The Tin Man brought up an arm to move a piece but its joints moved stiffly and with a mild grating sound. He looked at its hand and rotated it, opened the fingers and then closed them again several times. I don't think he had moved at all in the past forty years—and would likely have stayed here until the roof collapsed and buried him if we hadn't chanced by. There would be others like him still out there, just buried under accreted soil and debris or in pits or wells or lakes, awaiting rescue that might never come. He was old tech, and obsolete—just one more thing the Previous left behind when they died. He eventually clasped his chess piece and moved it, then said:

"Sorry, New Dorothy, I think you missed it. Queen to bishop three, bishop takes queen, knight takes bishop, checkmate."

"I think you're right," said Jane, staring at the board.

"Thank you for a very enjoyable game, Dorothy. Would you like me to mend something now?"

"No, thank you, Tin Man," said Jane. "You are to wait for me here until I return to give you further orders."

"Are you talking to me or Eddie?"

"You."

"Is Tin Man my name?"

"Yes."

"It is not a good name. I am not made of tin, nor am I a man. I am mostly tungsten steel and magnesium alloy on a titanium-molybdenum chassis. I have silicon-based ceramic bearings, and use much copper, aluminium, vanadium, iridium and almost all trace metals in some part or other."

"Would you like to be called something else?" asked Jane.

"I have no issue with the name," said the Tin Man. "I just said it wasn't good, as it is inaccurate, the same as Eddie over there who is named after a hydrostatic feature of watercourses—when he is not that at all."

"It's a shortened version of Edward."

"As 'Dot' is a shortened version of Dorothy?"

"Yes."

"That explains something that has confused me for a long time. A dot to me is a singularity which has no position or dimensions, merely location."

"I think you and Lucy would get on very well," I said with a chuckle.

"Who is Lucy?"

"Lucy Ochre. She's someone you would get along with."

"I like people I will get along with."

"We need to leave," said Jane.

"Do not," said the Tin Man, taking a step in the confines of the workshop to check his legs were working. "If you are absent I shall experience that word that describes the act of not wanting to be without others."

"Lonely?"

"Yes, I will experience lonely."

"You can't come with us. It is forbidden."

"I understand the word forbidden," he said. "If I cannot come with you, then you must give me a function to give meaning to the reason I am here. Otherwise I have no reason or purpose to be anything at all. Dorothy had me mend things; it was a function. I need a function."

Jane and I exchanged a look.

"Spoons," I said, "you are to collect spoons. Do you know what a spoon is?"

"I have repaired three hundred and two of them. They come in many sizes and are made of a variety of alloys, but mostly steel."

"Good. Search the village and find as many spoons as you can. But do not allow yourself to be seen by anyone."

"I understand."

"If you go to the sea to the west of here," said Jane, "you will find many spoons in a deserted place on the coast, visited only by the railway."

"'If I go to the sea' is ambiguous. Do you mean 'I should go to the coast,' or 'if I happen to find myself by the coast'?"

"I meant you should go to the coast."

"I understand. And what should I do with these spoons?"

"You are to store them here."

"I will undertake this function," said the Tin Man with what I detected to be a tinge of satisfaction, "and await your return."

We climbed back up the stairs out of the workshop and stood blinking in the sunlight. The Tin Man followed us with a halting gait and immediately started searching. Throughout the remainder of our time in Crimsonolia we heard him ferreting around among the ruins.

"Do you think he will find High Saffron?" I asked.

"I don't know," said Jane. "I've never met a Tin Man before and don't know what to expect. Won't the rain make him rust?"

"He didn't mention iron in his list of constituent parts," I said, "so I guess not."

We found a small open area and sat on the warm grass. We checked for swans and that our fingers were still covered, then sat in silence for a while.

"I'm still thinking of that Yellow's head coming off."

"Me too," she said, "and Hanson."

We lay down on the grass and gazed upwards at the grey sky and at the puffy doughnut-shaped clouds as they moved across. A flock of curlew passed overhead, and in the distance we could hear several peewits. The land was utterly peaceful, and we seemed an age away from the strictures of Chromatic politics. I could see why people left to join the Riffraff, or just left.

We stayed quiet for some time.

"Now what?" I asked.

"Jollity Fair. Your mother found a truth there, she spoke of escape and they killed her for it. If she was right about how gloves render one invisible to swans, she might be right about the Creator—the one who has all the answers, and controls our fortunes. The Angel Hanson proves it, so we need to meet the Herald and ask it some questions."

"If we survive the hearing."

"We'll survive the hearing," she said. "I'm just wondering in what form."

HOME AGAIN

Although fatal to the unwary, the carnivorous yateveo tree was easy to spot and easy to avoid—just don't go under its leafy spread. And if you do, don't tread on one of the sensitive roots or you'll be snatched at lightning speed and dumped in the central digesting bulb. A bag of copper nails attached to a hapless goat-bait would disable one, and from there they could be sawn down quite easily. But their berries were considered quite the delicacy and their wood too pulpy to burn or to fashion, so were generally left to grow unmolested, and avoided where possible.

—Ted Grey: *Twenty Years Among the Chromatacians*

"Hello, Tommo," said Jane as we walked up. He was unchanged in position and activity since when we last saw him, sitting cross-legged next to the Ford and engraving postcodes on to spoons. He'd also been rubbing the engravings with sandpaper and a wire brush to make them look as worn as the spoon, but that probably wasn't necessary—deMauve would have taken them in any condition.

"What ho!" he said when he saw us. "How did you get on?"

"We found four rather miserable examples," I said, showing him the ones from the repairers. "Everything okay?"

"Pretty quiet," he replied. "A ground sloth wandered through a few hours back. I jotted down the Taxa number for you. What happened to your fingers?"

He'd noticed we had handkerchiefs tied around our index fingers. We'd discussed what to do about them, and while Jane, practical and a little wild as ever, thought a pair of pliers to remove the nail or an axe to take off the finger, I'd suggested painting on a random code, which would be subtler and less painful, an idea she conceded had a lot more going for it.

"I got mine trapped between two rocks," I said, "busted the nail. *Really* painful."

"Bad luck. Jane?"

She paused, and with that pause nothing she said would have been believable.

"Same here," she said, "but different rocks."

"Okay," said Tommo, clearly suspicious but unwilling to take it any further. Jane and I had spoken about Tommo on the way out of the village, as the Yellows had said "they meant him no harm," which either meant Tommo knew what was going on, or they'd been told to leave him alone so the spoon laundry could go ahead as normal. Jane had said we needed to find out about Tommo's complicity one way or the other before we got home, which I didn't much like the sound of. Personally, I thought he didn't know—when he saw us returning there wasn't an atom of surprise. But then again, he was an astonishingly good liar.

So we packed up in silence and once we had topped up the radiator, checked the oil and coaxed the Model T's engine back into life—an undertaking that took nearly twenty minutes—we headed back the way we'd come. I wasn't sure how Jane was going to broach the subject of the Yellows, but she didn't need to, for he suddenly chirped up:

"By the way, did you bump into the Yellows?"

"No," I said, "what Yellows?"

"Five or six of them. They arrived by way of a Ford coming up from the Dog-Leg-Lake direction soon after we arrived. They parked a little way up the road. I don't think they saw me."

Jane and I said nothing. If he was in on our planned murder, it made no sense for him to mention this.

"Did you *really* not see them?" he persisted. "I mean, you were in the same village together all day, and there were at least five of them and they looked kind of purposeful and were carrying farm implements and a cricket bat."

We were in the front of the Ford and he was in the back, so Jane and I just glanced at one another and said nothing. But in that silence we spoke volumes.

"Oh shit," he said. "Did something happen?"

We still said nothing.

"You didn't . . . kill them, did you?"

"We didn't kill them," said Jane, "but they won't be going home."

"Oh," he said, "so those Yellows. I guess . . . I didn't see them at all?"

"Now you're getting it," said Jane. "So aside from not seeing any villagers, did you see anything else?"

"I don't know," he said doubtfully. "Did I?"

"This one you can answer truthfully."

"In the morning there was a Leaper," he said, "covered in a blanket, its face hidden from view. It had a scabby arm out begging for scraps, but it smelled of poo and I told it to be on its way. After that, a crew of colour feed-pipe engineers led by Green Adair going in the opposite direction towards Blue-town," he said. "Apparently a colour feed-pipe had burst and there was cyan gushing out of the roadway that needed to be capped."

"We didn't pass them on the way this morning."

"No, I thought that odd too—must have come over the mountain road from Ochre-in-the-Vale. Those Yellows. Was it an ambush?"

We said nothing.

"Look, just for the record, I had no knowledge of this. DeMauve asked me to launder some spoons, but that's as far as my involvement goes, right?"

"It's all right," said Jane, "we believe you."

"Okay then."

We drove on in silence, the occasional animal on the road to entertain us, mostly squarial or tree-nesting badger. We passed the Leaper on the way, their body and head covered by a rough blanket with only a hole to look out of, their two spindly legs only visible from the calf down. They carried a wicker backpack held in place by a forehead strap, and which contained their few possessions—a small block of Perpetulite that would morph into a domed one-person shelter, a water bottle, a musical instrument and on the very top an incongruously large hat "for best," and by which I could deduce they were female. Tommo said to hurry on past, but Jane stopped the Ford and I placed an apple on the road in front of her, then retreated so she could take it.

"Did you smell it?" asked Tommo once we were on our way, and I replied that I did, and yes, she stank. Food was generally left out for them at the Outer Markers, but they were usually pelted with stones if they tried to get anywhere near the village boundary.

Tommo spent the journey re-counting his spoons and calculating the bounty, while Jane and I simply looked at the road ahead, our minds occupied with what had just happened and quite how the disappearance of five Yellows would pan out, as they'd be logged missing at nightfall.

"So," I said after about an hour's travelling, without, it must be noted, any sign of a swan overhead, which presumably meant Angel Hanson so far did not suspect we had survived, "how did you fake so many postcodes, Tommo?"

He shrugged.

"Time was not on my side so I simply looked at the village roll and subtly altered the last few letters and digits to make new ones. Why are we slowing down?"

"I need some more water for the radiator," said Jane. "Would you help me, please, Tommo?"

If the "please" wasn't enough to make Tommo suspicious, the place where we had stopped would certainly do so: we were close to the river and between it and the road was a very large yateveo tree.

"Oh, c'mon," said Tommo, who surmised he was about to be killed, "I said I hadn't seen anything. What do you want me to do? Swear on the life of Our Munsell?"

"I just need help with the water for the radiator," replied Jane in an even tone.

But her denial just made it worse.

"I don't want to be eaten by a tree," he said in a plaintive wail. "I had no idea the Yellows were putting on a reception for you—if I had, I wouldn't have come lest I was included in the death list or hurt in the melee. The one thing everyone knows about me is that I'm a coward. Eddie? You can put in a bad word for me, right?"

Jane and I exchanged looks.

"He's a weasel and a coward and a n'er-do-well," I said. "I can vouch for that. I can help you get the water."

Jane glared at me, took a deep breath, said "okay fine," picked up the water can and walked off down the bank to the river. I followed her and we carefully skirted the empty earth beneath the yateveo, the sensitive touch roots just visible where they waited to spring the branches and catch the unwary.

"I'm not sure killing people willy-nilly is really going to help matters," I said once we were out of earshot.

"What do you mean 'willy-nilly'? How many people do you think I've killed?"

"That Duckegg guy."

"Oh, *please*. He was a reptile of the worst sort. If he hadn't have died when he did, he would have been sent to Reboot and died there—but not before someone had fallen prey to his toxic ways. Stop a sec, I need to have a pee."

So we stopped and she squatted down.

"I'm not sure killing people actually makes us any better than a Collective which *also* kills people."

"Don't give me that," she said. "To sweep all this shit aside, someone's going to die. Me, you, someone else. It doesn't matter. Results are what's important, and if someone essentially valueless like Tommo has to die to ensure we remain on track, then so be it. Help me up, would you?"

I gave her a hand and heaved her to her feet.

"But since there's a very good chance he won't talk," I said, "why should he have to die on a low probability?"

"Because we can't leave anything to chance."

"So where does that end up? Killing someone because they *might* know something they shouldn't?"

She glared at me with that sort of look that made me *really* nervous.

"What about Imogen and Dorian?" she said. "That was on you, wasn't it?"

"I didn't actually kill them," I said.

But I had, sort of. They travelled on the Night Train to

Emerald City and while the city was a place where young people like them *could* find a new life, the "Night Train" was the same as Reboot. I knew that, but couldn't warn them without putting myself at risk. I said nothing and let them go to their deaths.

"Have you ever actually killed anyone?" I asked as we carried on towards the river. "Proactively, by your own hand. *Intentional.*"

She stopped and faced me.

"Okay, no, I haven't. Happy now? My secret's out. Don't go telling anyone. Half of being able to do what I do is because people *think* I have killed people—and might do again."

We arrived at the river and Jane unscrewed the cap of the container, checked for any snapping toad in the vicinity, then filled it.

"But I *will* kill if necessary," she said, "as will you. If you don't think you can, we probably better part company right here and now."

"Jane?"

"What?"

"I think I'm in love with you."

But my words didn't have the response I was hoping for.

"For Munsell's sake, Eddie—don't spoil it by *telling* me. It's unsaid, and truer than ever when we both understand the silent bond. I mean really, I shouldn't have to explain this to you."

She glared at me, got up, screwed the cap back on and walked back up the slope.

When we got back to the car, Tommo was looking anxious and mouthed "okay?" at me and I nodded. We carried on the rest of the journey in silence, and Tommo made no comment even when we passed the rhinosaurus without pausing to take the rest of the teeth. We didn't stop again until we got to the stockgate, and Jane pulled the Ford off on to a grassy verge so we could wait for the two-hour quarantine period to be up. Tommo had brought a pack of cards so we started to play, but had only dealt when Tommo looked up.

"Hello," he said as he peered down the direction we had just come, "we have company."

RIFFRAFF

The Chromatacians' homes, like all communally owned property, were allocated strictly according to hue. If and when an individual died, everyone below them in the Chromatic Scale would move up a property whether they liked it or not. Conversely, a newcomer to a village could cause those beneath them to move house accordingly. If several citizens died in quick succession and there were some sporadic incomers, you might be doing nothing but moving home for a fortnight.

—Ted Grey: *Twenty Years Among the Chromatacians*

A figure had approached from the direction from which we had just arrived. As she drew closer I could see it was a woman dressed in the neat, hand-stitched and very recycled clothes of the Riffraff. She was young, perhaps late teens or early twenties, and her hair was long and plaited with flowers. She had a string of beads and a large seashell around her neck, and her legs and feet were bare. She was carrying an infant in a sling knotted behind her neck, and walked towards us without fear, which was unusual— they generally stayed well hidden. She was a Riffraff, or to give them their taxonomic title: *Homo feralensis*.

Tommo reacted the most predictably. He picked up a stone and hurled it in her direction, something she sidestepped easily. My own reaction was more circumspect, mostly due to our ongoing observations that Riffraff weren't actually dangerous at all, didn't eat their own babies, and may even see rudimentary colour. If Jane and I couldn't remain inside the Collective, we would almost certainly end up living a similar lifestyle, and maybe even with them—even if that meant losing a finger in their Offgridding ceremony, which I now realised must have its origins in swan and Angel avoidance.

"Where did she spring from?" asked Tommo.

"There's a colony two miles northeast of here," said Jane. "Is there?" said Tommo.

"They keep themselves to themselves," she said. "Quite wise when you're classified as 'vermin.'"

The Riffraff carried on her approach until she was less than thirty feet away.

"I've heard that Riffraff sometimes beg for food," said Tommo. "Do you think it's true they'll do *youknow* for the price of a cabbage? And this is really a two-part question."

"'I have no idea' answers the first part," said Jane, "and in the second, we don't have a cabbage."

"Hmm," said Tommo, looking around as if by magic one might be handy.

"Help my child," said the Riffraff.

I took a step forward, expecting her to back away, but the Riffraff stayed resolutely where she was.

"Help my child," she said again.

"Careful, Eddie," said Tommo. "Riffraff are usually festering with disease, and to be honest, this could be an elaborate trap."

"So close to the village?" said Jane. "I think not."

I approached slowly, all the time with her staring at me intently. Her child was a boy, I think, but looked pale and his forehead was hot to the touch.

"Mildew?" called out Tommo cautiously.

"I don't think so," I said, then, to the Riffraff: "We can't help you. Our colour-medicine is *for us*."

I pointed at her smaller eyes, then to mine, which were larger, the most obvious difference between our species. Accepted wisdom had them as a remnant of the Previous, survivors of the Something that Happened, but also, shockingly, interbred with us.

"Yes, yes," she said, nodding her head vigorously. I looked at the baby. It was harder to tell at this age, but the child's eyes appeared bigger and its skull more rounded.

"I think the child is one of ours," I called back.

"Child theft," said Tommo, "I *knew* it."

Riffraff stealing children was a common story, but like swan attack and lightning strikes, not bolstered by fact.

"Should we steal it back?" he added.

"No one's stealing children from anyone," I said.

"Technically speaking," said Tommo after a short pause, "it wouldn't actually be stealing and I know someone who would pay good money to avoid procreating."

I ignored him, had an idea and asked Jane to bring me the emergency swatch pack. She brought it over while the Riffraff woman eyed us both nervously.

"I hope you know what you're doing," said the one-year-old in the dry monotone they used until their personality emerged.

"Try the 6B," I said, which was a mid-blue for most types of fever, and was omnifunctional across all sight gifts. Jane did as I asked, and I lifted the eyelid of the child so he could stare at the swatch. We waited a couple of minutes but there was no change, so we tried a 7D, for more viral-based infections. The effect was almost instantaneous, and the child said that "he was feeling a little better, thank you." The mother, tearful with relief, smiled at us both, then gave me the bag that was around her shoulder. It was heavy and felt lumpy.

"*Diolch*," she said, and dashed away into the undergrowth with hardly a rustle.

"Someone's been having *youknow* with the Riffraff?" exclaimed Tommo once we had rejoined him and explained.

"It happens," said Jane. "I don't know whose that was, but Davy Mint used to hang out with the Riffraff. Boasted of it, in fact. When his behaviour came to Prefect Yewberry's attention, he said that Mint must go to Reboot—but gave him two days to pack, which was generous of him."

"What happened to him?"

"He married into the Riffraff," said Jane, "and has three children in a group near the Daclands. We occasionally get postcards. He said he didn't regret it for one moment."

"Should we tell the Prefects about this?" asked Tommo.

"Nope," said Jane. "Unless you want to be scrubbed hard with carbolic soap—the Prefects are obsessed with how filthy and diseased they are."

"Goodness me," said Tommo, "there's so much stuff I didn't see today, I'm surprised I saw anything at all."

"What's in the bag?" asked Jane, and I emptied the contents out upon the grass. Wireless telephones, about a dozen of them.

"Valueless," said Tommo with a snort. "Unless you think one might be of a colour we can't see?"

It was possible, since Tommo and I could see only red and Jane hardly any colour at all.

"We're gonna have to surrender these or dump them," said Jane.

Wireless telephones turned up quite frequently, especially when raking over old homesteads while looking for scrap colour, and it wasn't uncommon to build decorative walls out of them, but only if they didn't work. Wireless telephones that glowed could be used to read after lights out so were much in demand, but absolutely forbidden: wireless telephones weren't even Leap-back, but "Annexe III" technology—banned at the inception of Chromatic harmony.

Despite all this we went through the telephones, pressing the on switch in a hopeful kind of way until one made a welcomey sort of noise as it started up.

"I think we've got a worker," I said. "Let me see."

Jane turned the telephone over in her hands. It was about the size of a bar of soap and had large, highly visible number but-tons beneath a small viewing window. On the back was a name scratched into the plastic: Nigel. Possessing this was a five hun-dred demerit, and even knowing about one and not telling a Prefect was an offence.

"I think it was designed for the less dextrous," said Jane, "which accounts for the large buttons."

"Or a cheaper version," I said, "the manufacturing seems cruder than the others. What do you make of that?"

The little window had come alive with "Network" in very small letters, plus a series of bars in ascending sizes.

"I don't know," I said. "Try calling a number. The rendering shed. They're always seven three six."

She held the wireless telephone so we could both hear and then pressed a seven. Almost instantly there was a tone and we heard: "You have dialled incorrectly. Please hang up and try again." So we tried an eight and got the same thing.

"I heard you had to start with a zero," said Tommo.

"Where did you hear that?"

He shrugged.

"General knowledge of the Previous, I think, like the Taxa checksum, the format of postcodes and that there were two com-peting units of measurements, only one of which we now use."

We tried what Tommo suggested and he was right. Jane

pressed a zero, followed by the 736 for the rendering shed. After a long pause we heard a voice with a subtler message: "The number you have dialled has not been recognised. Please hang up and try again." So Jane tried 737 for the repairers shop, but we got the same message. "Three numbers should be enough to connect you to *someone*," I said, as the internal village network only ever needed three numbers—but admittedly, that was through a switchboard where you had to tell the operator which extension you wanted. Long distance telephone connections between villages hadn't been possible for over a century.

Jane tried a third time and received the same message.

"It's unlikely to connect to anything," I said. "It might be the only portable telephone of its kind."

"I had low expectations," said Jane, "but it was worth a try."

She turned it off, put it in her pocket and we lay back on the grass to doze in the sun until the quarantine was up.

THE DEBRIEF

Harmonic Resonance Energy Transference powered Chromatacia for almost two centuries until Leapback II. The hum pervaded the air like unheard music, transferring energy to a suitable receptor to power anything from light-globes to hotpots to the scrubbers up at the DAClands. Best of all, the hum also transmitted information—everything you might want to know about—instantly to a remote viewer. It was forbidden, of course.

—Ted Grey: *Twenty Years Among the Chromatacians*

As soon as the quarantine period was up we got back in the Ford, retrieved our spot-badges at the stockgate and slowly drove the remaining mile into the village. It was by now seven and we had missed supper, but we would certainly be able to grab something so long as we received a "late eating" chit from the Prefects—and there was actually something left to eat.

"Drive through the square on the way to get to Janitor's garage," I said.

"Why?"

"I want to confirm something."

As we puttered into the square we saw Prefects Gamboge and deMauve talking outside the town hall. A brief look of shock and bewilderment crossed their features before they composed themselves and nodded a respectful greeting as befits the debt owed to those who risk everything on a scavenge hunt.

"That's all we needed to know," I said as we drove across to the Janitor's workshop to return the Ford. We reported to Amelia that all was well, signed the paperwork and waited while she did a brief inspection to ensure no damage had been done, and we then walked across to the town hall. We passed the telegraph office on the way and noted that Yellow Prefect Celandine was hanging over Mrs. Ochre, the telegraph operator, doubtless passing desperate messages to Dog-Leg-Lake, asking what was going on in suitably coded language. The Yellows would not be posted missing until dusk, and they'd get a search party out to them at first light. They'd find the Ford they arrived in, but nothing else.

"Business?" asked the Clerk-to-the-Prefects at the reception to the Council chambers. This was Mrs. Lilac, who when not artistically attacking privet hedges with secateurs, plainly relished in the small power her job brought.

We gave our names and numbers, presented our merit books and announced that we were there to surrender spoons and undertake a debrief. Mrs. Lilac snorted, and asked us if we were hungry.

"We are actually," I said. "Thank you."

"Yes," said Mrs. Lilac, filling out an unrelated form, "so am I. There never quite seems enough to go around, does there? You can sit on those benches to wait."

So we wandered over and sat on the hard bench. Jane and I would doubtless wait on the same bench tomorrow, before our hearing. I saw Jane looking around at the smooth Perpetulite walls, then touch her blouse where the bronze bob was hanging around her neck. If we could open a door in the Crimsonolia town hall, we could do it here, too. We said nothing for half an hour until the exterior door opened and Mr. Celandine bustled in, holding a wad of telegrams. He glared at us as he walked into the Council chambers, and twenty minutes later the buzzer on Mrs. Lilac's desk went and she said we could go in.

They were all there, sitting in a half-circle behind the colour wheel table, which was decorated with each separate part of the spectrum coloured in—some visible to us, most not. At the centre of the table where all the sections of colour joined in the middle was a leather-bound copy of the *Book of Harmony*, while all the other associated volumes of Rules, appendices and acceptable Standard Variables oppressively lined the walls in bookcases.

Head Prefect deMauve sat in the largest chair with Yewberry and Turquoise to one side and Gamboge and Celandine to the other, although owing to the fact that Mr. Celandine was currently visiting, he had brought in a stool to sit on and was subsequently lower than the others by a head height, which made him look faintly ridiculous.

"Good evening and fair be the colours that bind us," I began. "My name is Edward deMauve and I and my team, Thomas Cinnabar and Jane Brunswick, recently went on a scavenge trip to Crimsonolia. All three returned safely, and aside from a minor injury to my hand, we are safe and healthy."

I showed them my bandaged finger, while Jane kept hers hidden—she'd painted the nail with off-white paint and it hadn't dried yet.

"I can report that Mr. Cinnabar briefly met with Green Adair and her crew who were moving on through to Bluetown to deal with a damaged cyan feed-pipe. We came across a rhinosaurus carcass that might be worth mining for render, and I would predict a Leaper will turn up in about three hours."

We'd agreed not to mention the Riffraff.

"Otherwise," I continued, "little happened of note. Crimsonolia is long abandoned and little or no scrap colour was noted.

We returned with a grand total of twelve spoons with postcodes, and thirty-two without. They break down as follows . . ."

I went through the tally, then added up the total bounty owed, which was three thousand and fifty merits. I concluded by saying that we were glad to be of service to the village and the Collective, and that we would happily answer all questions. I then sat down.

"This is all frightfully good work," said Turquoise in an enthusiastic manner, looking through the impressive pile of spoons. If he was part of the plot to have us killed, he wasn't showing it. "However did you find so many?"

"It was hard work," said Tommo, "and required much diligent and careful searching."

There was a pause as deMauve weighed up his response.

"The expedition has exceeded our wildest expectations," he said in a faux-congratulatory tone. "We will advertise for Greys and lesser hues first thing in the morning. Mr. Yewberry, will you cable the *Spectrum* offices and place an advertisement in the 'Transfers' page, offering two postcoded spoons for every couple willing to move out here?"

"I shall, sir. Will we offer the cost of the train fare too?"

"The coffers are empty," put in Mrs. Gamboge. "The spoons shall have to be enough on their own."

"Then it is agreed," said deMauve. "We will allocate the other spoons and postcodes within the village based on marital status, need and child-bearing viability. As for the Leaper, leave out food and some old clothes—but nothing of any quality or quantity on either count—we don't want to be seen as a go-to place for Leapers."

He paused and looked at us again.

"I think we can safely say that your actions today are highly commended, and positive feedback will be attached to your name in the town ledger."

We all nodded our thanks, but he wasn't done.

"We do, however, have a few questions we'd like to ask you. Mrs. Gamboge?"

The Yellow Prefect stared at us all intently.

"I have been speaking to the Prefect's Council over in Dog-Leg-Lake, and it appears that you were not alone in Crimsonolia today. A party of five Yellows, led by Yellow Prefect Celandine's son Torquil, were on a similar trip. Did you see them?"

We all answered: "No, ma'am."

"How is that possible?" said Gamboge, staring at us intently. "Crimsonolia is not large."

"Then I think it safe to say that they weren't there," I said. "If they were, you're right—we would have seen them."

"So what do you think happened to them?"

"I have no idea and it would be unwise to speculate," I replied.

"Speculate," said Celandine.

"Perhaps they—"

"No, I want Brunswick to have a go. Any ideas?"

"Well," said Jane, "they could have misappropriated the use of their Ford and then bunked off to Vermillion, got wasted on Lincoln, then gone to stare at Riffraff Novelty Dancers."

There was a sharp intake of breath from all four of them. "That's *highly* insulting," said Celandine. "All of the missing Yellows were well known for their probity, clean living and strict adherence to protocol. Besides, Riffraff Novelty Dancers are simply an urban legend with no basis in fact. Your accusations are malicious and you shall be fined fifty merits."

"According to Free Speech Rule 5.6.73.4.09," said Jane, "a citizen is permitted to speak freely when requested to do so. You said to speculate. So I speculated."

"Humph," said Gamboge.

"What about a mechanical breakdown?" I said, before an

argument really got started. "Perhaps they are still with their Ford, trying to get it—"

"You found a lot of spoons," said Gamboge, her temper rising. "Like a *lot* of spoons. Enough for eight people to find. You searched together, there was a fight, you took the spoons and . . . killed them. Let's face it, when it comes to killing Yellows, you do have some form in this field."

"That's a bit of a leap," I said, "on both counts. Besides, you don't *know* they're dead, do you? They'll probably turn up tomorrow having spent the night out in a Faraday's cage."

"It would have been five against two," added Jane. "You flatter us when you think we could beat them."

"There are three of you."

"I'm a notorious coward," said Tommo simply, "and well known to soil myself at the slightest sign of danger."

"That is true," said Prefect Turquoise thoughtfully. "I saw it happen during the Great Megafauna Incursion of '94."

"My son was among the Yellows," said Celandine. "If a hair on his head has been harmed, retribution will be swift and decisive."

"I reject your implied threats," said Jane. "We didn't see them. Personally, I think my 'bunking off to Vermillion' is a sound theory. It's happened before—they'll be back tomorrow, all with splitting headaches and the sort of rash that accompanies incautious passion with men or women of negotiable affection."

"You are disgustingly disrespectful!" yelled Celandine, getting to his feet, but deMauve rapped his knuckles on the table.

"This is achieving nothing," he said. "Is there anything else you want to say?"

We all answered: "No, sir."

"In that case I think we should wait until a search party has looked for our missing friends. We shall assist with that at first light—Fandango will take a search party of Greys, led by Daisy

Crimson, who seems an eminently sensible young lady. Will you arrange it, Mrs. Gamboge?"

"I shall do it now."

"Very well then," said deMauve, "we will adjourn this meeting until tomorrow, but the findings may be moot as Brunswick and deMauve have their hearings at noon. It only remains for us to pay for the spoons and we are done. Pass over your merit books."

"Wait, what?" said Tommo.

"Your merit books. So I can transfer the merits."

"You said cash," said Tommo.

"I did not."

"You most certainly did," said Tommo, forgetting himself for a moment. "That's why we risked everything to go to Crimsonolia."

"You went as part of your civic duty," said deMauve, leaning back in his chair. "If any of you had even the slightest sense of communal feeling you would have done it for free. If I did say cash—which I do not believe for one moment I did—then I must have mis-spoken. We do not have anything like that amount of cash. Take your book merits and be grateful for small mercies. As penance for your outburst you are to sit silent beneath His statue for an hour to contemplate the harmony that Munsell has graciously brought to the world, and that you have just bruised so thoughtlessly."

So we passed over our books and had them duly stamped. We were now quite merit-rich, but that didn't count for much. Book merits bought mundane, sanctioned goods at set prices. Scented candles, extra pudding and a reconditioned comb—if and when they became available. Cash merits, on the other hand, could buy you anything that had a price—and *everything* had a price.

"I suggest you put your new-found wealth to good use and put in some advance orders for linoleum," said Prefect Turquoise. "It would help hugely in our efforts to meet our manufacturing targets."

"That would be wise," added Turquoise, looking at Jane and me as he said it, "given that all merits are cancelled at death."

With nothing more to say, we gave our thanks to them, their wise counsel and to Munsell himself for his fine words and leadership, then filed out of the Council chambers and into the main square.

"Uh-oh," said Tommo. A small group of people were milling around the statue, looking in our direction. "This is going to be sticky."

"Let me guess," said Jane, "there are two dozen or so people who were expecting to be one hundred cash merits richer this evening."

"Yup: a lot of people who will need to be assured that I will make good on that debt. I may be a little bruised come porridge time tomorrow. Looks like deMauve played me good and proper. Wish me luck."

He strode towards the waiting group of people.

"Hello, everyone!" he said brightly. "There might have been a few bumps on the road, but it's not anything we can't work out . . ."

We left him to it and walked on down the square.

"It was useful you could remember that free speech Rule," I said.

"What Rule?" she asked. "I made it up. Not even Prefects can remember all the Rules—besides, I'm sure they do it all the time."

She yawned.

"I'm going home," she said, "to get a good night's sleep. It's been a long day, and tomorrow might be even longer—or curtailed abruptly if Gamboge makes those charges stick."

"Do you think we should just leg it now?" I asked. "Just in case?"

"Nope," said Jane. "Hold fast, Eddie—we can't battle this from the outside. If we're consigned to the Green Room, we can leg it *then*. Best wear your PE pumps, just in case—and pack a valise."

We stopped on the corner of Ochre and Main and kissed, without thinking, right in front of people on their way home. There were some tuttings, but not from anyone powerful or who we held any great account of.

"Do you have to sleep at Violet's?" Jane asked.

"It will greatly annoy her if I don't," I said. "So I won't."

We smiled at one another, and after hugging again briefly, went our separate ways.

"I'm going to tell your father," said someone I didn't know very well as I walked away, "and your wife."

"You do what you have to do," I said, "and so will I."

BREAKFAST

The Previous could see at night, and fairly well, it was thought. The lack of our night vision was thought to be a mechanism to ensure compliance of behaviour, and limit movement. All excursions had to be undertaken before nightfall, and everyone had to be at home in bed when the lights went out.

—Ted Grey: *Twenty Years Among the Chromatacians*

I woke up to find Jane next to me, the sun already up. She'd said she wasn't going to come over but had anyway, and this time, not just for *youknow* and then talk in each other's arms before leaving. She'd slipped quietly into bed and we'd snuggled up close, said nothing, done nothing, and gone fast to sleep.

"Good morning," I said, having never been in this situation before and finding it curiously appealing in a relaxing, warm, *partnery* sort of way.

"Good morning," she replied, stretching out beneath the bed-sheet. "Judgement day. Is it time to get up?"

I'd already heard the clock chime so had reset my internal.

"Forty-six minutes past six," I said.

"I bumped into Mel on the way home," she said, propping her head on an elbow. "Applejack wants her to relocate to Emerald City to take up a post as his domestic."

"That was quick work."

"Melanie doesn't mess about."

Despite National Colour prohibiting their operatives from associating with Greys, the Rules had been tweaked so that domestic servants, maids and fitness instructors could accompany operatives at National Colour social meetings. She'd basically be his wife in everything but name and legal standing.

"She asked me if we wanted her to go."

"It would be helpful. Give us an ally in Emerald City, and an address. But it's her decision."

She nodded.

"I told her the same, and she said she would."

We had a shower together—another first—and went downstairs. I think Dad had heard Jane come in, or knew of her presence, as there were three places laid for breakfast when we got down. It was also the first time he noticed my finger was bandaged.

"Not cut at all," I said when he asked. "Mother was right when she said that gloves make us invisible to swans."

"I . . . don't want to know anymore. How are you, Jane?"

"Very well, thank you, Mr. Russett," she replied as he slid two eggs on to her plate and then poured her a cup of warm puddle water with a hint of spiced apple.

"I hope you two know what you're doing," said Dad. "Even without the Red/Green complementary colour stuff, you're now married to the Head Prefect in waiting, Eddie, and you could be subjected to a 'non-specific cabbage pelting directive' from the Council if anyone sees you together like this."

We didn't have time to discuss the odd Rules regarding vegetable-based punishments as Mr. Baxter and Harry joined us, and the conversation ranged more freely. We learned that Harry spent most of his day reading, carving things out of wood and doing the crossword in the back of *Spectrum*.

"They must be copying them from a pre-Epiphanic list of puzzles," said Dad. "There's a lot of words no longer in usage."

"I've been figuring out meanings by reverse engineering the clues," said Harry. "A 'parakeet' was likely a sort of bird, a 'jury' a group of people who gave you advice, and 'equality' the sort of word that meant all people were equal, something I guess referred to anyone of an identical hue and sight gift."

"How's the Morse going?" asked Baxter, as Harry was practising his speed Morse code, as telling stories by Morse required a tap rate faster than we were born with, and he was hoping to replace *Renfrew of the Mounties* with something a lot more interesting.

"Pretty good," he replied. "Not quite at speech speed, but I'm getting there."

"What will you tap out instead of *Renfrew*?" asked Jane.

"We have a private library," said Mr. Baxter, "and we thought something called *Sense and Sensibility* might be welcome. Archaic and full of old words and phrases and unashamedly pre-Munsell, but quite amusing."

"Bunty will definitely drown out the code," said Jane.

"I'm not so sure," said Harry. "It's a good read, and everyone wants a rest from *Renfrew*."

He was right. The story had been repeated so often that it had ceased to have much meaning and instead was just a regular tapping on the radiators, much akin to rain on the tin roofs.

"I matched three comets," said Mr. Baxter, changing the subject, "as part of that dating exercise, and can say with a reasonable degree of accuracy that in pre-Munsell notation this year is 2803."

"It's 00496 now," said Dad, "so that places the start of the Collective in 2307."

"That's seventy years later than we thought," I said. "Anything else?"

"The Monday/Tuesday conjecture is wrong—it's actually Wednesday today."

"Does knowing that help you?" asked Dad.

"Not right now," said Jane, "but it might do, given time, I hope."

There was a brief pause, and I decided to quiz the Apocryphal Man further.

"If I said I'd met a Previous yesterday, what would you say?"

"You mean Riffraff? They're partly Previous. The Remnants, we think."

"No, I mean a full-blooded Previous, who wears a uniform like the Fallen Woman, and travels using unknown technology."

The Apocryphal Man raised an eyebrow.

"An Angel? From on high, and death follows with him?"

"Something like that."

"Is that what happened to the Yellows from Dog-Leg-Lake?"

"That could be . . . *conjectured* as a potential scenario."

"Hmm," he said, staring at me carefully, "I've heard stories, but nothing substantiated. Did this Angel speak to you?"

"Let's just pretend he might have," said Jane.

"Then you have questions for me."

I took a deep breath.

"If I said that we were all 'subjects' with Taxa numbers and lived on a 'Reserve,' would that mean anything to you?"

He thought about this for a moment.

"Not immediately. I was sent here to record history but without any prior or special knowledge. The words you use are archaic, but once had meaning. A 'Reserve' is an area of land which has been set aside for any number of uses. 'Subjects' might relate to people who are ruled by a single person, who own them or to whom they owe their freedom. But it might also mean . . . somebody or something that is *studied*."

Baxter paused for a minute, then added:

"This sounds like unguarded talk from this Angel you met—just supposing you did."

"It was. He thinks us both dead."

Dad dropped a cup in the kitchen area and we all looked up. "Sorry," he said.

I looked at Jane but she was staring absently at the tablecloth, tapping her finger.

"Swans," I continued, "they are not flesh and blood, but machines of aluminium, wires and old tech. Did you know this?"

"I think everyone knows it," said Baxter, "or everyone *once* knew it—but any apocryphal knowledge, without recourse to being discussed or recorded, is soon lost. That which is not spoken of does not linger in the resident's mind. Do you know what they do?"

"They are the eyes of Utopiainc the Creator," I said slowly, "to know exactly where we are. They read our barcodes from on high using a technology now lost to understanding."

Mr. Baxter looked at my finger with the bandage around it, then back at me.

"Gloves make one invisible to swans," said Dad, "and if gloves are forbidden by the Rules, then the Rulebook has been written either by Utopiainc, or with their guidance."

There was another long pause in the conversation as we all considered what we were discussing—it was as if someone had suddenly decided to merge legend and fact, and found them compatible.

"This is either very worrying or a flight of most ridiculous fancy," said Harry. "You need to be very, very careful."

"We will, but it's *our* necks we're risking."

"I wish that were true," said Dad. "There are two thousand seven hundred and eight people in East Carmine, and every one of them is at risk because of you two. From the eighty-three-year-old Widow deMauve all the way down to little Martha Grey who was born six days ago. This is why C-Notices happen. The Prefects, corrupt as they are, have a very great responsibility to the villagers in their care. They know they have to stick to the Rulebook, because if they don't, the very worst that will happen is the *very* worst that will happen—the *Book of Harmony* is not the final arbiter of justice and life and death. Send out the warning bells too loudly and it's the Pale Rider for all of us. I think that's what happened in Rusty Hill."

We fell silent. Life was always on a knife edge. We just didn't know it, nor that our actions could have such dire consequences. Others must have found this out, and those same others must have opted to say nothing and let the whole matter go.

"That's what we're doing this for," said Jane in a quiet voice, "so that we don't have to be beholden to rules we know little or nothing about. There *has* to be a better way—irrespective of the risks."

"Your mother said the same, Eddie," put in Dad, "and they killed her for it."

Jane and I looked at one another. Even though we were really only scratching the surface, we were in too deep to stop. Little was said after that. Baxter and Harry said they were going upstairs to read a book and maybe play a version of Scrabble where any word was allowed, not just colours, Jane headed home to change and go to work, and Dad sat down to update his notes before opening his consulting rooms.

I dressed very slowly, and combed my hair in all three regulation ways—parting right, left and centre—before I decided on the centre. I wrote up my harmonics report for Lucy, then stepped outside to carry out my Useful Work for that morning. Hearing or no hearing, I would still be expected to undertake my daily tasks as a high Red.

PATROL AND DEATH DUTY

I spoke my first word at two weeks and walked after a month. About average. I didn't exhibit any non-instinctual behaviour until I was two years old. It was a simple giggle, Dad had told me, and I was showing affection and inventing metaphors within another month. It was always a worrying time for parents, as running on core instincts alone can only get you to three or four years old, although some survived to eight—and were difficult or even impossible to deal with. Needless to say, the Mildew carried them off, too.

—Ted Grey: *Twenty Years Among the Chromatacians*

Now that I was a Significant Shade, I had my own pigeon hole in the post office, in which any special duties were posted for me to find. I would be expected to check two or three times daily as new responsibilities were added as the Council saw fit. I had my first Death Duty to conduct later on, which I wasn't looking forward to, and my ninth morning of Supervisory Boundary Patrol, a job I had taken over from Prefect Turquoise. He had not been reluctant to give up the responsibility: it was a boring job that no one ever enjoyed.

I directed the patrol from what was called the "incident room," situated underneath the post office and telephone exchange and accessed down a long flight of steps and past a large and heavy door, very like the ones that sealed flak towers. The door had long seized open so was not technically a door anymore, and the plotting room was the only room still in active use aside from the well, a wide cylindrical shaft about thirty foot wide, half filled with water. This was once open to the outside by two ceiling doors that slid sideways, but they were seized shut long ago as well, and by my guess beneath a row of houses. I walked along the corridor which was lit by lightglobes set into the concrete walls, an indication of its pre-Epiphanic origins.

The room was octagonal, and there were the remains of desks around the walls which once must have carried old tech of some sort, as there were wires sticking out of conduits in the concrete. Little was there to give any clue as to what the room had been originally used for, and aside from the fact that Boundary Patrols were *always* conducted from an underground complex if there was one, led one to think that this might have been something that was done in the times of the Previous, and just carried on in the manner of long tradition.

The patrol was without much drama: a slight breach to the clutching bramble in Delta Sector, possibly by glyptodon or woolly rhino, a crackly line on Dog Sector's telephone and the Leaper we had seen asking for food and water over at Able Sector. There was no sign of the Riffraff we'd seen the day before, and once the patrol was concluded I came blinking out into the daylight and took the patrol form off to the town hall to be processed, which in the context of what I now knew, meant "filed and then forgotten."

I had my first Death Duty in an hour, so sat on the bench from where I could observe the post office without being seen myself. Every ten minutes or so Mr. Celandine or Mrs. Gamboge would drop in to check for any new messages and there was usually a scrap of paper in their hand when they came out. I knew pretty much what the messages would say: that there was no sign of the Yellows in Crimsonolia.

At ten to eleven I went to Mr. Pink's house in the Red side of town. He was certainly above his seventieth year and although not suffering any life-threatening ailments that might have warranted a Mildew order, he was physically worn out.

"My knees are pretty much shot," he said when I found him alone in his sitting room, once introductions had been made, "and I am little but a burden—dead weight that the village cannot afford to carry."

The room had been cleared, his few personal possessions on the table wrapped in string and brown paper and ready to be recycled in the traditional manner—left on the exchange table in the town hall at dinner, where the trappings of life were left for others to make use of.

"Fifty-five unswerving years of devoted service to the Collective, I heard," I replied, using the soft, soothing voice that Death Duty demanded.

"Yes," he said in a quiet voice, "the Head Prefect mentioned me at breakfast when I retired two weeks ago, which was kind of him. He didn't remember my name and instead called me 'The Chutney Guy,' but I think the sentiment was there, even if the compassion or interest wasn't. How old are you?"

"Twenty."

"Are you married?"

"I am."

"Do you love her?"

"No."

"Negotiated union?" I nodded.

"I had one of those. We had the required children for the Collective but spoke barely at all for the rest of our time together. My daughter Felicity died, you know—drowned, they said, but I never believed it myself. I sought solace among chopped vegetables, seasoning and vinegar. I made chutney out of anything: runner beans, beetroot, onion. To be honest, I'd use whatever was grown. I was good at it, too. Do you know what my career total was?"

"Tell me."

"Twenty-seven thousand, six hundred and eight jars."

"That's a lot of chutney."

"Yes," he said, "and you know what?"

"What?"

"I don't even like chutney. Can't stand the stuff. Brings me out in hives. I prefer honey or jam."

He looked up at me for the first time, and stared at me with his large eyes that were filled with a sense of loss.

"Do you think a life spent on chutney was a life wasted?"

"The . . . Collective values everyone equally, and all play a small part to bring harmony to the whole."

"Yes," he said, "I've heard that often. Maybe a little *too* often. I've not ever left the village, you know. I'd have liked to have got to Vermillion, just once."

"To see the Colour Garden or the Badly Drawn Map?" I asked. "Or the Last Rabbit, Oz Memorial?"

"None of those," he said sadly. "I wanted to get wasted on the best green that chutney can buy, then go and stare at Riffraff Novelty Dancers. *Male* ones."

"I'm not sure there is such a thing—of any gender."

"I know, but we can always dream. Shall we go? I think they want to move in."

I helped him out of his chair, then downstairs where a family were sitting on boxes outside, waiting to take over his vacated house. They didn't look at him as we went past, just walked in as soon as we had walked out.

"It was a good house," he said as he left for the last time.

The Green Room was set aside from the village, traditionally the other side of the playing fields and conveniently close to the rendering shed. We took our time and Mr. Pink chatted quietly, mostly about recipes for chutney, the best way to parboil potatoes and the disappointment that no one would be taking on his job, or was even remotely interested in his extensive book of recipes collected over fifty years. He had it clutched firmly under his arm; he had decided it should be rendered with him.

The Green Room was a multi-faceted dome made of interlocking triangles and surrounded by a circular wall. Dotted about the grass lawn within were small plaques upon which were chalked the names of the recently departed, inscribed there for perpetuity or the next rainstorm, whichever was sooner.

Mr. Pink rummaged in his jacket pocket for a moment then handed me his merit book so his details could be entered into the village Births and Deaths register. He had amassed eight thousand merits during his life which he had assigned two days earlier to his remaining daughter, leaving the traditional two hundred and fifty merits to cover admin fees and a tip for the renderers. I opened the gate and we walked up the path towards the door, itself painted in a mild green euphoric to keep those of shaky resolve from turning away.

"On behalf of the Prefects and the citizens both present and future of East Carmine, we thank you for your long and illustrious career, your selfless adherence to duty and your unwavering respect of the Rules, which you have followed diligently and without mishap. We thank you for giving up the time you have left in order not to become a burden to the Collective, and to give up your place so that another may replace you. Your life was well spent and will serve as an example and inspiration to others, something of which you can be justly proud."

I had memorised the standard speech and it was timed to end when the resident reached the door of the Green Room. But Mr. Pink was slow to walk with his stick and had only got two thirds of the way there as I finished. Perhaps I should have spoken slower; I wasn't sure. I was new to this. He carried on to the door, then stopped and turned to face me.

"Thanks for seeing me off," he said with a smile. "Will you wait until I am gone?"

"I shall."

He put out his hand and I shook it warmly. I felt tears rising in my eyes and not because I knew him well or would miss him, but for the easy manner in which he gave up what he had left to support the Collective that cared nothing for him. He looked at the door, then back at me.

"That crap you just said," he asked. "Do you believe any of it?"

I was taken aback by his sudden change in demeanour.

"Of course," I said, firmly rattled, "we are all as branches and leaves and roots of the same tree, every bit as important as the—"

"No really," he said, interrupting me, "do you?"

He gazed at me intently. I think he wanted me to give him something of value that he could take with him into the Green Room: the truth.

"Actually," I said, "no—not a single word."

"Me neither," said Mr. Pink, "but I'm going anyway; I've had more than enough of all this. Will you tell the Prefects to all go and fuck themselves from me?"

"I probably won't, to be honest."

"Very wise," he said, "but the sentiment was there, and at least someone knew my mind before I had none."

He smiled, handed over his spoon—a small silver dessert with an SY6 postcode—then turned, opened the door to the Green Room and went inside. There was a pause as he fumbled his way to the central lounger, then a "clunk" as he pulled the lever that opened the shutters, flooding the chamber with light and illuminating the deadly shade of green within. There was silence, then a few "ooh's" and "aah's" as the green gave him a sense of wellbeing, but that soon changed to joy, then pleasure, then rapture. I listened to his moans as the multiple and cascading waves of intense pleasure went through his old and worn body, then, when the noise stopped, I waited the regulation twenty minutes, closed the shutters from the outside lever and called the renderers to come and fetch the body.

Thoroughly unnerved by my first Death Duty experience, I decided not to go to lunch in the communal area, so signed myself out of attendance and instead wandered over to the Fallen Man where I found Tommo in the corner seat, scribbling in a small notebook. He looked up and smiled through a face that was badly swollen. His spoon donors had taken badly to being fobbed off with book merits. They were promised, and wanted, cash. I sat down opposite him and ordered a cup of warm puddle water with a sprinkling of loam and shredded dandelion leaves.

"I'm telling everyone I fell downstairs," he said. "Twice. And if I don't find three thousand in cash by this time next month, I'll be found face down in a swamp somewhere, or drowned in an inexplicable shower accident. How are we going to find that money, Ed?"

"*We* don't need to find that money," I said, "*you* do. This is nothing to do with me. Cash merits are the smallest thing on my mind right now. I have a hearing at noon, and if Jane and I are found guilty, it's the Green Room."

"I could still take some pictures of Jane if she's game," he said, "but time is pressing so we'd really need to be at my studio by eleven."

I simply glared at him.

"Okay, okay," he said. "Just asking."

"Any news from the search party?" I asked as I stirred some second-best goat's milk into my puddle water.

"They went out at dawn. Daisy took two Penny-Farthings and riders with her so members of the team could ride back with news when they had some."

"And?"

"They found the Yellows' Ford, but no sign of anyone, and no reaction to yelling and whistling. They'll send another rider back with a message if there's any more news." He paused for a moment. "There isn't going to be any, is there?"

"No. What are you doing?" I asked, as he had been jotting in his notebook.

"Writing out copy for my first issue of the East Carmine *Mercury*. How does this sound: '*Found guilty of the charges laid before them, Eddie deMauve and Jane Brunswick took the news as any good citizen would, accepting their transgression with fortitude and bravery, and after thanking the Prefects for their fairness and due diligence, gratefully walked to the Green Room with a jaunty stride, their heads held high.*'"

"Thanks a bunch, Tommo."

"What would you prefer? '*Eddie and Jane wept like infants when they heard the verdict, then had to be tied, eyes stitched open and dragged to the Green Room and thrown inside?*'"

"What about us being found not guilty?"

"Oh," he said, staring at his notes, "is that even possible?"

I dropped into the Aspirational Living shop soon after, but Jane was nowhere to be found, so I headed home to change into my Formal #1s to look my best for the hearing.

DISCIPLINARY HEARING

The verdicts at disciplinary hearings were generally more arbitrary and political than nuanced or fair. It was mandatory for members of the public to appear, and these were chosen on the basis of a rota. They were there not to scrutinise proceedings but to see those punished as an example to everyone, and spread the news among the village. It was more theatre than court.

—Ted Grey: *Twenty Years Among the Chromatacians*

"The very apartness of the Collective is the glue that binds," said deMauve once we were all assembled in the Council chambers, "but the civic cohesion we enjoy comes at a cost. The Rules by which Our Munsell guides us are sometimes bruised by citizens who feel that the Collective has less to offer them than they can offer the Collective."

DeMauve had opened the disciplinary proceedings with a speech, as was normal for every event in our lives. Solstices, harvest, dinner, replacement of the public latrines, new calf, first cucumber of the season. He probably made a speech before opening his bowels.

"For those who stumble we will always find it in our hearts to help them fall easily and without undue pain," he carried on in a dreary monotone, "but for the malcontents who reject the Rules that bind there is the Disciplinary Panel, to judge those who would attempt to bring a serpent into this garden of Chromatic perfection." There was applause from all of us, even the accused—it made sense not to piss the Prefects off even more—but none of it sounded very enthusiastic, except from the Yellows, who really enjoyed this sort of thing.

It was now past noon and both of the Penny-Farthing messengers had returned with the news that none of Dog-Leg-Lake's Yellows could be found. The only evidence they'd been there at all was their Ford and a single knapsack, which contained uneaten sandwiches and a thermos. Daisy was due back soon but I didn't think there would be much else to report.

Aside from the accused, the public and the Deputy Prefects, there was the crusty-looking clerk and topiarist Mrs. Lilac, who recorded the hearings, and Tommo, who was busy scribbling in a notebook. I caught Violet's eye but she gazed through me as if I was already dead. I would have expected her to have already crossed out "married" in the back of her merit book and written "widowed" instead.

"Right," said deMauve, "let's get on with it."

We were not the only cases to be heard that day. First up was Nicola Lilac, who had got into a fight with Lottie Grey and broken her nose. After Nicola and Lottie's widely varying accounts were heard and witnesses attested to Nicola's often volatile temper and Lottie's good work for the community, it was decided that Nicola had been "subjected to a high level of impertinence from a lesser hue that would vex and annoy any normal human being." But to show that violence of any sort could not be tolerated, Nicola would be compelled to offer Lottie her pudding ration for a month. Equally, to show that forgiveness must be encouraged and that vindictiveness should not be tolerated, Lottie was compelled not to accept the puddings. They were both aged nine.

Next up was Cassie Flamingo who had been found with

banned technology. Bunty was the chief prosecutor in this case, which centred around a working gramophone, something I had seen in Cobalt's Museum of the Something that Happened, and advertised there as the last working example. Cassie was also found in possession of a circular musical playing disc by a performer named "Rick Astley." The case was not straightforward, and revolved around whether Bunty had a legal right to see into Cassie's overnight valise in which both were allegedly hidden.

Cassie was a sensible girl of good parentage, even if low hue, and made a good show in her defence.

"The Rules over the sanctity of the valise are clear cut and prescribed in Munsell's *Book of the Model Citizen*," she said in a respectful manner. "Under Rule 1.1.01.02.271 it states that: 'the personal valise of regulation size is a place for private possessions of whatever sort, to which no one may have access without the express permission of the owner.'"

Cassie pointed a finger at Bunty.

"Yellow Prefect McMustard only *maintains* she saw the gramophone and music disc in my case, but since she cannot furnish proof that I actually *have* said artifacture, then I call for this case to be dismissed over lack of evidence."

"Lack of evidence has never hampered this court before," said Bunty, "and I do not see why dangerous precedents should be introduced today. I swear I saw said gramophone with my own eyes, before Miss Flamingo rudely snapped the valise shut. What's more, the illegal artifacture is sitting before you."

The thing that was sitting before them was not the gramophone, but Cassie's valise, in which the gramophone was said to be stored. It was a mildly shabby leather case of regulation size, stained by water, knocked about a bit.

"Is the gramophone in your valise?" asked deMauve.

"It is not, sir."

"The punishment for lying to a Head Prefect is most severe. You understand that?"

"I do, sir."

"This can easily be remedied," said Turquoise. "Cassie, I request you to open your valise."

"I decline to do so," she said with a nervous tremor in her voice.

"The needs of law and order override your personal needs in this case. Cassie—*open your valise.*"

"I decline to do so."

DeMauve asked her, but she still refused, as was her right.

"Very well," said deMauve, "I declare that this case be adjourned while Miss McMustard continues her investigations. The valise, which has been entered in evidence, will be retained by the Council until the new hearing."

Cassie nodded her head graciously.

"I accept the judgement and will await the outcome of Miss McMustard's investigations."

The case would never come back to be tried again, and the valise would be retained indefinitely by the Council. If Cassie was smart—and she was—she would have foreseen this outcome and weighted a spare valise with river stones before the hearing.

The next three cases were minor infractions—running with scissors, uttering profanities and sneezing without putting a hand over the mouth. There was then Bunty's infraction of wearing work gloves, which was dismissed due to "lack of any reliable witnesses" and then, following that predictable outcome, it was our turn. The charge was simple: "the intentional taking of another's life." In this instance, Courtland Gamboge.

Mr. Celandine was the prosecutor in the case and had decided that if either of us was going to break, it was me. Once Sally Gamboge, Bunty McMustard and little Penelope Gamboge had all given lengthy and very tearful victim impact statements,

Celandine had me stand up and outline exactly what we had been doing when Courtland died.

"We were on a trip to High Saffron, a town on the coast. The Prefects asked us to go and see if the town was suitable for opening up for mining scrap colour. Many had gone on this trip, but none had returned."

"Your bravery is not in question here. And was it suitable?"

"I say not," I replied, "and we reported so. Thick undergrowth, a lot of megafauna, and Perpetulite only as far as Bleak Point. After that it's sixteen miles on foot. If High Saffron were to be opened up for mining, we would have to build a new road, or even railway."

"I see. And who made it to High Saffron?"

"Violet stayed at Bleak Point due to a sprained ankle, and Tommo went five miles further to a flak tower before turning back. From there, myself, Courtland and Jane walked down into High Saffron."

"And what did you find there?"

I wasn't going to tell him, but High Saffron was neither abandoned, nor unvisited. What we found was essentially the reason for the seditious work Jane and I were doing right now. A secret as dark as High Saffron shows that, despite deMauve's fine words, the Collective was irredeemably flawed.

"So," repeated Mr. Celandine, "what did you find there?"

"Nothing," I said, "it was overgrown, patches of clutching bramble and groves of yateveo trees. I would not recommend anyone return."

"And you expect me to believe that a yateveo took Courtland? He had attended a Health and Safety 'carnivorous tree awareness course' only the week before."

"He was rescuing me," I said, "when another took him. The trees were close packed and their roots overlapped."

"He rescued you?"

"Yes."

He stared at me for a moment, then at Jane.

"And you substantiate this tissue of lies?" he asked.

"Every detail."

Mr. Celandine turned to deMauve, and his tone changed.

"It is well known that Courtland despised the pair of you, and had said so on numerous occasions to his mother and sister. The idea that he would selflessly put himself—a future Prefect—in harm's way is so inexplicable an act that I can safely deduce he never did so, and instead offer another, more plausible explanation—that you pushed him under the tree while he was in an unguarded moment, an act that was both base and cowardly."

"That's not how it happened," I said.

"And how can we rely upon anything that passes the unreliable lips of Eddie Russett?" asked Celandine, who was really getting into his stride, "who came to the village to conduct a chair census, a ruse by his own Council to help him learn some much-needed humility? I can reveal Russett's own father was asked to leave the post of Swatchman at Jade-under-Lime over 'unspecified misdemeanours,' and I have evidence to suggest that Edward lied about seeing the Last Rabbit for financial gain. Do you deny any of that?"

"No, but how does that prove I've killed anyone?"

"It's a pattern of antisocial behaviour which if left unchecked—which it has been—leads to aberrant behaviour. We've seen this again and again and again."

"How many 'agains' was that?" said Tommo, who was struggling to keep up with the hearing.

"Three," said Mr. Celandine. "Now: Jane Brunswick, your partner in this outrage. This woman is a former *Grey* who has been familiar to the Disciplinary Panel since she was five, well known to exhibit aggressive and disrespectful mannerisms, and there are persisting rumours she killed a man."

"This is all irrelevant," said Jane. "You've got nothing. In fact, you've got less than nothing. Not a single shred of evidence links us to Courtland's death."

"You're wrong. You will not worm your way out of responsibility by the use of honeyed words and cowardly application of the strict letter of Rule. Luckily, more recent events have confirmed what we already knew: that the pair of you have a criminal propensity for disposing of Yellows."

He paused dramatically, then carried on.

"Five of our very finest, my son among them, were lost on a scavenger trip yesterday, at the exact same time and place that Jane and Edward were present. Coincidence? I think not. Was there any evidence that Jane *formerly Grey* and Edward *formerly Russett* had anything to do with it? No."

He paused for effect.

"And it is this pattern of lack of evidence that points the finger directly at them, for not only are they obviously very talented at murder, but equally very good at covering their tracks. One single scrap of evidence would be enough to cast a question mark over their guilt, or even be refuted and explained away, but there is nothing. The complete absence of anything at all to connect them with this crime was their fatal error: they had overthought it all, covered their tracks perfectly—and left us with no margin for doubt."

"That's an *extremely* good point," said deMauve, visibly impressed. "Well done."

Mrs. Gamboge nodded her head in appreciation, and I looked at Jane, who shrugged.

"An innocent person would also leave no evidence," said Jane. "I think that's pretty obvious."

"So *you* say," said Celandine, "but how can we believe a single word that comes out of your mouth when you have been lying all your life?"

"That's not true either."

"Another one! Is there an end to this girl's level of fabrication? I think we have heard enough; may I have a show of hands to decide guilt or otherwise?"

All the Prefects put up their hands with enthusiasm except Red Prefect Yewberry, who did so with reluctance. He looked at me and mouthed "I'm sorry."

The Yellows in the public gallery applauded politely, and Head Prefect deMauve cleared his throat. The room fell silent.

"The decision is unanimous," he said. "The defendants are guilty. There is only one punishment available to me: death by Green Room, and reduction to birth hue. Jane Brunswick is now Grey, Edward deMauve now Russett. In addition, due to a high flight risk and possibility of violence, I feel there is no other option but to invoke Special Ruling 1796-b/D whereby the guilty parties are to be bound hand and foot, have their eyelids stitched open and be dragged slowly through the Green Room on a rope attached to a donkey. This Council has spoken. Hold them, bind them, call for the seamstress—and fetch the donkey."

It explained why there were so many Yellows present, and my easy manner was replaced by a sudden sense of cold fear.

"I should like to see that Rule in black and white," shouted Jane as the Yellows moved towards us. "I do not believe it exists."

"You impugn the word of a Head Prefect?" said deMauve. "All you have done is confirm that our decision was utterly correct. And don't shout. It's unseemly."

We both put up a fight as eleven pairs of Yellow hands went to grab us. I only managed to hurt my hand as I punched the side of Geoff Lemon's head before being held down, while Jane's defence was considerably more spirited: she handed out two black eyes, a foot in the plums for Tommy Yellow and evidence of her overbite on several forearms before she was eventually subdued.

"I like a story with a happy ending," said Mrs. Gamboge with a rare smile as our hands were bound behind our backs. "The death of my son will be avenged, and most gloriously."

The seamstress then arrived, who was, unluckily for us, a Gamboge-by-marriage. She was ordered to sew our eyelids open and as she threaded a needle with some button thread, I started to struggle, but did not cry out. Jane didn't, so neither would I.

DAISY PULLS IT OFF

Not all food and vegetable waste was put in the biodigesters to be converted to methane. Although grass clippings, worn-out clothes, nail clippings and shredded copies of *Spectrum* could make up half the clutching bramble's food, it still needed some meaty matter, so unwanted offal was slopped on its roots, along with any diseased animal that chanced along; a dead bison too far gone for human consumption was considered an ideal snack.

    —Ted Grey: *Twenty Years Among the Chromatacians*

I was first in line to be stitched and the needle with thread was actually through my eyelid when the Council chamber door opened and Daisy Crimson walked in, followed by Carlos Fandango and Mrs. Ochre. Daisy had an abrupt, businesslike air to her stride, as one who had something to say and would not be happy until they had said it.

"Am I too late?" she said. "I have crucial evidence that the Council must hear—evidence of a compelling nature that proves beyond doubt that a dagger has been thrust into the very heart of Chromatic harmony."

"We've sort of finished," said deMauve.

Daisy looked at us both, and decided she would have to insist.

"Begging your pardon, sir, but I think that evidence of such criminality is best put on the public record, so that all may know the depth of depravity to which these people have fallen."

"That does actually sound quite appealing," said Mrs. Gamboge, "and although we can't Green Room them twice—worse luck—I would dearly love to besmirch their names further in order to more fully discourage anyone who might think to follow in their footsteps."

"Very well," said deMauve, "we will reconvene the hearing so the full details of what you have found can be entered into the record."

So everyone sat down again and deMauve placed the hearing back into session, temporarily setting aside the verdict, but keeping our wrists bound and the button thread still through my eyelid "to save the effort of doing it all again."

"I have just returned from Crimsonolia," said Daisy, "and although there was no trace of the Yellows from Dog-Leg-Lake, I did find evidence of a conspiracy so debauched that I was at first incredulous."

I looked at Tommo, who suddenly looked worried.

"To confirm my theory, I went looking for corroborating evidence and found it, here in East Carmine."

Tommo began to sink even lower in his chair.

"Marvellous," said Mrs. Gamboge with a grin, "tell us *exactly* how you know Russett and Grey murdered my son."

Daisy looked around the room.

"This is not evidence of murder, but *attempted* murder—by a posse of Yellows who were sent to ensure two people did not return to their village. And they did it on the express orders of Mrs. Gamboge and Mr. Celandine, with the likely tacit support of Head Prefect deMauve."

There was a sudden and very sickly silence. Only Tommo seemed to look relieved, and he sat up and started to scribble on his pad again. "This is *totally* out of order," said deMauve. "Miss Crimson, you will be forcefully confined to your house while we investigate the very serious charge of impugning without foundation the good reputation of upright and respected Prefects."

The Yellows who had so eagerly bound us made a move towards Daisy.

"Wait!"

It was Yewberry, the Red Prefect.

"I wish to hear what she has to say."

"Reds," spat Gamboge contemptuously, "always sticking together, like sewer rats."

"And Yellows do not?" he asked in an even tone. There was a long pause. The Rules were quite clear on minority dissent. Matters of "extreme gravity" had to be unanimous.

"Very well," said deMauve, glaring at Yewberry, "but your evidence better be ironclad, or you will find yourself charged with an attempt to pervert the smooth running of the village, and at least thirty other Rules—many of them punishable by the Green Room. I shall magnanimously give you the chance to withdraw your allegations right now, and in return we will forgive your little outburst and you can be on your way."

"I shall not," said Daisy, unfazed by his threats. "There was a telegram sent from this telegraph office to the one at Dog-Leg-Lake, with Jane and Eddie's description, explaining when they would be there, that it would be advantageous to East Carmine that they should not return, nor ever be found—but that Mr. Cinnabar was not to be molested."

Gamboge and Celandine looked at one another.

"This telegram was found in the wallet of Torquil Celandine," said Daisy. "Dropped in the ruins of Crimsonolia. Mrs. Ochre the telegraph operator will confirm that you, Mr. Celandine, sent several telegrams with Mrs. Gamboge by your side. She also heard you say that this would 'sort out Violet's marriage problems once and for all' and that Head Prefect deMauve had sanctioned it."

"Lies," said Mrs. Gamboge, "and eavesdropping on Prefect business is privileged information that is inadmissible as evidence."

"Not," said Velma, "when it uncovers corruption and wrong-doing."

"I have heard enough of this nonsense," said deMauve. "We will interview Mrs. Ochre in private to ensure her truthfulness, and you will surrender the telegram so we can establish whether it is genuine—which I suspect it is not. It is my view," he concluded, "that Daisy Crimson has been put up to this by Edward deMauve and Jane Brunswick in order to release them from charges. Mr. Cinnabar, stop writing."

"Yes, sir."

"The evidence you ask for, the telegram, I do not possess," said Daisy.

"Hah!" said Gamboge. "Just as I suspected. Bare-faced lies of the worst sort."

". . . because I sent it immediately with a rider to the Council at Vermillion, as required under Rule 1.4.69.20.88, when corruption of a Council is suspected."

There was another long pause.

"It is my suggestion you resign," said Daisy, "while you still have the option of retiring without punishment, citing over-work."

This was indeed true. The Rules permitted Prefects to essentially dodge retribution if they *instantly* resigned their posts—a reward, it was said, for the stressful burden of leadership and civic duty, and a way of dealing with corruption internally without protracted and damaging investigations.

"If Prefects do not resign and an off-village tribunal is convened," said Mrs. Lilac, finally doing her job as the clerk correctly, "and the evidence is proven, the punishment is enforced Green Room. Rule 1.4.69.21.31."

No one said anything for a long time. Turquoise was the first to speak, and simply said: "I am retiring from the Prefecture with immediate effect and renouncing all my duties and responsibilities. So make a note, Mrs. Lilac."

He then took off his Prefect badge and placed it in the centre of the table. There were no bad apples when it came to Prefects. It was the responsibility of all Prefects to maintain the integrity of the whole—a crime by one was a crime by them all.

"A conspiracy," growled Mrs. Gamboge, "by the Reds. They were never trustworthy, and so it has been proved. Mrs. Ochre, you have done a terrible thing here today."

Velma bristled at the suggestion and, her lips loosened by Turquoise's retirement and the injustice done unto her first husband, decided to speak her mind.

"*You* are the disgrace, Mrs. Gamboge. For too long your family has run roughshod over the lives of the villagers and seen fit to cajole and bully us all for personal gain. You applied for a reallocation of Travis Canary's postcode to your own daughter the day *before* he was found dead. I speak bold words, but they are not only mine, but from the pulse and core of the village, who despise you more than you can possibly imagine."

The deathly hush was broken by Mr. Yewberry.

"I am with Mr. Turquoise on this," he said, as he also removed his Prefect badge, "and I am appalled at what I have seen today, and for the part I played in allowing Mrs. Gamboge's excesses to multiply and darken. I too resign my position."

DeMauve glared at Daisy.

"I hope you know the damage you have done here today, Miss Crimson," he said.

"I have done only what the *Book of Harmony* asks of anyone," said Daisy, "without falsity or malice. It is those who bruise the harmony who have done the damage, not I."

DeMauve sighed, also removed his badge and handed it straight to Violet, who took it, pinned it on her dress and then sat in the warm seat that her father had just vacated. She then placed her hand on the *Book of Harmony* and repeated the oath that she had been practising daily since childhood.

"I, Violet Elizabeth deMauve, do hereby accept the responsibilities of Head Prefect and swear on the *Book of Harmony* to uphold the Word of Munsell to the very best of my ability, and protect the Collective and all within it from harm, without falsity or favour, for as long as I remain in this post."

The room was stunned into silence, as events had taken a very rapid about face. DeMauve had been in the Head Prefect role more than thirty years, and was gone in under a minute.

"Mrs. Gamboge," said now-Head Prefect Violet deMauve, "you are to voluntarily hand in your badge or it will be noted in the minutes that it had to be forcibly removed."

Mrs. Gamboge glared at everyone in the room, tossed her badge on the table and went and sat at the back of the Council chambers. Tellingly, only those Yellows who were family followed. The others simply waited for an opportunity to show their undying allegiance to their new leader. Yellows were like that.

"Bunty McMustard," said Violet, "as the next ranking Yellow, you shall become Yellow Prefect with immediate effect."

Bunty nodded graciously and took her seat, too.

"The role of Blue Prefect shall be Jerry Turquoise."

He had to be nudged awake, and it was hurriedly explained to him that he now had his father's job.

"Really?" he said. "Gosh."

Jerry Turquoise and Bunty also recited the oath of office—they had doubtless been practising—and Violet deMauve spoke again.

"Now: the Red Prefect."

It was just about at this moment that I, slow on the uptake after the recent events and still with a piece of thread through my eyelid, realised that *I* was the ranking Red after Mr. Yewberry. Violet knew it too. She picked up the Red Prefect badge, looked at it, then at me, then her father.

"As regards the recent disciplinary hearing," continued Violet, "I will submit to the Council that the charges against Jane Brunswick and Edward deMauve are unsafe and utterly without merit. They shall be released immediately with the Council's apologies and are immune from any further proceedings in these matters."

"Thank you, Head Prefect," said Jane.

"Thank you, wife," I said, "and I would be honoured to become—"

"—however," she continued, "the charges and verdict remain in place until I have, as previously stated, conferred with the Council. Until such time as that formality is dealt with, you are restored to hue but ineligible to become Prefect. Father?"

"Yes, Head Prefect?"

"Did Mr. Yewberry to your knowledge have anything to do with the outrage that was heard this afternoon?"

"No, Head Prefect," said deMauve, bowing politely. "Mr. Yewberry's conduct has always been exemplary."

"I second that," said Mrs. Gamboge, who could see where this was going, "even though we are innocent of the scurrilous charges against us, Mr. Yewberry knew nothing of what it's . . . alleged we did."

"Very well," said Violet, "it is my view that continuity of governance is required to maintain a smooth transition of power, and I invite Mr. Yewberry to be acting Red Prefect until such time as Mr. deMauve is released from the charges."

"Well done," I said, "spoken and acted like a true deMauve."

"I will interpret that comment favourably, husband," she said, "but caution you to mind your manners. We are married, true, but I *am* Head Prefect."

Despite the recent turn of events, all was not yet safe and clear for Jane and me in East Carmine. Mr. Yewberry agreed to Violet's request, and replaced the Prefect badge upon his lapel, but inverted, as the Rules required.

I very delicately pulled the thread out of my eyelid, which felt very odd indeed.

"As for Daisy Crimson," continued Violet, "whose adherence to the Rules was so amply displayed this afternoon, she has the thanks of the Council and will be rewarded five hundred merits and a day train pass to Emerald City to view the sights. Mr. Celandine, your presence in this village is no longer needed, nor required, nor desired. You shall leave on the next train, and I will send an account of your conduct to your Head Prefect in Dog-Leg-Lake."

"Might you reconsider?" he pleaded. "And simply write it all off as a simple misunderstanding?"

"I shall not," she said. "The deMauves once stood for probity and honesty and I shall see that they do so again."

Celandine could do little except dip his head in agreement, while flashing an angry look at Gamboge.

"Are you getting all this down, Mr. Cinnabar?" said Violet. "The prompt actions by the new Council as regards adherence to the Rules will be your front-page story."

"Yes, ma'am," said Tommo, who had the biggest scoop of the past half-century in his very first edition of the *Mercury*.

"Good," said Violet, looking around the room. DeMauve was staring at the floor and Sally Gamboge and Mr. Celandine were seething quietly to themselves. "This Council session is over. Father? I will see you in my chambers immediately."

NEW STATUS, NEW JOB

Breaks in the feed-pipes were not uncommon, but highly damaging as any Colour Garden downstream of the feed-pipe would be denied full CMYK colour gamut, and start to look off-colour. Feed-pipe fractures were easily discovered due to the large colour stain that would leach into the surrounding land and trees; I'd seen an oak tree stained entirely purple once.
—Ted Grey: *Twenty Years Among the Chromatacians*

We walked out of the Council offices and to the Fallen Man, our minds in something of a whirl. We ordered a round of butter and crumpets and a chalk latte each and then, after a long pause, I said:

"Jane, did you have a hand in any of that?"

"It surprised even me," she said, and we fell back into silence. I touched my eyelid, which was still sore from where the needle and thread had gone through. It had bled a small amount, but soon stopped.

"Close," I said.

"Close," agreed Jane. "Hi, Daisy."

Daisy Crimson had just walked in the door of the café. She saw us and came over.

"Trouble just seems to follow you around, doesn't it?" she said as she sat down next to us and took a sip of my latte. "All I want to do now is Lime myself into oblivion. I'm not doing that again. Do you think there will be reprisals?"

When a Prefect is removed from office all the details are sent to at least three other villages for oversight. If there were any discrepancies found, the matter would be sent onward for appraisal to Head Office. For that reason, a new Head Prefect would want to do everything strictly by the book, since they were being observed.

"I think probably not," I said, "but be careful. If you need help, we are here for you."

"I did it because a sense of justice tasked me to do so," said Daisy, lowering her voice, "not for you, although I'm glad you're not to be Greened. Sally Gamboge I shed no tears for, but Yewberry and Turquoise had done no particular wrong. Violet, however, worries me. Old Man deMauve wasn't possessed of the finest mind, but Violet I think is different altogether—and I don't mean for the better. I may have just upset a hornet's nest while trying to kill a fly." She took a deep breath. "Look, no offence or anything, but stay away from me from now on, okay?"

"I'll miss your friendship," said Jane.

"And I, too," said Daisy.

And she got up, smiled at us both, and walked away.

We talked around what had just happened, finished the crumpets and ordered some more, and then ate those. As we made ready to go, Bunty walked in and indicated for us to stay where we were.

"Good afternoon," she said.

"Good afternoon, Prefect McMustard," we said, pretty much in unison, with me adding: "Congratulations on your new appointment. I trust we can put aside old differences and move forward together?"

She ignored me and leaned closer.

"As the Head Prefect stated we can't touch either of you for any of that stuff, so what *did* happen to the Dog-Leg-Lake Yellows?"

"An Angel descended from on high and smote the Yellows as punishment for evil intent."

I don't know why I said it, but I did.

"Yes, of course," she said, "an Angel. I should have realised. Silly me. Sarcasm isn't against the Rules, deMauve, but it's easily defined as *backchat*, which is. But since it's customary for a new Prefect to *not* give out demerits on their first day, you can have a free pass on that one."

"Speaking of which," I said, "I was on Death Duties this morning and Mr. Pink had a last word message for the Prefects."

"Who's Mr. Pink?"

"The guy who made all the chutney. He was here about forty years."

"Ah, yes—what was it?"

"He said the Prefects should all go and fuck themselves."

She stared at me for a moment, not quite believing what I had just said, while Jane giggled audibly. Bunty looked at her, then back to me, then went bright red, like a radish.

"Outrageous. How *dare* you. That is the second most forbidden of words and—"

"It was a last word message, Bunty. I was honour bound to deliver it. Would you have me deny the final wishes of a respected member of the community, and the driving force of East Carmine's one-person chutney industry?"

She looked at the pair of us in turn, then lowered her voice. "You got away with it this time, but the next time either of you steps out of line, me, the Yellows and the Council will be down on you like a ton of bricks."

"Yes, Prefect," said Jane innocently, "I think we've learned our lesson."

"I very much hope you have. Jane, do you have somewhere to be? Mr. deMauve and I need to speak in private."

Jane nodded, gave me a kiss much to Bunty's disgust and took her leave, presumably to continue her work at the Aspirational Living shop—an acquittal didn't mean you got the day off. Bunty waited until Jane had left the café, then turned to me.

"Look," she said, trying to sound all conciliatory and understanding, "we understand that Jane can be . . . *intimidatory* and we want you to know that if you feel you are being coerced, you can always come to us and talk it through. My office door is open, and Jane never has to know. Sign an affidavit saying she lied while giving testimony and we can have her in the Green Room the same day—I've been authorised to offer a thousand merits as a reward. And in *cash.*"

"It all went down as we said, Bunts. I wish you and Vi could accept that."

"Final answer?"

"Final answer. I think we're done."

She consulted her ever-present clipboard.

"Not quite. Firstly, you will never refer to me as 'Bunts' again without a demerit, and 'Vi' shall not be used to refer to a respected Head Prefect. You may have pet names to use in private, but in public you can and will show all due deference. Now, what are your current duties?"

"Head of Invasive Alien Eradication, Boundary Patrol, Death Duties and Chief Red Colour Sorter," I replied, as coldly as I could.

"Not anymore. Doug will look after rhododendrons, for you are no longer permitted to go beyond the village boundary."

"And the Rule that allows this?"

"5.1.1.3.27 in the *Book of Marriage*: 'A resident who is deemed of high value in regards to breeding opportunities can be compelled by force to remain in the village if the Head Prefect demands it.'"

"Breeding opportunities?"

"I don't make the Rules," she said, "and they are implemented only for your safety."

I'd not heard of the Rule, nor knew if it even existed. I could always ask to see the Rule, of course, but by long and painful tradition, no one ever did. It was tantamount to calling a Prefect a liar, and right here and now, that probably wouldn't be a great idea. I sighed.

"For how long?"

"Violet says until she can trust you, as you slept away from the marital bed last night without written permission, contrary to Rule 5.1.1.4.09. There are also persisting and credible rumours of an extramarital liaison with Jane. You are to sleep only with your wife from now on, and pledge fidelity to your chosen spouse."

"Anything else?" I asked in a bored voice.

"Yes. Your new work allocation is head of the linoleum factory, with personal responsibility for targets and production. You shall keep the job as Boundary Patrol Overseer, and in addition become Completion Supervisor of the ninety-thousand-piece jigsaw puzzle, which is at least seventy years past completion target, and Head Prefect deMauve would like residents to see you doing it during all your leisure hours—she thinks it is an underused resource to stave off indolence on rainy afternoons. You are expected at the linoleum factory for handover in twenty minutes. I have assigned a trustworthy Yellow to be with you at all times to ensure compliance."

I looked around and there stood Penelope Gamboge, Sally's granddaughter and possibly next in line after Bunty to be Yellow Prefect. She was only nine and thoroughly detestable already, or, as the Yellows might describe it: "shaping up nicely."

"Any questions?"

"Yes," I said, "what's for dinner?"

"It'll be on the board, as usual. Good day, Edward—and remember: you can always come and talk to us about Jane. An affidavit implicating Jane in wrongdoing would be a very wise move. You better get yourself to the factory; they're expecting you."

THE LINOLEUM FACTORY was on the area of land near the railway station that was traditionally reserved for manufacture. As progressive technological Leapbacks made more and more industries redundant, the area had shrunk in size and importance. The derelict remains of other factories were dotted around the area, and since the closure of the enamelling plant six years before and the trouser factory eleven years before *that*, linoleum was all that East Carmine exported. I'd never been inside the factory building, just heard the clanking of machinery from within and smelled the whiff of hot linseed on the breeze.

"Do I call you Penny or Penelope?" I asked the third youngest Gamboge, who was following at a discreet distance.

"I care not a fig," she said, "and I don't wish to talk with you."

We were overtaken on the walk to the factory by ex-Prefect Sally Gamboge in a cycle-taxi going at double speed, and when I was shown to the factory manager's office with Penelope left outside, Sally was heaping papers into a case and clearing her desk.

"Is there a handover procedure?" I asked. "I have no experience of running a factory."

"Good to hear," said Gamboge. "The sooner you fall flat on your face, the sooner will be my rejoicing. I am glad to be done with it—attempting to draw any kind of productive toil from the workshy Greys is a soul-destroying endeavour that has given me nothing but grief. Good luck to you."

And so saying, she walked out.

"Oh dear," said Samantha Grey, who was the one who had shown me in and turned out to be the office manager and the person who actually did the day-to-day running of the factory. "She didn't seem very happy—but then she never was. Is it true that deMauve is out and Violet is in?"

I told her what had happened, and she took this all in, biting her lip anxiously. Births, marriages, harvest festival, plays, winter solstice celebrations, musical opera and Jollity Fair were big of course, but something that impacted our lives more than anything was a change of prefectural management, as it brought in a fresh interpretation of the Rules, and that meant uncertainty—something that was generally absent from our lives, as Our Munsell had long intended.

"Oh well," said Samantha with a shrug. "I can't imagine Bunty and Violet being worse than Gamboge and the Old Man, but I suppose it must be possible, at least in theory."

I sat down behind the large manager's desk. There were charts on the wall which displayed manufacturing targets, actual production, and demand—the first being high, the second low, and the last ambiguous.

"You're right, it is very misleading," explained Samantha when I questioned her. "The targets are for a demand that existed when Chromatacia was almost ten times the size it is now. I have it on good authority that unwanted linoleum is simply cut up and burned in the grate as heating fuel."

"Do sales of linoleum generate much revenue?" I asked.

"None at all," she replied, "and since our manufacturing targets are pegged at one hundred and five percent to encourage productivity, the penalties for those missed targets soak up any profit if we made any, which we don't. Manufacturing policy in Chromatacia is designed, it seems, for making no profit, an impossibly high output and the workforce working flat out to achieve nothing at all. We're simply chasing our tails."

"I think that's probably the intention."

I had a thought. The shabbiness of the village, lack of any colourisation and minimal linoleum sales figures pointed towards one thing.

"Does the village have any money at all?"

"None at all," she said. "All our spare cash went on that dumb crackletrap project of Sally Gamboge's—thousands of communal merits for something that is utterly pointless. In fact, we even *borrowed* money from the Red Sector Mutual Fund Society to finance it. It's hard to pay back a loan with no merits, and little chance to earn any."

It explained why deMauve wasn't ever going to pay cash for Tommo's spoons.

"Hello," said a Grey who had just walked in, "I'm Jethro, the foreman. You're Jane's fella, aren't you?"

"Not officially. You know her well?"

"I've been in love with her ever since—no, wait, I've been in *awe* of her ever since I was six. And I'm not the only one. She's taken a shine to you though. Why is that?"

"To be honest? I've not the faintest idea. I think I just got lucky. Now: you better show me how you make linoleum."

For the next two hours I was schooled on the way of linoleum, which is a relatively simple process and was basically linseed oil and pine resin mixed with sawdust and then pushed with heat into a canvas backing. I also learned that the power that ran the factory was exempted Everspins and harmonic induction coils for heating, and how Gamboge had worked everyone ridiculously long hours to try and meet the targets, and removed any safety features that she felt "slowed production."

"I think she had more interest in demoralising the workforce than meeting the targets," said Jethro once we had got back to the office and were having a chat over a glass of cloudy water while looking longingly at a recipe for custard creams. "I think she felt that increased toil would somehow make us better people."

"I think she's just mean and bitter and twisted inside," said Sam.

I liked their unguarded talk. They knew about Jane and me, and although they knew I had never been Grey, saw me as an ally.

"How many people actually work here?" I asked.

They took me through the staff rota, and outlined who was up for retirement, and how much holiday time was due. By the time the whistle had blown to announce the change to the evening shift, I had a reasonable idea of how the factory worked, the huge amount of linoleum produced, and the meagre income it generated.

"Okay," I said, "this is what we'll do. Anyone who is overdue for retirement is retired from the end of their next shift. Anyone *owed* holiday entitlement can take alternate weeks off starting today until the deficit is repaid. Given all that, how much production do we have to cut?"

Samantha and Jethro went into a flurry of what-if scenarios and production projections, and started scribbling on bits of paper and, after a while, had to break the "In Emergency Need of Calculations Break Glass" to view a light shade of maths skill ochre to check their results.

"We can deliver about one twentieth of what we're producing right now," said Samantha in a nervous whisper, absently doing complex sums on a pad, because she could for the next twenty minutes.

"Perfect," I said, "make it happen."

"Are you sure?" asked Jethro. "That's woefully short of our assigned production target. The Head Prefect will go potty."

"I'm her husband," I said. "She'll not punish me publicly.

Besides, we were never meant to hit the targets, and even if you do, they'll only raise them."

"But what will Head Office say?"

"I don't know," I said, "but we've not met our scrap colour targets for decades, and I don't see anyone punishing us for that. Call me if you need anything clarified, I'm heading back to town. Is there a back door? Penelope's shadowing me and I want to annoy her."

"It's this way," said Samantha, beckoning me down a corridor. "Is it true Bunty's got you on jigsaw completion duty?"

"Bad news travels fast."

VIOLET TELLS US HOW IT IS

Your position in life was fixed the moment you took your Ishihara. All life's uncertainties banished for ever, and your position, power, expectations and career all laid out for you. "Choice," went the Word of Munsell, "leads only to dithering and unhealthy speculation over alternative outcomes. The choice to have no choice is the best choice of all."

—Ted Grey: *Twenty Years Among the Chromatacians*

The Aspirational Living shop was closed when I got back to the village, so I changed into my Casual Evening #2s and went around to the Fallen Man to see if Jane was there. She was sitting at her usual table next to the window doodling on a pad with a glass of weak puddle water in front of her. When I pushed the door open several Greys nodded their heads in respect. It was incumbent on all citizens to show due deference to greater hues, but here it actually felt genuine. The news about the linoleum factory retirements and holiday allowances had gone around the village like a rash.

I sat opposite Jane and the table cleared of people in a respectful manner to give us some privacy, even though the café was quite full.

"Hey," I said.

"Hey," she said.

A warm muddy milk and a currantless currant bun were put in front of me.

"On the house," said Melanie who was on shift. "Mum's orders. I stirred in some liquorice and quinoa for good measure. My aunt said to tell you she was sorry about the eyelid. She was told to do it."

I told her there were no ill feelings, thanked her and had a taste of the muddy milk. It was surprisingly good.

"I hear good things coming out of the linoleum factory," said Jane.

"For the time being. Bunty offered me a thousand merits to dob you in for killing Courtland." Jane chuckled.

"They'll try anything. What did . . ."

Her voice trailed off as the door opened and Violet walked in. The tearoom, which up until that moment had been full of lively conversation, suddenly went deathly quiet, and everyone stood up and gave their new Head Prefect a less-than-enthusiastic three cheers. She gave a short speech thanking them, then made her way to our table and sat down. She looked at Jane, then me, then to the rest of the tearoom, who, wary of her power and demeanour, decided it was in their best interests to be elsewhere—in under a minute we were the only ones in the café.

Violet reached out and squeezed my hand with mock affection, then turned to Jane.

"Now," she said in a businesslike tone, and not at all with the silly girly affectation we had become used to, "we've had our differences in the past, Jane, and while I was willing to turn a blind eye to you and Edward here diddling away while you worked it out of your system, now that I am Head Prefect it must end. Edward's place is by my side, and he will live with me in my house from now on, as befits the consort of a Head Prefect, and undertake all husbandly duties—both official and conjugal—as I see fit, and when and where and how I command it."

"Your father, Mr. Celandine and Gamboge just tried to have

us killed," said Jane. "It is only by extreme good fortune that we are not working our way through a jackal's digestive tract right now."

Violet narrowed her eyes and thought for a moment.

"And they have paid the price for their alleged—not proven—connection to the crime. And by retiring in a timely manner to a life of quiet non-involvement, they have courageously and selflessly ensured that the transition of village responsibility is smooth and unbroken."

We didn't say anything, so she continued.

"A recent audit of the Chromatic distribution of the village has revealed that we are heavy on the Greens—six are to be repatriated to Green Sector East, actioned immediately. I will be asking for volunteers, but I have the power to repatriate non-consensually if I so wish. At this point I will not insist Jane is to go, but in exchange for this benevolence I expect not to be humiliated in my job or my marriage. Do we understand one another?"

"This is not a kindness, Violet—you need my win at Jollity Fair."

"Perhaps, but not at any cost. Besides, I've heard that Jamie 'Mad Dog' Juniper is dangerously insane and you would be very lucky to survive the race, let alone win."

"I'll beat Mad Dog," said Jane. "You can be sure of that."

They stared at one another. This was sort of meant to be about me and Jane and Violet, but right now I think it was more about Jane and Violet.

"So," said Violet, "do we understand one another?"

"I understand the emptiness of your threats. Eddie and I have no plans in giving one another up."

Violet looked across at me.

"Is this true?"

"What? Yes, I'm—um—sorry to say that it is."

I had intended to sound strong and assertive, but I gave off a mild squeak with my nervousness.

Violet looked back at Jane and was silent for some time.

"The job of Head Porter is up for review quite soon," she said, changing tack, "and a change might be beneficial, don't you think?"

Jane's father had been Head Porter for almost twenty years, and was the de facto Head Grey. It was an important job, he was popular among the Greys, and he did it well.

"You wouldn't dare."

"Wouldn't I?"

"There are seven hundred and twenty-two Greys in East Carmine," said Jane, lowering her voice into a tone that was only just above threatening, "and they may decide to withdraw their labour if they felt that my father had been removed from his job unfairly. Would you like that sort of fuss and bother in the village within a week of taking over?"

"That degree of fuss and bother," said Violet, also lowering her voice, "would be highly unwise."

They glared at one another dangerously.

"Listen to me," said Violet, "there was a certain degree of fuss and bother in Rusty Hill before everyone died of the Mildew, so motivating the Greys to an aggressive level of disruption could have severe consequences. Not to me, obviously, because my family and I can go to Purple Regis at the drop of a hat. A safe haven. If the Rusty Hill Purples had known what was coming to them, they'd have done the same."

What had happened at Rusty Hill was no longer a mystery. The *Book of Harmony* was often arbitrary and capricious, but at least there was a process of some kind. But in extreme circumstances, a new set of rules came into play: a mass killing brought from on high by a Pale Rider was without any process at all. A cull. Prefects with Greys, all equal in a final judgement—and by someone we couldn't see, we didn't know about and who lived somewhere we couldn't imagine: the Someone Else from Somewhere Else. I think Jane and I knew in that moment that we couldn't win against the system, because our fight was not with the system, it was with the unseen hand that *controlled* the system.

"Shit," said Jane as the enormity of this sunk in.

"Well now," said Violet with a smile, "I think we understand one another. It's far better for all concerned to follow the Head Prefect's orders. And perhaps it's a good time to mention that the village Swatchman, your father, Eddie, will be taking a two-week much-earned holiday, and his place is to be taken by the Supervisory Substitute."

I felt myself grow cold when she said it. A Supervisory Substitute, Dad had said, only came to administer one thing: Mildew to any people the resident Swatchman declined to infect.

"What's the matter?" she asked, sensing my disquiet.

"Nothing."

"Good. So to recap: Edward is mine and will remain so until I decide otherwise. Your father keeps his job and you get to ride at Jollity Fair. Do we have a deal?"

"You have a deal," I said, before this got any worse. The way I saw it, Violet held many of the cards, and I needed some freedom to play some of them when she wasn't looking—and to do that, I needed to be close. Just not too close, obviously.

"Okay then," said Jane, figuring what I was thinking, "you win, Violet."

"My favourite words," she said, reverting to the little girl affectation. "I just want us all to be friends. But to ensure discretion I will be monitoring dear Edward for a couple of weeks—I have an army of Yellows who simply love all that sort of stuff."

Violet smiled at us both, which we returned half-heartedly,

and then left the café, leaving us alone with the hissing of the tea-maker. But Violet and her deals and her concerns over humiliation were soon gone and replaced with more pressing issues: culls and the reason they happen, and the Substitute Swatchman.

"Fuss and disunity and disruption are only allowed to go so far before our Creator wipes outs an entire village—or even a Sector," said Jane.

"Why?" I asked.

"I don't know. This Creator of ours is judgemental rather than benevolent, vengeful rather than forgiving. Why create us, study us, track our progress across five centuries then kill us all on little more than a whim?"

"We don't know enough to say for sure it's a whim," I replied. "The Munsell Doctrine is about stasis. Maybe that's what our Creator wants too. Subjects on a Reserve doing little for a long period of time. So what do we do?"

Jane shrugged.

"Rethink everything—and take this argument to the Creator. We'll go to Jollity Fair with honourable intent to speak to the Herald, as your mother did. If they Mildewed her because of it, then that's the sort of information we need right now—the sort that can get you killed."

She looked up at me with her large inquisitive eyes and her oh-so-perfect retroussé nose. Getting to Jollity Fair was a sound idea, and as a bonus I might see something two-headed and anthropological human curiosities preserved in jars.

"The game's changed, Eddie."

"No," I said, having a rare flash of what I thought was keen understanding, "the game's *exactly* the same—it's just the target that's moved."

JIGSAW PUZZLE

There are three carnivorous plants in the Collective that could be hazardous to health. The most notable being the yateveo, which can grow large enough to take a small horse. It is thought to be related to the clutching bramble, more of a static "trapping" plant. The third is the bodyjack, a fungus that releases hallucinogenic spores which cause the victim to eat it, which then poisons the host and feeds on the body from within.

—Ted Grey: *Twenty Years Among the Chromatacians*

"I thought I'd find you here," said Tommo, who had dropped in to see what I was up to that evening. The jigsaw room was by a very long margin the most disused room in any of the villages across the nation. It was joked that someone might die doing the jigsaw and would not be discovered for years, and that the area beneath the large central table was a good place for illegal trysts if the Outer Markers were too far in a moment of libidinal urgency.

The solving table was large, perfectly smooth and tattered remnants at the edges suggested it had once been covered in felt. It had netted pockets at each corner and in the centre of the long edges, presumably for some puzzle-solving technique now lost to history.

"I'm just doing what I'm told for the moment," I said, staring at the unfinished puzzle. It was over ninety thousand pieces and it didn't help that there was a lot of sky and sand in the picture, and that sometime in the puzzle's life, water had leaked in and discoloured some of the pieces.

"A wise move," said Tommo, "and look, I'll come straight to the point: I'd like to get to Jollity Fair this year to exploit some business opportunities and I was hoping you might be able to swing it with your wife."

"I don't expect she would listen to anything I have to say," I said. "Take it to Mr. Turquoise—he's in charge of Jollity Fair passes. Stay a while and do a few pieces, why don't you?"

"Love to," said Tommo, backing towards the door. "You can totally rely on me."

And he was gone.

It was now an hour after dinner had ended, and my first sitting at High Table had been mostly ornamental. My status as Head Prefect's husband required me to remain in a demure and supportive role and not have much of an opinion on anything.

After Violet had performed a numbingly boring speech—like father, like daughter—we ate and then for after-dinner entertainment Bunty performed a solo on her subcontrabass tuba. Although spirited and demonstrating a considerable level of lung capacity, she passed out as she finished the solo, something she had expected as she had thoughtfully surrounded her playing area with cushions. Sadly, it was not fatal and she recovered quickly.

I managed a brief word with Tania, who thanked me for organising for Clifton to pop round the night before as it was, she told me: "the most fun I've had in the deMauve house ever." Once dinner was over, Violet had Penelope Gamboge escort me to the jigsaw room and to then sit outside on guard, which explained why I was here doing the ninety-thousand-piece puzzle, thinking of whether it had been the Angel Hanson who disposed of everyone in Rusty Hill with that odd floating globe of his, and how easy that would be.

I stared at the puzzle blankly. There was a lot of sky and a lot of sand. The only easy bit—a boat lying high and dry on the flats—had been completed when the puzzle was started, one hundred and seventy-six years before. I could be precise because the puzzle log said so. It also told me that the last piece had been placed six months ago, and for seventeen years before that no one had placed any pieces at all. Apparently Lucy Ochre had run the numbers and calculated that at current solving rates, it would be done in two hundred and eight years.

"You're sort of a hero in the Greyzone," said Dad as he walked in and stared with a dispirited look at the acres of unsolved jigsaw pieces. "How is being the husband of the Head Prefect going?"

"Not great. Listen, Violet told me earlier a Supervisory Substitute Swatchman is coming in."

I saw the blood drain from his face.

"Supervisory Substitute?" he echoed. "You're *sure* that's what she said?"

"Yes; the day after tomorrow."

He rummaged in his pockets for a scrap of paper, then started scribbling with a pencil stub.

"They'll be given a list by the Prefects," he said, "but I don't think you and Jane will be on it. You because she needs a Red husband to make her look good and for the dynasty, and Jane because Red Sector needs her to win the gyro-bike sprint."

He scribbled some more, thought for a minute, then added another couple of names. Once done he handed it over to me.

"All these people need to get out of the village before the Substitute Swatchman gets here, and keep the supernumeraries well hidden—the Substitute may decide to go house to house and do his work spontaneously and without recourse to prefectural oversight."

I looked at the list. It mostly featured old or damaged ex-linoleum workers, but several names stood out.

"Why is Clifton Grey on the list? He's about the only person working at the factory who isn't owed holiday or retirement."

"Not sure—but I think Old Mr. deMauve didn't like that he and Violet had a physical relationship, and wanted it to end."

"He could have just told Violet."

"I'm not sure Violet gets to be told anything, even by her father. In any event, Clifton needs to get out."

I pointed to another name.

"Lucy Ochre? Are you kidding? Why her?"

"Inquisitiveness is always problematical," he said. "You may want to warn her. But be careful how you frame it. The first rule of Mildew is that once you know what it is, you'll be given the Mildew. Do you understand?"

I think Lucy knew more than Dad thought, but I knew I'd have to be careful.

"I understand."

I looked at the list again. One particular name *really* stuck out.

"Penelope Gamboge?"

"All I can think about her is that the Mildew has to strike randomly at times, and of all colours—it would look a bit suspect if Yellows and Purples never got it."

I looked out of the window to where Penelope was seated, playing cat's cradle with a length of string.

"That's a whole new level of perversity—that you can be Mildewed for no other reason than to make the Mildew look normal and without pattern?"

He shrugged.

"What happens when you lift the carpet, Eddie?"

"You find dirt."

"Right. There'll be two others on the list also: Velma and myself."

"Tell me you'll both go and hide, Dad?"

He took a deep breath.

"Velma and I are not the hiding-from-anything sort of people. We have some moves. You take care of yourself, and leave me to me."

HUSBAND AND WIFE

Starter boy and girlfriends were permitted by the Rules, as part of "interpersonal training," and premarital *youknow* was encouraged—so long as all due discretion was observed. Munsell's *Book of Harmony* was of the opinion that a "speedy and incautious rush to marriage might instigate resentment down the years that would not be conducive to the overall wellbeing of the community." The Rule made for much merriment before one's Ishihara, usually beyond the Outer Markers, where cosy and romantic *niches d'amour* were fashioned expressly for that purpose.

—Ted Grey: *Twenty Years Among the Chromatacians*

Violet picked me up from the puzzle room just as the first prebedtime bell went, and we walked across the square towards the deMauve residence under the sputtering central streetlamp, the harsh shadows transforming the twice-lifesize statue of Our Munsell from the loving and paternal way he looked by day, to harsh and forbidding.

She insisted we link arms and I said nothing, a dull thumping in my chest speaking of unwelcome anticipation of how her possession of me would be manifested in the house and her bedchamber.

"You were right to allow the Greys at the factory to be retired," she said, in the weirdly alien tones of an agreeable person. "We'll make up the numbers somehow, and to be honest, there are bigger weasels to boil and we can blame the shortfall on the previous Council. How did you get along with the puzzle?"

"I was there three hours and managed one piece," I said.

"Sorry about ordering you to do that," she said, adding an apology to her new range of diplomatic skills, "but as the ranking member in this marriage, I have long-term issues to think of if we are to grow old together."

I didn't like the sound of that one bit.

"You've changed your tune. Yesterday you wanted me dead in the Green Room."

"Things are different now, sweetheart, and we need to put our differences to one side. We are married. We can't *unmarry* unless one of us dies—and I think you and Jane have demonstrated that when a non-consensual death event is planned, you are more than a match. Five against two? I'm impressed."

"I don't know what you're talking about."

"It's okay," she said, "I don't give a stuff about Celandine and his dopey Yellows—or any Yellow, to be honest. They are useful in the way a hammer is to a carpenter, or a knife to a butcher. If you killed them because they tried to kill you, then as far as I am concerned you were simply defending yourselves and the matter is closed."

It seemed convenient to let her think that; she wouldn't believe me if I told her about Hanson.

"Did you know about the plan to kill us?"

She paused for a moment, I think as she tried to figure out the best way to answer.

"I was . . . not *actively* involved but I figured out what might be going on," she said slowly, "and your death might have offered me certain . . . advantages back then, but no longer. I could have said something but I did not, and I regret this, and other *misjudgements* against you. I have been manipulative in the past, and while I do not expect you to forget this, I am hoping you will see that I was acting for the best interest of my family and the village."

I didn't know what to say to this. Violet being apologetic or even vaguely reasonable just sounded, well, *weird.* I stared at her, wondering what her play might be—pro-deMauve, I was sure of that, and once the Supervisory Substitute had been in and cleared out some dead wood, a new start. But this could work to my and Jane's advantage too.

"Did you really report Mr. Celandine?" I asked.

"I did. He will be obligated to resign his post and, knowing him, will attempt revenge on both of us. But with Bunty covering our backs, we should be okay."

"Do you trust her?"

"Bunty? Yes—not as smart as Gamboge, but equally as driven, and she *will* take orders, and is village-loyal. I'll keep her focused on her tuba, and try to persuade her to start more actively reading *SpouseMart.*"

"I thought she would declare."

"Yes, I thought so too; she stares wistfully at the other women when swimming. She'll have to make her mind up soon. The Council has already issued her two child-bearing exemptions. She'll be thirty next birthday—she won't get a third."

There was a pause.

"Violet," I said, "you do know I'm going to carry on seeing Jane and that you and I will never be intimate ever again?"

"I know you *say* that, darling, but love is something that will grow between us. It is the *product* of a successful partnership and how you end up—not how you should begin, with the flaming passion of youth beguiling you from a sense of proportion and correct Chromatic life balance. Jane is *Green,* Eddie. You're *Red.* It was never going to work. What I'm doing now, slowly separating you, is to simply accelerate a gradual drifting that would have happened anyway. It's the plaster you pull off quickly to avoid the pain."

I looked at her without speaking.

"Speaking of plasters," she added, "what's with your finger?"

I still had one wrapped around the barcode on my finger.

"I caught it between two rocks up at Crimsonolia."

"Really? That must have been very painful, lambkin."

We resumed our walk and the setting sun caught the shiny lightning attractor on the top of the flak tower.

"Did you know that Gamboge almost bankrupted the village over that stupid crackletrap?" she said. "I don't know what she thought she was doing, but she had a hold on the Council, so was tolerated far more than was healthy. This village has been neglected, Eddie, and my aim is to have the colour feed-pipes here within twenty years, and make the Red Sector Outer Fringes somewhere people might want to come, not where you end up if all else fails. The prize merits at Jollity Fair will help, but it won't be enough on its own. This village needs cash, Eddie—any ideas?"

"None whatsoever. But if you're after get-rich-quick schemes, there's really only one person who you could try."

"Good thought," she said, "I'll ask him. I do so enjoy it when we're being a team."

She opened the door to the deMauve residence and instead of leading me into the kitchens where I thought I would stay, she showed me around. Her brother was there, and welcomed me with a grudging sense of new kinship while Violet explained which deMauve was which in the many portraits that lined the walls.

"Where are your parents?" I asked.

"I moved them out," she said, "since I am now Head Prefect. Tania will remain here, as the presence of children softens a harsh demeanour that I am eager to shed, and dear Tania is perfect as a servant: hardworking, requires no payment and, most of all, doesn't bruise easily. I'm so glad you and she managed to cook up a spare the other night—she and my brother can claim it as theirs, it will amount to the same thing, ultimately."

"Then she gets to go to Jollity Fair?"

"Indeed she does."

She rang the bell for Tania and flopped on to the sofa.

"Say, Eddie, do you want to get horribly greenfaced? I have some Gordon's somewhere, a bespoke shade of Lime that makes you feel as though you're floating outside your body and is wonderful for reducing inhibitions. You know what they say: 'Prefects have the best Lime.'"

"No thanks," I replied, as getting greened out of my face with Violet was not somewhere I wanted to be.

"Then how about some stereographic views of the ancient gone world? I have pictures of the Inexplicably Large Pyramid surrounded by dust and humped sand-horses."

So we did, while Tania viewed a light shade of Pachelbel from the *Keyboard Hue-Book*, and played Canon on the Mellotron as well as any I had yet heard. After the entertainments, Violet's brother wished us good night and departed, along with Tania, who I noted went in a different direction, towards the linen cupboard.

"Time for bed, darling," said Violet.

"Tell me about . . . er . . . Purple Regis," I said.

"It's on the coast in Green Sector South," said Violet, settling her head on my shoulder, "called Lime Regis before the Epiphany. It is a place where the stones are infused with spiralled animals and sea-creatures long dead, a place of rest for those tasked with the highest office of Head Prefect."

"Have you ever swum in the sea?"

"No, too dangerous what with the Kraken and the Squidling and the Under Toad and stuff. Did you know the sea is salty?"

"I didn't. How salty?"

"Somewhere between unpleasantly salty and extremely unpleasantly salty. Paddling is safe and the beach pleasant, but we generally only go there to meet other Purples. After Jollity Fair you will come along and meet some other spouses, with whom you can talk about babies and soft furnishings and colour schemes while the deMauves discuss Chromatic politics."

"You'd allow me to come to Purple Regis with you?"

"Of course—so long as you demonstrate that this is a proper marriage, and not some sort of silly sham."

"By doing everything you ask?" She looked at me and sighed.

"No, silly, you've got it all wrong. I don't want you to do things simply because I tell you, I want you to do things I tell you because it's the best thing to do."

"I'm so glad we cleared that up."

"Me too," she said, and beeped my nose in a manner that she probably thought was either charming or affectionate or both.

The half-hour to lights-out bell went and Violet took my hand and led me upstairs to the master bedroom. My clothes were there already in the chest of drawers, and the large bed was already turned down, and now ours.

Violet undressed without hesitation or preamble, forgoing any of the three versions of Night Attire and then slid naked beneath the covers, inviting me to join her. The sense of entrapment that had been rumbling all evening now manifested itself in a dryness of throat and a dull thumping of my heart. I changed into my regulation pyjamas in the bathroom with the door closed and lay down stiffly on the bed. She moved up close and laid her hand on my *thingy* and I instinctively leaped out of bed, which she found amusing and laughed out loud, which I'd never heard her do before. Curiously, it wasn't an unpleasant laugh. It was a sort of chirpy giggle that from anyone else would have sounded mildly endearing.

"Okay, okay," she said, "I'll be patient—but it's not as though we haven't already."

"Things were different then, and you coerced me into it."

"Coerced? Nonsense," she scoffed. "You performed flawlessly, so you couldn't have minded."

I lay on the bed again and we listened to the chatter on the radiator for a bit, mostly gossip about the day's events, and arguments for and against Violet being the Head Prefect. It was mostly positive, or rather, we only heard the positive remarks because as soon as they turned negative, Bunty, ready as always, drowned out the comments with her wooden spoon. After a while, Violet got up and laid a towel over the radiator to muffle the sounds, and pressed the manual reset for the heliostat, which automatically tracked away from the central lamp post and towards a place that would eventually meet the rising sun in the morning. I felt Violet snuggle up close and tried hard not to recoil from her presence.

"I'll be honest," I whispered in the darkness, "I don't much like you, Violet."

"Few do, sweetheart," she whispered back very close to my ear, "and for my part I find you pathetically insipid and dreary, and regard your habit of consorting with Greys and low Greens quite revolting. The truth is, sweetheart, that if you didn't have so much Red between your legs, I can guarantee I would not have troubled to even learn your name. Now, do you want to properly sanctify this marriage in the traditional manner? I don't do fakery and like a good *youknow* as much as the next girl, so if you're not doing it right I shall offer up instruction."

"Not tonight."

"I understand, pumpkin," she replied, then kissed my shoulder and snuggled to get comfortable, pressing herself against me, but this time staying her wandering hands. But I could sense the pretence. I was only around for as long as I was of use. Disposal of me wouldn't be too much of a problem, once I was away from Jane's protective influence.

"Oh, and husband," she said with a yawn, "you never did congratulate me on becoming Head Prefect."

"Congratulations," I said, "and please don't call me pumpkin."

EVERYTHING'S CHANGED

Manufacturing was spread around the Collective with production and demand decided upon by Head Office. What was produced and where it was produced was something of a mystery, and the quality and availability changeable to say the least. Shoes were made only for right feet for ten years, and the waiting list for a new kettle was eighteen years. A Prefect once ordered a set of crockery when they were twenty-two, and died before it was delivered.

—Ted Grey: *Twenty Years Among the Chromatacians*

There was an odd feeling about the village the following morning. It was cool for the dry season but the humidity seemed higher and the clouds appeared in regular parades over the village, the puffy doughnut shapes stretching and twisting and breaking up as they headed east. Given that the shapes were still quite regular where we were, Lucy Ochre—who was always curious about these things—had suggested they may have formed quite close by, perhaps as little as thirty miles away.

Violet rose without waking me and was out of the house early, presumably to the Council chambers to study the *Book of Harmony* and deal with the hundreds of items of bureaucracy that come with being Head Prefect.

I had a bath and came downstairs, said good morning to Tania and asked her if there was a spare room on the ground floor, and she said there was a study that could be converted, and she'd get on to it.

"I'd lend you the linen room," she said, "but I've bagsied that for myself."

"Clifton came over, did he?"

"He did," she said with a smile, "and stayed until dawn. Nice fellow. Thank you again for arranging it. Do I owe you anything?"

"Nothing at all."

"There must be *something* I can do. Shall I juggle eight carving knives for you while eating an apple? It's quite dangerous but rather fun."

"Maybe another time."

I stepped out of the deMauve residence. Another Yellow— Graham Custard I think his name was—was waiting outside for me, idly reading a copy of *Spectrum*. I nodded a greeting and he followed me as I walked across to the communal eating halls, then sat at a Yellow table while I took my breakfast to High Table. I ate quietly on my own, then organised Boundary Patrol before making my way up to the linoleum factory, Graham Custard still close behind. I didn't expect there was much to do until everyone came back off leave but the plus side was that it freed up residents to spend more time training for Jollity Fair, and probably the reason Violet didn't go nuts.

The linoleum factory seemed cold and dark without the usual clanking and puffs of smoke from the chimneys. Samantha was doing cost projections when I walked in, and made me tea from an old teabag she had recently found under the filing cabinet.

"We could be up for a productivity bonus next week," she announced, "and every week after that until we start production again."

"How is *that* possible if we're not actually making anything?"

Samantha smiled and turned to where Jethro was standing at

the blackboard. They'd both viewed the emergency maths skill hue the day before, and their understanding of figures had lasted longer than expected.

"It's quite simple," he said. "Our current production is zero—so if we claim to have increased our productivity by twenty percent next week, the sums do actually work, because twenty percent of nothing is also nothing."

He wrote two zeros on the board and then added them together.

"I see," I said, not really seeing at all.

"We could even log an increase in production by two hundred percent," said Samantha, "but that might set the alarm bells ringing. We thought we'd only claim a modest increase in production and vary it each week so no one looks too closely."

"Okay," I said, "and what's this bonus worth?"

"Sadly, the bonus is based only on two percent of the increased productivity, which is still zero—but if we win a productivity bonus for ten increased productivity weeks in a row, then there's a thousand merits to be shared out among the workers."

"That makes no sense," I said. "We can earn merits by producing nothing at all?"

"It's in the Rules," she replied with a smile. "So by definition, it makes perfect sense. Jethro and I are planning to reopen the trouser factory with no workers at all and zero production, and we hope to earn at least two thousand merits in productivity bonuses before the year is out."

"But these are book merits, yes?" I asked.

"Sadly so," said Samantha, "but it might help pay food bills—some tea, maybe."

"Now," said Jethro, "we're inventorying all the stock today, do you want to lend a hand? It would make it quicker."

I agreed, so they gave me a clipboard and a pencil and told me to list everything in Room 409. I wandered up the staircase and to the uppermost floor, which seemed to be used for storage of village paperwork before it was recycled. I found the room and pushed open the door, expecting to be greeted with rolls of burlap or linseed oil or something—but I wasn't.

"Hello, Ed," said Jane from where she was sitting among stacks of filed-and-then-forgotten mealtime attendance records.

I knew I'd see her soon, but wasn't sure how she'd engineer it.

"Have you got a Yellow following you everywhere?" I asked.

"I *did*," said Jane as we hugged. "She was too frightened of me to get close, so easily lost."

In comparison, my tail was outside the factory right now, with a second on the back entrance so I didn't do what I did yesterday.

"I missed you last night," I said.

"And I you," she replied. "Did you spend the night in Violet's bed?"

"I did."

"Did anything happen?"

"Why," I said with a smile, "are you jealous?"

My words didn't have the effect I was hoping for.

"No," she replied, "why, should I have any reason to be?"

"Well, that is to say, I mean, aren't you just a *little bit* concerned over whether I had *youknow* with Violet?"

"Eddie, it would probably be a good thing if you did—it might fool the heifer into thinking you were on her side."

"Oh," I said, suddenly feeling deflated.

"Why," she asked, "would you get pissed at me if I gave myself to another for the struggle?"

"Have you?"

"No, and I have no intention of doing so. I just said I would, if circumstances demanded it. Eddie, if you're not going to even try, we might as well give up right now."

Her voice rose, but surprisingly, so did mine.

"Don't you care even the smallest amount whether I had *youknow* with Violet or not?"

"You have already."

"That was before you and I were a thing."

"Does that make a difference?"

"Yes, of *course* it makes a difference."

She thought for a moment.

"You know what I care about? Wanting to be in the kind of peaceful mindset where these sort of things matter to me. But right now, it's not a luxury I can afford myself. But if it's any consolation, I wouldn't give a fig if you *youknowed* her because you needed to maintain your cover—but I most assuredly would punch you painfully in the eye and never speak to you again if you did because you wanted her. I should be enough for you."

"And you are," I said, "in all ways. I just wanted for our relationship to *matter*."

My temper had subsided, and so had hers.

"It matters," she said. "It really matters. And it's why we must win—so that everyone is free to love the person they choose."

She stared at me, and if I didn't know right now if she loved me I was a bloody fool and never would. So we both calmed down and I related what had happened. About how the village was without any money at all, and that I'd probably go to Purple Regis for the annual deMauve Convention.

"There are over thirty villages run by deMauves?" she said when I told her. "Got to be something in the Rules against that."

I agreed and then showed her the list Dad had given me that contained the names that he thought would be on the Substitute's Mildew list.

"No surprises there," she said, scanning the list, "aside from Penelope, I guess. We can start moving people out today, but it would be a very brave Swatchman indeed who tried to search the

Greyzone. Lucy's on the hockeyball team, so it's not likely that Violet would order her Mildewed until that's over; she can stay in Vermillion for a while. Clifton can take a two-week sabbatical somewhere; he can claim he was kidnapped by Riffraff or something. What will your dad and Mrs. Ochre do?"

"Dad said he had some moves."

"What does that mean?"

"I'm not sure. Any news your end?"

"Melanie is off tomorrow to Emerald City, but I was really up here to talk to you about that wireless telephone."

She unrolled it from an "I've seen the Badly Drawn Map" tea towel and handed it over. I switched it on and it made the "welcome" noise and up came the word Network. I dialled a random number and almost immediately I heard the recorded message say: "You have dialled incorrectly, please hang up and try again."

"Any ideas?" I asked.

"Plenty. I took it to an old Grey who collects wireless telephones and she said that it was unusually rudimentary, as most wireless telephones were without buttons and were more like a remote viewer in form and function. She also said it appeared to be in a newish condition, as though manufactured quite recently. She did a brittleness test on the plastic and aged it from between thirty and fifty years."

"That's not possible."

"Maybe, but that's what she said. She also said that this telephone seemed to work on an eleven-digit system, as that's the number of digits from when the woman's recorded voice moves from 'you have dialled incorrectly' to 'your number has not been recognised.' She also said that wireless telephones usually started with the zero digit."

"Is eleven digits normal?"

"She didn't know. She'd been collecting telephones for fifty years and although many powered up, none actually *worked*. She said to just dial numbers until someone answered."

"What if there's no one there to answer it?"

"That is a likely scenario," she conceded, "but what if someone does? It's got to be worth a try, yes?"

Jane showed me a list of a hundred numbers she had already dialled, and we then wrote out another fifty, all headed up by a zero. We started going through them without much luck, receiving the same: "The number you have dialled has not been recognised" each time. Once we'd finished those numbers we wrote out another fifty, then worked our way through those. It was all we did for the next two hours until I took a break to make us both a loamy latte, and we sat and sipped it slowly as Jane talked about her chances on the gyro-bike at Jollity Fair, which she thought were not good, given the opposition.

"I'd be a fool to think I could beat Mad Dog Juniper without a fight," she said. "She's not just fearless, but also without scruples. At the Blue Sector heats two years ago Lizzie Azure died when a broom handle went through her front spokes and she high-sided it into the crowd. No one knew where the handle came from, but we all reckoned it was Mad Dog. What's that?"

It was the wireless telephone. It was ringing. *Someone was calling us.*

WIRELESS TELEGRAPHY

There were thirty-one Purple surnames, but only the deMauves, Magentas and van Purples held any power. The rest were decidedly *not* Head Prefects or anywhere close. The Lilacs and Fandangos and Lavenders had not led a Council for the best part of a century, and some surnames had even become extinct. Violet was only a given name these days, and no one had carried the surname Plum for decades.

—Ted Grey: *Twenty Years Among the Chromatacians*

We exchanged confused looks, and I then offered the telephone to Jane but she insisted I answer it. I said "Hello?" but it carried on ringing, so pressed several buttons until the ringing stopped.

"Hello?" I said cautiously, with Jane's ear pressed close to mine, and with her notebook in hand.

"Nigel?" came a man's voice.

"No," I replied, "I don't know any Nigels."

"Who is that then?"

"It's Edward," I said.

"Which station are you at?"

"We have a station in the village," I said, "and although I can see it from the window, I'm not actually there."

"That makes no sense. Where are you?"

"East Carmine," I said. "Red Sector West."

There was a pause.

"You're shitting me?"

I looked at Jane, who shrugged and made that circular motion with her finger that means "carry on."

"No, sir," I replied deferentially, because only those in authority would dare to use such language. "I'm definitely not."

"Then where did you get Nigel's mobile?"

I looked at the wireless telephone and figured that's what he was alluding to.

"I was given it by a Riffraff."

"A what?"

"It's a sort of wild human."

"You mean a Digenous. Okay, makes sense, Nigel *had* been sniffing around one or two—whereabouts?"

"Outside East Carmine, to the northeast by a mile, I think."

"You have a different naming regime to us. Do you know East Carmine's real name?"

There was a discarded "welcome to" enamel sign now cemented into the side of the rendering shed, but no one ever called it by that.

"It might once have been called Rhayader."

"I know where that is. He was seeing a woman named Meena near there. Tall and pretty, necklace, large sea shell."

"That's the one. She had a child with her."

"Hmm," said the man on the other end, "missing for eight months, his mobile turns up with Meena who now has a child. I'll come look for him but it doesn't sound good."

"Who are you?" I asked. "And are you on or off the island?"

"Oh, I'm on the Reserve," he said, "about thirty miles west of you, on the coast—I was brought out of the Reserve when a child so I'm like you—just not a subject. Not anymore."

Jane wrote a question on her notepad and showed it to me so I could ask him.

"Are you with Utopiainc?"

The voice on the other end of the phone laughed.

"Good God no. I'm an engineer on a cloud-seeding station on Cardigan Bay. Boring job, but it pays well. Six months on, Six months off. Nigel was the same, but five miles north of me. He liked exploring, and liked the Digenous. I thought it wasn't worth the risk. You know there are modified beasts on the Reserve and trees that can eat you?"

"They're easily outmanoeuvred."

Jane had written another question on her notebook. It was the deepest and most profound question I would ever ask.

"What happens on the Reserve and why are we subjects?"

The caller, whoever he was, suddenly changed his tune. It was one question too far.

"I've said too much," he said in a quieter tone. "Even ex-subjects are expressly forbidden from interacting with subjects, and I could be recalled for this. Forget everything I said and if you want my advice, ditch the mobile. I'm not saying they are tracking it or listening in, but it's within their power."

"I need answers."

"And you deserve them. But it won't be from me. You want answers, you go to your Creator. Confront them; they'll be legally required to tell you. But look, subjects that make it out are never let back in. You can have answers, but knowing them is all you'll have. Muse on that before asking."

"Then there *is* a greater power, one who watches over us and guides our destiny?"

"Always has been, but not for much longer. When the twenty-five generations are up, everything will change. I gotta go. Don't do anything dumb, and again, ditch the mobile."

The wireless telephone went dead. I stared at it for a moment, then at Jane.

"Did you get all that?"

"Most of it, but aside from the 'cloud-seeding' stations on the coast, there was little we didn't already know: we are subjects living on a Reserve, controlled and observed by Utopiainc, our Creator."

"True, but he also said that those that get out are not let back in. Is that 'out' as in 'off the island'?"

"I don't know," she replied. "He said we could have answers, but never be able to do anything with them."

"Did he mean that as a euphemism for death?" I asked "Hanson told us stuff that he knew we couldn't do anything with."

Jane shrugged.

"Here's something else," I added. "He sounded to me like an ordinary working man, and if so, the things that he knew about us must be ordinary, knowable facts. And that the truth is only a secret here in Chromatacia—in the Somewhere Else and to the Someone Else who lives there, everything here isn't unknowable at all—we could even be common knowledge."

We were silent for a few moments.

"He said everything would change after twenty-five generations, but Hanson the Angel said you were twenty-four. Thoughts?"

"If a generation is measured by the First Child Expectation age of twenty years, then twenty-four generations brings us back to—where?"

Since neither of us were as good as Lucy with complex maths, we had to get out a sheet of paper and work it out. Twenty-four generations back was essentially a shade under five hundred years, right at the start of the Munsell era. The next generation, the twenty-fifth, would be with mine and Violet's unborn child, and any like him who had that many forebears. But all this simply added questions, not answered them.

I voiced my thoughts to Jane, who pursed her lips and agreed that the Herald at Jollity Fair was still our soundest bet. She asked me if I wanted to go fishing for Angels.

"What sort of Angels?"

"Ones that go by the name of Hanson."

"Maybe," I said. "What's the plan?"

"Give your Yellow tail the slip tomorrow morning and meet me at the northern stockgate twenty minutes before the mid-morning swan."

"What do you think will happen?" I asked.

"Who knows?" she replied. "But I have a feeling we might learn something."

I didn't see Jane again that day. Once more I was expected to sit at High Table next to Violet, saying nothing and remaining quiet. And after dinner I was again consigned to the puzzle room, there to be watched over by my own personal Duty Yellow, this time Penelope Gamboge. I thought of telling her to avoid the Supervisory Substitute Swatchman, but I didn't.

Tommo was the first to drop by.

"Hullo, Eddie. Your wife wants to see me privately tomorrow in the Council chambers. Any idea what that's about?"

I told him it was probably to do with earning a massive amount of cash merits to pay off the village's crackletrap debt.

"Oh," he said, and already I could see his mind clicking over as he figured out some sort of scheme, "a Prefect-sanctioned scam could be my finest moment. I could place a sizeable sum on Jane to win the gyro-bike sprint."

"You wager for cash?" I asked, as any game where something of value could be transferred on the basis of an unknown outcome was one of Munsell's Ten Abhorrences.

"I know someone in Vermillion who will take a wager on almost anything. Do you think Violet might go for it?"

"If you ask her, make sure there are no witnesses."

"I think I might like this new Head Prefect," he said. "Did you hear that Melanie is to be transferred to Emerald City to work as a domestic servant for that National Colour guy?"

"I did, yes."

"I think he wants her there for more than just making beds, ironing and cooking."

"I think Melanie understands that."

Violet didn't fetch me that evening and instead sent Tania, who had a large dressing over one ear.

"Let me guess," I said, "Violet didn't like the idea of converting the study to my bedroom?"

"You could say that. She hit me with a broom handle and almost took my ear off. I'm planning on poisoning them all during that big deMauve get together at Purple Regis. Want to join in?"

"Okay," I said, in the same manner as if someone had asked me to play whist, "how are you going to do it?"

"Foxgloves," she said, "baked in a pie."

"You're going to need a lot of foxgloves," I said, "and their growing season is over."

"Next year, then."

I didn't think it was a genuine plan, although the sentiments behind it were real.

"Why did you want to sleep in a separate bedroom on the ground floor?" asked Violet as we were getting ready for bed. I thought of what Jane had said, about pretending everything was okay, but I couldn't even entertain the possibility.

"Why do you think?"

"It's bad form to answer a question with a question."

"Is it?"

I took a long time brushing my teeth and flossing, and came to bed when the lights were already out, and fumbled my way into bed. She snuggled up close, but to my great relief kept her hands to herself.

SUPERVISORY SUBSTITUTE & ANGEL FISHING

The Temple of Colour was a simple octagonal affair, with a domed roof of randomly selected coloured glass, each hue to dwell upon their own so as to strengthen their part in society, and for the Greys to look upon the colourless glass and muse upon the hard work and diligence that leads to eventual Chromatic betterment. Attendance was not compulsory but Yellows were often to be seen loitering around, making a note of who went in and more importantly, who didn't.

—Ted Grey: *Twenty Years Among the Chromatacians*

Violet left early once more and I had breakfast with Tania and her kids but not her husband, who ate over in the town hall and had little to do with his wife and children. I went to conduct morning Boundary Patrol as usual, once again from the incident room beneath the village. I'd found a couple of lightglobes while I was rummaging around in the deMauves' house, and I'd arrived early, so walked through to the large circular void within the incident room complex and dropped one of the lightglobes into the water. I watched it descend through the clear liquid, down and down, until it eventually stopped and illuminated some old tech at the bottom. I sent another one after it, then a third and a fourth, and they all looked very pretty far below, illuminating ladders and walkways and a heap of Tin Men, one of whom had picked up the first lightglobe I'd sent down to stare at it, then upwards in my direction. The circular hole was without ladders or footholds; I don't know how long the Tin Man had been down there, but he'd be there for a while. At the same time I wondered how ours was doing on his spoon quest.

There was nothing to report during patrol aside from a brief megafauna incursion, and a ground sloth who had apparently walked in and out, crossing the boundary of clutching bramble as though it wasn't there. On migration, probably.

My Yellow escort stood up as I came out of the underground complex and followed me to the Council chambers so I could log my report. I met Melanie on my way back, who was dressed in Standard Travelling #2s that looked as though they had been taken in to fit her physique more closely. Such alterations were disallowed, but I couldn't really see anyone complaining unless they had a grudge against Melanie and the way she looked, which nobody did. There was a small group to see her off outside the twice-lifesize statue of Our Munsell, and many tears shed and a lot of hugging, most from family members and friends, but a few from opportunistic young men and women who had for years dreamed of being briefly in her embrace. She hugged them all tightly.

"You okay?" I said as we walked towards the railway station.

"I've not been out of East Carmine in all my twenty-five years," she said with a smile. "Never left the home I was born in, never been on a train."

"Not even to Vermillion in one of the Fords?"

"I'm *Grey*, Eddie. This is the biggest adventure I'm ever likely to see—Emerald City—that's quite a gig."

"I hope it all goes well." She shrugged.

"Actually, it might be quite fun. There was nothing specifically wrong with Mr. Applejack, aside from a little dullness and a propensity to talk about colour a lot better than he could make it. But once I'm established in his house there may be further opportunities for advancement. He'll want to show me off, I'm sure."

We chatted some more on the way to the railway station where I found Penelope Gamboge already waiting for us as she was once again on Arrivals Monitor duty. She nodded a greeting to Graham the Yellow escort, who turned to walk back into the village, his shift over. There were a few passengers waiting to leave but no one I recognised aside from a travelling heliostat technician who had been here for the past week doing routine maintenance, and two of our renderers, who were part of the half-dozen being transferred to Green Sector East. Rendering wasn't a job anyone much liked doing, so those that enthusiastically embraced the work were much in demand.

There was a distant whistle as the train approached.

Mel smiled that winning smile of hers and gave me a tight hug with one hand just the tiniest bit close to my rear for comfort, then kissed me on the ear, told me to look after Jane and then turned to Penelope to give her name and postcode and destination. She then walked up the platform to where the Grey carriages would halt.

"That was a demeritably close embrace," said Penelope.

"Melanie's like that," I replied. "Who are we here to meet?"

She looked at the clipboard.

"An irrigation expert to give a talk on better water management, a chutney expert from Blue Sector East to take Mr. Pink's place, a pair of Greys eager to take up a child allocation, and the Supervisory Substitute Swatchman."

If Penelope knew of the purpose for his visit, she made no sign of it.

The Substitute turned out to be a genial figure with a large, bulbous nose and an easy smile. I had been expecting a darker, more sinister figure, and I admit I was a little put off by his easy jovial manner.

"Goodness, it's hot enough out here to boil a badger's bum," he said, mopping his brow. "Are you Eddie Russett? Pleased to meet you. Stephen Emerald, Supervisory Substitute Swatchman—most people call me Steve. Your father's most excellent paper to the Guild regarding bilateral body part swaps to extend civic use to accidental amputees was an extremely sound piece of research work and much admired back at Head Office—I will be eager to speak to him about it."

He gave his details to Penelope and produced his merit book. I looked over his shoulder at the forty thousand merits he had amassed. If he was over seventy years of age as I estimated, he didn't need to do the work—he was old enough and merited enough to retire easily. If he was still doing it, he either must like his job or feel it is his duty.

Carlos Fandango was busy on the gyro-bike, so Stafford took me and Steve into town on one of the cycle-taxis.

"I've not been out this way for a long long time," said Steve, looking around at the parched landscape. "Are there active Chromogencia meetings in the village? I'm quite keen on swan migration patterns. I move around a lot, so am able to take detailed timings. What time do yours move over?"

"Usually about 10:15 in the morning and 17:07 in the afternoon, but there is variability in the times and they are weather dependent."

"In pairs or singletons?" he said, making a note in a small book. "Swans mate for life, so I'm surprised not to see them in pairs."

It didn't sound as though he knew what they were, and he chatted amiably all the way into town, then asked Stafford to drop him at the library.

"We don't have many books," I said. "In fact, due to the

long-mandated staffing levels, the librarians outnumber the books five to one. And those books we do have are worn away to the central chapter, so understanding them is mostly guesswork and piecing it together from the recollections passed down from our forebears."

"The library in Emerald City is read-aloud to minimise wear and tear," said Steve, "which was accepted as a Standard Variable many years ago. Each week a new book is read to an audience by one of the librarians; the events are always at capacity. A book named *The Very Hungry Caterpillar's Chromatic Fulfilment* has only recently finished a sell-out forty-seven-week run, but then Emerald City has a lot of people in it, and many wanted to hear it more than once."

"What was it about?" I asked, as I hadn't heard of it.

"Oh, it's a highly allegorical story," he said with a smile, "establishing the clear advantages of the Munsell Doctrine against the old world of the Previous. A caterpillar represents the voracious consumer of materials, which begins simply enough as an apple, then rises incrementally to consume all around it. On the sixth day of a decadently indulgent lifestyle the caterpillar gets a stomach ache after gorging on chocolate cake and ice cream, and on the last day is the Epiphany, the rejection of the hedonistic way of the Previous when the caterpillar, consuming the nourishing yet more proletarian food of a leaf, emerges as the bright and colourful butterfly of modern Munsellian harmony, with equality and chromatic abundance for all."

"I think that sounds like a book our Prefects would be very interested in," I said cautiously. "Could we borrow it?"

"I believe National Colour want to republish the title and distribute it along with several others that convey a similar message."

We stopped outside the library and he brought a picture book from his bag and trotted inside to give it to them. I could see him talking to Mrs. Lapis-Lazuli, whose expression went from suspicion to disbelief to joyful rapture in the space of about ten seconds.

"That went *very* well," he said once he had returned to the cycle-taxi. "I am head of Emerald City's 'Suitable Reading for the Chromatic Betterment of the Collective' project, tasked personally by National Colour to reprint and modify books that are understood to be of significant cultural and social importance."

"I thought printing books wasn't allowed."

"It's also being put forward as a Standard Variable," he replied, "and I am currently testing the idea."

"Did you just give the library the caterpillar book?"

"No, it was another—an excellent work titled *Bill the Burglar's Chromatic Journey*, another allegorical tale of a ne'er-do-well who finds that rejecting the pathological acquisitiveness of the old way is the only possible manner in which society can move forward and find happiness within the rainbow harmony of Munsellian perfection. He gets to keep the baby, though, demonstrating that within every soul there is always room for improvement."

"Apart We Are Together," I said, as I now strongly suspected that Steve Emerald was a dangerously fanatical follower of the Munsell Way. "May I ask a question?"

"Of course."

"Does Emerald City actually have Flying Monkeys?"

It was an intentionally dumb question in order that he not look upon me suspiciously.

He laughed.

"The stuff of legends, lad—none that I have seen, but you can never be too careful."

"That's a relief," I said. "Shall I take you to your quarters or the Council offices?"

"Better drop me at the Temple," he said, mentioning it by

name which was not something we were allowed to do, "I like to repeat the words we have for all the colours at least once daily. Do you, lad?"

"Every day," I said, which was a lie. It was the sort of thing that only people like Bunty attempted.

"Once you are done here my father will be waiting at his office to receive you," I said once he'd climbed out, "but if you need anything, anything at all, please do not hesitate to call."

"You are most kind," said Steve, and he tipped both Stafford and me a shiny five-merit piece. This was very generous—enough for a week's eating out for six at the Fallen Man.

I asked Stafford what he thought as we went to park in the rank outside the Council offices, pedalling fast to keep ahead of Wesley Yellowhammer who was currently on Eddie escort duty.

"I heard Substitute Swatchmen are always charming," said Stafford, "to give everyone the impression all is well. This one's dangerously Chromocentric, so I think anyone not wholly committed to the Munsell Doctrine should consider themselves at risk, despite your dad's list. We've removed several people to better hiding places and plastered over some doorways so the supernumeraries can't be found, but I'll alert anyone in the Greyzone who I think might be *especially* at risk."

We parked just as Wesley caught us up, looking very red-faced after his run from the station.

"You don't lose me that easily," he said, panting to get his breath back. Jane had told me to meet her at the northern stockgate twenty minutes before the mid-morning swan, to go, as she put it, "Angel fishing." Losing Wesley would have been tricky as he was the smartest of the five who were tailing me, but Doug and I had worked out a plan whereby a small crowd of agricultural Greys gathered around him in a silent yet impenetrable knot of humans, saying and doing nothing. In the time it took for him to order them away I'd made off through one of the many alleyways that led out of the square. I donned a work coat I had left for myself and made my way swiftly to the northern stockgate to find Jane waiting for me. She was sitting on the grassy mound on the outside of the clutching bramble hedge.

"Hey," I said, "what's up?"

"See that oak tree about a mile away, poking up above the silver birch?"

"Yes?"

"I dumped Mr. Pink's body up there this morning before anyone was up. You want to know why, don't you?"

"The thought had crossed my mind."

"I copied out my finger barcode on a strip of paper and wrapped it around his finger. If what Hanson said was correct and swans track our movements, I want to see what will happen if he thinks one of us is still alive."

"Is that wise?" I asked.

"Almost certainly not. Did Mel get away okay?"

"Out on the train the Supervisory Substitute arrived on."

"What's he like?"

"A more genial old gentleman you could not possibly hope to meet," I said. "If I were wanting to put someone at ease before I slipped them the M-shade, that's exactly how I would act."

"Worrying. Look, see there, the swan."

It was heading in from the usual direction and eight minutes early, but well within tolerances.

"It's circling," said Jane once it was in the overhead. It wasn't the usual figure of eight, but a circular wing-down movement, centred over where Jane had deposited Mr. Pink. It circled for ten minutes, then carried on to do its usual orbits over the village, and after it had done that, it flew off in the direction of Rusty Hill.

"Hmm," said Jane.

"What were you expecting?"

"I don't know. And do you have to squeeze my hand so tight? You're hurting."

"Not me," I told her, showing both my hands.

It was the clutching bramble. Usually six feet is far enough away, but a tendril had crept out and latched on to Jane. She quickly freed herself and we edged a little further away. We chatted about Jollity Fair and some sort of strategy to get me a permit. The team were due to leave the following day to get some practice on the fields there, or in Jane's case, the Vermillion velodrome. It was also a good time to scope out one's opponents.

"In Free Practice we either underplay our skills to make our opponents overconfident," said Jane, "or overplay them to mess with their heads."

"What does Jamie do?"

"She rides full power, elbows out, all the time. She rides likes she's the only person on the track, and never yields."

"What will you do?"

"I ride in the same sort of way, so somebody has to blink first."

"I don't much like the sound of that. Hang on—is that another swan?"

I had happened to glance upwards, and a very small glint in the sky had caught my attention. Jane turned and followed my stare upwards.

"Where?"

"Up there."

It glinted again. It was so high it was impossible to see unless it caught the sun. Tiny, no bigger than a grain of sand. There could be dozens up that high and we'd never even notice.

"You're right," she said, "it's def—"

She didn't get to finish her sentence as the oak tree where Mr. Pink's body was sitting suddenly erupted in a ball of fire, with the sound and the shock of the event reaching us 5.02 seconds later. We were too far away to receive any damage, but parts of the tree—and presumably Mr. Pink—were hoisted high in the air and then fell to the ground in a shower of dust and soil and twigs that drifted sideways in the wind.

"So now we know," said Jane, getting up to leave. "If they think we're alive, they aim to make sure we're dead. And fast."

As we walked back into the village we saw the ball of fire that destroyed Mr. Pink had not gone unnoticed, and the general consensus seemed to be that it was ball lightning, even if out of the usual time we could expect them. But if there was one straggler—or early bird—it was argued there might be others.

We saw Preston Grey drive past in the crossbow-equipped Model T to have a look and hopefully electrically ground any others before more damage could be done, and he had Doug and Lucy with him.

Jane's Angel-fishing trip had been chillingly successful, and I clamped my fingers tight round my index finger, despite it being already covered. With fire descending from on high sent by an angry Angel on the orders of a vengeful Creator, you can never be too careful.

DINNER

The Green Room was purposefully left unlocked so all may choose to use it at whatever hour, for whatever reason. A book of remembrances was placed outside for any final words, as residents would often not tell anyone they were going, nor want to cause a fuss. It was called the "Green Way Out."

—Ted Grey: *Twenty Years Among the Chromatacians*

Steve Emerald sat at High Table with us, and was as polite and funny at dinner as he was on the trip out from the station. His copy of *Bill the Burglar* had gone down well with the library, and was so popular that the waiting list to the waiting list now had a waiting list.

In Violet's pre-dinner speech she spoke about the Jollity Fair team and how she expected excellent sportsmanship, and if anyone was disqualified by viewing a banned skill hue before the contests, they would be placed on rendering shed duties for a year. She emphasised the point about being punished for *disqualification*, rather than *using* enhancing colours, so I guessed the underlying message was "don't get caught."

Violet then introduced the Supervisory Substitute Swatchman, who stood up and congratulated the residents upon the quality and cleanliness of the village, thanked the recently retired Prefects for their unswerving devotion to duty and wished the new

Prefects success in their new jobs. He then went on to talk about his career as a Swatchman, and how adherence to the *Book of Harmony* and the Word of Munsell in its glorious entirety was the only way to full colourisation. He then related an amusing anecdote about a Swatchman who had the bright idea of experimenting with long jump skill hues on a domestic goat, and how the test subject escaped and bred in the wild, leading to the bouncing goat we see today.

This went down well and with a lot of laughter. Violet rose to her feet to give thanks to the Supervisory Substitute on our behalf, but stopped halfway when he gestured her to sit down again. Given she was Head Prefect and answered to no one but the Rules, this level of impertinence was unthinkable in any context, and the room abruptly descended into an uncomfortable silence. Violet, perhaps unwisely, sat back down without a word. When the Supervisory Swatchman spoke again, it was in a more sombre tone.

"You would all have heard there was a ball lightning strike this afternoon, and this is a clear indication that everyone is to be heedful of the many jeopardies with which our life is filled, and how they can be avoided by strict adherence to the Rules."

There was silence, so he continued.

"A crew has been despatched to look for other instances of ball lightning, but I took it upon myself to investigate the strike as part of my evening pre-dinner walk. I found a smoking hole in the ground, and these."

He took out some items wrapped in grease-proof paper. It turned out to be a few parts of Mr. Pink, but only recognisable bits, like part of a foot, a hand and an ear. Few people had been spared rendering shed duties, so it wasn't likely to put us off our dinner, but even so.

"My enquiries identified the victim as Mr. Pink, who took the

Green Way Out the day before yesterday and was accessioned to the renderers the same day."

This was a serious deal, and you could almost hear a pin drop in the town hall.

"Now," he said, "I took the liberty of speaking to the Head Renderer and she had no explanation as to how someone managed to steal a two-day-old cadaver—the property of the Collective, I should add—nor why it was transported a mile out of town, nor why a rapid conflagration event occurred, something which I am now inclined to believe was someone up to silly kicks and giggles who found and set off explosive devices to see what would happen."

Everyone remained silent. Violet retook the initiative and stood up.

"This is indeed a very serious matter," she said, "and we thank Mr. Emerald for his investigative skills and unswerving devotion to duty. The whole sorry story will be thoroughly scrutinised by the Yellow Prefect, but as usual I will ask the perpetrators to step forward now under the HP9-4FF Early Confession Forgiveness Directive and do nothing more than eight weeks methane-digester duties."

No one moved or said a word. I casually swivelled my eyes to where Jane was sitting, and her hand tapped the table. About to confess, was my guess.

"Last chance," said Violet, "or I will have to punish the entire village."

But before Jane could take the blame, one of the other Greys put up her hand.

"Very good," said Violet, "but I think this was not the work of one girl alone?"

Two more hands went up, which were quickly followed by two more, then another six after that, swiftly followed by the rest of the table and the rest of the Greys and most of the lesser hues, including Jane. I saw a look of supreme distaste move across Steve Emerald's usual genial demeanour. Violet looked like thunder, too, I think partly because of what had happened, and partly because the Supervisory Substitute Swatchman had been here to witness it.

"You will take *individual* names," said Emerald to Bunty, "for the permanent record. Such flagrant disobedience must be recorded so that repeat offenders can be identified and dealt with."

He turned to Violet.

"Would you not agree, Head Prefect?"

Violet looked at Bunty, then at me, then at the Greys, then at the Supervisory Substitute Swatchman.

"You presume much, Mr. Emerald," said Violet slowly, "and make orders and suggestions that are not yours to give. Life in the Outer Fringes is hard, and the pleasures limited. My Greys might be disobedient, but they are solid workers, and mine to punish as I see fit. The first four hands that went up will take the punishment for all of them, and I am willing to write this unhappy incident off as simply misguided high spirits and a need to let off steam."

"They stole and detonated a *corpse*," remarked Emerald. "Your lenience borders on the indulgent."

Violet's anger was up, now, and I have to say it was kind of impressive.

"The Rules, Mr. Emerald, give me broad powers to dispense justice as I see fit. My time in the job, age and experience is tender and *Harmony* permits a more permissive interpretation of the Rules until such time as I am fully comfortable with my new role."

There was another awkward silence until the Supervisory Substitute said quietly, between gritted teeth:

"I apologise without reservation to you, your Prefects and all those within your charge. I will say no more on the matter and instead reserve my energy for the job I am here to do."

Violet, who had gone quite beetroot, relaxed, gestured for all the Greys to put their hands down, announced that dinner could now be eaten, and sat down. I leaned across to her and whispered in her ear: "That was a fine piece of leadership, Violet."

She gestured me closer and whispered: "This outrage reeks of you and Jane. If I find evidence that you were involved, I will have Jane transferred to the furthest and seediest backwater in the whole of Green Sector—gyro-bike sprint or not. Do you understand me?"

"Yes, I understand you."

Dinner was otherwise uneventful. Twice I caught Jane looking at me, and I think she felt, as did I, that the whole Mr. Pink misadventure was probably the worst idea she'd ever had. Steve then engaged with my father upon his work regarding the grafting of body parts and the feasibility of moving hands and even entire limbs from one resident to another. They spoke about how this might benefit the workforce, with those with jobs of a sedentary nature donating a foot to someone whose work was more active. The Substitute Swatchman seemed especially taken—even so far as to jot the idea down in his notebook.

I went to the puzzle room after dinner, and didn't see Jane again that evening. Dad dropped round and actually managed to do two pieces in eighteen minutes, breaking a forty-six-year record. I asked him what he made of Steve Emerald and he told me I should just wait and see what the morning brought. Oddly, Tommo didn't drop by. In fact, I swear that he'd been avoiding me for the entire day.

Violet was silent and thoughtful as we prepared to go to bed, and once the streetlamp had been extinguished we sat staring into the blackness together.

"I shouldn't have said that to the Substitute," she said. "They have the ear of National Colour, and he will not shirk from reporting me unfavourably."

"You did the right thing."

"I did not. I was angry he challenged my newly gained prefectural authority. The Greys may be workshy idiots, but they are *my* workshy idiots, to do with as I please, not him."

"Even so," I said, "your outburst will gain you a more positive view from the Greys."

"I do not seek approval from the cattle," she said, "so why should I want it from the Greys? They are not to be negotiated nor to be made friends with, they are to be exploited for their own good in order that they may see that self-improvement is the only way to achieve Chromatic betterment. It is true that we remain . . . *tolerant* of their sometimes wayward escapades, but only up to a certain point. Still," she added, "the Greys taking collective blame was quite impressive in a deluded togetherness sort of way. Made one almost feel like respecting them. Oh, and by-the-by, I have a plan whereby you will come to Vermillion for the duration of Jollity Fair."

"Really?" I said, not expecting this. "How come?"

"Mr. Cinnabar and I will explain everything on the train to Vermillion tomorrow afternoon. Come, we need to get some sleep."

I lay awake for a while, beyond the time at which Violet's breathing became more regular and quiet. Going to Jollity Fair was good news, but Tommo having a hand in it had set the alarm bells ringing.

JOLLITY FAIR

Aside from a few dissenters—always Orange—the Munsellian Doctrine was so well entrenched that on trains the residents sorted into the perfect Chromatic Hierarchy without even thinking about it—and not just which carriage, but one's *place* in which carriage. Stops on the way usually meant a quick game of "musical chairs" as the carriage rejigged itself to accommodate the precise Chromatic placement of the new passengers. Supporters of the Doctrine cited this as proof that the Munsell Way perfectly integrated itself with the human psyche.

—Ted Grey: *Twenty Years Among the Chromatacians*

There were rumours about Sally Gamboge during breakfast, and the news was confirmed once I'd completed Boundary Patrol supervision. The ex-Yellow Prefect had caught the Mildew while out on her early morning run, and voluntarily took herself to the Green Room after scrawling a short note to her family. Her entire household were currently in the quarantine shed, a small wooden hut nestled against the eastern edge of the boundary, the furthest place from anywhere within the village curtilage.

"Sally Gamboge must have done a deal with the Supervisory Substitute," said Dad when I dropped in to see him on the way to the railway station, "to take her instead of Penelope."

It was the right call to make, especially as Gamboge's career and standing in the village had rendered her mostly irrelevant.

"There'll be others not on my list," said Dad. "I think once the Prefects knew I wouldn't flip anyone the Big M, they stopped asking. Villagers will be dropping like flies unless someone intervenes."

"Intervenes?"

"Yes, intervenes."

"In what way 'intervenes'?"

"Whatever it takes to stop him. I'm sure we can get him to see reason, once we spell out the alternatives. Look, Robin Ochre and I have spared this village of Mildew for as long as we've both been here—Robin gave his life for it. I'll be Greyed if all that were for nothing."

I made to protest, but he raised his hand to quiet me.

"*I will do what needs to be done*, Eddie. I am the Swatchman and the villagers' health is my responsibility, a responsibility that I will not abandon—come what may. Now, what's this plan to get you to Jollity Fair all about?"

I told him I had no idea, and we agreed to keep in touch by way of the telegraph office via Velma, whose position there was now untouchable. We shared a hug and I left him to his thoughts and his plans.

The importance of Jollity Fair required that the 10:07 stop for us instead of steaming through as it did every other day, and as it rocked to a halt the platform was unusually full. There were fourteen residents in the East Carmine team, one short of the maximum, as Yewberry had to stay back to deputise in Violet and Bunty's absence. There were three hockeyball players, Violet, Daisy and Lucy, and of those Daisy and Lucy were also competing in unicycle hockey. The Penny-Farthing contingent was led by Doug who was accompanied by Earl Grey and Oscar

Greengrass, neither of whom I knew well. They would tackle speed and endurance events but not urban freestyle, as the last East Carmine resident to try any sort of trick on the Penny-Farthing now repots seedlings in the greenhouse using the fullest extent of their intellect. Tania was the village's juggling hope, and the topiary events—speed and freestyle—were represented by Mrs. Lilac and Sophie Lapis-Lazuli, who would join the eight-person Red Sector team for the events. Jam-making was the preserve of Lisa Scarlett, with Bunty McMustard there with her subcontrabass tuba for the "lowest attained note" event. Not to be missed was the gyro-bike team of Jane, Carlos and Amelia as assistant engineer.

There were four "Jollity extras": Tania had requested her children to come along in lieu of their promised holiday, and Penelope Gamboge was "general assistant to Violet," a made-up title that was probably invented so she could go on a freebie. It was her very good fortune she hadn't been staying with her grandmother Sally Gamboge, otherwise she'd be quarantined with the others. Ex-Prefect deMauve, his wife, mother and son Hugo made up the rest of the travellers. They had decided to take a short break in Purple Regis before the deMauve convention.

I wasn't on the Jollity Fair list, and neither was Tommo. Violet told me we would be working in the city, independent of the fair, which made me more puzzled, not less.

The passenger manifest was undertaken by Wesley, who wasn't very practised at it and did it slowly lest he make a mistake. But once that was done and the Penny-Farthings, unicycles and gyro-bike had all been checked, weighed and loaded, we boarded and were away with an excited buzz and cheery waves from the villagers who had come to see us off.

"So, wifey dearest," I said, from the comfort of the "Prefects only" compartment, "what's this all about?"

Violet looked across at Bunty, who was obviously in on all this. The deMauves were at the far end, and studiously ignoring us, but even so Violet spoke in a hushed tone.

"In a word, Eddie, cash."

"To pay off the crackletrap?"

"The debt is increasing daily. It will stay with us for ever if we don't pay it back and soon."

"So you aim to win big at Jollity Fair?"

"Very big indeed. But there's a snag: any merits we earn from winning are *book* merits, and we need *bearer* merits, the hard currency to pay off the debt. So I was speaking to Tommo, and he has a contact in Vermillion who is willing to take a wager on Jane to win the gyro-bike sprint race."

The gyro-biker Jamie "Mad Dog" Juniper, it has to be said, had won twenty-eight of the thirty-two races she'd entered, two of them on the "default winner by surviving" Rule. We stood to gain much if Jane *did* win, but it wasn't that likely.

"What sort of wager?"

"We think maybe they'll offer between ten or even twenty times the returned wager as Jane's never raced against anyone, yet is known to be fast—Carlos made sure her times were published in the racing pages of *Spectrum*."

"If Tommo wagers a thousand," said Bunty, who had run the numbers, "and they are offering ten to one, we'll get back ten thousand. *In cash*."

I think I might once have had fifty-eight cash merits at one time, but that was it. Ten thousand was a huge sum of money. But Violet wasn't done.

"But we don't aim to wager a thousand," she said.

"No indeed," I said, "because Juniper is an aggressive competitor and Jane might lose, and that will be a thousand down the drain."

"Providence favours the bold," said Bunty, who was clearly in on this. "We're going to wager *five* thousand."

"That would be impressive," I said, before I suddenly realised there were two very big problems with this plan. The first was Munsellian.

"I'm no expert," I said, "but this is in complete opposition to the Munsell edict that forbids wagers—aren't East Carmine's Prefects in enough trouble already?"

"That's the best part of it," said Bunty. "We're not involved. This is all something that Tommo has cooked up. He will be undertaking the whole wager for a five-hundred-merit fee, and donate the winnings to the village in exchange for early retirement. If it *does* go wrong, Tommo Cinnabar is so well known for his dishonesty that no one will ever believe we had anything to do with it—and there is nothing written on paper or discussed aloud beyond the four of us."

"I . . . see," I said, getting to the second issue: "and just where are you going to get five thousand up-front cash merits?"

"Well spotted," said Violet, "and this is where you come into the plan. You are, quite literally, sitting on a fortune."

"In what way?"

"Have you heard of the Rainbow Room?"

It was a dumb question. *Everyone* had heard of the Rainbow Room, but especially me. Mum went to Emerald City on the pretext of a diploma course in how to fold fitted sheets, and came back pregnant, two thousand cash merits poorer and got a son who topped 86 percent red. The practice was thought unseemly but not *strictly* against the Rules. The fidelity guidance from *Harmony* recognised that without recourse to unmarriage, it was realistic that unhappy people would form physical attachments to others, and it was healthier if that were permitted. It was legal to barter "personal favours" for "tradable commodities," so cash for seed was allowed, even if at a stretch. What was *totally* illegal, however, was the one thing you needed to become pregnant at all: being flashed the ovulating shade without a chit from a Prefect was strictly forbidden. But cash would buy anything that had a price, and for cash, everything had a price.

I never knew the name of the man who fathered me, and my mother wouldn't have either. You didn't use names in the Rainbow Room; it was all business—strictly transactional.

I didn't speak for several seconds.

"You're kidding me."

"I am most deadly serious, sweetheart—as I said, you are sitting on a fortune. *Sitting*," she added, for emphasis, "on a—"

"—yes, thank you, I get it."

"Then that's all agreed, darling. Tommo has booked you a room at the Green Dragon and he's already got a few clients lined up, but he's also confident of a goodly amount of walk-ins. With your eighty-six percent, I think you'll be very popular."

"It's eighty-seven if we round the figure up," I said, "but I'm not breeding stock, Violet—like a prize bull or a ram or something."

"No," she agreed, "not until your first assignment—then you will be all of those things. Six a day is usual for the more vigorous of males, so I thought I'd put you down for three given your mildly weedy demeanour, with lots of liquids and snacks in between—unless you think three is too much?"

"I'm not doing *any*, Violet."

She looked confused.

"Why ever not? You get to have some guilt-free off-marriage *youknow*, it's all in support of your village, and just think, it will dramatically increase the strength of your own Colour Group."

"I have a feeling I might be seeing more low Purples," I replied. "Even a few deMauves eager to increase their progeny's sight value—just like you did, in fact."

"Honestly, Eddie," said Violet, smiling to make light of what had clearly been her plan. "Always thinking the worst of me. It had not crossed my mind at all—*plus* I will permit you one percent of gross as pocket money, all hotel expenses paid—plus a four-day pass to Vermillion's many tourist attractions. Between engagements you could go and see the Badly Drawn Map, Colour Garden or Oz Memorial."

"I've seen them all."

"The Last Rabbit experience, then, we know you haven't seen *that*. A few days off in Vermillion is not to be sniffed at. I hear they do some good Lime in the back streets, and off-Rule novels and periodicals can be read for as little as a merit."

"I'm not doing it, Violet. Although fidelity Rules are fairly elastic, *consent* Rules are sacrosanct."

"I'm not *forcing* you," she said in a shocked tone. "I am merely . . . making you understand it's what you must do."

"I'm not a commodity ripe for exploitation, Violet."

Her eyes narrowed, and her voice rose.

"Dear Munsell above, Edward—how can you be so selfish? We are *all* commodities to be exploited. The contents of your testicles don't belong to you any more than the contents of my ovaries belong to me—our reproductive capacity is as much a part of our obligation to society as the sweat off our brow, or our bodies to the renderer. I have a responsibility for two and a half thousand people, Edward, and like it or not, as husband of the Head Prefect, that responsibility falls on you, too—you should be honoured to spread yourself among women eager for their children to have social betterment, and doubly honoured to clear a debt the village can ill afford. If you refuse, I can only assume that you are selfish beyond measure, and utterly beneath contempt."

I looked at Bunty, who shrugged and said: "I think that sounds fairly reasonable, don't you?"

"I'm not doing it, Violet."

"Why not?"

"Because I don't want to: it's distasteful, I'm not that sort of person, and—hang on, why am I even giving you any reasons?"

"We *all* do things we don't want to, Eddie," said Bunty. "I wanted to play the trombone, but I was made to play the tuba. It's the same thing."

"How can that be the same thing? Look, my answer's final— and you can't force me. The Consent Directive is *extremely* clear on this matter, and you can get into a lot of trouble if you are found to have coerced *any* person, of *any* gender, in *any* relation- ship of *any* intimate contact."

Violet shuffled forward on her seat to get closer to me and laid her hand uncomfortably high up on my thigh. "I know the Rules, Ed," she said in a soothing tone, "I was just hoping you'd be reasonable."

She looked at Bunty, who nodded.

"Okay," said Violet, "here's the clincher: there have been rumours going around about supernumeraries hiding out in the Greyzone. Had you heard?"

I felt a cold chill go down my spine.

"I don't know what you're talking about."

"I think you do. Before Sally Gamboge caught the Mildew she took me aside and outlined what she'd suspected for years."

She put a faux-comforting hand on my forearm.

"Now don't panic, honey, because this is not currently a pri- ority, as it would vex the Greys, and Greys are better left unvexed. But," she added, "if you were to selfishly think that your out- dated concept of consent weighed greater than the disruption and almost *guaranteed* Rebooting of anyone caught harbouring, well, that's entirely a matter for you."

I didn't say anything, which was frustrating as Jane would

probably have some pithy counter-argument that would have both Violet and Bunty squirming, but I had nothing. We were alone in the Prefects' compartment, with no one else present.

"I don't know about any supernumeraries, Violet."

She sighed and gave me a patronising smile.

"Poppet, Sally told me one lives in *your very own house*. Harry Lime? Half a face? Ring any bells?"

I hoped my concern didn't show. Sally Gamboge was making sure her legacy was secure from beyond the Green Room.

"So technically speaking, *you* are harbouring someone—as is your father. Reboot, pumpkin—for the pair of you. Bunty, will you act upon this knowledge?"

She made a big show of being undecided.

"Not unless you ask me. I have many things to take up my time, and sweeping the Greyzone for supernumeraries is at present a very low priority."

Violet smiled at me.

"Over to you, pumpkin."

I took a deep breath. I had one thing in my favour: time. I only had to agree to the Rainbow Room; I didn't have to do any-thing—yet.

"Okay then," I said, "but if Jane loses, all this will be for nothing, you'll be five grand out of pocket and I will have spent four days doing non-consensual *youknow* for nothing."

Bunty gave out an unpleasant snigger.

"Then you better make sure she wins, hmm?"

THE RAINBOW BROTHERHOOD

The Rainbow Room, like many things in Chromatacia, was permitted and not permitted all at the same time. It was against the Rules, but of most value to those in need of social advancement and with ready cash, who were often the ones who administered the Rules. If you wanted a good example of the hypocrisy that governed the nation, look no further.

—Ted Grey: *Twenty Years Among the Chromatacians*

We said little in the carriage after that. We rumbled quietly along the track, the gentle huffing of the steam train a calming audio accompaniment to the vapour that drifted past the window.

We stopped briefly at West Cardinal, then East Cardinal where we were joined in the carriage by their Deputy Red Prefect, who seemed ill at ease and introduced herself nervously.

"Competing at Jollity Fair?" asked Bunty.

"No," she said, mildly flustered, "business to take care of in Vermillion. I will be returning home as soon as possible."

We said nothing more, and less than an hour later the train arrived at Vermillion's station. It had been less than a month since I was here last, but it somehow seemed an age—and one in which I had learned a lot and not much of it good, nor welcome.

We were met by the organisers, all wearing diagonal red sashes around their bodies and welcoming all of us to the "Red Sector

CDXCVI Jollity Fair" and how they hoped our stay would be a happy and enjoyable one. They were also there to direct the competitors to the houses in which they would be staying, and to the people who would be their hosts. Each house in the nation would be expected to have provision for the household's equal number in guests; a Sector capital like Vermillion could swell to double its size with little to no discomfort.

There was a horse and cart to take the gyro-bike straight on down to the Jollity Fair show grounds situated to the north of the town. Both Bunty and Violet were greeted by one of their opposite numbers here in town—I think Vermillion had three of each Prefect, given its size—and were whisked away in cycle-taxis after Violet had handed me an "All Sites Vermillion Tourist Ticket," then gave me a faux-affectionate hug and told me to do my duty diligently and professionally, and how she'd see me in a few days. She then went to see off her family, who were due almost immediately out in Purple Regis. Jane walked over when Violet had gone and straight away figured something was wrong.

"What's up, Ed?"

"Tell you later."

We agreed to meet later for a drink at the Badly Drawn Map Visitors' Centre and Tearooms, and she was off with Carlos and Amelia to ensure the gyro-bike's safe passage to the velodrome.

"Where to, guv'nor?" asked a Porter, picking up my bag.

"This and this and this to the Green Dragon," said Tommo, pointing at our cases as he approached me in a cautious sort of manner.

"Did Violet tell you?" he asked once the Porter had trotted off with our luggage.

"I should punch you very hard, Cinnabar. What gives you the right to start selling off my plums to the highest bidder?"

"Highest bidder?" he echoed. "What a great idea. I never

considered running the Rainbow Room like an auction. Do you think it would work better that way?"

I told Tommo I hated him and walked off in the direction of the town centre, with Tommo having to almost run to keep up behind me.

"Hear me out," he said, "this could work out very well for the pair of us."

"With you and your fixing fee?"

"And the rest. I told Violet that we could get five hundred merits a go from you, but given you're eighty-six percent, the price I can negotiate is nearer a grand."

"It's closer to eighty-seven, actually."

"Whatever. The Purples are wanting to balance the Red/Blue line in their children, and Reds always want to be Redder. We can do as much as you want to do—and that five hundred merit clear profit on each siring? I am prepared to give you a quarter of that."

"Only a quarter?" I replied sarcastically, increasing my pace.

"I'm doing most of the work," he said without a hint of how stupid that sounded, "getting the clients, fixing the timetables, bribing the Swatchman, keeping the hotel sweet and the bellhops on our side. All you have to do is, well, *youknow*. And the best bit is that we make a profit whether Jane wins or loses. I can't see how this isn't a win-win for all of us."

I stopped walking so suddenly he almost ran into the back of me.

"Look here, parasite, I've had my arm twisted by Violet to agree to this, but what you, Tommo Cinnabar, are going to do for me now is figure out a way to make five thousand cash merits without me having to bruise my fidelity to Jane. Do that for me, and when I'm Red Prefect I will owe you big time, and having a Prefect who owes a favour is somewhere I think Tommo would very much like to be."

He stared at me incredulously.

"You *really* don't want to do this?"

"No. Why don't you just pretend to be me, Tommo? This sounds further up your street than mine."

"Won't work. The clients are wise to that little scam—no one is going to part with so much as a button until they see your picture in the merit book and read your Ishihara rating. The risks are huge—they'll want to make sure the goods are rock solid. They won't know who you are: tradition maintains you hold your thumb over your name to maintain anonymity."

"Just shut up for a moment, Tommo," I said. "Don't you see how objectionable I find all this?"

"Truly?"

"Truly."

"Let me give it some thought," he said in the manner of someone who is not planning on doing any such thing, "but since we have rooms booked at the Green Dragon with all expenses paid, it makes sense to use them, right?"

"I guess."

So we walked on in silence, along the bustling streets of the Sector capital.

The city status of Vermillion necessitated a different set of Rules regarding communal eating and governance, and the city hall was proportionately larger, as was the city square in front of it, and certainly able to hold the entire population for speeches, celebrations, and the twice-weekly roll call. More impressive still was the thrice-lifesize statue of Our Munsell, here made of bronze and polished to a high sheen.

Jane and I had spoken about how a city of this size would be governed, and knowing what we now know, the higher-than-normal level of urban-related Mildew was never due to poor sanitation, high population density or reduced morals as *Spectrum* would have you believe, but a lower acceptable threshold of wrongdoing. Rule-breaking was eradicated almost as soon as it broke out, presumably by a network of Yellows who answered to the Prefects, then passed on swiftly to the Swatchmen, who did the necessary.

"This is my kind of town," said Tommo, excited to be back in a place that offered so many money-making opportunities. "I brought the negatives of that racy picture project I was telling you about, and I've just noticed a photographic studio which might be able to make multiple copies at a discount—and quite possibly work as an exclusive outlet, too. I'll see you back at the hotel."

He then departed, but instead of making my way straight to the hotel, I walked on to where the Last Rabbit Experience was located, just inside the city wall and opposite the Colour Garden. The attraction had lost some of its lustre since the Last Rabbit died, but was still offering tours. I used my "All Sites Vermillion Tourist Ticket" to go in and was conducted around by an enthusiastic guide who told us all about the Last Rabbit in a talk that was probably the same as when it was alive, but now in past rather than present tense. We saw its empty enclosure, the actual dandelion leaf it choked on, and a short play with a man in a rabbit costume demonstrating the rabbit's last moments as interpretive dance.

When the guide asked us if there were any questions, a man asked how old the rabbit had been, and the guide said it had been captured one hundred and six years ago, but in that time had shown no evidence of ageing, so was thought to be immune to the ageing process. A small child at the front then asked how we knew it was the Last Rabbit, and the guide replied that no one had ever seen another rabbit, so it was assumed that there were no more.

"What if there was a Somewhere Else?" I said in the

contemplative silence that followed. "Another island perhaps, across the seas from here. Could there be other rabbits there?"

Everyone just stared at me.

"Somewhere Else?" asked the guide.

"Yes," I replied, "somewhere that isn't here."

"This is all there is," said the woman next to me in a reproachful tone. "Our Munsell tells us so."

"Only idle dreamers fill their heads with abstract nonsense," said someone else, and the mother of the child covered her son's ears in case I said anything more.

"I think you better leave," said the guide.

I walked into the Colour Garden after that, and moved around the beds of perfectly colourised flowers. The promise of full colourisation never rang less true, nor seemed more like the aspirational system of control that it was. I sat on a bench, gazed at the green grass for a moment, then upwards where two swans were circling high above, but seemingly more over the Jollity Fair site than here. I looked at my finger that still had a plaster on it.

"EDWARD DEMAUVE," I said to the reception at the Green Dragon. "Three nights. I think you have a reservation."

It was the same manager that I'd seen the last time we were here. A thin man with a finely shaped nose and only one ear. He wore his Blue Spot high up on his lapel, an unofficial yet broadly accepted signal that he knew how to "fix" things. The badge had much more relevance today.

"Mister deMauve," he said with a disarming level of insincere charm, "how *too too delightful* to have you staying in our little hotel." He looked left and right to check there was no one present, but lowered his voice anyway. "We are expecting a lot of . . . *Rainbow traffic* this Jollity Fair, and require that all of our *special guests* conduct themselves with discretion. While *fruitful liaisons* with others is not unruleful, the passing of currency with which to make introductions is not permitted. I do insist, therefore, that all such transactions are conducted off the property so as to bring no disrepute upon the establishment. As usual, the Hoople Room has been reserved for our Rainbowers. I believe some others are already there."

"Others?"

It had not occurred to me there would be others working the Rainbow business this week. The manager indicated where the Hoople Room was, then introduced the bellboy, whose name was "Sonny" and was, the manager said, "as discreet as an oak."

I thanked the manager and headed for the Hoople Room. Even though I had told Tommo to find another revenue stream to raise the cost of the wager, I had little hope that he would do such a thing, and I was now at least partially committed to undertake what I was here to do—but I didn't want to, and needed to speak to Jane.

The Hoople Room had a sign saying "Private Party Members Only" on the door, so I paused, took a deep breath, pushed the door open and stepped inside. There were half a dozen men within, all well dressed, and they were talking animatedly as I entered, but then abruptly stopped when they saw me.

"This is a private meeting," said a man sitting at the bar with a glass of muddy water in hand. "Best be on your way."

"No," I replied, "I'm in the right place. I'm here to . . . Rainbow."

The man who had spoken got to his feet and strode towards me with a broad smile and outstretched arm.

"Then welcome to the Rainbow Brotherhood—first time?"

"Does it show?"

"Spot them a mile off. It's all right, lad, we all have misgivings to begin with—the first is always the trickiest. Make it over that hump and it's plain sailing from there on in. Usually. I'm Mr. Blue, by the way."

"Hello," I said, "Eddie—"

"We don't use our real names," he said quickly. "Just the colour you bring to your clients. So you are?"

"Mr. Red, I guess," I said.

"We've already got a Mr. Red."

"Mr. Crimson?"

"Got one of them, too."

"Can I be Mr. Russett?"

"Not bright enough. We sell big promise here, my lad, upward mobility for your client's family. You can be Mr. Hollyberry. Gentlemen," he announced to the room in a louder voice, "this is Mr. Hollyberry, new to the trade. Over there is Mr. Crimson, Mr. Green, Mr. Yellow, Mr. Purple and Mr. Navy. That's Mr. Red sitting by the yucca plant with Mr. Lime, and Mr. Cardinal is seated at the pianoforte."

"Hello," I said, and they gave varying levels of enthusiasm in response.

"Drink?" said Mr. Blue. "The Hoople Room serves some of the best puddle water in the Sector."

Vermillion had fully embraced tea and coffee alternatives and was now a place where the mixing of puddle water and its derivatives had reached something of an art form. I thought I'd test the barman's skill.

"Can you mix me up a 'Fringe Hoof Print'?"

The barman was impressed.

"Sir knows his puddle water," he said. "One Hoof Print coming right up."

"So where are you on the scale?" said Mr. Red, settling himself next to me at the bar.

"I'm sorry?"

"How much Red are you offering?"

"Steady, Reddy," said Mr. Blue, who seemed to have made himself the leader of the small group, "you know we don't ask that. Leave the deals and the other unseemly aspects to the agents, eh? All we want to see is the timetable—and one that's not too onerous."

They all laughed about this, but the second Mr. Red didn't.

"It's no laughing matter," he said. "Every time I come down here there's someone Redder than me and I invariably get to offer cut-price seed to those on a limited budget—and my family do have to eat."

"That's because your plums are a bit lacking in the Red, old chap," said Mr. Crimson, the enmity between them clear, "perhaps your career lies elsewhere?"

"Let's keep it cordial, shall we?" said Mr. Blue. "We're all in this together, remember."

"There'll be a lot of clients," said Mr. Green. "There's work enough for us all, you'll see."

"It's not the volume of traffic that worries me," said Mr. Red. "It's the volatile price structure."

"One Fringe Hoof Print," said the barman, placing a glass of cloudy water on the bar. "Tell me what you think."

It was in a tall glass, chilled and with a crust of dark earth stuck to the rim. I sniffed at the glass and then took a mouthful.

"That's good," I said. "*Very* good. Peaty with a touch of clay, a rim of sun-dried lake bed and then a hint of shire horse urine right at the end as a kicker. If you'd told me you'd scooped this from a hoof print I'd believe you."

The barman nodded an appreciation of my praise, then went back to polishing glasses.

Mr. Yellow spoke up.

"Local boy?" he asked me.

"East Carmine, other side of Rusty Hill."

"Did you know Courtland Gamboge?"

"Not for very long."

"Odious little tick—gave Yellows a bad name. Is it true about Sally Gamboge resigning over corruption and then dying of the Mildew?"

"Every word."

"She had it coming, from what I heard. Want some advice, lad? Lots of rest and plenty of liquids, eight hours sleep and a good breakfast. Don't get greedy and think you can do more than four a day, or by the tenth appointment conception may not be guaranteed." He put a friendly hand on my shoulder. "Whether you do this once or make it your career, professionalism should always be your watchword."

"Professionalism?" said Mr. Green with a snort. "Oh, *please.* There are no refunds or recourse to the Prefects."

"The clients remember faces, you clot," said Mr. Yellow, "and we all need repeat business. Remember what happened to Mr. Azure during Cobalt City's Jollity Fair, six years ago?"

They all nodded sagely, but no one expanded on what had happened.

"Doing this for yourself or the village?" asked Mr. Blue.

"The village. I have a Prefect hanging over me, threatening me with the harm they may do unto others if I say no."

"That's how most of us get started," said Mr. Yellow. "Persuaded to pull a solid for the community. Next time out you're simply an export commodity. Mr. Navy over there does this full time and earns more cash for his village than their hat factory."

"Sixteen years now," he said.

Given how much the linoleum factory earned, that would be probably true for me, too.

"Don't let what you're doing get about in your home village," said Mr. Green kindly. "Rainbowing doesn't sit well with everyone—least of all with the partners of the clients who have been here. We remind them of what they didn't do, and don't have, the children who aren't really theirs."

The others nodded sagely and the conversation switched to Jollity Fair, and in particular the gyro-bike race. They'd heard of: "a blazingly fast newbie from the Outer Fringes' but didn't think she would be able to unseat Mad Dog who was "dangerously insane." They'd all left a gap in their schedules so they could go out and watch.

The door opened and Tommo popped his head into the room.

"Psst, Eddie," he said, "can I have a word?"

"You an agent?" asked Mr. Blue, and Tommo nodded.

"Then you can wait outside in the Fordpark."

"I just wanted—"

"I don't give a shit," said Mr. Blue. "Can't you read? This is our safe space in which we give each other mutual support in between assignments. Which means if we're in here, we're untouchable—get it?"

His manner was so aggressive that Tommo didn't say another word and hurriedly closed the door.

"Agents," snorted Mr. Yellow. "The lowest of the low, scraping their profit from the sweat of our gonads."

And they all laughed heartily and I nodded in agreement. I spent the next two hours chatting, and a more supportive and understanding group of men I would be unlikely to meet again. Yet I could sense buried resentment; there weren't many things in life that we could refuse to give, but consent was one of them, and few of us were here by choice. Most were in the brotherhood out of fiscal necessity, coercion or both.

"Are you a Rainbow child yourself?" asked Mr. Red, who seemed to have softened towards me.

"Yes."

"Most of us are," he said. "I think it's a cycle."

While I was there another Red came in, two more Greens and, unusually, a Grey. It seemed that in the Rainbow Brotherhood there was no hierarchy of any sort.

"Welcome," I said. "I'm surprised to see you here."

"Don't be," replied the Grey as he ordered a Pine Forest Puddle with a hint of moss. "My services are much in demand, just in an inverted sort of way."

"How so?"

"If a Grey woman marries up hue but they decide between them that they want their children to remain Grey, then she comes to me to negate any possible colour vision from her off-spring. I'm unusual in that I'm pure Grey—not an ounce of colour in me. Sometimes it's as difficult to stay Grey as it is to stay a high colour."

"How do they afford you?" I asked.

"They're always freebies," he said with a smile. "I don't make a bean."

"Then who pays for the room and your meals?"

He looked around the Hoople Room but it was Mr. Blue who answered.

"Everyone chips in," he said. "You'll be asked to make a contri-bution. The Brotherhood looks after its own."

THE SIDESHOWS

At Jollity Fair the teams were Red, Green, Yellow and Blue. Despite your individual hue, you competed under the Colour of your Sector. Someone had run the numbers and found that it was Greys or ex-Greys who made up almost two-thirds of the winners. If the Grand Prize was based on personal affiliation alone, the Greys would have been the outright winners seven years in every ten.

—Ted Grey: *Twenty Years Among the Chromatacians*

I told Tommo I didn't want to talk to him when I eventually came out of the Hoople Room, and he said that was totally fine but I had my first client at 9 P.M. that night, just before lights out. She was staying in the hotel so quick and easy. She'd come to me.

"I could have booked three for you today," he said, "so I'm really on your side."

"I bet you are. Have you thought of an alternative plan to make the five thousand merits for the wager?"

"Hang on—are you *serious* about not doing this? I thought it was just Eddie being a goody-two-shoes."

"I've never been more serious. If you don't cancel my nine o'clock I'll simply be a no-show—you can tell her I had an accident in the revolving door."

"You wouldn't dare."

"Wouldn't I?"

He narrowed his eyes and stared at me.

"Perhaps you might. What will we tell Violet? She's asked me for a daily financial report."

"Tell her what you want. Just cancel my nine o'clock."

"I can't. I've already taken the money and she's been flashed the ovulating shade. You wouldn't want her to get all hot and bothered for nothing, would you? It's all arranged, Eddie, you can't back out now."

I glared at him, then walked out of the hotel and down the street to the central post and telegraph office. Tommo, quite wisely, had decided not to follow me. I still had six hours to think of a way out—or just not show up.

I walked into the post office.

"Edward Russett," I said to one of the telegraph clerks, using my old name to simplify things, "anything for me?"

"Postcode?"

"RG6 7GD."

The clerk went through the files and said there was nothing. I said I'd like to send one, so quickly scribbled out a note on the form. The clerk counted out the words and charged me two merits. The message read:

++ DEAR FATHER ARRIVED SAFE IN VERMILLION ++
VIOLET HAS INSISTED I HAVE AN ALL-EXPENSES ROOM AT
THE GREEN DRAGON TO HELP WITH VILLAGE FINANCES
++ KEEP ME POSTED ON DEVELOPMENTS AT HOME ++
REGARDS EDWARD ++

He'd be able to figure out what was going on, and if he knew me, he'd know I wouldn't want to. The Badly Drawn Map Visitors' Centre and Tearooms was opposite the post office, and that's where I found Jane waiting for me. She was wearing a Red spot-badge in place of her Green, which was an unthinkably grave misdemeanour, but I reckoned we were past caring. We kissed right there in front of everyone and headed off towards Jollity Fair.

We walked along Widemarsh Street, past the colour shop, saddlers and repairers, then exited via the North Gate. Although Jollity Fair was outside the scope of the Rules and essentially governed itself on the ingrained sense of obedience we had all followed since birth, it still needed to be outside prefectural jurisdiction so was always situated beyond the Outer Markers.

"How are things?" I asked. "Seen Mad Dog Juniper yet?"

"I'll meet her at First Practice later."

Jane outlined what had happened so far, which wasn't much— mostly the teams looking at the facilities and prepping the gear after transportation. They hadn't been out on the track yet, and she said if I were doing nothing, to come and watch First Practice that afternoon.

We ambled past apple orchards on one side and pig-maize on the other, then removed our spot-badges and placed them in our pockets once we had passed a wide gate set into a grove of clutching bramble that delineated the Outer Boundary. Competitors would be expected to wear an upper garment of their team colour and in a Univisual hue so that all would know, but no individual Chromatic affiliation would be shown. Here, you played only for your Sector.

"So," she said, "what are you doing here and what's Violet and Tommo's big plan?"

"Oh, nothing massive," I replied, thinking perhaps the Rainbow Room was something I should handle on my own, just in case there was no way out of my first assignment that evening. "Just Tommo wanting me to use my connections to peddle those naked pictures of his, and to try and recruit anyone willing to act as models."

She tipped her head on one side and stared at me.

"So why is Violet involved?"

"They need to make some—um—quick bucks to wager on your race."

"They can make that much?"

"Apparently."

The apple orchard ended and we found ourselves at the edge of the Jollity Fair show ground, an area that encompassed Vermillion's horse-racing track, playing fields and banked-track velodrome. All the Penny-Farthing riders were out testing their machines on the Perpetulite, getting the feel of the surface, their machines, and each other. Our velodrome back in East Carmine was almost perfectly smooth, but Vermillion's example was suffering from *Perpetulitic Necrosis* that resulted in several unsightly bumps, scabs, undulations and dips—especially on the exit of turn three, where you had to ensure your exit speed was fast enough in order to stay high on the banking to avoid the hole.

"What sort of wager is Tommo looking at?" asked Jane.

"He thinks you'll be around twelve to one to win, but we won't know for sure until the wagerers see you ride. On a five-thousand-merit wager that's a potential payday of, hang on, I've got it written on a piece of paper somewhere—here; sixty thousand cash merits."

She whistled low.

"That's enough to make a big colour splash in the village, and Violet would be known as the Head Prefect who delivered. Does Tommo really think he can raise five thousand on a few dozen pictures of naked people? That boy needs to be punched hard and often."

"He has been. It makes not the slightest discernible difference."

As we watched, a Penny-Farthing rider on the velodrome attempted to clear the damaged section of Perpetulite at full speed, but the large front wheel buckled with the impact and deposited the rider flat on his face, knocking him unconscious. There was a murmur from the small crowd who had gathered to watch the practice sessions, and while no one wanted to see anyone badly hurt on the velodrome, it wasn't uncommon and added greatly to the excitement.

"Good job he's not one of ours," said someone close by as the groaning rider was loaded on to a hand cart to be taken to the Emergency Swatchman for treatment.

We walked away from the velodrome and towards where the other competitions were being held. Vermillion had not hosted a Jollity Fair for five years, so the privet hedges had grown in lush profusion, perfect for the topiary speed event. Already we could see Mrs. Lilac and Sophie eyeing up their allocated privet bushes to figure out what shape could be achieved and whether any exciting "overhangs" or "voids" could be successfully cut, always a favourite with the judges.

The rest of the events—field and track, unicycle events, urban freestyle Penny-Farthing, hockeyball, competitive shouting, musical superlatives—were in a huge marquee in which the colour-mixing events were also held. Inside we found Bunty polishing her subcontrabass tuba among a sea of other outsize instruments and seemingly oblivious to us or anything else.

Beyond this were the traders, who were buying and selling items of interest: some legal, but most not. People here to trade carried their valises with them, so goods bought or sold could be transported free from the Yellows' judgemental gaze.

The first trader we came across was selling potted clutching bramble and bonsai yateveo trees, and further on were tables of old tech—hundreds of portable telephones, adding machines and grooved discs. There were also books, periodicals, paper ephemera and various items of scrap colour. Next to this was a floaty table and a dealer in Taxa numbers who happily gave me a merit for the zebra foal I'd spotted. There was then someone who had barcodes to sell, and next to him was a woman trading Everspins and lightglobes, all of which were either glowing or whirring quietly to themselves. After that was a dealer selling parts that belonged to one of the twelve known creatures of manufactured origin. The centrepiece on display was the head of a Tin Man which would, a sign stated, "blink the answer to simple arithmetic."

"Cash paid for functional Tin Men parts," said the trader, seeing that we were interested. "A merit for five pounds of scrap, ten merits for a pound of anything functioning. I can collect, too," he added, "if the part you have is too big for your valise."

"What do you think they were used for?" asked Jane.

"It's unclear," said the trader. "There are three types that I know of, the largest one will actually carry a man inside and increase your strength tenfold, so perhaps just heavy work. The two other types didn't need a person anywhere near them, and might have been designed for fighting."

"Fighting what?" I asked.

"I don't know," he said. "Large animals, perhaps—something like a rhinosaurus, only bigger, maybe."

"I think they were fighting humans," said Jane.

"Why would a Tin Man fight a human?" asked the trader.

"They were used by humans to fight *other* humans," she said in one of her flashes of inspiration. And once she'd said it, nothing seemed more obvious. The land-crawlers, the flak towers, the flying machines, the small things that pop when thrown in the incinerator, the discarded things that explode, the buried cans that can kill.

"It was a long fight, and brutal, and there were many dead. The teeth of the Previous we find might indicate thousands. In fact, maybe *thousands* of thousands."

It was unguarded talk, but that's what Jollity Fair was all about.

Still eager to find the Herald, we moved on to the sideshow tents with their luridly painted hoardings advertising the grotesques within. The tents were arranged in a circular fashion around a large open area, at the centre of which was a fire-pit with large logs arranged for seating. The ill-dressed people who were sitting and cooking maize and bits of meat looked as though on the very edge of society, people who had either rejected or been rejected from the Munsell Way, but had not chosen to descend into the more unsophisticated trappings of the Riffraff. I could see how Harry Lime with his facial injury could find this a safe place to live.

Beyond the side shows were pigs, goats and other wildstock tethered to stakes in the ground. There was a butcher's table with a recent pile of offal upon the grass, the choicest parts of which several blanket-covered Leapers were sorting through, ignoring the flies and the jackals who were sitting close by, awaiting their turn. Beyond this were corralled the pull-oxen, a dung heap, piles of rubbish and two bodies on a hand cart ready for the renderers, one of them the Penny-Farthing rider we had seen earlier, who clearly did not make it. There were more Leapers further out, living in tents that consisted of only a sheet of dirty canvas, crudely draped over a framework made of sticks.

"What does a Herald look like?" I asked.

"Like the one we saw in our heads, I guess," she replied. "Neat and polite and with a monotone voice."

One of the Leapers came closer to us and thrust a grimy hand from her blanket. I could smell it from where we were standing ten feet away, and the sores on her arms were running with moisture.

"Help my child," she said, and showed us, very briefly, the child that we were meant to help, held against her emaciated red-blotched naked body. The child was small, dirty and lifeless and had been, I think, for some time. I recoiled at the spectacle, as did Jane.

"Renderers won't take her," added the Leaper. "Quality control. Help me?"

Jane pulled a coin from her pocket and dropped it in front of the Leaper as was the custom, and we quickly moved away.

"Wow," I said, looking over my shoulder as the Leaper rummaged in the grass for the coin, "makes the Riffraff seem positively hygienic by comparison."

"Focus, Eddie. The Herald."

We slowly walked around the sideshows in an attempt to find the Herald and even surreptitiously enquired, but aside from it being reported that others had asked too, we had no luck.

"I could check inside the two-headed sheep tent," I said in a hopeful tone of voice, "or among the anthropological specimens kept in jars."

There was no time for that, however, as somewhere in the distance three trumpets sounded a shrill alarm and we returned to the playing field in time for the first event: lowest note sustained on a brass or wind instrument. This was Bunty's time to shine, although as a spectator sport the event was somewhat unexciting, as it involved a player going very red in the face and needing a lot of puff to produce a note that was below the threshold of human hearing. Fortunately a trained elephant was on hand to indicate what it could hear, and when. Bunty came in a creditable second, with the Green competitor managing to go even lower on a super-sub-bass saxophone, and emitting a note so low that the elephant made off in fright, crushing the Blue's sub-bass clarinet in the process.

Soon after that it was the hockeyball team try-outs to see who was to be selected for the Sector teams. The East Carmine contingent acquitted themselves well, with Violet in possession of the ball for quite a long time until she was taken out by an opponent on the Green team and carried off the field on a stretcher, clasping her shin and screaming in agony.

"Music to my ears," said Jane. "Coming to the gyro-bike First Practice?"

"Wouldn't miss it for anything."

FIRST PRACTICE

Gyro-bikes were the only technology to have progressed within the past two hundred years. The primary reason for this was that Prefects liked to watch the spectacle.
—Ted Grey: *Twenty Years Among the Chromatacians*

Two of the four bikes were out and ready for action with the engineers fussing over them. Both of them were having their gyros run up to speed by the use of an exempted Everspin and a low hum was already filling the air. It was felt more than heard, up through the ground and our feet. Carlos and Amelia were clustered around Jane's bike and as soon as we arrived they all started to converse in their impenetrable language—something about spindle shafts or gigglepins or magnetic bearings or something. The onlookers, of which there were a great many, seemed to be enjoying the preparations as much as they would the race itself, while nearby a reporter from *Spectrum* magazine asked the Yellow team's Janitor what they should expect.

Someone stood next to me, and I turned to find Lucy, direct from the hockeyball try-outs.

"Congrats on making the team."

She nodded her thanks, and we chatted about whether Lisa Scarlett was as good at competitive jamming as we had hoped, when a sudden hush fell upon the group of spectators and competitors. The reason was soon clear.

"That's who Jane has to beat," said Lucy as she pointed towards where a gyro-bike was being pushed to the start line by an engineer. The rider she indicated was walking behind: a tall, elegant woman with luxuriant gloss-black hair tied up in a tight bun. She was wearing well-worn kneepads, gloves and a heavy jacket. Her nose, I noted, was worn down at the tip, doubtless due to some racing mishap or other. She caught no one's eye and just concentrated on the bike.

"Jamie 'Mad Dog' Juniper," added Lucy in case I hadn't guessed, "about to show us what she can do. See those people up there?"

She pointed to a group of men and women sitting in the stands in a small huddle.

"Yes?"

"Wagerers. They're here to see how Jane compares to Mad Dog before they fix the level of payouts. Jane's never been in a race, but has blisteringly fast times—better even than Juniper—so they'll be watching both of them this morning and fix their wager levels on that."

Once Mad Dog's bike was charged up and the air filled with the whine of flywheels at dangerously high speeds, she flung a leg across the machine, readied herself for a moment and the start official dropped her flag. The whine lowered in pitch as Mad Dog accelerated off around the circuit while hunched down into the fairing to reduce air resistance. The crowd was utterly silent as they watched her take the first bend and go high on the banking, still accelerating until she was almost horizontal, wheels planted just below the white safety line.

"That's daring," said Jane.

"She'll never keep this up," added Amelia, also staring at the spectacle.

Mad Dog came off the banking, passed the outside of the

hole which had caught the Penny-Farthing earlier, then accelerated fast down the straight until she hit the back curve, then planted herself once more against the white line, expertly came down from the banking and passed the start line with a speed that was almost a second faster than Jane's best. This continued for another lap until about midway through the penultimate corner when the gyros, depleted of their speeding mass, began to slow the bike down. Mad Dog came down off the banking at a lower speed, steered *inside* the annoying hole, then crossed the finish line where her engineer and team were waiting for her.

"That was at eighty-five percent of maximum gyro speed," said Carlos. "She'll be running ninety-eight percent for the race and will take the last bend without power, yet with enough energy to stay high on the banking."

"So you're saying the race is hers?" I said.

"Nope," said Lucy, "but as good as."

"Okay," said Carlos to Amelia, "let's power her up."

They connected a large Everspin to a splined shaft and the heavy weights began to slowly come up to speed. I left them to it and went and stood next to Tommo, who was also watching the proceedings.

"Good afternoon," he said. "Think Jane can beat her? There's no cash or glory for second prize."

"You know what?" I said. "I'm not sure it matters if she does or she doesn't. All we're doing here is working to pay off an unwanted crackletrap debt that was ordered by a corrupt Prefect who's now on her way to becoming tallow and bonemeal."

"Does that mean Jane won't push to win?"

"She'll bust an ovary to win—just not for the village. For herself. She likes to win. You may have noticed."

"Ah," came a voice, "Mr. Hollyberry. You have an interest in gyro-biking?"

It was Mr. Blue, from the Brotherhood. He was accompanied by Mr. Green, Mr. Red, Mr. Navy and Mr. Grey. Most men at Jollity Fair had loosened their collars and removed their ties due to the relative freedom, but the Brotherhood were still impeccably dressed, which made them stand out.

"Sort of," I said, suddenly flustered to see them. "Jane's an—um—ex-girlfriend."

"Is she now?" said Mr. Grey.

"Is this your agent?" asked Mr. Green, staring at Tommo. "Thomas Cinnabar at your service," said Tommo. "I'm always on the lookout for new clients if any of you gentlemen—"

"Can I stop you right there?" said Mr. Green, and then, while Tommo waited to see what he would say, Mr. Green added: "No, nothing more. That was a complete sentence."

And they all laughed.

"I'm Lucy," said Lucy, introducing herself, "a friend of Eddie's."

They all tipped their hats politely, and since she was a friend of mine and logic might suggest she was Red too, Mr. Red gave her his business card. She looked at it, raised her eyebrows and then looked at me. I shrugged and suddenly felt a little hot, but didn't have to say anything as Alice Blue's practice was up next and she squealed off the line with an unwelcome wheel spin. She slewed sideways for a moment, but soon straightened up and took the first banked corner—yet a good six inches lower than where Mad Dog had taken it.

"I'm not sure Alice Blue has much of a chance," I said.

"It's about stored energy as much as it's about speed," said Tania, who had also turned up to watch with her children. "Mad Dog rides full out, but it makes her gyros run down quicker. The trick is to get the best mix of speed and energy depletion. If you still have some spinning mass when it comes to the last corner and you're heading for the finishing line, then that's where a race is won."

"The higher up the banking, the faster you're going," said Tommo, who seemed to be in conversation with Mr. Grey, "but go too fast and you'll be over the top. I wouldn't rate a rider's chances if that happened, nor any spectators she hit."

Having the Brotherhood so close was feeling increasingly awkward, especially with Jane around. But they made no signs of moving away from me, so I moved away myself, making it look as if I were finding a better view. It didn't work. Tommo joined me, and Lucy and Tania and her kids too, then the rest of them.

We watched as Emma Yellow had her turn, and although faster than Alice off the line, her bike had smaller and less efficient stream-lining, and she came in slowest.

It was Jane's turn, then, and there was silence from the hundred-plus crowd as she climbed on to the bike that Carlos and Amelia had pushed up to the start line. I noted that Mad Dog Juniper and her team were also there, arms folded, waiting to see what Jane had in her. There was barely a squeal from the tyres as she accelerated off the line, but she took a different approach to the race—fast into the turn and about as close to the white line as Jamie, but then backed off the throttle and came down from the banking before the turn had ended, then fast down the straight and repeating this through all the corners. By the time she had come off the last corner it was clear she still had spinning mass in hand as she crossed the finish line in third, three tenths of second behind Alice. If she wanted to beat Jamie she'd have to find almost a second and a half a lap from somewhere.

"Based on that performance," said Tommo, "she's probably something like a fifteen- or twenty-to-one outsider. Good news if we win, but given the odds, they aren't expecting her to. She's going to have to do better in the race."

Tommo walked off to negotiate the wager while we walked over to where Amelia and Carlos were pushing the gyro-bike back towards the workshop. Annoyingly, I could sense the Brotherhood following me.

"That was a good speed," I said to Jane. "Think you can beat the Mad Dog?"

"Maybe," she said, "maybe not."

We'd reached the workshop by now, and at about the same time as Jamie Juniper made an appearance. She had a strange, featureless sort of expression and eyes that didn't seem to blink much, if at all. The two of them made formal introductions, shook hands, but the pleasantness pretty much ended there.

"So, newbie," said Jamie, "what was that pantomime all about?" Jane stared back at her impassively.

"I know what you're up to," continued Mad Dog. "My guess is you were running at seventy-five percent spin speed, and were doing that lazy-eight way of riding to make me think you're no good—I've seen your times, Brunswick: you're better than that."

"Guilty as charged," said Jane, "and I'm sorry, the point of this conversation is . . . what?"

Jamie leaned closer.

"Oh, I don't know," she said, suddenly not sounding dangerous at all. "I thought I'd come in here and sound like I'm menacing you as it plays well with the crowds outside. Do you aim to ride faster than that on the day?"

"It's quite likely," said Jane.

"Hmm," said Jamie, "well, don't try too hard because although I quite like flower-arranging and playing with puppies and talking to trees when I'm not riding, when I *am* riding a sort of green mist comes down and I'll do anything to win. Literally, I mean *anything*. I feel quite bad about it to be honest, but something just clicks in my head. I'm sort of here to apologise in case I kill you or cause serious injury."

"That's very thoughtful," said Jane, who seemed a little rattled by Jamie's odd understanding of her ruthlessness, "but I do quite like to win myself."

"It won't be enough," said Jamie with a smile. "I don't *like* to win, I accept nothing else. Get in my way and you'll feel my elbows. Look, I'm glad we've had this little chat and now I better get back into character."

And she scowled and marched out of the workshop. Unwisely, Mr. Green stepped into her path to offer her his business card and the benefit of his services. She didn't take the card, and instead glared at him.

"Stop me when I'm walking again," she growled, "and I'll crush your livelihood with my bare hands. Got it?"

"Yes," he said meekly, quickly getting out of her way. "Sorry."

"Was any of that true?" I asked Jane. "About seventy-five percent spin speed and stuff?"

"All of it," said Jane. "Jamie's way better than I thought, and curiously unhinged. Who are they?"

The Brotherhood had gathered behind me, presumably wanting to be introduced.

"A few guys I met earlier. They wanted to meet a real live gyro-bike racer. Jane Brunswick, these are . . . the guys."

"Hello," said Jane suspiciously. Mr. Green reached into his pocket for a business card but I shook my head at him and he turned the gesture into removing an invisible piece of fluff from his coat.

"You seem very well dressed for Jollity Fair," said Jane, "and I can smell soap even though it's well past bath time. Eddie, are you mixed up with the Brotherhood? Was that Tommo and Violet's money-making scheme?"

"That's very insulting," said Mr. Blue, who could think on his feet and was clearly used to this sort of thing. "We're a shantymen quartet due to entertain the spectators between events tomorrow."

"There are five of you."

"I'm the understudy," said Mr. Red, who like them all, knew when to stick together with a cover story. "Mr. Grey has been a little hoarse recently."

Mr. Grey coughed to lend credibility to the lie.

"We'll be off now," said Mr. Blue. "Rehearsals. Pleased to meet you, Miss Brunswick, and good luck tomorrow."

They hurried off, but Jane was still staring at me suspiciously. "What's going on?"

I thought of Violet's threat to unmask the supernumeraries if I didn't go through with this.

"Nothing's going on. Can you beat Jamie?"

"Don't change the subject. Tommo, you tell me what's going on." Tommo had just returned.

"The wagerers are offering you fifteenfold on your stake," he said. "They know you were holding back on the speed, but still don't think you have the experience to win."

"Is that a fact?" she said, almost between gritted teeth. "And how, *precisely*, are you going to get the money to do this wager anyway?"

A look of terror crossed Tommo's face and he looked to me for explanation.

"I told you," I said, "Tommo's naked pictures. Vermillion is a big market. I don't want to act as a salesman, but what the hell—I get to come to Vermillion and visit Jollity Fair."

Jane narrowed her eyes.

"So those men weren't Rainbow Brotherhood?" she said.

"No."

"What do you think, Tania?"

Tania glanced at me, then at Tommo. She *definitely* knew they were the Brotherhood.

"I think," she began slowly, "that sometimes you have to take people on their word."

Jane looked at Lucy, who also nodded agreement.

"Okay then."

The matter wasn't resolved in any way, shape or form, but it was barely four in the afternoon—I still had five hours to wangle my way out of my first assignment. Providence, however, had other ideas.

"Is that *you*, husband?"

It was Violet, and before I could say anything, she added:

"Why are you not at the Green Dragon, putting Red babies into Red ladies?"

"Oh-oh," said Tommo, trying to move away, but Lucy trod on his foot so he couldn't. I thought Jane would go ballistic, but she didn't. She looked at Violet, then at Tommo, then at me and said in a quiet voice:

"Why did you conceal the truth from me?"

There was no point in lying anymore.

"Because if I don't do this Violet will have supernumeraries shaken out of the Greyzone and all the harbourers sent to Reboot."

"Is that true?" said Jane to Violet.

"It most certainly is," said Violet, "and you better win tomorrow, because if you don't and Eddie's well-earned five thousand gets wasted, the same thing will happen. What's the wager, Tommo?"

"Fifteenfold."

"So on a five-thousand-merit wager we could make . . ."

"Seventy-five thousand," put in Lucy.

She smiled.

"Enough to pay off the crackletrap and lay down some feed-pipes. Listen," she said, trying to sound conciliatory, *"personally,*

I do not want the supernumeraries out of the Greyzone. Live and let live, I say. I respect the Greys and everything they do for us, but I *will* move the village forward now I am Head Prefect. Do we understand one another?"

"As clear as day," said Jane.

"Then I shall leave you. Husband, don't you have somewhere to be right now?"

And she departed.

"Sorry," I said, once Violet was out of earshot, "but I'm—"

"Have you had an assignment yet?"

"This evening is my first, at nine."

Jane signalled to Lucy to get off Tommo's foot, which she did.

"Do you want to?"

"No, but there's really no choice in the matter."

She said nothing and gave me a hug, then left to see where she could make a few improvements to the gyro-bike.

"Well," said Tommo, "that went a lot better than I imagined—I thought Jane would punch you, then me."

"She may still," I replied.

"Never mind. At least we're still on track."

"You and Violet are still on track. Me, I'm little more than breeding stock."

THE VALUE OF NOTHING

Since long distance telephonic communications were Leapbacked, the telegram was the primary method to communicate between villages. It was generally reliable, but was not secure—to ensure Yellows weren't reading your messages, it was safer to use the post, although that could take between five days and eighteen years, depending on how many times you had moved.

—Ted Grey: *Twenty Years Among the Chromatacians*

I walked back into town with Tania, whose children seemed a lot better behaved here than in East Carmine. She was chatty and friendly but the trepidation over what I had to do that evening gave me a feeling of heaviness, and the conversation was muted. She asked me if everything was okay, and I told her I was fine.

I stopped off at the post office to pick up a telegram from Dad, who'd answered the one I'd sent earlier.

++ DEAR SON ++ MILDEW HAS TAKEN DONALD BLUE BUT IT WILL GO NO FURTHER IF WE CAN HELP IT ++ SEND BEST LUCK TO LUCY AND JANE AND THE TEAM ++ REMEMBER THAT NO IS A COMPLETE SENTENCE AND REQUIRES NO CLARIFICATION ++ TRUST THAT WHICH YOU SEEK YOU WILL FIND ++ BE OF HONOURABLE INTENT ++ REGARDS FATHER ++

It didn't tell me much more than I knew already, but I didn't want either him or the Greys to take matters into their own hands.

++ DEAR FATHER ++ WOULD BE GRAVE MISTAKE TO TAKE RADICAL ACTION TO STOP SPREAD OF MILDEW ++ SUGGEST QUIET AND REASONED APPROACH ++ SOFTLY SOFTLY CATCH DONKEY ++ JANE THIRD IN FIRST PRAC-TICE ++ BUNTY SECOND WITH TUBA ++ VIOLET LUCY AND DAISY ON HB SQUAD ++ NO SIGN OF WHAT WE SEEK ANY CLUES AS TO WHERE QUESTION MARK ++ LOVE TO VELMA YOUR SON ++

I read it back, handed it over to the telegraph clerk and paid them three merits. At this rate I'd be skint before I got home. I returned to the Green Dragon where I met Mr. Blue in the lobby, chatting to the hotel manager, and he broke off when he saw me.

"That meeting was a little awkward," he said. "Jane your girl-friend?"

"She's kind of a bit more than that."

"Wife?"

"Still more."

"Oh," he said, "you're each nothing without the other? Two hearts beating as one?"

"Something like that."

"And she didn't know about the Rainbowing?"

"No."

"Does she now?"

"Yes."

"Did she get angry?"

"No."

"Oh dear. So are you being coerced into this?"

"No. Kind of. Actually, yes, yes I am."

I rubbed my eyes and he put a fatherly hand on my shoulder.

"I was too, for the first three years. Then it got easier, especially when my wife would no longer touch me and moved in with an Indigo. I think of her every day; this business has taken everything from me." He paused for thought. "Tell me, what currency is this coercion measured in?"

"If I don't earn five thousand merits then people will start to die."

"Ah," he said, then thought for a moment before asking: "How much Red have you got, if you don't mind me asking?"

"Eighty-seven percent. So long as you round up."

He raised his eyebrows.

"You're kidding me?"

"No," I said, and showed him my merit book to prove it. He gave out a small chuckle.

"With plums that rosy, lad, I think you and me can sow a little magic to make some easy gravy and find a solution to your issues. Meet me in the Fordpark in half an hour."

Behind the Green Dragon and next to the city's long unused ice-house was where all the Ford Model Ts were parked, as many outlying villages were not serviced by the train, and Ford was about the only other realistic method of transport. There were about a dozen people milling about when I arrived a half-hour later. Either agents, clients, agents for Rainbowers, agents for clients, clients who also acted as agents for other clients, and even agents acting for other agents, eager to strike the best deal possible.

If you factored in all the agents, the hotel, food, drink and the Swatchman for the ovulating shade, the Rainbow Rooms generated a lot of revenue, and not just for the donor.

Tommo was talking to the Deputy Red Prefect we'd seen on the train, and seemed to be about to strike a deal.

"Would you excuse us for a moment?" said Mr. Blue who had also just arrived, addressing the Deputy Red. "Mr. Hollyberry has recently had a change of management. We can talk again soon. Five minutes?"

She looked relieved and quickly made herself scarce, much to Tommo's dismay.

"Wait, what?" he said.

"You heard me. You are no longer representing Mr. Hollyberry."

"You can't do that."

"I think I just did. Who represents you, Mr. Hollyberry?"

"Sorry, Tommo, but Mr. Blue does."

Tommo's eyes opened wide and he made to speak, but Mr. Blue cut him off.

"Observe carefully," said Mr. Blue to Tommo, "and learn."

He turned to the other agents.

"Who here represents the selling of Redness?"

Three men and a woman put up their hands, presumably each of them representing a Red Rainbower. I'd only met two, so more must have arrived today.

"We need to talk for our mutual benefit."

All the agents nodded, interested to see what he had to offer.

"Most of you already know me as Mr. Blue," he said, "but I'm now Mr. Hollyberry's agent. His previous agent Tommo Cinnabar here overreached himself with assumed authority, and you are now talking to me. Yes?"

They murmured their agreement.

"Good. Mr. Hollyberry, show them your merit book."

I opened it on the back page where my Redness was logged: 86.7 percent. They all looked annoyed, one threw up her hands and the two others swore under their breath.

"That might be so," said one of the agents, "and while Mr.

Hollyberry might get the lion's share of trade there is a limit to how much and how often. There'll still be enough for all of us."

"It's worse for you than you think," said Mr. Blue. "Mr. Hollyberry may not look like much, but he has it where it counts. His recovery period is almost non-existent, the goods are always delivered perfectly, and so long as food and drink are ample, this man has a gift that will keep on giving."

"I don't believe you," said one of the agents.

"Scepticism could render you bankrupt, my friend, so listen up: Mr. Hollyberry here can easily do ten or twelve clients a day without breaking a sweat, and we plan on a means-tested cost basis to service *all* clients, irrespective of budget. The way I see it, ladies and gentlemen, is that the Red Seed business is closed for you this year. You might as well pack up and go home right now."

"Then why are you even speaking to us?"

"I'm speaking to you," said Mr. Blue slowly, "because Mr. Hollyberry had to marry up-colour and he and his former girlfriend want to enjoy a little quality time together before they begin their separate lives. With eighty-seven percent Redness, Eddie can easily command seven hundred and fifty merits a go. Over the three-day period with thirty clients—minimum—there's a potential payday of twenty-two and a half grand."

He paused for effect and lowered his voice.

"That business, his business, can be yours for a measly six thousand. Give us that *up front* and my client agrees to stay out of the market, trousers firmly buttoned, his talent exclusively reserved for his loved one. Do we have anyone scheduled for Mr. Hollyberry yet, Mr. Cinnabar?"

"One tonight at nine o'clock, and nine others pencilled in so far. I'm expecting more."

"Okay—so you get his client list, and his nine o'clock

tonight—you'll offer her a partial discount for switching the sire. Decide among yourselves who takes the job. Yes?"

The agents looked at one another, said they needed to talk and then went into a huddle on the other side of the Fordpark. Tommo made to say something but Mr. Blue pressed a fingertip to his lips.

"Okay," said one of the agents after they had chatted for ten minutes, "looks like you've got a deal. We'll get the cash to you first thing tomorrow."

We all shook on the deal, Mr. Blue said it was a pleasure doing business with them, and we walked back towards the hotel.

"Wow," said Tommo in admiration, "that was hugely impressive. Can I ask—"

He didn't get to finish as Mr. Blue grabbed his wrist, twisted him backwards and pushed him hard against a wall, then grabbed his ear and started to pull just hard enough so I could see a tear beginning at the top. I'd never seen anyone *intentionally* tear an ear off—or not outside a sporting fixture, anyway.

"This is the last time you trade on the fidelity of others," said Mr. Blue in a low growl. "Mr. Hollyberry was coerced, and that means you were complicit in coercion. You'll collect the six grand and give it all to Mr. Hollyberry. Nod if you agree or I'll pull your ear clean off and choke you on it. Don't think I won't."

Tommo nodded and Mr. Blue let him go.

"You okay, Mr. Hollyberry?"

"Yes," I said, "thank you."

Mr. Blue told me I probably shouldn't hang around the hotel lest the others thought I was moonlighting. I asked him how I could repay his kindness, and he simply told me "the Brotherhood looks after its own" and to "pass the kindness on and sooner rather than later," then smiled again, shook my hand and walked away.

I looked at Tommo, who was pressing his ear to his head with a handkerchief.

"You could have arranged all that," I said. "Why didn't you?"

"I didn't think of it. I'm not in Mr. Blue's league, and I now feel hopeless and inadequate. In truth, you should feel sorry for me and offer support and sympathy."

"That's one thing I will never do. As soon as you get the money, wager it all on Jane to win, yes?"

"Really?"

"Yes."

I went to the post office just before it closed and sent a short telegram to Dad:

++ DEAR FATHER ++ GREEN DRAGON SLEEPING ONLY NOW ++ THANK YOU FOR ADVICE ++ HAVE NOT YET SEEN TWO HEADED SHEEP MAYBE TOMORROW ++ REGARDS EDWARD++

After that I went and sat in Hoofprint, a fashionable puddle water bar around the corner from the hotel, ordered myself a double cloudy with fresh grass and chatted to someone who was curious to know why I was here and asked a lot of questions. I figured out they were a Yellow on a fishing trip for infractions. After engaging them for as long as possible so they had less time to quiz a *real* Rule-breaker, he asked me if I knew where he could get some Lime, and I dutifully referred him to a health re-education programme. He then revealed himself, gave me five merits for being a good resident, and went on his way.

I stayed at Hoofprint until the last bell, then hurriedly made my way back to the hotel and sneaked in by the rear stairs. Surprisingly, I slept rather well.

PUT ON NOTICE

Cities, towns, villages and hamlets all ran on subtly different Rules. The ideal size of a settlement was 2500 people, Munsell said in his writings, so that: "Each may know another, and by familiarity trade courtesy more easily." Cities were, Munsell told us: "a necessary evil, where needs of commerce outweighed that of companionability."

—Ted Grey: *Twenty Years Among the Chromatacians*

I got up late, had a bath and a leisurely breakfast before venturing out. The town was quiet and warmer in the morning than I had been used to, the result, Lucy told me, of the paving slabs and buildings retaining heat. There was a breeze, which helped, but the city wasn't somewhere I would have chosen to live—the Outer Fringes suited me better. It was unsophisticated, yes, but full of trees and rivers and not quite so strict with the Rules.

I walked towards the post office and noted a few Yellows doing their trademark "busy but not busy" walk that made them appear to be on an errand, when actually on patrol. None of them made eye contact, but that didn't necessarily mean I was unobserved. It was rumoured that Yellows on Vermillion's streets were *meant* to be seen, a distraction from the ones who were really keeping an eye on us all. I waited in the queue outside the post office until it opened, then picked up a short communication from Dad that was shocking and to the point:

DEAR EDDIE ++ SUPERVISORY SWATCHMAN DEAD ++
FEAR WORST ++ TAKE ALL NECESARY PRECAUTIONS ++
MAKE ME PROUD ++ COMMS MAY PRVE DIIFUCULT ++
LOVE U FATHR ++

I read the message twice as I stepped away from the queue and suddenly felt hot and angry and at first curiously in denial. I quickly got back in the queue, but by the time I'd reached the front and written out a request for clarification I was told that the East Carmine telegraph office was temporarily closed until further notice due to an ongoing health issue. As the news confirmed itself, I felt a nasty sick feeling rising inside of me. Unsure what I should do, I staggered out the door and found Jane on her way in to look for me.

"The hotel manager told me you'd be here," she said. "Come with me."

"Don't run," I said as she picked up speed. "It's not permitted and they're quite hot on enforcing it."

She slowed down and I handed her the telegram.

"This came in last night, but I only got it ten minutes ago." She quickly read it.

"The misspellings look like it was sent in a hurry. An operator could lose their licence for that. Over here."

We took a left turn down an alleyway, then a right and another left and stepped into the Sarah Siddons tearoom. It had presumably been opened just for us, and the staff had made themselves scarce. Lucy, Amelia and Tania were sitting at a table at the back along with Doug. Daisy, I noticed, had positioned herself on the far side of the street to keep an eye out for any Yellows.

There was one other person present: Clifton, Jane's brother. He wasn't on the Jollity Fair manifest and had been left behind in East Carmine, so he'd have to be here illegally. I noticed that he was sitting next to Tania and holding her hand, while Tania's kids were playing on the floor with an evermouse they had found, oblivious to the drama.

"Hey, Ed," said Doug, "I heard Violet sold you into Rainbowing. Sorry to hear about that."

I told him that I'd got away with *not* having to be breeding stock—but would still get the six thousand merits as the Brotherhood looked after its own.

"But if you didn't Rainbow you're not brotherhood," said Jane, "so why did they help you out?"

"Because they knew I *would*, in order to save lives. To belong, all you need to do is show intent. A fine bunch, and I'm honoured to be counted among them."

Lucy said she didn't get that at all, but there were bigger issues on the table so we moved on, although I did note that Jane gave my hand a squeeze when she found out what I hadn't been up to.

"Clifton?" said Jane. "What's going on?"

He took a deep breath.

"Okay, so yesterday morning the Substitute Swatchman asked several retired Greys to come to see him in the Colourium, and when they refused he marched down to the Greyzone to make some house calls, portable swatch-case in hand. His way was blocked, and after arguing for a while Dad—I mean, the Head Porter—told him to leave on the next train or face irreversible consequences. The Swatchman said he was not going to be spoken to like that by a Grey, and told Dad he and the rest of the Greys were a stain and dishonour to the Munsell Way and he'd see them all dead of the Mildew even if it took an army of assistants."

"What happened then?" asked Jane.

"There was a scuffle, the Swatchman was pushed over and he hit his head on a kerb stone, killing him instantly."

There was complete silence in the room.

"Did Stafford tell the Prefects it was an accident?" asked Doug.

"He tried to, but all Yewberry would do was repeat: 'oh dear oh dear oh dear' and 'you and your Greys have cost us the village, Stafford' and stuff like that. He had to send the telegram to Head Office himself as Mrs. Ochre refused to do so."

Clifton paused for breath and took another sip of tea.

"The word spread quickly to take what you could and get out of the village, but only the Greys and the lower hues actually took heed of what was being said."

"And you?" asked Jane.

"Mum and Dad told me to reach you, Sis. I took a lightglobe, then hid near the rendering shed until nightfall—and that was when the fire came from the skies, destroying everything. The village burned so hot I could feel it from the rendering shed, and I think even escaping individuals were found and killed as small balls of fire sporadically lit up the hillside. At about two A.M., once all was quiet and using the lightglobe to illuminate my path, I started on my journey here and arrived soon after dawn."

"What about my father?" I said.

"I don't know what happened to him, nor your mum, Lucy. Nor your folks, Doug. As far as I know I'm the only one who got out, but I can't know that for sure."

We all fell silent and I felt a hollow, empty sort of feeling inside me. For the whole village, sure, but mostly for Dad. He and Velma were smart and savvy and knew stuff, but so did Hanson, and Clifford's report of the escapees also being individually targeted suggested a precision and resolve that was chilling. Culls were what Hanson and others like him did, and they'd be good at it.

"We remember those recently lost," said Lucy in a quiet voice.

"Friends and family and colleagues and workmates. They will be missed."

We all bowed our heads. It felt better now that Lucy had said it. Vocalising what we all felt brought it out into the open, and was something on which we could all agree. I thought of everyone I knew, and although in the short time I'd been there I'd got to know less than a tenth of the village, those I had met I had liked. It was hard to comprehend that those who had seemed so alive and resilient yesterday—working in retail or the factory, kitchens, fields and workshops—were now no more.

"There will be ample time for grief later," said Doug in a quiet voice, "but what happens now?"

It was a very good point.

"The Vermillion Prefects will know the names of all members of East Carmine who are here," I said, "and the news of East Carmine's destruction will not take long in getting out. The Rules state we will either be resettled or relocated where needed, so prepare to be interviewed as part of the Resettlement process."

"Does Violet know?" asked Lucy.

"Almost certainly," I said. "I'll be interested to see how she reacts when I see her."

There was a whistle from Daisy across the street and we tried to make ourselves look as though we were *not* talking urgently about the mass murder of an entire village, while Clifton, who was here illegally, ducked into the toilets. It was a small group of Yellows that Daisy had alerted us to, but after a brief conversation, only the most senior walked into the tearoom.

"Good morning," he said in something of a sombre manner and respectfully giving a faint nod to all of us. "Dustin Colman, Vermillion's Yellow Deputy Prefect. You look as though you've heard the news—?"

We nodded.

"Can I offer my sincerest condolences?" he said. "I can't imagine what you are going through right now and I will only momentarily interrupt your very individual grief. The Head Prefect Angela Van Purple *herself* has asked me to send her sympathies, and wants you to know that the city welcomes you all with open arms."

"That's very kind," said Jane. "We appreciate the gesture."

"Good," he said, unfolding a sheet of paper with a list of names on it, several already with ticks against them. "I've been tasked with telling all ex-East Carmine residents personally of the welcome, and once you're ready, make your way to City Hall and visit the Resettlement Bureau in Room 101, where we can register your change of address and discuss work opportunities and accommodation details. Oscar Greengrass and Sophie Lapis-Lazuli are being inducted over there as we speak, and I can personally guarantee there you will be resettled internally and with no enforced relocations. You need to do this today, though, so we can release emergency pocket money to tide you over before your re-employment—is that okay?"

We nodded and Mr. Colman ticked our names off the list to show he had spoken to us. He wasn't at all cagey about us looking over his shoulder and I noted that Daisy, Tommo, Penelope Gamboge and Bunty were the only ones not already contacted.

Once done, Dustin reiterated on behalf of the Head Prefect how sorry they all were, and said that in these dark moments our apartness always brought us together, then left.

"He seemed genuine enough," said Lucy.

Doug asked for the third time what the plan was, so we decided to just carry on as we were for the moment, and stick close to one another until we knew how to proceed. Clifton would have to wait for three days, then present himself at the town gates as an "orphaned brother of the Collective" to be then resettled like the rest of us.

"I'll go up to Head Office now," said Amelia. "Plenty of time before the race starts."

So while Amelia headed off to the Resettlement Bureau, we walked towards the Jollity Fair site, each of us lost in our thoughts. There didn't seem to be anything we wanted to share right now so all wondered silently if perhaps, by a miracle, our immediate friends and family had somehow got out. Although I wanted to feel confident that Dad and Velma made it out to safety, I knew I couldn't be sure. Lucy's Grey boyfriend and other people I didn't know that well like Jethro, Samantha, Mr. Baxter, Harry and Bertie Magenta would all likely be dead, too, and it was all so wrong on so many levels. In among the tangled wreckage of grief and loss there was a sense of terrible and palpable injustice—and a rising anger. But it wasn't an anger that could be directed anywhere, as there was nowhere it could be directed. Hanson was safe in the Somewhere Else and nothing could touch him. I also strongly suspected that what he'd done would not actually be considered a crime at all—and he was simply directed to do it by another.

East Carmine had not been culled because it had done wrong, or was beyond saving. It had been culled because it had become mildly troublesome.

TWO-HEADED SHEEP

All residents are the property of the Collective and it is
the duty of all to ensure that shared property is fully maintained and able to fully and productively discharge their
duties to the Collective.

Rule 76.2.45.23.1 of the *Book of Harmony*

Jane and I held hands as we walked towards the Jollity Fair site.
We'd lost people before, but this was on another level entirely. I
outlined how I escaped Rainbowing and she said that was impressive and yes, as Mr. Blue had said, I should pass that kindness on.
She said she was glad I hadn't Rainbowed, and I said I was glad
she was glad. We squeezed each other's hands and moved out past
the city walls.

"I'm not racing to win," she said after a pause. "There's no point."

"I don't blame you. What will you do?"

"Just enjoy it. My first proper race. I'll take it easy and sail in
close formation behind everyone else."

"Seems a safe option. Tell Tommo not to lay the wager and we
can keep the six thousand."

"Will do."

We walked on in silence until we reached the gyro-bike tent.
Usually, Carlos would be busy stripping down the bike in pursuit
of some small gain and surrounded by hundreds of components,
but this morning he was sitting on a chair and staring into space.

"You heard the news then," I said. "I'm sorry."

"Thank you," he replied without looking at me. "Did your dad and Velma get out?"

"I don't know."

"Your dad's smart and so is Velma. They'll make it out. Seen Amelia?"

"Went to the Resettlement Bureau."

"Ah."

"My race is at midday," said Jane to me. "Will you go and check in at Room 101? If they're allocating accommodation it might help to know where you are so I can at least be somewhere close, perhaps in the same block."

I weighed this up for a moment or two.

"Okay," I replied, "but I think I might go and look at a two-headed sheep first to take my mind off things."

"Give them both my love."

I walked away from the tent, past the cycle teams getting into practice for the "greatest distance covered in an hour Penny-Farthing event." Doug and Earl were warming up, but Greengrass wasn't yet back from City Hall. Usually wild horses wouldn't have dragged me away from this event but today was different, and I headed off to the sideshows as a welcome distraction. The "amazing two-headed sheep" was every bit as astounding as I imagined it to be. After viewing some dead specimens—either stuffed or in jars or as skeletons—I was brought into the presence of a real two-headed sheep that was alive, healthy, and actually bleating. Weirder still was that it had a shared barcode—the two of them merging into one that was unreadable. I spoke at length to the keeper and he said it was born that way, and if ever I came across anything with two heads I was to contact him straight away and he'd offer me a good price.

"I thought I'd find you here," said Violet, who had just

walked into the tent. "Goodness, does that sheep really have two heads?"

The sheep turned to look at her with both its heads and all four eyes.

"I guess it does," she continued. "Look, Eddie, I'm sorry about your father."

I turned to face her. "You knew, didn't you?"

"Knew what?"

"That East Carmine would be destroyed."

"Shit, *NO*."

"Your family got out."

Her face fell as she realised how bad this looked.

"That was a coincidence."

"Was it?"

"Yes. Look, if I'd known that was going to happen, I'd have done anything to stop it."

"Really?"

"Yes, really. You want proof? I've wanted the Head Prefectship since I knew I was in line for it, and now I've got nothing. Yesterday I had a village to command, today I'll be lucky to ratify Council agendas for the rest of my life, the loss of my village hanging over me like a millstone and precluding me from advancement. Yes, I knew what the Substitute was up to, but no, I didn't know what would happen if he was killed."

We stared at one another for a moment, and I had an uncomfortable feeling that this bore all the hallmarks of a marital argument. "It looks," I said, "as though your father had a very good idea how this might pan out."

She looked doubtful for a moment; it seemed this was an idea that she could clearly not entirely dismiss.

"I can't speak for him. This is how the Munsell Way functions, Eddie. Nearly five hundred years of peace, and all we have to do is follow the Rules."

"And that makes mass murder okay?"

She looked left and right to check no one was about and then lowered her voice.

"Okay, I agree with you to a certain extent. The Word of Munsell *is* flawed. We can make it better, we can *tweak* it. We've been planning this for generations. The Purples led by the deMauves can be in charge. What happened to East Carmine and Rusty Hill and Crimsonolia doesn't have to happen. We're thinking of building a better, more Purple-orientated future. The Collective will be eternally grateful for their deliverance from an unjust leader, and in return all we'll ask is for the Collective to swear allegiance to the one true colour."

I was too tired to make any argument. Leadership under the deMauves would be exactly the same, only with more insufferable Purples. And there would be no defence against Utopiainc and the Pale Rider, either—but that, like much else, was unknown to Violet and almost everyone else.

"Maybe you're right," I said. "Maybe it would be better under the Purples."

"I'm very glad you said that," she said, missing the obvious sarcasm, "and I wanted to say that you can join me as we try to effect change and put an end to any mass Mildewings. With the deMauves in power and father a bigwig at the deMauve convention I can get another Head Prefectship. But," she added, "we will have to be husband and wife, as Purples are big on marriage and family unity, so I'd be willing to make some sort of arrangement that would include Jane. Run it past her, will you? It might work for all of us."

"Okay," I replied, "and by the way, Jane won't be racing to win, so please don't think there's any cash coming your way."

"It doesn't much matter now," she said thoughtfully. "East Carmine's crackletrap debt died with the village."

She thanked me for considering her proposal and we walked blinking into the sunlight to come across the same Leaper I had seen the day before. She was still wrapped in a hair-blanket, her scrawny and diseased hand pushed out in front of her, and making low guttural noises about her dead child, which I presumed was still within her blanket.

"Disgusting," said Violet with a shudder.

"Here," I said, and not wanting to chuck the coin on the ground in front of her, placed it into the Leaper's palm. I regretted it almost immediately as her bony hand, surprisingly quick and strong, grabbed me by the wrist and pulled me closer.

"Help me," she said in a low husky voice, "to bury my child."

"Sorry, no," I replied and pulled myself away.

"You better wash that," said Violet. "Mimi Orange accidentally touched a Leaper last year and didn't have a firm stool for three months."

Violet took me to a washing station and insisted on scrubbing my wrist and hand with a nail brush until it was almost raw.

"Okay then," she said at length, "I'm going to watch the games. Bunty went over to Room 101 just now, and I'll be going this afternoon. Will you come with me? We'll get better treatment if we present as husband and wife."

The Collective was very big on robust marriages whether sham or not, so I agreed to meet Violet at City Hall at 3 P.M., which would give me a chance to consult with Jane. As a parting question she asked me if I'd seen Oscar Greengrass as he'd missed the team Penny-Farthing event. I said I hadn't seen him since yesterday and we said goodbye.

With a couple of hours to go until the gyro-bike sprint I went to look at specimens of anthropological interest in jars, which were weirdly captivating in a "you can't really *not* look" sort of way. The murkiness of the liquid in which they were preserved added to the spectacle, as did the size of the jars—mostly tall and narrow, enough to preserve an entire human in a standing position. The collection was predominantly humans like us, except two, which were Riffraff, and one, a Previous.

"How did you get hold of a Previous?" I asked the owner, who seemed dazzlingly uninterested in the collection, and instead complained bitterly about how difficult the jars were to move, and how barely a year went by without one being dropped, or springing a leak, or some other "human-in-jar"-based mishap.

"I don't know," he said. "Maybe he was preserved at the Something that Happened. Do you want me to screw off the lid so you can touch his head? It'll be two merits extra."

"No thanks. What does 'anthropological' mean?"

"I don't know. Maybe the . . . study of humans preserved in jars?"

I looked at another specimen, this time one of us but dressed in a uniform similar to Hanson's. He carried a badge that said his name was Nigel Williams under the acronym CSS, so quite likely the same Nigel that vanished from the cloud-seeding station, who'd been seeing a Riffraff named Meena and had a son that he'd never see. He had an odd smile fixed on his lips and his eyes were open and milky white.

With nothing more to be gained here I thanked the collector and returned to the Fair for the speed topiary event, which Green Sector won with an excellent "squarial holding a nut" where the nut in question was the sort that fits on a bolt. It was an astonishingly good effort. The Red team came in last, and for a good reason: Sophie Lapis-Lazuli had been a no-show.

"Young people today have no commitment to the Great Art," said Mrs. Lilac, who then added: "But understandable I suppose, given the circumstances."

I met up with Lucy at the urban freestyle Penny-Farthing

event, where we watched a whole series of insanely dangerous tricks performed with a daring that was beyond foolhardy and well into the realms of outright insanity.

"I don't even know how they do that," said Lucy as one of the Yellow Sector Farthingists managed to complete a double back somersault from a ramp of banked earth, while also letting go of the bike mid-air, swizzling the tiny wheel around the large wheel before grabbing it again and coming down for a perfect landing.

"Lots of practice and a slender grasp on the concept of risk," I said. "Have you been over to the Resettlement Bureau yet?"

"Not yet. Earl went over after his Penny-Farthing sprint heat ended. I've not seen him to hear how it went."

I asked her if she was going to carry on her work with harmonics, and she said that although all her notes went up in flames, she'd be able to piece it back together—but in secret this time. She didn't want to be back on any Mildew list.

"How did you get out of the Rainbowing?" she asked.

I told her all about it, and she was interested in the idea of paying the kindness forward rather than back, then asked me when I was going to do that, and I spotted a shovel leaning against a fence.

"You know what," I said, "I think I might do it now."

"Don't be long," she said. "Jane's race is at midday."

THE HERALD

Heralds had been seen from the earliest times in the nation, but existed only in the oral tradition, as reporting them was specifically forbidden, and known by the slang term Pooka. Anecdotally they were seen quite often: here and there, now and again, to this one and that one.

    —Ted Grey: *Twenty Years Among the Chromatacians*

I took the shovel in hand and went back to the Leaper, who was still sitting in the same spot. I stood back and watched for a minute or two, and everyone she asked for help either moved away or hurried past, or attempted to shoo her away as you would a stray goat. On six occasions she was kicked for being too close to the sideshows, and twice was kicked simply for fun. I waited until the crowds had thinned, then walked up to her.

"Hello," I said, speaking slowly as I didn't know if a Leaper's skin condition also affected their mind or their hearing, "my name's Eddie deMauve."

As it happened, it affected neither.

"Hello, Edward," said the Leaper, using a normal tone of voice, "my name's Lyndsey. Lyndsey Green, although I don't use my surname, not anymore. Do you have any liquorice on you?"

"No."

"Shame. I can't buy it and no one ever thinks to give me

liquorice when I'm begging—it's always cash or food. Begging's a bitch. Have you ever begged?"

"No."

"Everyone should, at some point in their lives. Once you've begged, it puts a whole new spin on how you treat others."

"I expect it does."

The folds of her hood momentarily fell away and I saw her face for the first time. She was emaciated, dirty, and her skin was almost peeling off her, but she was young, certainly in her twenties and had bright, alert eyes. Her nose was small and pert and marred only by an open sore right on the very tip.

"You can speak normally?" I asked.

"The voice you heard earlier was my begging voice."

"Does it work?"

"Usually. Are you here to kill me with that spade?"

"No, you asked me to help you bury your child."

She stared at me for a few seconds.

"Wow, I so read *that* wrong. I accept your offer."

She put out her hand for me to hold and I paused only momentarily before I did so, and she led me towards where the latrine trenches were located. The smell was bad, but I made every attempt not to make it show. I could feel the rough skin of her hand chafing mine, and the dampness of a sore. She stopped behind a grove of silver birch where there was some privacy, and said:

"Here will do."

"I'm sorry for your loss," I said, pushing the shovel into the soil.

"I haven't lost anything," she said. "Never even been pregnant, or felt another's skin on mine. Look."

She showed me the child, which wasn't a child at all, but a large, flesh-toned doll with a leg missing.

"A doll?"

"For some reason the children of the Previous used to play with them," she said. "I think the infants of the Previous were soft and vulnerable for a lot longer than ours; they may not have been able to fully converse in an adult fashion until three or be capable of a useful job until they were eight."

"I'd heard the stories," I said, "but you want me to bury your doll?"

"No," she said, gathering up the small mannequin and replacing it in the folds of her cloak, "but I have two questions: How did you know what I have isn't infectious?"

"I didn't."

She nodded, pleased by my answer.

"Then here's the second: Did you come to Jollity Fair looking for something?"

I understood, now. I had shown honourable intent, and this would be my reward. My mother must have done something similar to someone very like Lyndsey all those years ago.

"I came looking for a Herald."

"Then you need to go and speak to him."

She pointed to where a man was sitting on a log near a wagon, watching us.

"Thank you," I said. "Here."

I gave her a ten-merit coin, the largest and least worn that I had. I wished her well and walked over to the man, who was dressed in a well-worn but ill-fitting Outdoor Adventure #2.

"Mr. Baxter?" I said as soon as I recognised him. "What are you doing here?"

He made no sign of recognising me, although he understood my confusion.

"You mean," he said slowly, "*another* Baxter has survived?"

It wasn't *our* Baxter, *our* Apocryphal Man, it was another. There had originally been ten, and our Baxter thought all the others were dead. So too, it seemed, did this one.

"One that I know of," I answered. "Baxter #4."

"I remember him. Sort of quasi-enigmatic and a little whiny."

"That's him. When did you last meet?"

"Hoo," he said, thinking hard, "got to be one hundred and twenty years, maybe more. Does he prefer men?"

"He does."

"I prefer men. Must be a Baxter thing. How is the old fellow?"

"I don't know. He lived in East Carmine and we had a Mildew epidemic."

"We don't get the Mildew."

". . . which was then consumed by cleansing fire from on high."

"We are not immune to the predations of a cleansing fire," he conceded. "I'll go and have a look for him, though. Which village did you say?"

"East Carmine."

"Ah-ha. Lyndsey signalled to me that you are of honourable intent. She's a good judge of horseflesh. Do you want to meet your Herald?"

"*My* Herald?"

"They tailor themselves to the individual. Whatever it is you want to know, better ask the correct questions. The doors of your perception are about to be opened, but you only get two minutes."

"That's all?"

"Swiftly gained knowledge leads to impetuosity of action. Come back next year if you want another shot. Are you ready?"

"No."

"That's okay; no one ever is."

He produced a compact from his pocket, the sort you might have about you for a flash of calming Lime to get you through the day. But it wasn't Lime, it was a pale tangerine colour, and with a momentary shifting of my reds into purply-blues accompanied by a loud G-major chord, there was another me standing opposite. He was dressed as I was, only with tie done up, and was faintly transparent. Like the other Heralds, he was in my mind, yet *interacted* within my sight. When I looked momentarily to Baxter, the Herald stayed planted where he was and became only peripherally in my vision.

"Hello!" other me said. "And welcome to Herald Configuration Module One. I can see that you are over twenty years of age and have advanced social skills, so will not require basic infant orientation. I can also see that you are HE-315-PJ7A-M. Is there another name you would like to be known by?"

"Eddie."

"Thank you, Eddie. The default gates are set for me to appear as yourself, but would it help to take the form of another? Many people choose a loved yet deceased or absent relative or friend. I can use your memories to build them, or you may specify changes. You may also ask me to create a randomised amalgam of people you have known. What would you like?"

I didn't need to think.

"My mother."

And there she was, as I remembered her from the only two photos we had of her. It was as if her picture had suddenly come alive, and I felt my eyes moisten.

"Hello, Mother," I said.

"I'm not your mother," she said, "I just look like your mother. I am currently defaulted to plain response, would you prefer me to act motherly so interactions are easier?"

"I'd like that."

"Two minutes, remember," said Baxter, and walked away. Lyndsey had already wrapped up the doll and was wandering back towards the sideshows.

"I see you are also defaulted to lose timecode during sleep cycle," said my mother. "Would you like me to reconfigure your internal clock to retain accurate time-keeping during sleep? A side effect is random waking and bad dreams if you have eaten cheese or other dairy products."

Mum had been plagued with bad dreams. She must have chosen this when she first met her Herald.

"That could be useful."

"It is so done. Did you have a bath this morning?"

"Yes, of course. I have one every morning."

"Just checking. I see night vision is also defaulted to *off* along with your internal positioning, which will require switching to the metric system. Would you like to access these too?"

"Sure."

"It is so done. Would you like access to cosines, sines, logs, tans and advanced geometry?"

"What are they?"

"You'll find out."

I'd used almost a minute of my allotted time. This must have been why my mother returned to Jollity Fair each year.

"Can we pause configuration?"

My mother smiled at me.

"Configuration so paused, Eddie. Did you clean behind your ears and would you like to move on to Module Two, 'Advanced Configuration'?"

"No, thank you. Can you answer questions?"

"You didn't answer about your ears."

"I did."

She looked confused.

"You did answer already, or you did clean your ears?"

"I cleaned my ears."

"Good. About answering questions: you are currently defaulted to core knowledge, so my responses will be limited."

I now had less than a minute so I had to think fast. "What is the Mildew?"

"It is a fatal reaction to hue DFE799 known as Necrotising Turburcoloursis and uniquely deadly to the engineered sub-species E698b *Homo coloribus*. To all other humans it is an insipid green roughly the colour of gooseberry fool. The Mildew is kept in reserve as a last resort against wrongdoers who have shown themselves to be a hazard rather than a benefit to the colony. It can be administered by light or paint and is always fatal."

"Who uses it?"

"I'm sorry, I've no information on this. Do you have someone, Eddie, a special someone?"

"Yes, she's called Jane. So . . . what are we doing here on the Reserve?"

"I'm sorry, Eddie, information is limited. This girl, is it serious?"

"Yes, it's *very* serious. What's a subject?"

"A subject is both a noun and a verb. It has five meanings as a noun, and one as a verb. Would you like me to run through them?"

"No, cancel that."

"So cancelled. So this girl. Sort of serious in a marriage proposal sort of way?"

"No, I'm already married—to an ex-Head Prefect named Violet whom I despise. It's complicated."

"Oh," she said, pulling a face, "yes, that does sound *very* complicated. Do I have any grandchildren?"

"One on the way."

"Goody," she said, clapping her hands together, "from Jane?"

"No, Violet. As I said, it's complicated."

"How do you feel about that?"

"Why are you asking me all this?"

"I'm sorry," she said, "I have to work up an offworld colony psychology report. I know it's a bit silly."

"Are you part of me?" I asked.

"Research has shown a companion to talk things through with when facing challenges when possibly alone in a hostile environment can be extremely useful. I am an independent consciousness within your own consciousness. I die when you die, but I am here, whenever you need me. You will not have had the benefit of parents for skill acquisition and communication offworld is not possible, so all knowledge has to be carried internally from one generation to the next."

"I don't understand."

"I'm sorry, that query *really* lacked specificity. You have to be clearer, Eddie. Let's go back to your bath this morning. Did you wash your hair?"

"There wasn't time and I didn't feel like it."

My internal clock told me I had twenty-two seconds left, and I was beginning to get desperate.

"Is there a Somewhere Else?"

"Eddie, sweetheart, it's that specificity issue again. Of course there's a Somewhere Else. It's easy to find—it's anywhere that's not here."

"How do I get to speak to you again?"

"With practice, you can access me whenever you want."

I now had only a few seconds left, but I had to ask *something*, so I said the first thing that came into my head.

"What was the Something that Happened?"

"What did I tell you about being spec—"

She didn't get to finish, as with a sharp stab of pain behind the eyes I was once again alone on the wasteland beyond the Leaper tents, while the smell of woodsmoke mixed with cooked offal and the latrine trenches wafted past my nose.

Deep in thought, I moved slowly back towards the competition grounds, past the side shows, trade stands and what looked like a Riffraff Novelty Dancer—maybe they existed after all. I stopped to have something to eat and ordered some random meat on a stick and, once paid, sat down to eat it. The Herald hadn't really answered any questions at all—just added a whole host of new ones. My Herald was an entity within me and had always been there, and at some point, she had told me, I would access her on my own. It made very little sense, but as an odd aside, I could now do maths whereas before I couldn't. I took two random numbers of six digits each and multiplied them together. I didn't do any workings out, I just seemed to know the answer in the same way as I could suddenly do needlework with the quilting skill hue. By way of an experiment, I took this large number and worked out the prime factors. It turned out to have eight, and I figured that all out in 3.76 seconds. I also knew that I was 526 metres from where I had spoken to Mr. Baxter, and knew in which direction to go to get there, and precisely how long it would take me.

"Eddie?"

FADING YELLOW

Floaties once dislodged from the earth or released from their boxes would float to their approximate floating height of 3' and then meander downhill until they reached the lowest point on the earth, reputedly somewhere far out to sea where the material had accreted, been covered in soil and was now replete with grass, palm trees and reputedly the nesting place of the Kraken.

—Ted Grey: *Twenty Years Among the Chromatacians*

It was Penelope Gamboge. She'd never called me "Eddie" before, so something was up. She looked frightened, and I initially thought that might be because of the loss of East Carmine and everyone in it, and while that was part of it, that wasn't all.

"What's the matter?" I asked, trying to be pleasant, despite how little I thought of her, and how much I had loathed both her grandmother and her uncle.

"We've lost Bunty."

"She'll turn up," I said, "in the music marquee, most likely, or at the Yellows' Club, figuring out new ways to be hideous."

"No," she said, "we've lost her as in . . . *she's dead.*"

"Okay," I said, not overly concerned or filled with remorse, "what happened? A fight? A lucky fall? An aneurism while playing that dumb tuba?"

"No," said Penelope, "budge up. We can't allow ourselves to be overheard."

So I shuffled up on the bench.

"I accompanied Bunty to the Resettlement Bureau," she said in a low voice, "and she told me to wait outside City Hall, and if she wasn't back outside in an hour she was dead and to find you or Violet for guidance."

This did not sound good.

"How long has she been gone?"

"Seventy-one minutes and eight seconds. The Resettlement procedure takes barely ten; I did them myself from time to time back in East Carmine."

"Shit," I said under my breath.

"I'm worried, Edward."

I was worried too. Now Penelope mentioned it, nobody who had gone to the Resettlement Bureau had reappeared and Deputy Colman wanted us all to check into Room 101 as quick as we could. It looked as though there was another Rule about the C-Notice, one that we didn't know about—until now.

"Bunty took my hand and squeezed it before she went in," said Penelope. "I think she knew there was a chance she wasn't coming out again, and wanted to warn you all."

"Have you seen Sophie?" I asked, and Penelope shook her head, tears welling up in her eyes.

"What about Earl, Mrs. Lilac and Greengrass?"

These were the ones I knew of that had headed off to Room 101. Penelope shook her head again.

"I know about the Mildew," said Penelope. "I heard Gran and Courtland talking about it. Gran took my place on the Mildew list, but she also had concerns about the Substitute Swatchman overstepping his power and coming to a sticky end. That's why I got to be on the Jollity Fair list, so nothing would happen to me.

I think the deMauves thought the same. But if we don't go to Room 101, then they'll find us and give us the Mildew anyway. Eddie, I don't want to die."

She stared at me with her large eyes, and all of a sudden she didn't seem like an obnoxious Yellow at all, but a frightened child who also happened to be Yellow and quite obnoxious.

"Neither do I, Penny. But we need proof before we take this to the others. This is what you're going to do: go to City Hall, hang around outside and tell any East Carminers who approach that they are to skip Resettlement and meet at the Sarah Siddons. Don't tell them why, and don't leave City Hall until you hear word from me. Can you do that?"

She said it was the most important task she had ever been given, and ran off.

There were twelve minutes and nine seconds before the sprint race was due to start, but I instead headed for the renderering shed.

It was a four-minute-and-nine-second jog-trot away and was considerably larger than the one back in East Carmine, but then there was more organic waste in cities—and more of the Mildew. "Edward deMauve," I said as I walked into the hot and foetid atmosphere of the rendering shed, where large cauldrons of what might best be described as "gloop" were bubbling away over a gas flame, the slowly revolving ceiling fans yellow with accumulated gick, and the walls and windows dripped with condensation, "I'm here to do an inspection."

The Overseer told me they'd already had one this year, but I insisted and he told me to help myself, but to watch out for the floor as it was slippery.

It didn't take me long to find Greengrass, Mrs. Lilac, Sophie Lapis-Lazuli and Bunty, all unceremoniously dumped at the "Goods In" shed among a pile of cow and pig carcasses, food

waste and a well-rotted bison that looked as if it had been partially absorbed by Perpetulite. Sophie was lying face down, but
the tendrils of Mildew still showed around Greengrass's nose and
mouth and the whites of his eyes. Amelia Cinnabar was here too,
and Earl Grey. I stared at them all with a certain detached numbness that was difficult to describe. The anger again, I think, and a
certain level of increasing hopelessness—that the Mildew would
come for us all no matter what, and if the good Yellow folk of
Vermillion failed to kill us all, then Hanson would be sure to do
so. Worse, that this had been going on for a very long time and
the people who did this were good at it.

Taking a deep breath, I quickly removed the spot-badges from
their lapels and discovered—astonishingly—that in their hurry
they'd left Bunty's merit book in her petticoat pocket. I quickly
left the rendering shed and made my way towards the velodrome
to speak with Jane; the race wouldn't take long to complete and
we could thrash out a strategy together. We had the six thousand
cash merits from the Brotherhood deal to use as bribes, but that
wouldn't go far between us.

THE GYRO-BIKE SPRINT

To be truthful, the gyro-bike contravened so many Leap-back regulations that it should have been banned over a century before. But like a few other things that were just too useful to lose such as steam locomotion and the wireful telegraph, it simply stayed, contravening the regulations by tradition. Some said it was proof that the Regime, however rigid, would one day collapse.

—Ted Grey: *Twenty Years Among the Chromatacians*

I arrived at the velodrome just as the riders moved off the start line with a faint squealing of tyres and the soft whine of their gyros as the energy shifted from the spinning weights to forward motion. There would be two more laps in this race than at practice, so the movement off the line was more reserved. As Jane had said, racing a gyro-bike was as much about energy management as it was about speed and handling. Mad Dog Juniper edged swiftly into the lead, quickly followed by Alice Blue and then Emma Yellow. I headed off to the start line from where Carlos, Lucy and Tommo were watching.

"How's it going?" I asked.

"They're all running one hundred and two percent above optimum spin in the gyros except for Emma Yellow's team, who have overspun them to one hundred and twelve percent."

"Is that wise?" I said.

"It's borderline insane, but it's the only chance she has of a second place."

We watched as the riders took the first bend, always a telling manoeuvre as, the bank of the track notwithstanding, the gimballed gyros have to not only swivel to enable the bike to go around the corner, but tilt in opposing directions to cancel out the forces. This was a well-understood phenomenon, but the first and second turns were always the most dangerous as the gyros were at full spin and errors in balance would be vastly magnified. That turned out to be the case; Emma Yellow was in trouble almost immediately. Jane had hung back so they weren't dangerously bunched, and whereas Mad Dog and Alice Blue easily rose high up into the banked turn, Yellow's bike took a different trajectory and you could see her pushing hard on the right handlebar to try and control it.

"One of her gimbals has jammed," said Carlos, and we watched as the bike shuddered with increasing violence until it tore itself into pieces with an angry metallic shriek.

The crowd instinctively threw themselves to the ground as the five big and heavy gyros broke free of their housings, fell still spinning to the track and were then catapulted off in all directions at lethal speed. One cut through a small group of spectators as though they were barley, and another shattered a wooden flag post just to the right of us before it passed through the timekeeper's hut, taking the hat off one of the judges. A third and fourth went bouncing off towards the sideshows where their progress could be tracked by screams and yells, and the last one took a section off Jane's fairing before bouncing on the infield, sailing over the opposite banked track and taking out a spectator in the grandstand.

Jane wobbled for a moment but held her course and the three remaining riders were soon off the banking and flying down the back straight while the marshals struggled to remove the bike wreckage and drag Emma Yellow to the infield. She was still alive, but had lost a foot.

"Jane's not going to win at this rate," said Tommo. "Unless she has a clever plan up her sleeve."

Carlos and I looked at one another.

"Didn't Jane tell you she was going to sit this one out?" I said. "And to not do the wager?"

"No," said Tommo, his face falling, "I gave them six thousand for Jane to win, as we said. Wait, she's planning to come in *last*?"

This was problematical, to say the least. If Jane lost, we'd lose everything and have to face the Yellows of Vermillion with little more than our wits and the clothes on our back.

I quickly chalked a message for Jane on the message board and held it up so she could see as she rode past. I had little time to compose a message, so simply wrote:

New plan: Win!

She acknowledged me with a brief nod of the head as she shot past, but in alerting Jane to the new plan, I was also alerting Mad Dog and Alice Blue, who both looked over their shoulders to where Jane was following, four bike lengths behind.

"We can't stay another day in Vermillion," I said to Tommo. "How quickly could you claim the wager money if Jane wins?"

He told me: almost immediately, so I told him to hang around and then—whatever the outcome—to meet us all at the Sarah Siddons tearooms as soon as possible. He understood from the tone in my voice, and hurried off.

"Why do we need to leave town?" asked Lucy above the whine of the bikes as the riders went up and round the banked curve and past where the marshals were attending to Emma. "Besides,

Jollity Fair isn't over yet, we have no travel permits and where would we go anyway? Not back home—it's a smoking ruin."

"You're going to have to trust me. You need to go and find all the East Carminers, tell them not to go to Resettlement and meet up at the Sarah Siddons tearooms. Don't worry about finding Penny, she's making sure no one else goes to City Hall. And don't trouble yourself with Sophie, Oscar, Earl, Amelia or Bunty. They're already dead."

"How could you know that?"

I showed Lucy and Carlos Bunty's merit book from the rendering shed and the small collection of spot-badges. Their faces fell.

"Oh please no," said Carlos, pointing to one of the badges. "That's Amelia's."

There was a pause.

"All that stuff you and Jane get up to that I try to ignore," said Lucy in a quiet voice, "it's all about this, isn't it?"

"And the rest."

"I'll go and find everyone," she said and hurried off.

The riders came off the banked corner and tore down the back straight once more, still in the same place order. I'd seen a gyrobike race a few times, and often the action didn't really start until the penultimate lap and the final two corners, when the benefits of good energy conservation really kicked in.

"Where will we go?" asked Carlos. He'd been around long enough to know that things were not all rosy in the Garden of Munsell.

"Anywhere but here," I said. "We'll figure out something."

As the riders negotiated the next bend I noted that they took the banking a little higher in expectation of a late overtake. They were riding nearly a foot under the white line, with Juniper leading and Blue just behind. Jane, meanwhile, had decided that three turns from the end was the time she wanted to make her move, and accelerated rapidly in the last third of the straight and took the banking high and fast, placing her front wheel just behind Juniper's and startling Blue, who, expecting a collision as the tight knot of riders swept around the high corner almost horizontal, rolled off the clutch, which dropped her a foot down the banking where she was easily overtaken. As they descended the banking to the back straight Jane was less than a bike's length behind Mad Dog. Alice, though, was not out of tricks and overtook with a surge of power, then swerved in front of Jane in order to make her brake.

Jane, however, was made of sterner stuff and held her position and the two bikes collided with a screeching of rubber. They held this for a moment, locked together, tyres smoking and both now backing off from the leader until Alice's bike flipped sideways and catapulted rider and bike through the outfield, knocking over spectators as they cartwheeled out of the track.

The crowd had fallen silent and the cheering that was heard earlier—most from the Greens, it seemed—had now given way to a sense of numbed awe as the two remaining bikes swept around the track at breakneck speed, with Jane closing dramatically upon the leader until she was millimetres from the other's rear wheel. As they made their way along the back straight, Mad Dog glanced behind her and when she did, Jane made an attempt to pass on the outside. Juniper was too canny for this, though, and jinked sideways to block Jane, and seconds later they both hit the next corner at a far greater speed, this time rising so they rode *upon* the white safety line. The radius of the bend was short and the speed high, so they were both forced hard down into the saddle.

On the next straight Jane attempted to overtake Juniper to the left but then instantly moved to the right, anticipating Mad Dog's attempt to block her. She accelerated and started to overhaul

Juniper on the straight, both of them crouched hard down on the bikes to keep air resistance to a minimum. By the time the straight ended Jane was half a wheel ahead and with both of them reluctant to cede the corner, neither had decelerated enough and both went high on the banking. The white line that lay a foot from the edge was always considered a safety line that it was unthinkable to go above, but that's exactly what happened as they tried to out-corner each other—locked together as one with Jane still a half-wheel ahead and with her tyres perilously close to the top of the banking. If she went over the edge, she'd be badly injured—and lose.

But that's exactly what Juniper attempted to make her do. With a gasp from the crowd, Mad Dog accelerated with a whine and as she went faster, it pushed her higher on the banking and since Jane was to the right of her and they were now touching, this pushed Jane further up, too, and right to the top of the banking. Jane could have rolled off the clutch and dropped back down to safety, but this was about who blinked first and I don't think Jamie or Jane were blinking-last sort of people.

This was all or nothing.

Jane's tyres were now right on the top of the banking, then partially off it, and I closed my eyes and waited for the sudden silence, the crash, the cries of dismay from the crowd, then the Green whoops of adulation as Juniper came off the banking and powered around the remaining corner to go straight to the finish line and glory.

But that didn't happen. There was a large sigh from the crowd and I opened my eyes. Juniper had pushed her gyros too far and too fast, and with her stored energy now depleted, her speed had slackened and she dropped down the banking to give Jane a half-bike-length lead. I thought it would be an easy win now, but Jane's power was depleted also, and with clutches in they could rely only on their stored inertia to make the finish. It was about mass, now—the heavier rider and bike would sustain the power-off coast the longest, and Mad Dog, a larger woman on a bigger bike, looked as if she might have the edge as they rolled at considerable speed towards the final turn.

The banking drained their speed and they entered the final straight with Jane only a wheel ahead. They tucked themselves in tight behind the fairings and delicately controlled their now powerless vehicles towards the finish line, every wobble or turn of the wheels a small increase in friction, and with that, a loss of energy. They rolled on for what seemed like an age, the race now as slow as it had earlier been fast, but no less nail-biting. Juniper slowly gained on Jane, and if the finish line had been ten yards further away, Juniper might have taken the lead, but she didn't. She regained some distance, but not all, and Jane eventually won by the width of a sidewall—about ten centimetres.

The crowd erupted in something of a frenzy with the exception of the Greens, who had thought that Jamie "Mad Dog" Juniper's winning streak would continue unbroken. The racers coasted to a halt and left their bikes where they had stopped, their temporary usefulness over. I thought Juniper might be angry at being defeated but she was a better sport than I had thought as she hugged Jane, then went over to see how the other riders had fared.

"So what's up?" asked Jane as soon as she found me. She was hot and sweaty and I think the penultimate corner had scared her a lot more than she had expected, but as far as I could see, winning the race was not a big deal, or at least, not a big deal for her. It had been fun, nothing more—the consequences of the outcome meant little to nothing.

"Drop everything," I said. "We're heading to the Siddons. They're killing anyone who goes to the Resettlement Bureau—we've lost Amelia, Earl, Sophie, Oscar, Bunty and Mrs. Lilac.

Lucy's rounding up everyone, Penny's stopping anyone else from going to City Hall, and Tommo's picking up the winnings."

"Oh—I forgot to tell him I was coming in last."

"Best mistake you've ever made."

We pushed the bike off the track and into the tent and Carlos immediately connected the Everspin to speed up the gyros.

"I'm leaving," he said as he strapped his toolkit and valise on to the back of the bike. "I'll keep the Everspin attached. I have friends in Greenville. It's been fun, thanks for the warning, and Jane, you made me proud today."

"Here," said Jane, taking some tape and wrapping it around his index finger. "No time to explain, but keep your barcode hidden and they shouldn't find you."

I saw Tommo running towards us holding a valise.

"Do you need cash?" I asked Carlos.

"I'll be okay. I have some saved and a Janitor has multiple skills. I daresay we won't meet again. Good luck, the pair of you."

We shook hands and a moment later he was off, heading towards the west across the open grassland. We watched him go for a moment, then headed back towards the city, Jane signing autographs and giving an account of the race to one of the *Spectrum* journalists until we got to the city boundary where that level of self-aggrandisement was no longer permitted. I told her everything that had happened as we walked and she shook her head several times, but was unsurprised.

"East Carmine has been culled," she said, "and the Prefects in Vermillion are mopping up. What's your plan?"

"My plan was to ask if *you* had a plan."

"I don't have a plan."

"We'll go with that."

GET OUT

Escape from society is considered utterly impossible until you need to do so, and it's then you realise that it's not only possible, but many have tried it before—annoyingly, with varying degrees of success.

—Ted Grey: *Twenty Years Among the Chromatacians*

Thirty-six minutes later we were in the Sarah Siddons basement storeroom, kindly offered by the Grey staff who understood that things need to be spoken about privately and away from prying Yellow ears. Lucy and Penelope had done a good job, and the surviving thirteen members of East Carmine were present. Tania's children sensed something was badly wrong and were silent.

Jane and I had spoken a lot over the past half-hour, and I'd told her all about the Herald, and how basic maths and an uninterrupted time base had been added to my core skillset, along with a new system of measurement.

"I can also navigate to anywhere I've already been," I said, "blindfolded—and I can see at night."

"We knew Heralds were in our heads," said Jane, "but as an accessible addition to one's conscious mind? Why?"

"I don't know. I think we are more capable and adaptable than we think, and that we have a greater purpose, perhaps something that requires varying skills and an ability to function on one's own without training."

We started the meeting by telling everyone what had happened and what was going to happen if anyone went up for Resettlement, then told them about what I'd seen in the rendering shed, and showed everyone Bunty's merit book and the other effects I had gathered. Spot-badges, merit badges, even a picture of Greengrass's kids and wife I'd found in his pocket. There was no doubt as to what was going on.

The reaction from the small group was less of grief, as the loss of East Carmine had already dulled our senses, but more of anger—and fear. Everyone looked nervously at everyone else, attempting to find someone who appeared even remotely optimistic, of which there was none.

"They wouldn't do that to me," said Violet after a short pause. "I'm a Purple. A *deMauve*."

"Did they warn you not to go to Room 101?"

"No," she said in a quiet voice, "no, they didn't."

"They took Bunty," said Jane, "and a more zealous and enthusiastic adherent to the *Book of Harmony* it would be impossible to find. If they can kill her, they can kill anyone. There are no exclusions for merit or name or colour. We're to die because the Rules say we have to."

"Shit," said Violet.

She rubbed her temples and stared at the floor. Penelope, who was standing close by, mistook the gesture for grief and placed a hand on her back, which was instantly shrugged off. Violet wasn't consumed by the loss of friends and the village, but the loss of her Chromatic privilege.

"But we have a play," said Jane. "Thanks to Tommo and Eddie and Violet we have seventy-five thousand merits in cash from a wager. Take it from me that most Prefects and petty officials— Yellows included—can be bought. It's risky, but it's pretty much all we have. We'll split the cash equally, which means each person gets . . . um—"

"—five thousand, seven hundred and sixty-nine," I said, "remainder three."

It was a huge sum—the most any of us might reasonably expect to save in a lifetime was never more than three or four hundred. We were not fooling ourselves as to how long such a huge sum might last, or even if it would work.

There was silence for almost a minute as everyone took this in, processed what it meant, and considered their next move.

"Does this mean I won't get to compete in the speed jamming event?" asked Lisa.

"To have any chance of survival," said Jane, "all of us need to be out of Vermillion or in hiding by tonight. If Yellow Deputy Prefect Dustin Colman has his way, we'll be clutching bramble fodder before the day is up."

"You're all talking nonsense," said Lisa, who was still in denial. "I only came here to make some jam and maybe win a prize or two. I've had enough of this. The *Book of Harmony* knows best and will protect us all. You're insane—*dangerously* insane. Especially you, Eddie. And Violet? You should know better. Why are you not defending Vermillion's Prefecture?"

"Because Eddie's right?"

Lisa gave out a massive *HUFF* sort of noise and walked out. Daisy ran after her, but Jane and I exchanged glances. Knowing Lisa, she'd not give up the chance of a loganberry jamming prize for anything—not even death.

"I consider myself something of an expert in dishonesty," said Tommo, to which no one could or would make any argument, "and as Jane said, all officials can be bribed. I'd suggest you use some of this cash to obtain a replacement merit book in a false name in one village, then move villages immediately before the person you bribed tries to milk you further. Once you've got a false name, things will be easier. Most of all, don't flash the cash around—it will make people jealous, and tongues will wag. Low-key is the trick."

"Replacement merit books can be obtained," piped up Penelope in the thoughtful pause that followed, "by using little-known Rule 2.4.65.99.2, which not many people know about as Prefects and Yellows keep it quiet. All it requires to get a merit book in *any* name is a self-declaration, a photograph and a witness or written statement from a Prefect."

"I'll sign anything for anyone," said Violet, without looking up.

There was a sharp intake of breath. Breaking any of these Rules was so unnatural that even the *suggestion* of such a thing was unthinkable.

"Useful," said Doug, who had been making notes, "thank you."

"Whatever we do needs to be done immediately," said Jane, "as soon as Colman or his Yellow cronies realise we are no longer going to the Resettlement Bureau voluntarily, they'll come for us directly."

Daisy came back in and shook her head.

"Lisa's going to compete in her jamming event," she said. "It's all she's ever wanted, and nothing will sway her from the perfect set of loganberry jam in front of an appreciative crowd."

"Even if it means death?"

"Yup."

"Crazy," said Jane.

"You risked death on the gyro-bike, Sis," said Clifton. "It's the same thing. Death or glory. Jam, gyro-bike, track, kitchen—what's the difference?"

"I'll concede that," said Jane, "and it's her choice. But will she blab to the Yellows?"

"She's focused on jam right now," said Daisy, "but she might, if asked. Time is not on our side."

"There's a train in an hour," said Tommo who had been consulting a timetable, "and five hundred merits should get a ticket without a travel order. Departures Monitors are usually low Yellows; a hundred merits will easily suffice to get past them, especially somewhere like Vermillion. People come and go all the time, and not all of it is recorded."

"Gates in the walled town are unguarded," said Jane, "and lightglobes are cheap in the Fair markets—so if anyone wants to walk out and keep walking after dark, that's a possibility too."

"Utter madness," snorted Violet. "I will be heading to Purple Regis. I shall present myself to my father and my hue, fine reputation and adherence to duty will protect and promote me. Perhaps you will join me, Edward? Married Purples travelling together are rarely questioned or stopped—we often walk past Departures Monitors with simply a dismissive wave of the hand."

I looked at Jane. We had no plans at all beyond leaving Vermillion—and hiding out in an all-Purple enclave had a certain attractiveness about it. I nodded to Jane, and she said:

"We'll go to Purple Regis with you. Edward will be your husband, I shall be Jane Fandango, your personal assistant."

Violet looked at us both in turn. Jane probably wasn't part of her plans, but it didn't much matter. She knew, as we all did, that getting out was the most important thing right now.

"Tania?" said Violet. "Will you join us? A united deMauve front might be helpful, and as a widow with reproductive ability and bearing a Reddy-Mauve child at present, you may be able to find yourself another Purple husband of considerable wealth and influence."

Tania shook her head.

"I've had enough of being Purple to last me several lifetimes.

Clifton and I and my children will strike off in the direction of Blue Sector North. Damson City is notoriously relaxed when it comes to Rules and is somewhere where we might find a place to live with few questions being asked."

It seemed like a good idea, so long as they could get up there unmolested.

"What will you do, Daisy?" I asked.

"Doug and I will take a Ford and head off towards East Carmine to check for survivors; visit the Riffraff camp, perhaps, see if any Greys made it out that way. After that, who knows?"

"How will you take a Ford?" asked Tania.

"We'll just take it," said Doug, "*without* asking."

It was a uniquely audacious plan, and I'd never heard of anyone taking a Ford without asking before.

"We could pretend to be a Red couple," said Tommo to Lucy, proving that he was still hopelessly besotted, even in a time of crisis. "The Cinnabars are a big family and might give us safe harbour. You could carry on your work regarding harmonics."

Lucy looked at him and I think realised that as bad as he was, Tommo's uniquely dishonest skillset might offer at least a reasonable chance of survival.

"Okay," she said, "but a Red couple in name only—none of the other stuff."

"I agree," said Tommo.

"No, I'm serious—none of that stuff, like, *ever*. A kiss in public to allay suspicions, perhaps, but that's it. Not a top-rack squeeze, shared bed or other intimacy. We're talking *nothing*, Tommo, and we need to get that straight right now or we go our separate ways."

He sighed.

"Yes, I get that—and I agree."

"Where will you head?" I asked.

Lucy and Tommo stared at one another.

"Yes," said Lucy, "where will we go?"

"You'll go to Crimsonolia," said Jane, "and seek out a Tin Man who is rich in spoons."

"I'm sorry?" said Lucy.

"Tell him your name and he'll know that you are friends of ours," I said, "and your need for spoons will give him function."

"I'm not sure I'm following."

"You're going to have to trust us," said Jane, then turned to the rest of the room and held up her taped index finger and added: "another point we should mention is that swans can see you with your barcodes uncovered. Tape it over and you'll be invisible to the swans that track our movements—but you have to keep it that way for life."

"Swans, Tin Men rich in spoons, index fingers, invisibility," said Daisy, "I'm finding all this a little hard to swallow. But I'll go along with it because you've been right so far and we have few options."

"Penelope?" asked Doug. "What do you want to do?"

The former Yellow monitor seemed increasingly lost, and looked at us all in turn with a mournful expression. She was the youngest, so when it came to a death event, had the most to lose.

"Can I come with you, Violet?"

Violet looked up from where she had been staring sullenly at the linoleum flooring.

"Sure," she said after a moment's thought, "why not?"

Jane picked up Mrs. Lilac's spot-badge and handed it to Penelope. "As soon as we're off-Sector you'll be Penny Lilac, orphaned daughter of a dear friend, now Violet's handmaiden. You lost your merit book at Jollity Fair. Yes?"

Penelope looked shocked at the possibility of being party to such flagrant and immoral Rule-breaking, but managed to nod her agreement.

Our patchwork of plans now complete, there was only the need to implement them.

"Okay then," I said. "Lucy, divide up the money and good luck, everyone. Better assume we'll not be meeting again."

Everyone nodded and we said our muted goodbyes and good lucks and discussed plans and details and ideas while Lucy shared out the cash. It took her almost forty minutes.

UPSET ON DOWN TRAIN

Rail travellers were only monitored at point of departure and point of arrival. With sufficient cash reserves it would be possible to stay travelling within the network indefinitely, so long as you had access to an All Stations Super Season Apex ticket. It's thought as many as a hundred souls may be using this measure to avoid the authorities.
—Ted Grey: *Twenty Years Among the Chromatacians*

There were two trains out of Vermillion that afternoon, one hour apart. Tommo, Lucy, Clifton and Tania and her children made it out on the first with apparently no issues—Jane and I watched from the hat shop opposite as they bought their tickets and walked to the platform. The Departures Monitor, after speaking briefly to Tommo, left them alone and went to check on someone else. Daisy and Doug also made off with little difficulty using their novel "taking without asking" plan and presumably had a good choice as the Fordpark was packed with vehicles.

Jane and I absently window-shopped around town to soak up time before meeting up with Violet and Penny at the ticket hall. Tommo was right about the ticket office being corrupt and so, two thousand merits lighter and four one-way tickets to Purple Regis heavier, we made our way towards the platform and the Departures Monitor. Jane had a thousand merits in the pinafore of her Outdoor Casual #1s, but all optimism evaporated when we found ourselves face to face, not with a lowly Yellow Monitor, but Dustin Colman, Vermillion's Yellow Deputy Prefect. It wasn't his usual job; that would be too far below him. No, he was here for us. Someone must have tipped the Yellows off.

"Well, well," he said with a faint smile, "going somewhere?"

Violet was still shocked into silence by her loss of privilege, so I intervened.

"Purple Regis," I said, "to attend the deMauve Convention. We shall happily attend the Resettlement Bureau upon our return."

"Is that a fact?" said Colman. "You cannot leave unless the Council permits it. You can take it from me that they do not."

"Here," said Jane, holding out her fist, palm downwards. "This should take care of things."

"Are you offering me a cash inducement to ignore my duties, contrary to Rule 6.09.78.44?"

"You can all be bought," she said. "All we're doing is haggling over the price."

He smiled.

"You cannot buy *me*, Miss Brunswick."

He said it in the sort of way that meant he really wasn't kidding.

Jane and I looked at one another, then at the train, which was just pulling in.

"I have the power to stop the train from departing," he said, correctly guessing our intentions.

"These aren't the travellers you're looking for," came a voice.

We all turned to see who had spoken, and found Mr. Baxter standing at the door of the waiting room. It wasn't our Baxter, obviously, but the one I had seen earlier. Since he would be Apocryphal in Vermillion, too, we all turned smartly back by force of long habit to ignore him. The Rules that Deputy Colman was so eager to enforce were from the same stable that stated Baxters could not be seen. That being so, a Baxter could do anything they wanted without interference or consequence. When Colman once more told us we weren't leaving, Baxter walked smartly up, took hold of Deputy Colman's right ear and tore it off in a single swift movement. Only he didn't, of course— he couldn't have because he was Apocryphal. According to the Rules, Coleman had spontaneously and inexplicably lost his ear.

"These aren't the travellers you're looking for," repeated Baxter as Colman winced in pain and placed a handkerchief against the wound to staunch the bleeding. "Ignore me again and I'll pinch off your windpipe."

Baxter's intent was clear: he could choke Mr. Colman to death on a crowded platform, and the Yellow's death would have to be logged as "unexplained."

Colman stared at Baxter for a moment, then at us.

"These aren't," he said in a subdued, frightened voice, "the travellers I'm looking for."

"They can go about their business," said Mr. Baxter in a low voice. Colman bit his lip but could do little. He wanted to uphold the Rules, but he didn't want to be dead. And he couldn't do both. "You can go about your business," said Colman.

"Move along," said Mr. Baxter.

Colman stepped aside and waved us past.

"Move along."

Baxter handed Colman his ear and we all boarded the train, or rather, Violet and I went to the Prefects' compartment and Jane and Penelope sat in the "notable hues" carriage behind. We didn't speak until we were through the stockgate and steaming across open countryside.

"My father and the rest of the deMauves will pull some

strings," said Violet in a brighter mood, "and all these problems will disappear. I will not be ungrateful for my deliverance back there in Vermillion, and there will be some sort of position for Jane and Penelope. A united front here is essential, Eddie. I may have to commit to a lowly job to begin with, but so long as I show due diligence to my work and demonstrate sound reproductive value, you and I can be at the sharp end of the Collective within ten years at worst."

"You just can't seem to stop trading on my breeding possibilities, can you?"

She looked up at me.

"Let's not fool ourselves, Eddie, it's all you've got—and could take you great places. Make some sign you'll think about it, Eddie, and as a sweetener, I'd be willing to tolerate your infatuation with Jane. She can stay your Grey-on-the-side until you tire of her, or she of you—but for you and I to survive and prosper, I need your cooperation."

"I'll speak with Jane."

"Eddie, you know you don't owe her anything?"

"You're wrong," I said. "I owe her *everything*."

She paused for a moment, then said:

"I'm carrying your child. Does that mean nothing to you?"

"It was only a planned pregnancy on your side, Violet—I had no say in the matter."

She made to say something more but instead lapsed into silence. But she was right, I suppose, in part. It *was* my child, and that had to mean something. Maybe not right here and now, but at some point. Violet and I, like it or not, would always have a connection. We carried on the journey in silence, the only interruption when we had to change trains, wait on the platform, then catch a connecting train, with each passing moment an opportunity for us to be halted, and detained, and taken to Room 101 or its nearest equivalent. That this didn't happen was due to Jane's persuasion skills and several healthy wads of cash. We made it to Emerald City by the evening three thousand merits poorer.

"That's twenty-seven years' salary," noted Penny. "Eighty-eight for a Grey."

We all checked into the Emerald City Railway Hotel in order to stay within the "Passenger Transit Zone" so we neither had to book in or out of the city. We were allocated rooms according to Spectral Affiliation, which meant Violet and I had our own room, while Penelope and Jane—wrongspotting as a Fandango and a Lilac—would spend the night in the "Sub-Chromogencia Lower Purples (Female)" dorm, ten to a room. We could eat together, of course, and did, but for some reason a Yellow was assigned to the dining room, and he moved without any form of sublety around the tables, keeping an eye out for infractions. Trying not to appear suspicious, I talked about the Last Rabbit in lavish terms while everyone looked bored with little acting required—and the Yellow moved on to another part of the room. The between-courses entertainments were an Orange conjuror who demonstrated how to saw a volunteer in half and then restore them, then a Grey male voice choir singing hits from *Ochrlahoma!* Violet sang along—she had quite a good voice—and after we had settled into our main course I spotted someone familiar near the serving counter. She was Grey and wore a waitress's uniform over her tall and willowy frame. I nudged Jane to have a look, and she stiffened. It was Melanie. The Yellow was busy demeriting a Blue couple for "heaping with undue highness a bowl from the salad bar," so Jane moved forward and whispered to us all:

"Act like you don't know her."

"Act like I don't know who?" asked Penny, a little unhelpfully.

"Work with me," said Jane, "and treat her like a Grey."

"Treat who like a Grey?" asked Penny, still really not getting it. But then Violet also noticed Melanie and laid a calming hand on Penny's arm.

"Hello," said Melanie in her waitress voice as she joined us. "Are we done here?"

I told her we were done and she gathered the plates, while talking in a low voice.

"Your father and Velma survived and are holed up in Blue Sector North," she said, while keeping a careful eye on the Yellow, "along with Adrian Crimson, Roddy Carrot, the Turquoise twins and Jeb Grey."

I knew the Turquoise twins—idiots the pair of them—but not the others.

"Jeb could run faster than anyone I know," breathed Jane. "What about your parents, or mine?"

Melanie shook her head.

"Jeb's the only Grey we know who got out. There could be more. Don't know."

I laid a hand on Jane's thigh under the table, and momentarily saw tears in her eyes, a rare show of emotion. But then she blinked rapidly a couple of times and they were gone.

"How did you know we were here?" I asked.

"I came here once I'd heard the news about East Carmine— and will keep on coming in case anyone else got out and needs help. I'll be able to harbour you all, but it will be in Emerald City's Greyzone and movement in and out is restricted."

Jane and I looked at one another.

"How restricted?" I asked.

"The Greyzone is a closed off city within a city. Access to Emerald City on work business only. East Carmine was a *lot* freer. It's not ideal, but I can get you in there while you figure out options."

We all pondered this for a moment.

"Thank you, Melanie," said Violet, the first to speak, "but Penny and I are heading to Purple Regis; Jane and Edward may do as they wish, but I'd advise them to come with us. I am a deMauve. I have contacts. My father is there. I can make things happen."

I couldn't imagine Violet ever taking up life as a Grey—or even doing manual work, come to that. I looked at Jane and she nodded. Entering Chromatic society at the top made more sense for what we wanted to do.

"We'll try our luck in Regis," said Jane, "but might be back, thank you."

"Okay then," said Melanie. "Good luck, everyone. You know my postcode; send me a letter if you change your mind. I will take your pudding order in a jiffy," added Melanie in a louder voice as the Yellow had once more hove into view. "The Munsell chocolate fudge sundae only contains forty percent actual mud, so is as palatable as it is economic."

She didn't come back for the order, someone else did, and we didn't see her again. I think she had plans, and didn't want to be caught by the Yellow either.

"Will we get out tomorrow?" asked Penny. "The Vermillion Prefects *must* have alerted the Emerald City Prefects."

"Red Sector wouldn't lose any sleep over disruptionists moving off-Sector to cause trouble elsewhere," said Violet.

"And Baxter may have harassed Colman into inactivity," added Jane.

"Do you know any of that for a fact?" I asked.

"No," said Violet and Jane, pretty much together.

"Then we stay on our toes and look to luck, cash and our wits to keep us safe."

We didn't have any pudding, paid the bill and retired to

our separate rooms. Before lights out Jane and I took a bath together, not because we needed one but so we could talk. We did paper/stone/scissors to see who got the tap end, and after a long silence Jane spoke of her loss. Her parents, she knew, would not have taken flight before helping everyone they could, and I think in this manner she was at least proud of them, and could draw solace from that.

"I'm glad your dad got away," she said. "If we knew where Lucy was we could tell her about Velma."

"They may be okay now," I said, "but day-on-day safety is now a thing of the past, especially with Hanson and Utopiainc wanting them all dead. Us too. Do you want your hair washed?"

Jane looked at me oddly, told me that no one other than her or Mum and Dad or Melanie had ever done that, then said that she would, very much.

So I undid her plait and washed her hair, and although we had been *youknow* intimate twenty-seven and a half times now, somehow the very mundanity of this small act made what we had that much stronger.

"Did you ever think a C-Notice would happen?" I asked as I rinsed her long auburn tresses.

"In retrospect," she replied, "I think it was always going to happen once Robin Ochre refused to show anyone the Mildew and your dad continued that policy. Perhaps a village is on probation once the Supervisory Substitute Swatchman is called, and if he or she goes missing or is killed, then that's it."

We were silent for a moment.

"What are you going to do about Violet?" Jane asked. "The Purple facade she wants to maintain with you will have to be close, lest anyone gets suspicious."

"What does that mean?"

"A family. She's carrying your child, and if you don't have

another that will be suspicious, too, and Violet won't want it fathered with anyone less Red than you."

I found some shampoo and started washing her hair.

"We'll figure something out that you're happy with."

But Jane didn't want to let this go.

"You'll still need to live closely, with all the trappings and privilege that high colour brings. It could be a comfortable life. It *will* be a comfortable life."

I used a jug to rinse out her hair.

"Look," I said, "I have to get close to her to make this work for you and me. That's what we wanted, right? That's what *you* wanted. I mean, how can we even *begin* to tackle someone like Hanson and the Creator, Utopiainc and all the rest without being at the top of the stack? This could be the best and only chance we'll ever get to effect any sort of meaningful change: you and me, together, using Violet and her connections. This was your suggestion, Jane."

She thought for a moment.

"And I still think that's the way, Eddie, but one dead village gives one pause for thought. I think we . . . should part right now so you can live your life to the Purple without let or hindrance. There will be no Jane, no hiccups, no creeping around—you'll be embedded so deeply in Purple society that in ten or twenty years no one would suspect you to be anything other than a compliant Purple husband. Then we strike."

I stopped rinsing her hair.

"You're kidding, right?"

"I'm deadly serious. The cause is everything, and everything can be sacrificed to that end."

"Without you there's no reason for me to do this," I said, suddenly feeling a tautness in my chest, a sense of impending loss. "I can't do this on my own. I don't *want* to do this on my own."

She climbed out of the bath and stood on the "Welcome to Emerald City" bath mat, water dripping from her naked body.

"I think this is a test of our commitment," she said, no longer catching my eye.

"Then I've failed that test," I said, my voice rising. "We're in this *together*. Always."

She wrapped herself in the towel and gathered up her clothes.

"Was this your plan all along?" I asked. "This thing I've shared with you, these moments we've been together, risking everything, has all been some sort of play?"

"Maybe I was wrong about you," she said. "That when the big decisions arrived you'd falter and fall by the wayside."

"Oh, c'mon—!"

"No," she said as she pointed an accusatory finger at me. "Live a good life and I'll be back sometime in the future. Don't make this worse than it needs to be."

"I'm not doing it, Jane."

"Then you're valueless to the struggle. I should have let the yateveo take you that first time."

"Yeah," I said, "maybe you should have. Would have saved me a lot of grief."

"Don't give me the homeless puppy routine, Edward—you're better than that. I'll be in touch."

She made to kiss me but I pulled away, so she opened the door and left me feeling empty and abandoned. I sat on the edge of the bath for several minutes, wondering if what she said made sense—and it did, annoyingly. I just hated the finality of it all, and a life with Violet instead of Jane filled me with an unfathomable layer of dread.

I dressed slowly and made my way back to my bedroom. Violet was still awake, but sensed I'd just been in an argument and said nothing. I stared at the ceiling once the light outside extinguished, angry with myself and angry with Jane. I desperately wanted to go and talk to her, but the female dorms were strictly off limits and I would have shoes thrown at me if I stepped inside. It took me a second or two to realise I could now see in the dark.

TRAVEL TO PURPLE REGIS

There was no precedent for an all-Purple enclave, it just came into being once the deMauve and von Purple dynasties gained sufficient power and influence. It is assumed that someone Purple ended up in a position of power at Head Office, or that Head Office thought it a good idea. It is not known which.

—Ted Grey: *Twenty Years Among the Chromatacians*

We were woken by a noise outside in the corridor but it turned out to be the bootboy, replacing the shoes that he'd diligently shined in the early morning. We both breathed a sigh of relief, but it showed how on edge we were. Violet did not catch my eye and we dressed facing away from each other.

Breakfast was a muted affair, but was at least eaten, even if the kippers had seen better days.

"Where's Jane?" asked Violet.

"She left early," replied Penny, "with a packed valise."

She glanced at both of us in turn; she knew what it meant. Violet could have said something crass at that point, but used what little tact she had to remain silent.

We returned to our rooms to pack, then mustered in the lobby to pay our hotel bill five minutes before our train was due to leave as we didn't want to spend a second longer in public than we had to. I thought of walking away and taking up Melanie's offer as I presumed that's what Jane had done, but I didn't. She'd been right about stuff in the past, and perhaps she was again. Besides, I couldn't think of a way of meeting her there that didn't make me look *exactly* like a homeless puppy.

WE SENSED THERE were problems almost immediately when we entered the station, as there were two Yellows in the booking hall. There wasn't an Arrivals or Departures Monitor to contend with as we were in transit, but spot-checks were common. Beyond the Yellows and beyond the booking hall, tantalisingly, we could see our train at readiness, doors open and with passengers boarding.

"How are we going to do this without Jane?" asked Penny. "She was very good at handing out bribes."

"I'll have a go," I said, without much conviction.

"We'll be tallow before we know it," said Violet, taking a deep breath. "Follow my lead."

She took off across the concourse with a speed and gait that might be described as imperious.

"Those kippers were the worst I've tasted," she said in a loud, outraged tone. "As though soaked in urine. Further, I counted eight cockroaches last night when the Bed Vermin Threshold *specifically* permits only four."

"I will make a note," said Penny, who had picked up on Violet's obvious gambit: a high Purple *not* complaining bitterly about something would be highly suspicious, and a Purple in a temper was a Purple worth avoiding.

"Is it really worth your valuable time, my dear?" I said, doing my part for the charade.

"Standards *have* to be maintained," she said, "or we might as well all be Grey—feckless, filthy and unsophisticated."

The gambit worked. We remained unmolested, showed our tickets at the barrier and moved on to the platform.

"Very good," I said.

Violet gave a rare smile.

"Principal girl at the theatre group six years running," she said, "but I'm not doing that again."

We made to board the train but an altercation behind us made me turn and my heart sank. Jane had followed us on to the concourse and was arguing with the two Yellows.

I touched Violet's elbow and she turned, then sighed and pulled a face.

"She'll be fine, Eddie, Jane's a born survivor. Don't you *dare* go over there and try something. United front, remember? Mr. and Mrs?"

I stared at her, then down at Penelope.

"What do you think I should I do?"

Penny bit her lip and looked up at Violet, then back at me.

"I'm surprised you're not over there already."

"Whose side are you on?" asked Violet, and Penny shrugged.

"Go then," said Violet, "we will take our seats—the train leaves with or without you."

She turned to board and I marched over to where Jane was being questioned.

"Hello," I said to the Yellows in a chirpy voice, "what seems to be the problem?"

The Yellows looked at me up and down.

"You know this woman?"

"Of course. Miss Fandango, my wife's assistant. We are heading over to Purple Regis, part of the deMauve Convention."

"She has no merit book and claims it was stolen by a casual liaison while insensible on Lime. Does that sound plausible?"

"*Very* plausible. Can we leave? Our train is due out any minute, and my wife would—"

"I'd like to see your merit book, too, sir. A deMauve, are we? Some people of that name departed Vermillion illegally yesterday. Edward, are you?"

"Torquil, actually. Would I really be so stupid as to travel under my own name?"

He looked at me carefully and decided that yes, I might well indeed be that stupid.

"You need to show me your merit book, sir. We can do it here or at City Hall. You decide."

"That's not necessary," I said, "and if I am delayed any longer you will incur the displeasure of Mrs. deMauve."

He narrowed his eyes.

"That'll be City Hall, then, I take it?"

"Miss Fandango?" came a loud voice behind us. "Where in Munsell's name have you been? Making colour under a Grey, I'll be bound. Can you not keep your legs closed for even one second?"

It was Violet. The combination of volume and vulgarity had a shock effect on not just the Yellows, but everyone on the concourse, which had fallen silent.

"I'm very sorry, ma'am," replied Jane meekly. "He stole my merit book. It won't happen again."

"It had better not, you little fool. Get on the train. Husband, you too."

We made to move off, but the Yellows were not totally convinced.

"And you are?" the elder Yellow asked.

She turned back, her eyes boring into them, her lips compressed into a thin line.

"How *dare* you?" she said in her haughtiest tone. "I had an unhappy fish-related incident this morning that led to multiple visits to the toilet; I have dealt with enough shits this morning without you two adding to the compliment."

They were both taken aback by this, and Violet's gambit was clear: shock them with such outrageous language that they would forget almost everything, and only want to be finished with her.

"You . . . you . . . should not talk to us like that."

She leaned closer and lowered her voice.

"You dare question me, a deMauve? I am a close personal friend of your Head Prefect. Back off now or I swear on Our Munsell's life I will devote the rest of my days to having you both allocated to the rendering sheds . . . *for ever*. Get it?"

"You can't do that," said the Yellow who hadn't yet spoken.

"Want to put it to the test?"

They both decided they did not wish to do so and bowed politely. Violet turned on a heel and walked briskly towards the train, yelling at the guard as she did so.

"Don't you dare blow that whistle until we are on board!"

He didn't, and a few minutes later we were comfortably steaming away from Emerald City.

"Thank you," I said as we sat in the Purple carriage, but Violet didn't answer. Instead, either from the stress or the bad kipper or a combination of the two, she rushed off to vomit in the toilets.

THE TRIP TO Purple Regis required only one change at Aquaminster to access the short Purple Regis branch line, and required an hour's wait. It gave me the first opportunity to talk to Jane, so we went off to the station café. As we entered, a couple of retired Blues were talking about East Carmine's destruction. News like this travels quickly; the official report would make the front page of *Spectrum* next month, doubtless with some story about how Mildew outbreaks always correlate with low morals, lack of industry, or other less-than-enthusiastic embracing of the Munsell Doctrine.

We bought some red-soil water and a biscuit each and sat down by the window. We said nothing for a few minutes.

I said: "Violet was pretty good back in Emerald City, wasn't she?"

"We used to be best friends when we were little," she replied, "before Chromatic politics kicked in. My mother was Violet's nurse. I think it's why I survived as long as I did. We're closer in personality than I think we'd like to admit."

There was another pause.

"What changed your mind?" I asked.

She took a deep breath.

"Mel changed my mind. Said you and I were better together; that we needed each other; the parts greater than the whole; we were a good team; gave mutual support to one another; regular and meaningful *youknow*; yadda yadda, that sort of nonsense. Wait, are you smiling?"

"No, yes, well a little—look, I'm just glad you're back."

She thought for a moment.

"I *hate* compromising. I wanted to effect major change—and instead we have to negotiate through Violet and use her position as a springboard to get where we want to go. But you and Mel may be right—this could be the best and only play we have, and it's something we need to do together, for mutual support."

"We're still young," I said. "Violet will get another Head Prefectship and we can set things in motion for a new plan under the safety of a Purple umbrella. We've got a good contact in Emerald City with access to National Colour, and perhaps that's the route to success: to the Creator themself through National Colour and Head Office. If we'd known then what we know now, that might have been our plan all along."

"I think it probably was even if we didn't know it," said Jane. "Just derailed by the C-Notice and Jollity Fair."

She punched me hard on the arm.

"Ow. What was that for?"

Jane shrugged.

"For making me care for you. I *hate* emotions when they make me act illogically."

She took a sip of the red soily drink, then pulled a face.

"Wow, that's pretty terrible."

I took a sip as well. She was right—it *was* terrible. Earthy but in all the wrong ways. I found her hand under the table, squeezed it and she squeezed mine in return.

Once back on the train I told Violet that her plan was sound, and that I would become a model deMauve husband for appearance's sake and we could promote ourselves as a young Purple power couple, heading ever upwards in the Chromatic Hierarchy. I told her that Jane and I would remain a couple, and that a second child might be possible in some manner.

"You and Jane will be discreet?"

"Since we can both see in the dark, night will be our time, and never the day."

"Looks like we have a deal," she said, and we shook hands.

The track was wooded and curved and just before our arrival at Purple Regis fifteen minutes later we traversed a pretty viaduct which crossed an inland tidal lagoon. The station was just outside the town, which allowed non-Purple travellers to use the line without entering the strictly "Purples only" enclave. We found no Arrivals Monitor on the platform, which Violet assured us was perfectly normal, and we walked with the other Purple passengers along a path to the boundary of the enclave, which was delineated by a gate, a hedge of clutching bramble and lots of warning notices that told would-be trespassers that only shades of Purple may pass. After another hundred metres we arrived at the lodge where the Porter and her staff greeted everyone and handed out bedroom allocations.

Violet explained who she was and asked where her father might be, and how she needed to see him as a matter of urgency.

While the Porter made enquiries, we read the noticeboard and learned the deMauve Convention wasn't for another week, but delegates had already started to arrive and had almost spontaneously formed sub-committees, with titles such as "The burden of Leadership" and "How to extract the best and most from your Greys" and, most revealing of all, "Redefining Loopholery in the Age of the Purple."

The Porter returned and said that Violet's father was in a meeting, but would join with her in an hour at the Mary Lavender Museum and Tearooms.

"Perfect," said Violet, "show us to our rooms and we will freshen up."

The Porter explained that the rooms were not yet ready as she was four days early and her party was bigger than expected, but they would be ready as soon as possible and we were welcome to stroll on the beach until Mr. deMauve would receive us all.

We took the Porter's advice and walked down to the shore. The tide was out to reveal a slippery foreshore that was ugly and untidy and smelled of salt, dead fish and rotted vegetation. Violet went and sat on a rock and stared out to sea to consider, I imagine, how best to engineer her return to power. She looked happier now than I had seen her since Vermillion, but I would have to be on my guard—her father would have renewed authority here, and have plans of his own—ones that might not necessarily include Jane or Eddie. Penelope for her part, poked among the rocks for spiral fossils while Jane and I chatted to some fisherfolk.

They were a crusty-looking bunch, with wind-weathered faces, thick-knit sweaters and were apt to break into sea-shanties at the slightest opportunity, which while initially entertaining, did get a teeny-weeny bit annoying after the third time. The fisherfolk were all mostly low-hue Mauves and Periwinkles, and were as much ornamental as they were practical, as the Purple Prefects liked to see the vessels going in and out of harbour, even if there was no ready market for the catch beyond the town. They fished only within sight of land, partly for said ornamental reasons and partly because of the wide array of jeopardies uniquely related to the sea. From the way they spoke, drowning was one of the more enjoyable things that could happen to them. We knew the waters around Chromatacia were fraught with perils, but the fisherfolk seemed to have an almost perverse delight in relating lurid tales of giant octopuses that could crush a boat, the Kraken that no one could describe as no one had ever survived, and ripping tides and whirlpools that could shred boats. To this was added, as we had long been told, the danger of the Under Toad—a large, venomous frog-like creature that lurked in the sea beyond chest-height water, and would grab at your heels and drag you under to be devoured at leisure. Little wonder that fishing was an underused resource for the Collective—it was just too hazardous.

They showed us their boats, which were 6.2 metres long, made of Perpetulite and with a small cabin up front to protect one from rain and spray. The motive power was a large Leapback-exempted Everspin housed in the centre of the boat, which turned what they called a "propeller," a sort of three-bladed knife that rotated under the water, pushing the water behind and propelling the craft forward, and controlled by a pivoting device that sat behind the propellor to direct the mass of water. They then showed us their nets, of which they were inordinately proud, and gave a series of demonstrations about knots of a bewildering variety of uses.

"Were they showing you their knots?" asked Violet as we walked back up towards the town.

"They did."

"They do love their knots."

We ordered some tea and currant buns in the tearooms, which we found were served with fish, as was everything. We waited another half an hour until the door opened and Violet jumped up, expecting her father. But it wasn't, it was the Enclave Head Prefect. He looked very grand in Univisual robes of the clearest and most perfect purple I think I had yet seen. He was an Ultra-Violet, the very highest Chromatic ranking there was.

"Your father will join us presently," he said in an amiable tone. "My name is Jethro deMauve. Why not introduce me to your companions?"

ALL CHANGE AT PURPLE REGIS

The existence of Purple Regis, as far as anyone can ascertain, was to give dynastic Purples a place to plot so they could weaken the hold of Munsellian Doctrine. It remains, so far, the only viable attempt to do so in nearly five hundred years.

—Ted Grey: *Twenty Years Among the Chromatacians*

"This is Jane Fandango, my personal assistant from East Carmine and due to start her Janitor training next year. The young lady is Penelope Lilac, orphaned daughter of a dear and close friend and now my handmaiden."

Violet had really no choice but to maintain this deception until a better strategy chanced along. "And saving the best for last," she carried on, "this is my husband, Edward. We are expecting our first child this winter."

The Ultraviolet congratulated us both, shook all our hands warmly and invited us to sit in a private room away from the chatter and bustle of the main eating area.

"News of East Carmine's Mildew outbreak was swift to reach our ears," said Jethro deMauve as he beckoned for the waitress, "but then to also suffer a devastating multiple ball lightning strike at the same time—most unfortunate and my sincere condolences for the loss of your Headship and village. It was by a very good fortune that your father, my brother, took his holidays when he did. He is a good and fine man, brought down by an overzealous Yellow. They can be troublesome and do have to be watched."

"I agree," said Violet, "and when will my father be joining us?"

"Soon."

Jethro deMauve professed how lucky Violet was that she and I had been at Jollity Fair during the Mildew outbreak, and then asked me in what event I had competed.

"None," I said. "I was there in a supportive capacity. Violet was playing hockeyball."

"And you?" asked Jethro deMauve to Jane.

She glanced towards me for a moment, unsure of where all this was heading, but like Violet knew that we had to carry on.

"My father is Carlos Fandango, sir, the Janitor. I was at Jollity Fair as gyro-bike engineer."

"Then you must know Jane Brunswick, who rode East Carmine's bike to victory? We heard the news over the telegraph."

"Beat Jamie Juniper by barely three inches," said Jane. "It was an exciting race, and edged Team Red ever closer to the Grand Prize."

"I've seen Jamie Juniper ride and I never thought she would be beaten. What's this Brunswick woman like?"

"Determined," she said. "She was Grey before she was Brunswick, and I think that never left her."

"Ah-ha," said deMauve. "And where is she now?"

"We left her in Vermillion," said Jane. "I personally saw that she would be well resettled as befits someone who has brought glory to the Sector."

"Good, good—and you, Penelope? Why were you at Jollity Fair?"

"I was in charge of the kit," she said, voice trembling. "The team gets through a lot, and constant mending is required."

"And you think washing and needlework are appropriate work for a Lilac?"

They weren't, of course. For a Yellow *maybe*, and certainly for a Grey—but a Lilac, never.

"It was to get her on the squad," said Jane without missing a beat. "Everyone should have a chance to visit Jollity Fair at least once in their life. The village Swatchman flashed her the skill hue for the occasion."

Lying seemed to just get easier and easier. Little wonder it was so aggressively outlawed. Jethro deMauve regarded Jane for a while, then me, then Violet again.

"This is fascinating," he said, "for I am an Ultraviolet, and that position comes with expectations. Not only in what I am expected to do for others, but what others are expected to do for me."

If he was wanting us to say something, we didn't, so he carried on.

"The Collective functions on the understanding and appreciation of hierarchy, unity, and trust," he said. "Without trust, then society collapses to the dark pre-Munsellian age of mendacity and violence. Munsell's great vision ensures that those who seek to manipulate truth for their own benefit are removed from society's pool before they have a chance to poison it. Do you understand what I am saying?"

This did not sound good, but delusive hope is strong, so we waited for him to spell it out.

"We were alerted by the Prefects in Vermillion that you might be headed this way, and I had my brother, your ex-Head Prefect, observe as you walked back from the beach and at my instruction, identified you all."

There was a deathly silence from us all, and I felt an odd sense of relief that the subterfuge was no longer necessary. Violet even gave out a nervous snigger, then apologised. Jethro deMauve looked first at Jane. "You are not a Fandango, you are a Brunswick. But to show that I understand sporting worth, my congratulations on winning the sprint."

"Thank you," said Jane, as denial seemed pointless.

"Penelope so-called Lilac," continued deMauve, switching his attention to Penny, "you are a Gamboge. You are wearing the Spot of another and have lied to the face of a Head Prefect. While I hope you are horribly ashamed of yourself, I believe it is because you are a child, and have been poorly influenced by those of a reckless and dissolute demeanour."

"My lying was all my own," said Penelope in a contrite manner. "I accept sole responsibility for my actions as any good resident should, and will embrace the demerits as you see fit."

Admitting your ills quickly and with full and frank disclosure was always the best policy, and she knew it.

"We know less of you, Edward Russett, other than you are the son of a man who shirked his responsibilities with tragic consequences, and was shunned by your first village for having the impertinence to suggest that queuing might somehow be improved."

"That was wrong," I said. "I see it now."

"And Violet," he said, finally turning to her, "my own dear niece. While you cannot be wholly to blame for the loss of East Carmine, you were Head Prefect when it was taken. You left a Supervisory Substitute Swatchman—a notoriously volatile presence—unattended while you sought personal aggrandisement on the field of hockey."

"I was inexperienced; I accept that."

"Youth and inexperience are not an excuse; if you thought you could not accept the responsibilities of the job, you should have applied for a replacement. A Prefect always puts the village ahead of their own ambitions."

"Yes," she said, "you speak wisely."

There was a pause. Our wrongs had been outlined, the future was his to determine. But we were in a Purple enclave and Violet had connections. This could go any way.

"Luckily," he said, "you still have a use to the Collective."

"Tell us how we may serve," said Violet.

Jethro deMauve rested his hands on the table. He had big palms, I noticed, and fingers like sausages.

"Your escape from Vermillion created a stir over at National Colour. I have reported you are here and they are sending out inquisitors. You will give a full and frank disclosure of what you know, how you came to know it, how you escaped Vermillion, and who helped you get all the way here."

We exchanged nervous glances.

"It's not unusual," he continued, "for residents with an inquisitive mind to achieve a limited degree of unnecessary awareness. Most people are sensible, ignore it, and live on. The system failed when it allowed you to slip through the net, and your function now will be to ensure that this does not happen to others. Your disclosures will ensure the Collective is made stronger and more resilient."

Jane spoke first.

"I will tell them nothing."

"No, you will tell them *everything*. Your choices are limited to fully cooperating with the inquisitors and being allowed to take the easy way out in the Green Room, or you can stay obstinately quiet and let the Mildew take you naturally, drowning in your own fluids. I've seen the latter and it's not pretty."

"Everything about the Munsell Doctrine is wrong," said Jane, "and it *will* be dismantled."

Jethro deMauve paused for thought.

"If you truly want betterment, then gain it by obedience,

hard work and a sound breeding choice, not a lazy demand for unearned freedoms."

"And Reboot?" I asked. "Or the Night Train to Emerald City, C-Notices and the Mildew? If the Rules are as perfect as you so imagine, why do they have murder as a form of social control?"

He turned to me.

"Humankind, my young friend, is a flawed, imperfect animal, and requires flawed and imperfect regulation for effective governance."

There was a pause, and with all credit to Violet, she hadn't yet given up the fight.

"It does not need to be this way," she said. "It is within your powers to hide us here, and tell the inquisitors we departed, or died, or have been rendered. Our names can be changed, our duties lessened. It may interest you to know that I am carrying a child with a potentially large purple sight gift. He and I and others yet to be conceived have much to offer the deMauves dynastically. My father will vouch for my solid adherence to the Way."

"A good point. Brother, would you join us, please?"

DeMauve stepped out from where he had been listening out of sight, just behind the door. We all stood up dutifully and bowed respectfully except Violet, who against protocol ran up and hugged him tightly.

"Daddy," she said in her annoying little girl voice, "I've had *such* a beastly time."

"There, there," he said in an unusually fatherly manner, "all is well now."

We all sat at the table.

"There is a part for me to play with the Purples, Father?" asked Violet. "I admit I have fallen, but you can help me recover."

DeMauve looked at Jethro who nodded.

"We have big plans," said deMauve, "and Jethro here wants me to be a part of that. But the new Chromatic order cannot be built with crumbling brick and substandard mortar."

"I am a deMauve," said Violet, who could see this didn't sound good. "Your daughter."

DeMauve laid his hand on his daughter's in an affectionate manner.

"My dear Violet," he said, "as soon as you decided to take matters into your own hands, that was the moment you demonstrated you were unfit to hold the privilege of leadership. A good and upright Head Prefect would follow all orders placed upon them, as they know without hesitation that the Rules are right and proper and just. We would have spared you Room 101 had you attempted to go there, but to be given life, sometimes you must be willing to show complete adherence to the Rules."

"I would have been stopped had I tried to enter the Resettlement Bureau?"

"You would. As soon as you abandoned the Munsell Way, that was the moment when we had no use for you."

"Dad?"

"We need to demonstrate to National Colour our compliance, to alleviate suspicions," said Jethro. "Revealing everything you know to the inquisitors will be your contribution. Your sacrifice will push your hue further and higher. Do you see that?"

Violet gave a sigh and tapped a fingertip on the table.

"I see that now. Thank you."

We all looked at one another. Violet's plans—and by extension, ours too—were in tatters. There was no safe haven in Purple Regis. The endgame here would be with the inquisitors, then the Green Room. We would have to move on.

"Cosying up to National Colour will not save you," said Jane. "You will be crushed as East Carmine was crushed."

"The Creator," I added, "sees all."

Both Jethro and deMauve gave out a guffaw.

"Myths and nonsense," said Jethro. "The future is Purple."

Violet unclipped her Purple badge and placed it gently on the table.

"I won't be needing this anymore. Is there a Green Room here?"

"I cannot allow that," said Jethro. "Not for you, nor any of the others."

"The use of the Green Room is the resident's prerogative," piped up Penelope, "and may be used, according to Rule 1.2.4.17.31, whenever an individual feels their usefulness to the Collective is over. Do you feel your usefulness to the Collective is over, Mrs. deMauve?"

"I do."

Jethro deMauve smiled.

"The Collective really has lost an asset in you, Miss Gamboge. You better hurry if that is your decision, Violet, I will grant you this small favour. The others I will not permit to take the easy way out. I have instructed muscular Lilacs to tail each of you, lest you try and escape again. But you are free to wander within the enclave to better muse upon your shortcomings."

We all got up and walked slowly out of the tearooms, then the short distance to the town square. Already we could see the Lilacs that deMauve had mentioned. They were leaning in doorways, staying mostly hidden, but tailing us. We mingled among the other Purples out walking and taking the sea air, and paused by the twice-lifesize statue of Our Munsell.

"Are you really going to take the Green Way Out?" asked Penny.

"What's the alternative?" replied Violet. "I don't see myself on the run for the rest of my life, nor ending up giving birth on the dusty floor of a hovel somewhere, attended by lice-infested

Riffraff, then working as some skivvy to a toothless old crone without manners or breeding. I despise you all for what you have allowed me to do to myself."

She spoke quietly and without emotion, and I couldn't help but feel a small amount of sympathy at her dramatic fall. She sat down on a bench in the square beneath the Munsell statue, head in hands, while Penny went to look at some doves as she'd never seen one before.

"Now what?" I said to Jane.

"I'm not sure. I can see four Lilacs watching us, how many you got?"

"Six," I replied. "Yours plus two in the door of the foot spa lounge."

"What's a foot spa lounge?"

"I don't know. It's written above the door."

"I guess we just make a run for it," she said, "and hope we can pay them off when they catch us up. Swan."

"Where?"

"Out at sea, heading this way."

She looked up and there it was, about a mile away. She had an idea, smiled, then pulled the plaster off her index finger. It was an audacious and aggressive move, wholly based on a deep loathing of those in authority who had unfairly sentenced us to death. *Exactly* why I loved her, in fact.

"You're a terrible person, Jane Brunswick. If Hanson detects that you're alive for a third time, he may just get annoyed enough to rain some fire down on you."

"True," she said. "Imagine how even more annoyed he'll be when he spots yours too?"

I needed no more persuasion, and pulled the tape off my finger. We held them aloft and waited until the swan had passed overhead. It dipped its wing, flew a couple of tight orbits, then headed off towards Aquaminster.

"We've got an hour if Mr. Pink is anything to go by. We should warn those that matter. Hey, you!"

We walked over to where one of the Lilacs was hiding badly in a doorway.

"Hullo!" said Jane in the overly bright and sunny manner of the not-quite-sane. "You've probably been told we're dangerous and been instructed to use physical force to keep us in Purple Regis. Am I right?"

"We've also been told not to talk to you," she said.

"I'll do the talking, then. You've heard about East Carmine? How it suffered a Mildew outbreak, then was destroyed by a cleansing fire from on high?"

"They said ball lightning."

"They lied. In an hour you'll see a swan high up in the sky, and a second or two later, Purple Regis will be destroyed in a pillar of fire, and everyone in it."

"I don't believe you."

"You don't have to," I said, "but deMauve said we're dangerous and this is why. You're about thirty; you'll have two kids, maybe ten and eight. Be worried for them if not for yourself. Again: you've got about an hour."

She said nothing more, and turned to leave.

We walked back to the twice-lifesize statue of Munsell, and rewrapped our nail-beds. Penny was there, now at a loss since Violet had decided to take the Green Way Out. She sidled up close to show she was with us.

"So," said Jane, "which direction do you think would work best?"

The town square was on a raised bluff which gave a clear and uninterrupted view up and down the coast. To our right there were cliffs and rugged coastline which led to a headland about a mile away, and to our right there was more of the same—just with a headland perhaps six or seven miles distant. On top of the cliffs were mature beech and sweet chestnut but there was little else to be seen in either direction, and no sign of life. As far as I was concerned, no particular direction had any advantage over the other.

"Eddie? What do you think? Strike east or west?"

"What about," I said slowly, "going somewhere else?"

"That's what I'm asking you."

"No," I said, nodding in the direction of the sea. "I mean somewhere else as in *Somewhere Else.*"

Her eyes followed where I'd indicated—to an empty horizon, the billows of the water shimmering brightly in the sun, with only a few seabirds and scattered clouds to break up the desolate emptiness.

"It could be thirty miles or a thousand," she said.

"No," I said, "it's one hundred and fifty-one point nine nine two kilometres away on a bearing of southeast by south."

"What's a kilometre?"

"It was a present from my mother. About ninety-four miles to you."

"And what is out there?"

"Shareborg."

"What's a Shareborg?"

"I don't know. I just know it's there."

I touched my finger to my head.

"And before you ask, I think it's also from Mother. I think it's how inspiration works. A Herald, *my* Herald. You up for it?"

She looked out to sea again, then to me, then the remaining Lilacs. She beckoned Penelope closer.

"Penny, ever wanted to take a trip in a boat?"

"Nope."

"It's either that or the inquisitors and the Green Room."

"They can't put a minor to death in the Green Room. It's contrary to Rule 2.34.1.1.88."

She said it almost mechanically.

"Think that's going to stop them?"

Penny thought for a moment.

"Are the stories of sea beasts real?"

"The stories are real, yes. The beasts themselves—not sure, possibly not."

"'Not sure, possibly not' sounds like quite an encouraging outcome right now."

Our minds made up, we walked in an unhurried manner towards the harbour mole, a large breakwater made of Perpetulite that was reached by a causeway. It was one way in and one way out, so we would have to hope that the Lilacs would not trouble to follow us. I turned to look at Violet but she was gazing into the middle distance, doubtless contemplating her loss of fortunes and impending self-Greening. She caught my eye, and I waved goodbye, and she waved back, then stared at the ground again.

We walked slowly across the causeway, hoping not to arouse any suspicions. There was a viewing pavilion on the harbour mole, and the Lilacs would most probably think this our destination. We were right, for they stopped at the causeway, and sat down to await our return or the arrival of the inquisitors.

"Ahoy, fishermen," said Jane when we found them playing cards behind a large upturned boat and a pile of discarded nets. "An odd request: How much for your boat, right now? We're paying cash and we are in a generous frame of mind."

They stared at us, laughed, and pulled a number out of the air.

"Eight thousand and it is yours, young lady—and we'll even throw in some sea shanties for good measure."

"Ten thousand," I said, "if you leave out the sea shanties."

"The boat is yours. You need to leave now as the tide is about to turn."

"Suits us fine whatever that means," said Jane, and we trotted down the steps to where the boat was moored. We stepped gingerly inside and as one fisherman told Jane how to work the steering gear and the Everspin and something called a "directionator," I counted out the cash and handed it over to the other.

"Where are you headed?" asked the fisherman, the first time he'd thought to ask.

"Shareborg," I said.

"Where?"

"Ninety-four point four four miles southeast by south," I replied.

"Ninety-four miles?" he echoed. "You are deluded and you will die."

"Maybe. Oh—and stay out of Purple Regis. In about fifty minutes it will be destroyed by a pillar of fire brought from on high by agents of our Creator."

They exchanged glances and moved off quickly. I suppose anyone with ten thousand merits in cash is probably someone you should listen to.

"I'd like to come too."

It was Violet, who had followed us.

"You sure?"

"If I die by Green Room or Kraken, it's no matter to me—but at least this way there's a better view and I won't be alone."

Jane and I looked at one another.

"Your call," I said.

Jane stared at Violet with her head on one side. They had been friends when they were children and maybe they could be again. Perhaps that was what the politics of harmony lacked more than anything else: flexibility.

"Sure," she said, and offered Violet her hand so she could climb aboard.

And without any fanfare, Jane started the Everspin by the

movement of a lever and we pushed off from the harbour wall. The fishermen waved us away and despite the extra two thousand merits I'd given them, sang a sea shanty about how our expedition would end in failure, that Krakens and octopuses and the Under Toad would take us, and how they hoped our death would be painless, or at the very least, quick.

THE WATER

The waters surrounding Chromatacia were an underused commodity both for fishing and recreation, and for a very good reason.
—Ted Grey: *Twenty Years Among the Chromatacians*

Jane steered the small boat using something called a "tiller" at the back of the craft and we made our way towards the entrance to the harbour, where the sea became more choppy. Once clear of the mole she increased the speed as the fisherman had suggested "in order to have more control" and once in open water we took up the heading of southeast by south on the "directionator," which seemed to jiggle and rock in a manner that made it seem entirely unsuitable for ocean navigation.

I watched as a lone pair of Lilacs appeared on the mole and yelled at us to return, but their imploring voices were soon drowned out by the lap of waves on the hull.

We made steady progress and drew further away, Purple Regis soon small, then a blur and finally a smudge. We didn't see the high-level swans arrive, but an hour and eighteen minutes after the first swan had seen our barcodes we saw the effect: leaving nothing to chance this time around, Purple Regis erupted in a huge fireball, the concussion of the blast soothed into a dull rumble by the distance. The survivors would have been those with doubts, the arrogant and immovable incinerated where they stood.

"I'm sorry about your father and mother," I said to Violet, as Jane laid a comforting hand on her shoulder. She said nothing, and simply stared. Pretty soon all we could see was fire and smoke, then only smoke, then just a wisp of coastline. The weather was clear with only a light wind, and so far there were no sea beasts, no Under Toad, no Kraken, no giant octopus.

Jane and I took it in turns on the tiller while Penny and Violet sat in the cabin up front, huddled in some blankets they'd found, I think more out of fear than cold. I navigated solely by staring at the compass for a good ten minutes, trying to work out the best average as it jiggled about, but then I gave up and just steered where I thought southeast by south lay, and when I occasionally looked down I noted I was more or less correct.

We followed the coast for four hours, then struck off into open ocean. Without thinking, I changed the bearing to south by west and when Jane asked why, I replied "because of wind and current" and referred to my Herald when she asked how I knew. We were soon out of sight of land, a state of affairs that was far more worrisome than I'd imagined. Before it was simply an adventure of mild peril, but now it seemed like a decision of almost manifest stupidity. Although none of us verbalised it, a wiser course of action might have been to follow the coast around and to try and make a landing in a place where we could settle as supernumeraries—and given the cash we still had with us, that was probably a sounder plan than the one upon which we were currently embarked.

As dusk fell I decided to be the one to say the unsaid, and asked Jane if we should carry on. Violet and Penny looked at me and by their expressions they were definitely for turning back, but knew better than to say anything. This was our show now, and they knew it.

"We carry on," she said, "and trust in your Herald. If we haven't found Shareborg in a hundred miles, we turn back and take a bearing to make landfall further to the east. How far have we come?"

"Thirty-one miles so far," I said. "If Shareborg *is* there, at our current speed we will arrive at oh-nine-oh-seven tomorrow morning."

The night was overcast and without a moon and the wind dropped, so I altered course to south by east to compensate. Jane went for a rummage in the storage boxes up front and found some lightglobes. She stood them on a pole in the centre of the boat, from where they illuminated our anxious faces and the dark sea all around, where the crests of small waves seemed to morph into a tentacle or toad with every fatigued blink. There was a keg of water and some biscuits, but the water felt metallic and the biscuits like cardboard.

There was no sleep for anyone, and given that we were lightly dressed we were now cold, too, and as dawn broke and vision returned to our world, I noted with dismay that there was still no land in sight, but agreeably, no sea beasts either. Finally, almost three hours after dawn, we sighted something directly ahead. First it was a wispy glimpse, then a crust, and finally it was land. More excitedly and unexpectedly, as we drew closer we saw another boat making straight for us at some speed. It was larger and sleeker than our craft and as it grew closer we could see it was crewed by . . . *Previous*, all tall and small-headed and dressed in matching uniforms with "Coast Guard" written upon them. They were also smiling, which I hadn't expected. We all looked at one another nervously.

"Stop your spinner, we are coming alongside," yelled a woman, and pretty soon they did so, and helped us to board their vessel, where we sat in a warm cabin and were given blankets of incredible softness with which to wrap ourselves, and a warm drink that tasted like chocolate, but about twenty times sweeter. I'd not tasted anything quite as good, ever.

"You are now in the Union of Federated States," said the

woman as she perched herself on a seat as the boat switched direction and sped back towards the land, "the UFS. Can you all understand me?"

We all nodded and I said: "We can understand you."

"My name is Sabine," continued the woman, "and I will be your Citizen Induction Officer. How long did it take you to cross?"

"Fourteen hours and nine minutes," I said. "Are you going to send us back?"

"Good Lord, no," she replied. "Over there you were the Property of Utopia Inc, but as soon as you crossed the Reserve demarcation limit, you became free citizens of the Union. You have *exactly* the same rights as any of us. Are you hungry?"

We nodded and were given sandwiches. Again, they tasted amazing.

"Is it okay if we read your barcodes?" said Etienne. "You don't have to let me, but your citizenship papers become a lot easier if we have your subject codes."

We all dutifully peeled the tape off our nail-beds and by some sort of tech that beeped when it was pointed at them, Etienne was satisfied.

"We'll have your citizenship cards ready for you when we dock—it's a point of honour for us that your first steps you take on UFS soil are free steps."

"We have a lot of questions," said Jane, "beginning with 'what's a Citizen'?"

"And we'll answer every one," she said, tapping her remote viewer, "but I'd suggest asking them slowly, and taking your time to process the answers. It's a lot to take in."

"You said we were property?" I asked. "Is that allowed?"

"Yes and no."

"You can't own anyone," said Penny. "It's a contravention of Rule 2.3.8 . . ."

Her voice trailed off.

"Who were we owned by?" asked Violet.

"It's a long story, but simply put, the very first version of you were sequenced rather than born, and for a very specific purpose."

"Sequenced?"

"I'm so sorry," said Etienne. "You're only the seventh escapees I've met in my career—'sequenced' means 'built, created, manufactured.'"

"Like a Tin Man?" I asked.

"Wow," said a crew member who was standing near us. "Sounds like the AVMs are still active. Airbus Robotics will be pleased."

"Ignore Franc. You are not like a Tin Man, you were built *organically*."

"Like chutney?" asked Penny, still confused.

"Closer, but no."

"What were we created for?"

"I'll give you a quick and dirty answer and we'll go into specifics later, but you were on the Reserve to test genetic resilience for hard-wired hue-extractable skills and auto-repair systems. We Legacy Humans have to learn everything we know, have trouble being expert in more than two disciplines, can't do much at all for our first fifteen years and don't repair well and sometimes not at all. You guys are born with skills and knowledge beyond anything any of us could acquire in twenty lifetimes, have a potential life span of over a century and knit back together like a dream."

"I still don't get it," said Jane.

"Lots of time to explain," said Etienne, "but there's no point in designing a human to go to the stars if none of you function beyond three generations when you get there. Most of you are twenty-four generations from Couple Zero, and as far as we know, there are no major faults."

"Our ears come off quite easily," mused Violet.

"Aside from that," said Etienne.

"Why are we going to the stars?" asked Jane.

"Because we can't stay here," said Etienne, "and impending disaster brings forth focus, ingenuity and unprecedented levels of collaboration."

The phrase slipped off her tongue as though a mantra, a watchword, a mission statement. She said it like we used to say "Apart We Are Together," but here it sounded like she actually meant it.

"I'm still not getting this," said Violet.

"But we will and we shall," said Jane, "in time."

"Wise words," replied Etienne. "*Homo coloribus V3.4*s are kind of rare. You'll be in demand—but only if you want it. Some go on the lecture circuit, others retire to gardening and an easy life, others return as part of infrastructure support. It's totally up to you. Now," she went on, consulting her remote viewer again and pointing at me and Jane, "it says here that you two are both dead twice, one of you three times. What's that all about?"

"We found a way to game the swans to our advantage," said Jane. "We call them drones, and it's not a problem being dead—many escapees figure that one out."

"Can we ever go back?" I asked, thinking of Dad.

"I'm afraid not," she said. "All Reserves are out of bounds to ordinary citizens. No one agrees with *everything* that Utopia does, but their importance is recognised as 'vital to continuation of species' so they have a broad remit."

"What about the *Book of Harmony*?" asked Penny. "Munsell, Chromatic Hierarchy?"

"We'll cover that fully at the debrief. Now: What are your names? I've only got serial numbers in the database."

"Violet Elizabeth deMauve," said Violet, and Etienne tapped it out after getting her to spell it.

"Penelope Joan Gamboge," said Penny, "but they call me Penny."

"Okay. And you?"

"Jane Grey," said Jane, who never liked the name Brunswick.

"O-kay," said Etienne, tapping the remote viewer to spell out her name before turning to me. "And you are?"

"His name's Edward Grey," said Jane without a second's hesitation. "Eddie. We're married. Two days ago."

"Is this true?"

"Yes," I said.

"On-Reserve marriage does need at least one witness, or we'll have to do it again."

"I witnessed it," said Violet. "I think they'll be very happy together."

"Then congratulations," said Etienne, followed by a similar commendation in chorus from the crew. "Your marriage is henceforth officially recognised."

I felt a weight suddenly lift, and not just simply at the idea of being married to Jane at her insistence, but for the sudden and abrupt *freedom*, and being treated as an equal, and people in authority asking me what I wanted, and reacting positively to my needs. Jane took my hand and squeezed it.

"Can you log me down as Ted?" I asked. "Always liked that name."

She did so, then asked if any of us had any health issues she needed to be aware of.

"I'm pregnant," said Violet, "but early days."

Etienne made another note and said how sorry she was that Violet's partner was not with her.

"It's okay," she said. "He was my husband but it didn't work out. Given time it might have if I'd known then what I know now, but he's happier with the person he's with, and frankly I don't blame him."

Etienne, sensing this was a sensitive moment, said:

"That's enough questions for now, but before we get in and you're taken to a hotel for a rest before a more in-depth induction and full debrief, would you like to see in full colour?"

"How long for?" asked Jane.

"We can refigure your cortex here and now to see full colour for ever," she said. "That option has always been open to you with the correct hue, and it won't cost you any losses in skill acquisition at a later date."

"Full colour vision has *always* been open to us?" asked Violet.

"I'm afraid so," she said. "I know that must sound sort of disappointing."

She wasn't kidding. Everything that we had ever experienced, our expectations, our aspirations, our order in society—all predicated on a massive lie.

We all nodded vigorously.

Etienne tapped her remote viewer a couple more times with an elegant finger, and told us to look at the screen.

I can't really describe the colour we saw, but this time there was no stabbing of pain, no barking dogs or crinkling paper, just a slow leaching in of our missing hues. I saw Jane stare at her hands, then at me, then at the boat we were on, which was a pale green.

"Oh my goodness," said Violet, "look at the sky!"

We looked up, and there it was, a deep blue of almost unfathomable perfection.

Etienne smiled.

"I never get bored with this bit. I'll leave you to enjoy yourselves until we get in."

So we all sat on the back of the boat and watched with a new, sort of childish fascination as we approached the port and slowly moved past other boats, all with flags of every colour you could imagine fluttering in the breeze. On land there were trees of green, *real* green, and the people who had gathered to see our boat dock were wearing an almost infinite array of chromatic shades, more subtle and varied and beautiful than I could possibly have imagined. As we moved closer we could see that while most of the crowd was composed of Previous, there were two just like us—shorter and with big eyes and a large head, grinning fit to burst and holding a hastily written placard that simply read "Welcome." We were, by that time, all of us, in tears.

Jane held my hands tightly in hers.

"Oh, brave new world," she whispered in my ear, "that has such colours in it."

ACKNOWLEDGMENTS

My thanks to Carolyn Mays, my editor for the past sixteen years at Hodder in the UK and now moving on to publishers anew. Carolyn did not just supply wise counsel, but also intuitive editing: she knew not just how I wrote, but also how I edited, and could thus achieve a large quantity of improvements in very few words. Always supportive, always enthusiastic. My books have been far better with her involvement.

My thanks are also due to my new USA editor Juliet Grames and the team at Soho Press, who have so enthusiastically welcomed me into their fold, and who will continue the excellent relationship with my large number of valued North American readers.

My thanks to Katie Keily for taking on the responsibility of "Continuity Reader" a role in which she excelled and helped me in several areas, most notably in that Tommo's sister Fran was invented by him in SofG to give more weight to East Carmine's Red marriage market—a detail that I had forgotten and developed her as a character. Fran's part has been taken over by Amelia, a cousin.

I would be remiss not to mention the passing of Dr. John Wooten, who was for many years my Official Scientific Consultant, a role he fulfilled perfectly as he had a mix of knowledge and humour, so could advise on how my ideas might better have

ACKNOWLEDGMENTS

a "whimsical air of scientific plausibility," a distinction that gave those parts of my books a depth that they would otherwise not have possessed.

And finally, my thanks to Ozzy, whose blunting of teeth and dimming of sight has not diminished his enthusiasm for sticks and walks.

Jasper Fforde
September 2023

READ ON FOR AN EXCLUSIVE SHORT STORY FOR THE AMERICAN EDITION

Strictly Private and Confidential

To: The Prefects of Beizeminster, Green Sector South

From: Alfred Peabody

Regarding: Submission to Spectrum magazine approval

Rule Reference: 9. 502. 76. 23. 6b

Date: 17th Summer, 00422

Esteemed Prefects:

Please accept the following account of a recent encounter with the Riffraff which I think may be suitable, with your editing and guidance, for publication within the pages of 'Spectrum' Magazine.

Delete

'...As Beizeminster's representative of National Color for Green Sector South, it is my duty to investigate potential color Feed-Pipe leaks in the area, and I was alerted by an off-hue discrepancy in the village's Color garden, which I found had been caused by a drop in pressure of the Cyan Feed-Pipe leading into the village.

A telegram to my opposite number at Greendale confirmed that the pressure was holding fast at her end, so this suggested a leak somewhere in the Feed-Pipe on the seventeen mile section between us.

My Feed-Pipe network map revealed two maintenance
stations on the route between our villages, and after
seeking permission from your good selves and dressed in
appropriate attire as befits a representative of the
village, I ordered a pack lunch and walked out of the
village at dawn one month ago on the 14th Day of Summer,
00422.

The day was warm and bright, the perpetulite roadway
clear and undamaged and aside from the rustle of
creatures within the woods I noticed little sign of life. I
found the first maintenance station with some difficulty
as it was a little way off the roadway and in poor repair.

Inside I noted that it had been used in the recent past as
a depository for thousands of glass beads, buttons, coins
and other shiny objects, as though the work of a large and
very industrious Squarial, presumably of a type unknown
to the Chromogencia. Of whoever had collected them there
was now no sign, and the heaps of finds had been covered
by dust, cobwebs, moss and the skeletal remains of a Grey
travelling brush salesman, who had Thoughtlessly
Chosen This Place to expire.

I entered the mixed broadleaf forest beyond the
maintenance station and followed the 500 yard interval
marker stones that traced the route of the Feed-Pipes.
Knowing that these stones were often missing, overgrown
or buried under leaf litter, it took me over an hour to
cover the mile until I found what I was looking for: A
large beech of quite considerable age which was, from the
bark to the leaves and even the soil around its base, a
deep synthetic Cyan. The leak was beneath it, and had
caused all manner of color mischief.

I sat and made some notes for the repair gangs and
attempted to pinpoint the area on a rudimentary map, but
when I stepped back to better sketch the beech, I trod upon
the sensors of an unseen Yateveo, and with the unnatural
screech that will be familiar to any poor fool who has
wandered so thoughtlessly close to such an arboreal
terror, the branches lifted to strike and then waited,
ready to sense the slightest tremor in its root sensors to
accurately pinpoint the position of me, its prey.

I stood there without moving for half an hour, hoping that
the tree would ignore me and reset – but it did not,
presumably because it was hungry, and did not wish to
risk the loss of such a hearty meal. I waited another ten
minutes, then carefully took my bag from my shoulder and

tossed it closer to the trunk, hoping to fool the tree. It
did not fall for such an obvious subterfuge and I waited
again, my muscles trembling and my legs beginning to
shake. The only course of action was to bolt for safety,
the only and likely last plan I would make, as Yateveos
were staggeringly fast - I would likely be grabbed before
I'd taken a single pace.

It was as I was steeling myself to this desperate plan when
I heard a voice:

'You, idiot under the Yateveo. Stay exactly where you are.
'

I then heard the rustling of feet and a second or two later
and with a terrifying swoosh the branches of the tree
descended - but not on me; they grabbed a goat two yards
to the right of me, and with a creak of the boughs and a
plaintive wail, the goat was deposited in the digesting
bulb in the centre of the tree. The strike completed and
the tree now safe, I turned to face my rescuer - and found
myself face to face with a child no older then twelve.

She had a grubby face, was dressed in a mix and match
style of clothes and had wild and unkempt hair. She was
clearly of the sub-human species known as 'Homo

Feralensis', or, to give her type the more usual term: The Riffraff.

I was, as you might imagine, taken aback by this. The only Riffraff I had seen before this were either at a distance or safely dead, and irrespective of the vastly different social stations of our kind, I decided to demonstrate the importance of politeness so gave gratitude where it was due and thanked her and asked if there was anything I could do in return, ~~expecting her to ask not to be boxed about the ears and be allowed to go on her way.~~ *Delete*

Instead, she unsheathed the bush cutlass that was strapped to her waist. I took a step back as Riffraff of any age can be dangerously unpredictable and wholly without morals, ~~but instead she held the cutlass with the handle toward me. I asked her is she was surrendering her weapon, and she said that if I wanted to show my gratitude I could get her goat back as she'd lost one the week before and didn't want to get into any more trouble.~~ *Delete*

And she tried to stab me until I took the cutlass from her

And Then

~~I hesitated for a while and~~ she then said in an angrier tone: 'you better hurry before Buttercup drowns' so demonstrating the sense of fair play that the Book of Harmony demands we show in all situations, ~~I took the~~ *Delete*

delete

~~cutlass and~~ sliced open the bulb of the Yateveo, something
that I had never done before and won't hurry to do again.
Aside from the foul-smelling gelatinous liquid that
flooded out there was an unconscious goat, a half digested
badger, a human leg and, unusually, a functioning Tin
Man of a smaller variety I'd not seen before. He sat up
and looked around, surprised by the events as much as I,
but seemingly none the worse for his experience, except
that all his paint had been burned off by the caustic
digestive juices of the Yateveo, and he now had a
burnished appearance that shone with a sort of dull
purity.

Delete

'Is that you, SID-5?' asked the girl, and the Tin Man
replied that it was he, and they set about talking in an
animated fashion as old friends, and I learned that SID-5
had been missing for about four years, and it had been
very gloomy and dark in the digesting bulb with only the
odd terrified animal and screaming human to alleviate
the tedium.

Delete

Boring
Delete

It was he who had been collecting the buttons and coins
that I had found in the maintenance shed, so I asked him
why he did this, and he said he had been finding objects
that were lost so they were not lost any longer, as he had
been lost himself for as long as he could remember and

page 6

I Deactivated The tin man and it was Then

knew what that felt like. I said that those items were not alive and did not know they were lost as they had no way to experience lostness, and the Tin Man replied that he too was not alive, but believed he felt lostness – and if him, then why not other things too? His arm then fell to the ground with a thud – loosened by the immersion in the digestive gloop most likely – and after he said 'I'm not sure that was meant to happen' I noted that the Riffraff child had vanished along with the goats and my shoulder bag, which contained not just my notes and my lunch but my irreplaceable National Color manual on Color Feed-Pipe engineering.

I asked SID-5 where he thought she had gone, and he replied that I should probably just forget any of this had happened and return to my home wherever that was and to keep my lips 'firmly buttoned' which I took to mean say nothing. But since I knew there was a 1000-demerit for loss of National Color property, I would have to get my bag back or risk forgoing a new three-piece lounge suite next year, something of which I had been looking forward to for a decade.

Now mildly irked (but within temper tolerance parameters of Rule 8. 9C) I told SID-5 that I did not care to be given advice from anyone whose recent life experience revolved

Delete

~~around being trapped inside a tree, and~~ walked off in the
direction the child had taken ~~with the Tin Man following~~
~~behind, complaining about the loss of his arm.~~ *Delete*

I followed a poorly defined path between the trees and the
corroded remains of a flying machine and soon found
myself faced with an impenetrable hedge of Clutching
Bramble that looked too dense to be natural growth but
was also tactically starved, as several of the fronds made
hungry clutches in my direction, one of which took my hat
off and tore it into several pieces.

There was a path of sorts so I followed this around the
perimeter, and soon found an area of Clutching Bramble
that had been recently pruned of its catching spikes, so I
pushed my way through and found myself in a clearing of
perhaps one hundred yards in diameter, and behind a
central cooking pit there were several dwellings built of
scrap metal and sheeting, *And all looking very shabby.*

Delet

The ground in the clearing ~~had been brushed meticulously~~ *WAS covered in Litter*
~~clean,~~ and tables had been set up upon which were *objects*
stolen
suitable for trading – Hotpots, LightGlobes, a couple of
negative pounds of floaties in a net and Remote Viewers.
Essentially, illegally held technology. There was also a

small pen for goats, and several animal hides drying in

the sun, AS well as several riffraff undertaking unspeakable acts in full view of everyone.

I was ~~also~~ being watched meticulously by ten or twelve

faces, who seemed as surprised to see me as I was to see

them. It appeared I had wandered into a Riffraff

encampment, and one, contrary to what was generally

thought, of relative permanence, and less then three miles

from the village, ~~something at odds with the popular view~~ which might explain the recent SPATE of Baby Theft

~~where it was generally agreed that any Riffraff within~~

~~five miles or so would be constantly stealing either food~~

~~or babies, and no thefts had been reported around here for~~

~~years.~~

Delete

The most prominent Riffraff was a woman: tall, elegant

and ~~not unpleasing to the eye,~~ very ugly and she strode up to within

ten feet of me without fear. I noted that she was pregnant,

but did not hide the bump beneath the mandatory gingham

maternity dress, but had her bump outrageously on full

display, and she rested a hand upon it as she spoke.

~~'It's good to see you again after such a long absence,' she~~

~~said, 'we welcome you back to the village.'~~

Delete

~~I started to say that I had never been here before, but she~~

~~rudely spoke across me to say she wasn't speaking to me,~~

Delete

~~and SID-5 who had followed me in, thanked her for her welcome, and he asked her to put the word about that he had lost an arm and would be grateful for a replacement.~~ *Delete*

'And you?' asked the Riffraff woman in ~~the silence that followed,~~ 'so' *A slovenly tongue,* 'Who are you?'

I gave her my name and status of which she was entirely unimpressed, and said that a young girl had rescued me, but that I was seeking the return of my shoulder bag, as theft was viewed dimly by my village, and punishment would surely follow.

'I have it here and I am impressed by your bearing so

'You left it under the Yateveo,' said the young girl whose name I learned was Bethany. Am deeply sorry' She said

~~'Is this true?' asked the Riffraff leader.

'I think it might be,' I replied, suddenly feeling very foolish that I had mislaid my bag only to assume it stolen.

'Then you owe Bethany an apology.'~~ *Delete*

~~I didn't say anything, and she asked again, but added that if I did not, it would be unlikely I'd be heard of again, so I readily apologised, and Bethany nodded in acceptance,~~ *Delete*

I told The riffraff woman I was Hungry

~~and the Riffraff woman stared at me again for a moment~~
~~and then asked if I was hungry, and I said I was,~~ so she
beckoned me to sit at their cooking area, which consisted
of several HotPots nestled together in which there was a
ghoulash that ~~bubbled tantalisingly, and of which the~~
~~aroma was exceedingly good.~~ smelled awful.

All the Riffraff of the village sat down to eat together,
and once everyone had appeared from the houses and other
workplaces, I guess maybe there were thirty or forty
individuals, and all seemed in ~~good~~ Poor health and ~~good~~ Poor
humour, ~~although~~ AND each, I noted, were missing an index
finger. I was asked where I was from, and I explained that
I was peripherally important at Beizeminster, and that I
was sometimes listened to by the Prefects, but was wholly
in charge of the color Feed-Pipes, and entrusted by
National Color to do so, and had been invited three times
to Emerald City on training courses, and even though work
kept me at home village, the invitations were a clear
indication of my importance.
                          very   and
If they were impressed by this ~~they made no sign, several~~
asked what or where was Emerald City, but when I tried to
explain their attention wandered, and they passed out the
food. Ever cautious of the Riffraff's habit for poisoning
visitors, ~~I watched carefully as the food was ladled out~~
                          I Did Not Eat anything,

~~but was assigned a plate at random which could not have been poisoned, so I ate it, slowly at first and then with greater gusto, and it tasted better than anything I had ever tasted at the village kitchens, and finished it all up.~~ *[handwritten: Delete]*

There did not seem to be any strict hierarchy at dinner, or indeed, anywhere at all, with many people speaking at once and with interruptions and outbursts of laughter, ~~(a far cry from mealtimes in the the village, where conversation was kept to a minimum, and manners carefully observed with Yellows on hand to mete out infractions.~~ *[handwritten: Delete]* *[handwritten: And other rude interuptions as befits their low status.]* They asked me about the village and the life I lived there, and made faces and laughed when I spoke of the intricate nature of my polite and ordered society, and why such order was essential for civilisation, and how a descent to anarchy and sloth and the associated bestial urges that would be forthcoming without it, *[handwritten: which They then agreed with.]*

[handwritten: I Demanded] ~~The leader asked if they all seemed barbaric to me, and I had to admit they did not, but there was always an exception to the rule, and that this village was clearly one that may have found some guiding principal from the Chromotocracy with which they had risen above the ignorance of their kind.~~ *[handwritten: Delete]*

The leader looked at me and gave what I can only describe as a patronising smile, and I felt distinctly ill-at-ease, as though I were somehow missing something, and that whatever it was they could see it clearly while I could not.

I Demanded

~~I was then given~~ a guided tour of the encampment, and everyone appeared (well)-fed, (healthy) and (happy), with tasks *chaotically* spread amongst everyone, rather than the ~~more usual~~ *better method of* allotting (of) particular tasks to particular individuals, which ~~did seem to work.~~ *works much better.*

[*ill* / *unwell* / *un* written above well, healthy, happy respectively]

They showed me tech that was forbidden, of remote viewers intact and functioning, and explained past histories of the Previous which were recorded upon them, and available for all to see so long as we had the want to do so, which I told them I did not, but when I spoke of Munsell and his magnificent aims and goals and triumphs, I heard them giggling, so decided not to say anything more on the subject.

At one point in the afternoon I was shown the body of a villager who had recently died, and joined with them as they bore the body with (great) solemnity to an area beyond the boundary, and there to a hole in the ground in which the dead man's vessel was placed with (great) reverence.

FALSE [above first "great"]

MISGUIDED

There was then a display of emotion as if the body in some way represented their lost companion, and an attachment and respect to the vessel seemed to be made. The hole was covered with earth, and no effort it seemed would be made to harvest any part of their friend, which while initially seeming a waste, suddenly spoke to me of a greater reverence to the memory of the departed than a simple plaque, and I found my eyes moisten as I observed the sadness of the others.

The leader told me I should probably leave at that point, and said me I was a good person, just misguided, and asked if I would endeavour to keep the Riffraff village secret, as it had taken many years to build up the Clutching Bramble and they liked it here, and were loathe to move.

I said in all honesty that I was bound by oath to report them to my Prefects, and that if that required them to kill me and put me in the ground, then so be that, too, and the Leader told me they did not do murder without just cause, no how, no where, and they hoped that I would think carefully upon my visit and all that it meant, and would I like to take SID-5 with me, as his talk of his lost arm was beginning to become tiresome.

page 14

[handwritten margin notes:]
WAS
Delete
I TOLD
Delete
AS I had seen enough of their BASE ways, and bestiae habits, The worst of which Propriety would compel not to mention here.
Delete

Delete

I said I would say nothing for a month to give them time to move as they would most assuredly be visited once I had reported them, and the leader smiled and wished me well, and gave me a seashell of exquisite beauty.

clear

I came away from the visit with a better understanding of the Riffraff. I collected my bag, retraced my steps and kept my word to my new friends. I think you will note from my small stay amongst the Riffraff, that there are a great deal of question marks about the way in which they are perceived, and my observation suggests that contrary to popular opinion, the Riffraff are not unsophisticated or as bestial as is supposed, but hold similar values to ourselves, and that further study as to the peaceable nature of these people should be undertaken as a matter of some importance, as potential assimilation may be preferable to continued extermination.

And

delete

NO

AS

And

Abandend as useless.

They are utterly without redemption and deserve to remain as 'vermin'

I remain always your respectful servant,

Alfred Peabody

NINE MINUTES

Possible title: 'An afternoon among the riffraff'

Note to SWATCHMAN:
A. Peabody to be DIAGNOSED with Tennis ELBOW ASAP

By ORDER
BEIZEMINSTER
HEAD PREFECT